LOVE'S FIERY RESOLUTION

LOVE'S FIERY RESOLUTION

Flynn's Crossing Romantic Suspense Series
Book 10

Yvonne Kohano

Nanokas Press

A Division of Kochanowski Enterprises

LOVE'S FIERY RESOLUTION
FLYNN'S CROSSING ROMANTIC SUSPENSE SERIES BOOK 10

Nanokas Press/KE Press books may be ordered through booksellers or by contacting:

Kochanowski Enterprises/Nanokas Press
PO Box 1274
Clackamas, OR 97015-9594
www.yvonnekohano.com
yvonne@yvonnekohano.com

Love's Fiery Resolution is a work of fiction. People, places, events, and situations are the product of the author's imagination. Any resemblance to actual persons, living or dead, or historical events, is purely coincidental.

This book contains an excerpt from the forthcoming book *Love's Fiery Prescription* by Yvonne Kohano. This excerpt may not reflect the final content of the forthcoming edition.

Any people depicted in stock imagery provided by Thinkstock are models, and such images are being used for illustrative purposes only.

Certain stock imagery ©Thinkstock
Cover design: John Kochanowski

ISBN: 978-1-940738-40-6 (sc)
        978-1-940738-87-1 (e)

Nanokas Press First Edition: 06-08-2016

Also by Yvonne Kohano

FLYNN'S CROSSING ROMANTIC SUSPENSE SERIES

Pictures of Redemption, Book 1
(Serena & Dane)

Flashes of Fire, Book 2
(DK & Vince)

Naked Intolerances, Book 3
(Gabby & Rick)

Tastes and Consequences, Book 4
(Mac & Roxy)

Blooms on the Bones, Book 5
(Tess & Powers)

Wine Into Water, Book 6
(Marguerite & Deke)

Love and the Christmas Tree Nymph,
A Flynn's Crossing Seasonal Novella

Love's Touch of Justice, Book 7
(Jake & Marlee)

This Proposal Between Us,
A Flynn's Crossing Seasonal Novella

Measure Twice, Love Once, Book 8
(Geno and Agnes)

Love's Fiery Prescription, Book 9
(Noah and Nicolle)

Love's Fiery Resolution, Book 10
(Gideon and Danielle)

And more to come!
Learn about upcoming releases at
www.YvonneKohano.com.

Subscribe to Yvonne Kohano's enewsletter to be among the first to learn about new releases and special offers. Visit www.yvonnekohano.com for more information.

Follow Yvonne at www.yvonnekohano.com, on Facebook as Yvonne Kohano, and on Twitter @yvonnekohano to learn what tickles her about being a writer, and at www.GooseYourMuse.com for creativity tips.

LOVE'S FIERY RESOLUTION

Prologue – Last Autumn

Blisters formed where heat baked bare skin. Dense smoke made vision of more than a few feet impossible. Gid's tongue had long gone dry from scorching air penetrating his breather. Twin sensations of power and fear rippled through him. Conditions were beyond the realm of reason, and he loved it.

He brought the Pulaski down with a surge, intent on digging a scratch line in partially burnt ground. The understory had disappeared on the first flash and they thought they had this front contained. Madame Fire had other ideas. A gust of wind built into a flame devil, tearing a new hole in their line and racing away, even as it left behind torches skipping from treetop to treetop. There was no way down, and no way up. They were left to fight the monster, cut off from help.

Still, he felt powerful. Perhaps there was something wrong with him. Part of him fought the fire with the last surge of energy he had. The other part, the part he'd like to think was wise and objective, jittered in knowing they were five men alone in hell, and despite their best efforts, they might die on this ridge.

"Hey, hey, over here."

The disembodied voice sounded urgent but controlled. Training surpassed fear in circumstances like this. Over the roar of combustion, he heard a keening scream, and his eyes swung to the dim shape of a small building. Sparks lapped its roofline and the shingle siding smoldered.

Instructions poured over his comm unit faster than slippery retardant falling from planes above them. A fresh rain of red spattered around the team, but it made only marginal difference. Their yellow turnouts had long since turned a mixture of gray and red, making locating his men harder by the moment. Pines engulfed to their tops outraced their efforts.

"Clear a path. One evacuee, a little girl. Anyone got a spare hand?"

Gid stepped toward two waving figures. Two more flanked them with their backs turned, their faces to the advancing fire.

"Honey, we're here to help you. Please stop struggling. We'll get you out."

He heard the words of the rookie. He and the other firefighter carried a child between them. A fire shelter protected her head and shoulders, making her unrecognizable. Her feet would soon suffer from the heat in those sneakers. He wondered if she could run.

The rookie said, "She was behind the cabin. I didn't get a chance to check inside. You take her and I'll go back."

Gid shook his head. "Nah, keep moving. Might be safe in the streambed between the bounders. Head down. I'll check the cabin."

He rushed forward over their protests. Who left a child alone in a tinder dry forest? Behind him, he heard the child's startled cries. "Binky. You have to get my Binky."

Figures. Binky was probably a dog or a cat. But if it was a living thing and he could catch it, he'd bring it to her. The girl would have precious little else left.

He rammed the head of his Pulaski into the door and heard splinters of wood where the hinges left the old frame. The interior was darker than the forest, and he struggled to see through his visor. Smoke twirled in the light from the blaze outside. The space was meager but crammed with belongings. He heard his name called over the comm and acknowledged the directive to move out. It would only take another minute. There weren't many places to search.

Lifting his visor, he peered into the corners. "Here, Binky." He felt stupid, but he did it again anyway. "Binky, come on. You don't want to be a roast, do you?"

The impact came from nowhere, settling with a hard thump between his shoulders blades. Pain radiated down his arms. He tightened his grip on his equipment automatically. Whatever Binky was, it was huge. He wouldn't put it past the kid to keep a pet bear. People in these backwoods locations where never predictable.

He prepared to face his attacker when he heard shouts. The voices magnified in his earbud grew urgent.

"Kid, stop struggling. You can't go back. He'll find it. Honey –"

"Shit, she's running toward the cabin. Kid, are you crazy or –"

"Gid, get outta there. Roof's gonna go."

The cacophony of noises, the men's voices mixed with the pitched howls of the child, accompanied the raging voice of wildfire. He dropped his visor and turned toward the open doorway.

A large form filled his view of freedom. Raised like claws on the ends of arms extending from a big body, something loomed over him. Outside over the shrieks of the inferno, he heard the child's plea.

"Binky. I need Binky."

Something slammed into his face, cracking the visor's surface in a snowflake of fissures. What the hell? Another crash and he recovered his protective instincts and raised his tool to shield him from the next impact. This time, the swipe of a strike closed on the handle with a determined yank.

"Get out of my house," said a deep raspy voice, with enough rage to convince him he was hearing things. Everyone knew bears didn't talk.

The large hands closed on either side of his and pulled the handle away as if he'd been holding on with a single finger.

"Binky. Binky." The girl's sobs registered in his comm and echoed from the doorway, and he realized she was inside.

"Kinkead, outta there now. Gid, get out."

Frantic shouts in his ear went unheard when a flash from the woods lit the interior with an unearthly glow. In the light, he saw his attacker. A man taller than him by a good foot and more and with shoulders so broad, he probably needed to turn sideways to enter the door. But what scared him the most were the man's eyes. Even in the dimness, he could see their whites and the crazed expression in them. The bear of a man raised the Pulaski in the air with the fine point aimed for Gid's head. It bore down and he heard his own voice scream with the impending collision.

"Wake up, man. Kinkead, wake up. Gid?"

Rough shakes tumbled him over until his face bit into dirt. Something heavy pressed against his back, holding him in place. He struggled to free his arms, but they were pinned at his sides.

"It's okay, man. Gid, it was a dream. You're safe."

The voice penetrated. He wasn't fighting for his life. The weight on his back wasn't the bear-man. He drew deep breaths, feeling the douse of unhealthy sweat soak his sleeping bag. He stopped fighting, letting his body go limp as he turned his head.

"I'm okay." His voice came out weak without conviction and he tried again. "I'm awake."

The pressure eased, and the face of another firefighter swam into view as the man knelt next to him. Shaking his arms to stop their trembles, Gid drew a deep breath and pushed himself up to his knees. Feet shuffled in the small group surrounding him. He lifted his gaze to meet sympathetic eyes, but something else lurked behind those expressions.

Pity.

Fear.

Embarrassment.

This would never be over.

Chapter 1 – Mid-Spring

"Who's the redhead?"

Gideon Kinkead tracked the woman's progress across camp, waiting for someone to respond. A braid down her back swung in time to her hips. Fit, built, and from what he could tell, gorgeous. A lazy grin filled his face.

"I can't believe there's a woman left in the county, single or otherwise, that you haven't hit on, Gid. I mean, they chase you like bees to flowers. Like that curly-haired number the other night, the brunette. Why didn't you go home with her? She sure seemed eager to get her hands on you."

Gid shrugged, his grin fading as he thought about the real reason he'd chased after every woman in the county. One night and only one night for any of them. More than once, and they might learn his secret. Just leave them smiling, that was his motto. They always were.

It helped that their elite team stayed busy, which was also a bitch for the communities where fires burned. In those months since he'd nearly lost his mind and his job, fires raged up and down California and the surrounding states, even if the official start of fire season was more than a month away. Rare were the times he had more than two days strung together off-duty. That was more than good enough for him.

He forgot about his problem and the redhead a second later when a claxon sounded in the compound, shrill and insistent in the morning calm. Gid followed Curtis jogging into action as Cap, their commander, shouted orders. Men and women scrambled off picnic tables as they suited up in gear and slammed hoods and doors loading into trucks. A man burst out of an office at a run, handing Cap a single page of paper. The older man studied at it with a grim expression before passing it to Gid.

"This looks suspicious, Kinkead, so keep an extra eye out. No weather and a fast start. Could be related to that drug lab cooking crap all over the place, or it could be another arson. Watch everyone's back."

A suspicious source of origin would never be taken lightly. Gid suited up in the passenger side of the two-seater as it tore down the gravel road, Curtis at the wheel. When the man started about the chick in that bar again, Gid waved him silent. That was fun. This was business.

Once he coordinated their attack with the other units, the interior fell silent for the first three miles. Another suspicious start. A pattern had emerged, one he didn't like. It was one thing to blame dry lightning strikes or other natural causes. Deliberate acts weren't something they needed in red zone conditions.

Cursing the logging road's poor condition, Curtis said, "So what do you think, Gid, the druggies or a stupid human trick?"

Gid drew a breath but never replied when they rounded a bend in the one lane road to a wall of flames already forty feet high. They both swore at the same moment. On the other side of the flames, an old car sat next to a small structure that would soon be engulfed. A flash of memory of another cabin in the woods blocked his vision, and he shoved past it.

He got on the radio, breaking through communications in his urgency.

"Cap, we've got a possible evac. Can you find out if this cabin is usually occupied?" He read off their coordinates.

Others fell silent over the airwaves, because they all probably had the same sinking feeling. Gid's gut ended up in his boots as he and Curtis hit the ground at a run, already holding their Pulaskis in front of them for rapid response to falling debris. Without a water cannon, they weren't going to breach the wall of flames. Putting a glove on Curtis's arm, Gid guided them away from the worst of the flames to get a better assessment of their options.

"Kinkead, negative. That cabin is not listed as occupied year round, but someone might be holed up there. I'm routing more manpower your way."

Next to him, Curtis nodded as he too heard the update. The kid seemed jumpy, and behind the helmet visor, his eyes shown fire-bright. Too young, too eager, and too hot under the collar and ready to take action. Gid could read the signs.

Between them and the cabin, whatever dried grasses and small bushes in the line of fire had burned to char. Pine needles sucked little fingers of flame across the ground as if inhaling the smoke. Wind from their backs kept it moving toward the car and cabin. Gid cursed under his breath.

"What'd ya say?" Curtis turned to him, his voice distorted through his breathing mask.

Gid waved him off. If the kid heard his words, Cap did too. So did everyone else on the network. The comm remained quiet until two other units reported they were within four minutes of their location.

"We can't wait. We gotta go in and make sure." Curtis paired his words with an advance on the fire. Gid grabbed him before he could get too close.

"You see that wall? No break in it. No way to get through, and going around it will only trap us on the other side. We have to wait." Much as Gid hated the idea too.

He examined the fire's base more closely. The place where it started, closer to them than the actual flames, ran in a straight line across the clearing. While some lightning strikes could carry energy in a line if conditions were right and something lay on the ground to conduct the shock, a random origin scribed as a single straight line was rare. Plus, there wasn't a cloud in the sky.

He let go of Curtis to creep forward himself, keeping his gaze primarily on the flames while glancing down at his feet. "Keep an eye out for me," he said, waiting for a nod from the other man before dropping to a knee.

Fire presented different effects based on what burned. Wood, for example, left ashes, as did other materials. A very hot fire could incinerate almost everything in its path, while a cooler fire burned slower and left behind more debris. And then there was a case like this.

A thick black line, about six inches in width, showed discolored mineral earth and a glint of what could be heat-related melting. Only a closer inspection when things cooled would show if the glints were particles of metal, burnt clean by the fire. Glancing right and left, the symmetry of the line was unmistakable.

But that wasn't even the most interesting factor. He ran a cautious hand over the line, testing the surface for anomalies. Even through gloves, his fingers detected the change in grade. The cleaner surface marked by the thick black line gave way to markedly fluffier ash.

It would take a fire investigator to confirm this, but Gideon hadn't spent his adult life fighting fire without learning more about how it could start than could fill a textbook. The thick black line indicated ignitable material. It burned hot and quick before debris covering the dry forest floor blew in on the prevailing wind. On either side, ash signified normal forest burn debris. Signs pointed toward a deliberate source of ignition.

A hand touched his shoulder and he looked up to find other crews had arrived. He faced the others as they stared over his shoulder at the wall of flame, cabin and car. Linking his comm to theirs, he said, "Okay, this is how we're going to do this."

Time moved in slow motion in his experience, unless you were trying to knock down a fire. Then things ran quick. Every passing second could mean life or death to whoever was caught on the wrong side of flames. They worked fast, but it never felt fast enough.

When the water pumpers were able to break a gap in the fire's wall, Gid and the crew ran through. He checked the car as others slammed shoulders into the cabin's thick dark door. Wood splintered on the second impact and they barreled in, Gid on their heels. The interior stood empty of occupants and almost bare of furniture and supplies. Nothing gave an obvious clue about recent inhabitants or activities. He stepped back outside to scan the area.

He keyed his mic. "Cap, nothing here. No signs of recent activity."

Static filled the silenced before Cap responded. "Copy that, Kinkead. See if you can get a handle on the source. Safety's on his way to you. Save the structure."

Gid didn't need to check on the other crews to know they were already in motion. He lifted a chin to Curtis, and they worked their Pulaskis into the ground, snuffing sparks with raw dirt and knocking out remaining flames. The work was monotonous but necessary. Where possible, they protected human property.

But something felt off about the whole thing. To Gid, it looked intentional, but he wasn't a specialist. The flames continued their dance up the hillside, heading toward the efforts of another fire crew. The initial mop-up here would fall to his guys.

Gid turned away to work an area beyond the cabin, smothering spot flames between boulders large enough to block his view of the structure. His crew worked strung out in a line, with a couple of them keeping their eyes on the burning forest and the trees left standing around them. Someone always had the crew's back.

It left him time to think, and with each passing minute, his suppositions grew stronger. The growing circle of protection led him around to the cabin's front view an hour later. A Federal investigator wearing a bright yellow helmet with the word 'safety' emblazoned on the front examined the ground. Gid always thought they had a cool job, the fire version of crime scene investigations. It was unusual to see the guy this close to an active line, though. The string of probable arsons had everyone working overtime. Safety would gather samples of soil in the thick line and around it. Photos supplemented physical evidence. Gid would share his impressions, but only after Safety performed his initial assessment.

A hand on his shoulder made him turn, and he faced the fire investigator. The man looked like he'd seen a few decades of combustions and more than his fair share of problems. Thick white eyebrows bushed over tired red eyes and stubble covered his face as if he hadn't had a chance for a break in days. "So which of you jokers left me the present?"

Gid paused, unsure of the man's intention. "What the hell are you talking about?"

"Come on, Kinkead, don't mess around with me. I'm old, I'm tired, and I don't need additional shit. So who the blazes left me the flower?"

Gid thought perhaps the guy had been eating smoke too long. He said, "I have no idea what you're talking about."

The investigator stepped to the side, gesturing down the ignition line a few feet. "That is what I'm talking about."

Gid stared past the outstretched hand, encased in a sterile glove over fire resistant material. It made the fingers look like sausages in casings that were too tight. Between whiffs of smoke, he noted a bright color marring the otherwise dull, ashen ground.

"What the hell?" He strode forward, careful to place each foot with caution. He didn't know why the discordant color made him wary, as if each step could be a trap.

"A flower. Who the hell brings a flower to a fire? Are you guys nuts?" The investigator took bolder paces and passed Gid to stand over the offending item, continuing his grumbling.

When Gid reached it, he knelt low. With the handle of the ax, he nudged the thing. It looked like a plastic flower, a red rose. It should have melted in the fire. His brain scrambled to process how it could be laying there. Without rising, he toggled his comm switch and called the team together.

The investigator's rant slowed and eventually stopped as the men and women of the hand crew assembled and stared at the ground by Gid's feet. His gaze went from face to face, hoping for a sign of the culprit for this prank. He said, "Anyone?"

Some made off-color comments, but soon they fell silent as one by one, they came to the same conclusion Gid had.

They hadn't been alone at this fire scene.

Chapter 2

Danielle Trajan spit her mouth guard into her wrapped hands and grinned. "Now that was fun, wasn't it?"

Her twin did the same and grimaced. "The only fun part about exercise is getting it done. You enjoy this way too much. You're sick, you know that?"

With a widening smile, Dani watched Nicolle stalk away, her braid swinging down her back with each hard step. In all truth, her sister was good, almost as good as Danielle was herself. She didn't need to say that. Their trainer, a retired mixed martial arts pro with enough belts to start a metal factory, mentioned it more than once. But Nicolle lacked one thing Dani had. The kill instinct.

She wasn't sure if this was a good thing or bad. When Nicolle began self-defense training, Dani joined in to support her sister, finding she loved the take-no-prisoners attitude and the intellectual aspect of the workout. But when it came time, she'd pin anyone to the mat or knock their flaying bodies into the cage without batting an eye. Nicolle still worried she'd hurt someone. Wasn't that the effing point?

She began the process of unwinding the wrap protecting her fingers, tossing pieces into the gym bag at the base of the stairs. Their trainer gave her a thumbs-up. Yeah, it had been a good workout, all the better because Nici was pissed about the arsons, making her a demon to spar with today. Dani smiled again.

"Why do you keep grinning?" Nicolle punctuated her grumbling question with a sharp yank on a boot.

"Oh, I don't know. Maybe I'm grinning because you, Little Miss Sunshine, are pissed, and when you're pissed, you leave it all on the mat. I like that side of you. You even had me pinned a few times."

Nicolle froze in her movements, her face suddenly stricken as she raised troubled eyes. "Oh god, I didn't hurt you, did I? I'm sorry, Dani, I wasn't controlling myself well today."

Dani flashed her another smile. Their attitudes, one of the few things people could use to tell them apart, were reversed today. "You didn't hurt me, and being out of control isn't necessarily a negative."

Because Dani knew about control. Control equaled power. She'd been powerless to stop the one person who'd hurt someone she loved more than her own life. The thought put a sudden downer on her elation.

Nicolle resumed dressing, offering a small grin. "Pot, meet kettle. Lieutenant Control, that should be your name. When was the last time you were out of control, sis?"

Dani shrugged, wishing she hadn't directed the conversation on to such shaky ground. She was always in control, even when she swore at work or threw something at home. Each action had a purpose. It was how she rose to her current rank in a sheriff's department not known for its equal opportunity advancements. She'd always be in control in the future, particularly when lives depended on it. When she wasn't, the consequences were extreme.

"And, while we're on the subject, when was the last time you had a date? Like a real date, as in with a guy you aren't pals with and maybe a little woohoo at the end of the evening?" Nicolle escalated her grin into a chuckle.

Dani flipped her off, grateful no one overheard their exchange. Aiming for levity, she said, "I could say kettle, meet pot, but I won't."

She fell silent as Nicolle's grin disappeared. Shit, she felt like a monster at the swift change in expression.

"Sorry, sorry. I shouldn't have said that. Sorry." She dropped to the bench next to her twin and put an arm around her shoulders.

"It's okay. Really. I've grown a pretty tough skin over the last couple of years. Maybe someday, I'll see things differently. But for now?" She shrugged as if she didn't think things would ever change.

Dani wanted to kill all bastards of the male variety every time she considered how much hurt her twin had been in. She'd felt it like it was her own pain, and she still did, on those occasions when Nicolle chose to open up. It was the twin thing, the connection of identical siblings.

Nicolle continued while pulling on jeans. "Besides, just because I don't date doesn't mean you shouldn't. You need to give some of these guys a chance. They're not all bad."

Dani picked up an abandoned wrap and began to coil it to calm her thoughts. "Well, it could be that I either meet cops, who I won't date because we work together, or criminals, who I'd never date. Or the rare hottie, who I do date, but then for only one night so I can get some. Wham, bam, and ma'am is out of there."

Nicolle giggled, and Dani's lips lifted at the sound. Nicolle said, "Only one night stands, even for hotties, huh? And never someone you work with or might have to arrest. You're strict, Lieutenant Trajan. Too bad there aren't any other men out there."

Dani hefted her bag on to her shoulder and fingered her keys. "Nope, it's a good thing. Do 'em and dump 'em, that's my motto. Just don't share that with the parental units, okay? Mom has her heart set on one of us getting married and producing grandbabies."

Nicolle's face fell once more, and Dani cursed herself. She might be in control on the outside, but her mouth sometimes had no filter, and she hurt the one person she never wanted to mistreat. Zipping her lips into a tight line, she dropped the duffel and grabbed Nicolle in a vice. She hugged hard, wishing she could take back every bad thing she'd ever said and done to her little sister from the time they shared a womb.

"You know I'd do anything for you, right?" Dani heard the painful ache in her whispered tone, but she was powerless to control it. She would do anything for Nici, anything at all. No limits. No questions. And she'd protect her to the very end.

Nicolle squeezed her once before pushing away. When their eyes met, Dani read the hard-won wisdom she wished she could wipe away. Nicolle turned toward their gear bags and hefted both in one hand with proficient ease. When Dani reached forward to relieve her of the burden, she swung her body away.

"You don't need to coddle me, sis. I take responsibility for my past, as you do. I was partly to blame for what happened. I knew better, but somehow, I let it slip." She headed for the gym's door.

Responsibility for the past. The phrase kept running through Dani's head, even as she drove them back up the hill. The town appeared before she realized the miles they'd covered. Nici's silence wasn't censorious, and she didn't attempt to read anything into her twin's sudden need for an early shower and bedtime. Still, when the door to Nicolle's room swung close with a distinct click, Dani felt shut out.

Who was she kidding? She was as responsible for what happened to her twin as if she'd been beside her on that mountainside. She wished she had been, to bear the brunt of the pain.

Restlessness left her twitching for any kind of activity. A bad guy to take down. A crime to solve. Even administrative paperwork would have been a welcomed distraction. Anything to divert her from her worry that someday, she would have to share the only secret she ever kept from her twin.

She lifted a set of free weights and pumping her arms with overzealous vigor, but the actions did nothing to change her reality. The evidence was clear. Would Nicolle be so generous with her forgiveness once she knew Dani was the cause of her fear?

Chapter 3

The barracks were hardly luxurious, but they were a damned sight better than sleeping on the ground. Gid didn't mind the snores, farts and packed quarters. Over a decade on the fire line, this felt like home. Cots had been broken in by years of worn exhausted bodies and felt as welcoming as a hammock swinging in the breeze. The men and women around him were his comrades in arms. He wouldn't need his sad little apartment any more, and that idea didn't bother him in the least.

He stretched, feeling the tightness in his shoulders from wielding a chainsaw for hours on end over the last few days. Another arson. He swiped his hands across his eyes, wishing he could wipe away the memory of carcasses of animals they'd come across the day before. A barbed wire fence, tall and impenetrable, had blocked escape for a small herd of what had probably been deer. It was a horrible end he didn't wish on any creature.

With his eyes still closed, his memory flashed back to another set of charred remains. That time, there were two legs, not four. The barrier had been manmade, walls that did nothing to deter the fire in its horrific progress. Wood fell to ash, as did skin and muscle. Only dental charts and DNA testing confirmed identities.

Gid flinched and sat up abruptly, opening his eyes wide to cut away from the scene. He blinked at the rush of light in the room. Noon, and most of the crew was still dead asleep, worn out from too many difficult days on the line. There hadn't been a break since that stupid prank at the start of this blaze. They came in yesterday just before dark and stayed awake only long enough to chow down. To a person, they'd collapsed on to the cots and passed out.

He wished he could fall back, pull the blanket over his eyes, and find rest again. But with the memories came hurt. With hurt, responsibility. With responsibility, agitation. Sleep would not be his friend. If he did doze off again, he might wake up screaming from a nightmare, and then what would squad crew think?

He dropped his feet to the floor, jerking on his boots but ignoring their laces. He'd grab a shower before the rest were awake. With luck, he might be able to score an extra ration of hot water. Clean clothes would be a decadent luxury. He kept a spare set in his gear bag left here at base camp. After a week on the mountain, he thought he might have to dump everything down to his skivvies. Coffee dense enough to hold a spoon upright would be nice too.

The light was worse outside, a bright sun making its way through a sky clear of any layer of discoloring smoke. The wind had shifted, a low-pressure system coming in with moisture that raised the humidity and turned the fire back on itself. He hoped they'd finally caught a break. It put a spring in his step as he paced across the compound toward the mound of duffels.

The number of people milling around the covered area was unusual. Gid didn't think that many crews were turning over today. A new fire two days ago sucked up all extra bodies, and the only reason his squad was getting downtime was because they'd been out for a week straight and earned a mandatory rest period. Tomorrow, they'd be back on the line too.

His feet slowed as he approached the area. Yellow plastic tape hanging at waist height blocked his progress, and he stooped to duck underneath it. That's when he noticed the peculiar composition of the crowd. Lots of uniforms, and most of them weren't firefighters. A sheriff's deputy glanced over at him and frowned, putting up an arm to block his path.

"Sorry, but you'll have to wait on the other side of the line."

Gid put up his hands and backed up, but looked past the uniform. Curiosity dug at him. Had someone broken into the gear bags while they were gone? What kind of person would do that, stealing from firefighters while they were saving someone else's stuff? His anger rose as he thought about how sick that individual could be.

"Kinkead, over here." Cap's voice rose above the noise, causing Gid to squint past the huddle to a group standing to the side. Cap waved him over, and the deputy dropped his arm and waved him through.

He approached the men, noting the mix of law enforcement and fire brass. He didn't recognize most of them. One face did stand out, though. Jake Kermarrec, a drinking buddy who currently frowned at Gid like he'd done something stupid. The deputy was on medical leave. What the hell was he doing here?

Okay, whatever had everyone's nuts in a knot wasn't his problem. He'd been miles away, with Madame Fire wheezing her scorching breath in his face. He almost veered off, the smell of coffee drawing him like a siren. But Cap scowled and yelled, "Haul it, Kinkead." Gid broke into a jog.

No one spoke as he joined the circle of onlookers. Cap stared at him with laser intensity. A man with bars of senior fire command on his lapels glared and sniffed as if the lack of a shower offended him. An impatient pen tapped a tablet in the hands of an unknown deputy. Jake shook his head, but this time, sympathy shown in his expression.

Since no one seemed inclined to enlighten him, Gid said, "What's up, Cap?"

Cap's dense eyebrows drew tight, making a single line across his forehead. "You think this is funny, Kinkead?" If Gid had any doubts, the bark in the question let him know Cap was pissed.

But Gid hadn't been grinning as he walked up. He was sure of that. A huff of disbelief sounded from the top brass, who turned back to Cap. "This is his bag?"

Cap glance between Gid and the duffel at their feet. Gid looked down too, taking in the dark blue nylon identical to his. A mound of other gear partially concealed it.

"Kinkead?" Cap's voice demanded an answer, so Gid leaned into the circle and tried to check for a hanging tag. He kept multiple identifiers on his bag, from bright Day-Glo luggage types to his name written in white marker on the web strap. He didn't like to think about the next-of-kin data in the inside pocket.

"Well?" Top brass's increasing impatience radiated through the small tent.

Gid directed his question at Cap and ignored the rest of them. "Is there a problem?"

Cap's eyebrows hit his hairline and his face morphed from incredulous to thoughtful. He stepped forward until he stood a foot away and scrutinized Gid's face with so much concentration, Gid fought not to twitch and fall back.

"Where've you been?" Cap narrowed his eyes with the question.

Gid felt that anger rising again, but he tamped it down and answered as best he could. "The mountain for the past week, then dead to the world in the barracks for the past few hours."

Cap nodded as if this was the correct response. "And now?"

Gid forced down the sigh he felt rising with his frustration. When he was tired, it was always harder to mind his manners. Today was no exception. But one snap of warning from Cap's eyes and he knew he'd better try harder.

"Thought I'd get a shower, Cap, some clean clothes, and coffee. Lots of bitter, dark, hot coffee. If that's okay, sir." He realized he stood at parade rest without even being aware of shifting his position.

Top brass huffed as if he didn't believe it. "So you weren't anywhere around this area any time recently, Kinkead? Is that what you're telling us?"

Gid shook his head, willing his mouth to keep from saying something that could be taken for insubordination.

"No sir, not around here. Though I would like to find a change of clothes." He paused, meeting the man's eyes. "As you can probably tell, sir, I haven't enjoyed a shower in a few days."

Cap snapped into action, pointing at a probationary recruit hovering on the sidelines. "You, find something for him to wear." To another, he barked, "Coffee, and lots of it." And to the top brass, he said, "I think we're done here."

He strode away, leaving the rest of the group staring after him. Over his shoulder, he growled, "Kinkead, with me."

Gid fell out and trotted to catch up. When his stride matched Cap's, he said, "What the hell, Cap?"

Cap shook his head and said, "What the hell, Gid. What the hell."

Scant minutes later, Gid didn't feel like a new man, and he didn't things would get better soon. The pants were too long. The shirt, too tight. Thick socks filled his boots. His briefs were the only thing left of his own, and yes, he'd definitely want to send those to a trash pile as soon as he scored a shower.

"So you last saw your duffel before you headed out a week ago?"

Gid nodded, sipping coffee that hit his system like a miracle drug. His blood zoomed through his veins and he wondered if they added speed to it these days. "You still haven't told me what this is about," he said.

Jake and another deputy leaned against the wall. Top brass had abandoned them, saying they expected a full report. Cap sat behind a desk covered with enough paper to cause a conflagration by itself. He tapped a pencil, the kind you needed to sharpen, with his mangled hand. How he held the pencil and produced that accurate a tattoo given his missing finger, Gid wasn't sure.

Cap shoved his chair back and glanced at Jake, who nodded and said, "Someone left a message. We're wondering what you know about it."

Gid blinked at the comment. Maybe it was the combination of exhaustion and amped up coffee, but he felt confusion wrapping around an intense nervous buzz. "A message?"

Cap nodded, motioning to the mystery deputy. The man came forward with the tablet computer and ran his finger over the screen. When he placed it in front of Gid, a trace of a smug smile lingered on his face.

Gid's eyes dropped to the screen, focusing on the mound of duffels they'd left a short time ago. A few were tossed to the side, some with apparent disregard for where or how they landed. In the center of the pile, Gid could clearly see white lettering on dark blue webbing. His name stood out in bold letters.

He didn't get it. His eyes drifted from Cap, who watched him carefully, to the deputies. Jake had that sympathetic look again, and the other guy seemed too sure of himself, eyeing Gid as if he expected him to dart from the room.

"Show him where we started."

The deputy swiped his finger across the screen a couple of times, stopping when he came to another shot of the mound. In this one, the duffels were neatly stacked and hadn't been moved. Gid's bag wasn't on top of the pile, but a hint of bright red marred the otherwise bland photo.

With a nod from Cap, the deputy swiped again, and the duffels appeared again, from a different angle. The mass of blue, gray, and dark green still appeared to be untouched.

The dark red blob was larger now. A sick sense of intuition settling in Gid's stomach made the coffee churn.

"Look closer," Cap said.

Gid tilted the screen to change the light. The dark red mark was buried under the top layer. It might be the spot where Gid's duffel was buried.

"What is it?" He glanced between the men.

Jake said, "Next shot."

This time, Gid slid the photo and the red filled the screen. A red rose, sticking out of the open zipper of a dark blue duffel. A duffel that could have been his.

"Again," prompted Jake, and Gid slid his finger once more. The top layer of bags had been cleared off, and the location of the rose was now evident. It stuck out of a duffel with white lettering on it, lettering that read Kinkead.

>>>>>

Jake maneuvered the SUV with ease despite the congested traffic of emergency vehicles and support equipment. Gid wondered what he was thinking. Hell, he didn't know what he thought himself. He just hated being sidelined because of what was being labeled suspicious circumstances.

A plastic red rose at the ridge fire.

A plastic red rose in his duffel at camp.

Had he screwed up with some woman who now wanted to send a message? That didn't make any sense. Women didn't complain when Gideon Kinkead left their beds. Or if they did, it was only because he had to go, but he always left them smiling.

The silence hung as dense as smoke from a new fire burn, and yet Jake didn't seem to feel the need to break it. Gid's nerves pulled into a tight knot and he wished he'd taken Cap's advice and hit the chow line. He wasn't hungry, but the steady cups of coffee had taken their toll. And now, he was being escorted to his sterile apartment with the prospect of an investigation looming over his head.

"Who do you think it is?" Jake's question rose out of the silence like a sudden gust of wind.

Gid shook his head. "No clue. I don't think it was anything about me, particularly. It could have been for anyone. The rose landed in my duffel by chance."

Jake tipped his head to the side as if considering this.

"Granted, it could have been any bag. But the weird thing is that those bags were piled up three days ago, according to support staff. No one moved them since. Someone picking up their gear noticed the flower. Your bag was near the bottom. Why not put the rose near the top?"

Gid didn't have an answer for that.

Jake continued, "And then there's the fact that your duffel was partially unzipped. A whole four inches, to be exact. The crime scene kids didn't find any obvious prints. Someone unzipped the duffel and placed the rose there. Or the duffel became unzipped." Jake fell silent, shooting a quick glance at Gid.

He didn't need it spelled out for him. If the duffel became unzipped, its contents could have leaked out. Contents like a plastic flower. As if Gid had been carrying a fucking flower in his bag, exactly like the one found at the arson site.

Jake pulled to a stop in front of the apartment building, scanning around as if by habit. "I should escort you inside, check things out. You know, just in case."

Gid hated the fact that he was probably right. He didn't respond, merely shoving the passenger door open with the minimal gear bag he had been allowed to leave with. His duffel and the rest of his things would be returned to him at some point, he had been assured.

Jake fell in beside him. "For the record, I don't think this is about you. I think it's random. It just happened that you were at the site, and it was your duffel. It could have been any of the other guys too."

Gid didn't say anything. He appreciated the show of support, but only Jake had expressed it. Cap had regarded him with questions in his eyes, as if he thought Gid kept secrets.

His mind flashed to the three white envelopes buried deep in his bedroom, inside dress socks he rarely wore and under the two ties he owned. Their presence was a constant reminder that things were not jolly and merry in his life, but he couldn't bring himself to destroy them.

The grammar was lousy, like the person writing them had minimal education. They seemed to come from a computer printer, not a typewriter. Their words burned into his brain like the wildfire scars on the mountains above Flynn's Crossing.

'You think I wouldn't find you, asshole? Well I did. And I know everything about you. Where you work. Where you live. I even know where you drink.'

This was ridiculous. The letters didn't mean monsters hid in the apartment's shadows. He jogged up the steps to his second floor unit, Jake following behind at a slower pace. No view of the landing was possible from the stairs, and he hesitated for a moment, unsure of what he'd do if something strange waited for him. But the front door was its usual beige blank and nothing waited at its base. He turned his key and almost shoved inside when Jake put a restraining hand on his arm.

"Why don't you let me?" He had a weapon in his hand and turned the knob slowly, pushing it open and waiting.

Waiting, as if he expected gunfire from inside? This bordered on absurd, like a bad movie.

Gid strode past him into the small apartment. The rented furniture looked like it had when he'd left, slightly worn and dingy but serviceable. Dust motes rose in the gusts of outside air. The place smelled stale and unused.

He turned back to Jake, ignoring the punch of relief he felt. "Satisfied?"

Jake shrugged, moving across the floor to peer into the bathroom. His hand rested lightly on the closed bedroom door. Gid froze. Had he left the bedroom door shut? He couldn't remember, but it wasn't something he usually did.

Jake turned the knob in a deliberate motion, swinging the gun up fast when the door disappeared inward. He paused as if scanning the darkness, then advanced. He was gone for scant seconds when he called out.

"Gid, you'd better see this."

Chapter 4

Out of reflex, Dani's gaze swept the bakery's interior before she pushed through the glass door. The jingle of bells accompanied its swing, and the young couple feeding a baby in a stroller glanced up and shared contented smiles. Dani nodded back, her eyes lingering on the open tourist map spread next to their plates and cups. Guests in her little town, and as such, they were under her protection.

Two middle-aged women continued their intense discussion hovering over a computer tablet. Something about pictures and a vacation. A woman Dani recognized from the social services program engaged in a lively debate with a suited man who looked decidedly uncomfortable. As if they reached a decision, they shook hands, the woman's smile sunny while the man gave a rueful hesitant nod.

Satisfied as was as it should be, Dani advanced toward the counter. Peace reigned on Main Street on this May morning, which was a blessing since she was hungry. She scanned again, inhaling the rich scents of coffee and sweets in anticipation. She wasn't on duty for another half hour, and she planned to make the most of her time. Taking her wallet from the pocket of her jeans and shifting her jacket to cover the spot where a gun nestled against her spine, apparent interest triggered her awareness.

Seated in the corner of windows, a man faced her behind sunglasses, with the rest of his features almost hidden by a deep-brimmed cap. The logo marked affinity for an east coast sports club. His clothes did nothing to give away his occupation. But he had time to sit in a bakery on a weekday at mid-morning. Dani recorded what she could of his face, noting that he now smiled with a less than savory appearance. There was something familiar about him, but she couldn't place it.

The whiff of butter and sugar focused her on what was important. Brew Bank Bakery. Her not-so-secret addiction. Breakfast, and some really kick-ass coffee. She made it a habit when Nicolle was out of town.

"Morning. What's your pleasure this fine day?"

Behind the counter, Sarge waited with the ever-present tongs in one hand and bag in the other. It wasn't as if she frequented this fine establishment all that often.

"Your usual?" Stiff paper rustled with provocative patience.

Okay, maybe she was here more than she thought. It helped that she and her twin loved the same thing.

"Hey Sarge. Yeah, two of the usual, and coffee. A big coffee. A fifty-five gallon drum of coffee."

Sarge laughed as he retrieved two chocolate croissants. The sound of them slipping into the bag shivered through her like a seductive whisper. That man could bake. His delicacies were destined for her hips, and she couldn't bring herself to care. When he poured coffee into the largest to-go cup they had, she almost hummed in anticipation.

She moved down the counter to Stuart, his solemn gauntness an abrupt contrast to the jolly round man at the other end. The two couldn't appear more different, and their partnership in business and in life seemed unlikely. That is, it did until they smiled at each other. Then their love was obvious to everyone.

She cut off the envy before it took full hold. There was no time in her busy life for a relationship. She barely had time for sex.

That line of interrogation would only bring her trouble too. Every cop found their way to cope with the stresses of what they saw each day, the effort to remain neutral and fair, the difficulties that came with shifting threats, and the constant need for vigilance. The balanced ones had family, religion, or sports, something healthy. On the other end of the continuum, drugs, booze, and violence ruled lives intended to protect and serve.

Dani found comfort in telling herself she fell closer to the good mechanisms end than the bad. Sex, her outlet. Only willing partners. Nothing kinky or strange. What harm was there in that?

She knew she tried to fool herself, and sometimes it worked. Other times, the stark emptiness of it hit home. One night stands. Men she never saw again. And the worst part? She tried to hide it from Nici.

And why wouldn't she? Nicolle had been through enough. She didn't need to see her twin's addiction. Because it was an addiction, and Dani could admit it. She was addicted to sex.

Across the counter, Stuart cleared his throat, interrupting the dark path of her thoughts. Better to focus on the addiction to chocolate pastry and caffeine. Maybe she should buy a second set for later.

His voice low, Stuart said, "And how are you today, Danielle?"

The man was good. Almost everyone had a hard time telling them apart. But Stuart, with his serious gaze telling her he'd seen and experienced more than the majority of the population, always identified them accurately.

She nodded, wondering as she often did how he pegged them. Today, she had time to learn. She leaned a little closer and asked the obvious. "How do you know?"

A rare grin flashed across his face before he tapped the side of his nose. He regarded her with a knowing expression before leaning in too. "Years of training. The one thing I took away from the service I chose to hold on to."

That explained it. He must have been in intelligence. She'd watched him scan people as they entered as if cataloging their characteristics. He never forgot a name if he learned it. If there was anything going on in the town, it passed by the bakery's windows. Stuart probably noticed that too.

"Anything interesting happening on Main Street, Stuart?"

His eyes flashed behind her and back, the movement quick and imperceptible to most people. But she wasn't most people.

"Not much. Good tourist season, despite the fires. Lots of people coming to taste the wine. Restaurants are booming. It keeps us in dough." He smiled as if appreciating his joke.

She gave him a genuine smile in return, until another thought chased it away. "You heard about the arsons?"

He nodded, his face falling back into its usual graveness. "It's a terrible thing. As much as I've seen, the darker side of human nature can still surprise me."

She reached for the bag of pastries, closing the top against the alluring aromas. "Have you noticed anything or anyone unusual recently?"

His eyes flicked again, and she noted the location. The man in the corner.

"It's hard to tell for sure, of course, because of the tourists." His eyes flicked again, to the couple with the toddler this time. His voice dropped to a conspiratorial level when he continued. "But take that guy in the corner, for example. He's been in a few times. Doesn't talk a lot, other than to get his food. Always takes a table by the window where he watches the street. I've seen him take off fast, leaving a plate of food barely touched, but I can never tell what or who sets him in motion."

Dani shifted, turning sideways to the counter in an effort to glance at the man.

"Not now." The intensity of Stuart's sudden whisper made her pause with the obvious warning. "He's watching you." He never moved his lips as he spoke.

She picked up a package of premixed nuts stacked by the counter and read the back as if engrossed in the list of ingredients. Her eyes flicked up to glance at the area behind the cash register, hoping to find a reflective surface to examine the watcher more closely. Nothing at the right angle.

In his normal voice, Stuart said, "Why sure, you can step in the back and see how your order is coming, but I'll warn you, it isn't anywhere near ready." His sharp gaze on hers urged her to play along.

With a brightness she was far from feeling, she said, "That would be great." Rounding the counter at its end, she stole a look over her shoulder to find the sunglasses faced in her direction, but it was impossible to see precisely where the man's eyes might be focused.

Stuart ushered her into a small office and shut the door, leaning back on a desk strewn with papers and books.

"He's been coming in here every other day. He isn't local. Asks general questions about the people, the area, the climate, the culture."

The hairs on the back of her neck lifted, more in response to his tone than the simple words. "How long has this been going on?"

"Less than a month." Stuart didn't blink as he stared back at her.

"And you didn't think to report it?"

He shrugged. "I worked intel in the military, Danielle. Yes, he ignites my spidey sense, but what would I report? Someone likes to sit in the corner, examine Main Street, and avoid personal topics."

The door opened and shut behind them, and Sarge's bulk filled the remaining space in the room. "Did you tell her about the questions?" His usually jovial demeanor had vanished.

"I didn't have a chance." Stuart turned from his partner to Danielle, his face graver as lines creased his forehead. She'd never seen him this intense, and worry seemed to pulse in the air around them.

"What questions?"

His expression didn't change at her question. "A couple of days ago, he wanted to know if there were many redheads in town. Said he has an affinity for redheads, and would love to learn where they hang out."

Sarge added, "His eyes never left you since you walked in the door."

Her cautious cop side argued with her emotional half, saying this could be completely innocent. A guy comes to town, gets to know the lay of the land, and asks other guys running a popular local hangout where the redheaded women were. No big deal.

Intuition told her otherwise, though she would have preferred evidence. She eyed Stuart more closely. "How reliable is your spidey sense?"

Sarge elbowed his mate and said, "You told her about your spidey sense? Man, now she'll be here every time she needs to solve a big case."

Neither Danielle nor Stuart smiled in response. She continued watching the usually silent man act as his usual self. Silent. Then she turned to Sarge.

"How reliable, Sarge?"

The big man didn't hesitate. "Very, as in save your life very. I get a bad feeling too. I can't tell you why, but it's there in the air around the guy."

Dani nodded, her mind weighing options. She had nothing to go on, and no reason to call for back up. Sarge and Stuart were ex-military in so many secret ways that she had long ago given up trying to pry it out of them, and they would be solid replacements. Her mind could only settle on a single option, engage the man in conversation and see for herself if he was harmless. She swung the door open and headed for the front.

"Thanks guys. I can see this will be a terrific success." She kept her tone light as she passed from the back to the storefront, the men on her heels without another word spoken. It wasn't usually her way to play nice, so channeling Nicolle's energy, she pasted a big smile on her face in the hope that she looked interested and encouraging. She swung around the break in the counter, readying herself to entice the man into a discussion about his purpose in Flynn's Crossing.

Her eyes froze on the table. A plate of crumbs and crumpled napkin sat next to a used mug. The chair stood at a distance from the table, as if the man had left in a hurry. Or was he simply impolite and sloppy and nothing was unusual about him?

It wasn't in her nature to be indecisive. Something didn't sit right about this. If Stuart truly had a sense about these things, something was off. She turned back to the men behind the counter.

"Do you have a clean plastic bag?"

Chapter 5

Gid finished typing out what he remembered from the fire. It might well be the very last fire he was ever on, if Cap had his way. To say his chief was livid would be a description that lacked adequate color.

A plastic flower. A fucking plastic red rose in the middle of his bed. When he'd been gone for over a week. When red roses seemed to be dropping from the sky everywhere he was. When anyone and everyone barked demands for an explanation, he could only shake his head.

He closed gritty eyes and leaned his chair back, wondering if perhaps a change in profession and location might be on the horizon. But that left his doctor brother Noah and his nieces. They moved here only months ago to be closer to him. He'd landed on their doorstep last night when the cops blocked off his apartment and began to tear it apart for clues.

Noah wanted to beg off work at the hospital, worry drawing his usually calm face into a dense set of creases. Gideon urged him to go, saying he would willingly babysit. Elena, his older niece said she was too old for a sitter and hid in her room. That left the younger to entertain him, and she made him promise to play any game she wanted.

Yes, he'd made a promise to a princess dressed in a pink tutu and tiara, surrounded by miniature teacups and dolls. His niece Charlotte, age nine, was already a manslayer, and he was powerless to deny her request. She batted her eyes at him and delivered her decree in her best royal tone.

"Uncle Gid, you have to behave yourself. You make Daddy sad, and I don't want Daddy to be sad."

He didn't want to make Noah sad either. It seemed his little brother carried a load of grief on his shoulders these days, even as he remained kind and caring and the best damn doctor this town probably ever saw. His smile wasn't the easy grin of their childhood. He no longer looked at Gideon with adulation either, and that bit in a big way.

Charlotte continued her proclamation as she regarded him solemnly. "If you behave yourself and make Daddy proud of you, I'll grant you three wishes."

Despite the implication, Gid had smiled at her. He probably looked incredible dorky in the feathery blue boa she demanded he wear as dress-up to her tea party, but what the hell. This was his niece, and he was here to make her happy.

"Any three wishes?"

Char inclined her head. Damn, she did that almost as well as the British royal family. Then she gave him an impish nod. "But I get to pick them."

"That's not fair. What if you wish for something different from what I want?"

He was rewarded with a giggle for his mock protest. "I know what you want, Uncle Gid. You want rain to make the fires go away, and you want Daddy to smile again."

She had both of those right. Noah seemed to spend too outside of work with miserable worry written on his face. Gid wanted to have a talk with him, man to man. A failed marriage had to hurt, despite Noah's declarations to the contrary. His brother needed to get a life again, and his daughters deserved a break.

God, he loved his nieces. Elena was a pill at the enlightened age of twelve. But he understood. She hated Flynn's Crossing. Why Noah had moved the family here wasn't completely clear. He said he'd received a good offer for the house in LA, and he wanted to be near Gideon so the girls could get to know their uncle. Gid thought it was because

Noah's ex-wife was in LA and nothing killed a guy's hook-up buzz faster than exes.

That was why Gid had no exes.

"What's the third wish?" He stuck out his pinkie and took a make-believe sip of mock-tea. The soda in the cup tickled his nose instead. Char's peal of laughter when he sneezed made him warm and fuzzy inside.

"Why, you get to marry a beautiful princess, Uncle Gid. You and Daddy both get princesses. They're brave and strong and wise, and they will love you forever and ever."

Amen to that for Noah. He himself wasn't going that route. Besides, he still hadn't taken care of his problem, and it loomed over him with more urgency each day. Still, Char's proclamation was sweet beyond words.

"Why are you smiling, Kinkead?"

Cap's boom rattled pens in a cup on the desk, and Gid opened his eyes and struggled to his feet, weariness making the move difficult. "I'm not smiling, sir." He was in so much shit, it didn't hurt to lather on extra respect.

Cap stood in his office doorway, staring not at Gid but across the room where an outside entrance opened, letting in the noise of trucks and commotion. Gid turned to follow the gaze and immediately wished he hadn't.

A redhead in a dark regulation fire uniform strode across the room with purpose in every step, as she had in the camp a little over a week ago. She smiled at Cap but made a point of ignoring Gid. He wasn't sure why he felt grateful it wasn't a woman he'd known in the biblical sense. He'd remember those chiseled cheekbones anywhere.

Cap said, "Kinkead, Trajan, my office."

Gid grabbed pages of explanation out of the printer and an unopened bottle of water off his desk. The office door already sucked in the redhead.

Cap slapped his hands on the desk just as Gid walked in. The redhead didn't jump. It figured that a good-looking woman like that would have ice in her veins. And it was too damned bad, because she was gorgeous. Not that he was going to do anything about it, but his reputation would suffer if he didn't at least try.

Gid mirrored her stance and looked at Cap. Cap shook his head, as if he knew exactly what was on Gideon's mind. Then his gaze shifted back to the woman.

"Nicolle Trajan, meet your new investigative partner, Gideon Kinkead. Gid, Nici. She's our origin and cause investigator on this recent rash of fires." He leaned back in his chair as if he now expected them to play nice.

Gid turned, meeting her unflinching gaze and feeling like he didn't measure up. He stuck out his hand, and her grip crushed his for only a moment. She didn't answer his welcoming smile. Yeah, ice in her veins.

Trajan turned away and said, "I don't think this is a good idea, Cap."

Cap said he thought it was a damned good idea, and if Gid read it right, he gave her a pointed glance she was supposed to understand. The woman sighed.

She sighed a lot over the two days since as they studied report after report. Yeah, she was easy on the eyes, but that was it. They had about as much attraction as fire and water. She was hot, but something was missing. At least she'd warmed up to him enough to give him occasional smiles, occasional being the key word.

It didn't help that they found nothing to go on either. Too many assumptions, as if people hadn't time or energy to do their jobs and find answers. It bugged him, making him mumble under his breath, as Trajan reminded him on a regular basis.

She flipped through stacks of files yesterday, and he did the same. Today, they traded stacks. Theirs were supposed to be the fresh eyes finding patterns or links between the fires. A hell of a lot of suspicious fires of every variety had occurred over the past couple of years. If they didn't find something soon, they'd be going back even further. He hated the idea of being stuck behind a desk when there were fires to fight. Trajan didn't see too pleased about it either. At least they were on the same page about that.

Because they argued about everything else. Or she argued, and he merely nodded. The woman made too much damned sense, not that he wanted to admit it to her. She had his grudging admiration, because icy and gorgeous or not, the woman knew her firebug shit.

He tossed his pen at the lined yellow pad, slapping the folder shut with enough force to blow other papers to the floor. "This doesn't make sense."

"What now?" Her pissiness showed. He knew why she was pissed too. She'd told him right off the bat. She thought Gid was involved in these arsons and couldn't figure out why Cap assigned him to the case.

He pushed his pad toward her, pointing at the table he'd drawn from his analysis. "A different accelerant in each fire. A different combustible fuel. Varied structures. Geographically different locations. I'm not convinced we're looking at a serial."

He eyeballed her over his boots, propped on the table in the cramped room. How she'd wrangled a place in the sheriff's evidence locker, he wasn't sure. There was nowhere else for them to work at fire command. Her gaze flicked between his face and his boots, as if she saw something nasty in both places.

"You forget the common denominator, Kinkead." She waited for him to comment, and when all he did was return her intense stare, she added, "You."

He said nothing. What would be the point? He'd already argued she wasn't being objective. She kept pointing to what she deemed to be evidence. Not for the first time, she yanked forward a case file he already knew by heart. Even though he expected it, he couldn't hide the flinch or the jerk of his foot to the floor when she threw down a photo on the table like a gauntlet before battle. The manifesto, delivered to his squad during a particularly hellacious blaze, and again, one of suspicious origin.

'Justice will be mine. Punishment will be mine. Revenge will be mine.'

The page-long single-spaced rant had been analyzed to death by experts, with no answers other than it was the work of a nutcase. Gid had it memorized, with a copy of it now tucked with the letters the team searching his apartment had thankfully missed. They burned a figurative hole in his duffel.

Gideon dropped his other boot harder than intended, drawing a disapproving shake of Nicolle's head. He responded in kind, but he didn't meet her eyes.

"It could be a coincidence. We've been at many strange fires this year. You know, since we're the elite squad."

"That doesn't explain anything. The same kind of rose was found at the scene of a manmade fire. It was in your gear the next time. Another one found on your bed in your apartment. Why is that, Kinkead?"

He jumped up because he couldn't control his jitters anymore. He was a big strong firefighter, and he wanted to cry like his little niece sometimes. He fingered something soft, realizing with another twitch that he held fuzzy handcuffs in his fingers. If they ever strapped a pair on him, he doubted they'd be of this variety. The messages, sick and threatening, held proof of his innocence.

Or they might not see it as proof. Cap might believe him. Noah certainly would, and would be damned pissed Gid hadn't said anything sooner. But the rest? That pack of vultures flapped eagerly as they readied to dismember his firedog body and eat his still-beating heart.

He kept his face to the fuzzy cuffs, not wanting to read whatever disbelief filled Trajan's face when he said the words. She might call for a deputy and arrest him on the spot. He said, "Have you ever felt like you're being watched, Trajan? Like someone's drilling their eyes in your back, except when you turn around, you can't see them?"

She didn't respond, probably texting for help even as he spoke. He couldn't blame her. This wouldn't sit well with Cap or the brass.

She cleared her throat, and he waited for the condemnation. If their positions were reversed, he wasn't sure he'd react any better. But at least he had documentation to back up his theory.

Trajan said, "I have felt that, Kinkead. What are you trying to tell me?"

Chapter 6

The glass had long since lost its earlier chill and the beer inside tasted tepid at best. No matter. It was beer. He figured he'd earned the right to a little down-low time. Running his fingers up and down the glass's familiar shape, he skimmed the room for a likely candidate for the evening. The list of possibilities seemed to grow shorter each night over the past month he'd been stuck in town.

A nice looking woman at the end of the bar flicked her fingers at him with a hopeful smile on her face. Nope. When had he gone home with Debbie? Two months ago? He returned a grin, but moved on.

That curly-brown-haired chick eyed him with needy hope on her face. Every time he saw her, he found her unsettling in a way he couldn't identify, like she was trying too hard. No way.

Ah, there was Janice. But she wasn't watching him now. He'd have to work some magic there. She liked to play hard to get, and he hadn't gotten to her yet. Did he even feel like playing games tonight?

Gid sobered with the thought. Back to the front lines of danger tomorrow, a place he usually felt in control. It was better than staring at files in an office, and he was thankful Cap had finally seen the wisdom in deciding to put him back where he belonged.

Despite the dangers, on the line Gid felt whole. Vulnerability shifted faster than wind direction when looking into the explosive maw of Madame Fire. Things escalated on a daily basis. You never knew when your number was up. Just look at those hotshots in Washington and Oregon. His turn could be next. It was time to tell his brother the truth while he could explain. Then he'd find a nice girl and give her a few hours of distracted bliss.

"You're making a pretty good dent in that beer," Jake said, his tone neutral. Good old Jake, always a buddy to count on for a distraction. He'd known the man to get plastered a time or three in the recent past, but tonight he nursed a soda until the fizz had gone flat. Thank the fire goddess the corner they occupied was dark. Gid had a reputation to uphold, and soft drinks weren't part of that persona.

Gid took a sip, a longer one than he actually wanted to make his point. "Back to the fire line tomorrow. When do you return to full duty?"

Jake didn't respond, his face falling into a dark glower with a sharp inhale. He twisted in his seat, and Gideon felt a moment of remorse. His friend carried his pain as if it was something he'd never be able to lose. The unknown of trying to heal from an injury that might end a career must be a bitch.

"There he is."

Turning to follow Jake's chin lift, Gid saw his brother glance at the blaring flat screens. His eyes tracked high on the walls to take in the stuffed trophies with their vague eyes. The tightening of his lips radioed his air of disapproval.

"Noah, hey, over here." Gid waved an arm, sliding up from his slouch in the chair. At least he could look like he had his act together.

Noah's gaze traveled back down, settling on Gid. Sports games lit his expression in stunning technicolor, and it wasn't hard to read. Relief. Worry. Tension.

Gideon kicked a chair away as he approached, gesturing to the pitcher and an empty glass. His brother didn't respond, standing and staring at the tabletop and the array of glassware with a frown.

Gid tried again. "Hey bro, glad you could make it. Girls get off okay?"

Noah crumpled into the chair as if the words sucked the energy out of him. Sending his daughters to their mother's for the summer must hurt more than Gid could imagine. He didn't understand much of what made his brother tick anymore, but he knew he loved his girls more than anything and the next few months would be lonely for him. Gid tried to ignore the guilt his own leaving would add to that burden. He'd introduce his brother to some of the ladies, and maybe someone would click.

Gid scanned the room again with quick eyes, trying to find suitable prospects. A woman who could give Noah a good time, but was smart and intellectual. Almost any of them would love to date a doctor. Hell, most of them would love to play doctor. The thought made him smile.

He looked back at his brother, ready to spring the idea on him. On second thought, let Noah think it was the lady's idea. Or that he himself made the first move.

"Noah? Everything okay?"

The question came not from Gideon but from Jake. The cop's gaze carried a hint of wariness.

"Yes, but I miss the girls already."

Jake nodded with understanding in his expression and pushed the beer pitcher and empty glass across the table. Noah stared as if debating the merits of a drink, finally reaching out with a decisive nod. Gid drained his and pushed his empty across the table as encouragement, meeting his little bro's direct stare.

The examination was thorough, as if Noah could see through skin and muscle and bone to the heart underneath. Another shift in expression pulled his eyebrows in and small lines radiated from the corners of his eyes as he paused there. Gid wanted to rush him along, but he kept silent. Something told him he was on the receiving end of an assessment that wasn't flattering. When Noah finally turned his attention to the beer, he only filled Gid's glass halfway.

Pulling in a breath to protest, he met Noah's gaze once more and read the message. He did not approve.

Well screw that. He didn't need Noah's approval. He grabbed the pitcher and filled the glass to the top.

Gid lifted the drink. "Cheers," he said, and barely waited for responses before he put the glass to his lips and drank heavily. When he stopped, only a quarter of his pour remained.

Frowning in turn, Noah took a brief sip. When he set the glass down on the scarred table, his touch was almost gentle, like he was caring for a fragile patient. Yeah, his brother could send messages without saying a word and be a total pain in the ass at the same time.

But he couldn't leave things this way. Call it a niggling sense of doom, but Gid didn't want any bad blood between them, not tonight. The thought sobered him faster than an explosive eruption in a dead zone. He inhaled, wishing he smelled clear sweet forest instead of the stench of booze and sweat.

"Thanks for coming out tonight, guys, really, thanks. I wanted a sendoff. I can't tell you why. Just a feeling I have." Gideon drained his beer and reached for the pitcher.

Noah pushed his nearly full glass to the side with a resigned sigh, one Gideon could hear over the noise of the games and voices rising and falling. It pushed his buttons. His brother, all righteous and solemn, had no place to be judging. Sure, he saved lives on a daily basis, but so did Gid. How the hell could he ever live up to his little brother's example? Remorse and anger warred inside him, forcing his hand down on the tabletop hard enough to make everything jump.

Was someone watching them even now? The bar's corners could hide secrets in their darkness. His eyes darted to those spaces, wondering if they guarded his stalker. The letters said the person knew where he drank, and he usually drank here. The idea made him squirm, sliding low in an effort to make himself invisible.

His behavior was crazy, he knew. Inside his head, he had a running conversation with himself, and its reasonable voice sounded remarkably like his brother's. Noah was only trying to look out for him. He, Gideon, should be looking out for little bro instead. But what could he do when he was on a fire line? Noah would be on his own, and everyone knew he didn't have a violent bone in his body. He could suggest Noah carry some kind of knockout drug in a syringe. The idea brightened his mood.

Gid toasted himself for the idea and drained his glass, letting it land back on the table with a wobbly slam. He caught the sadness on Noah's face, and he remembered why he'd wanted to talk with him tonight. It killed his buzz without so much as a whimper.

Gid alternated between seething and sorry. Both emotions pointed back to him. Sorry he dragged his brother out and then turned into such a looser of a host. Sorry he'd let things go too far, so far that Noah vetoed the new pitcher idea and a couple of sexy blondes and dragged Gid to his minivan.

His brother's mouth settled into a thin line of disapproval, one that didn't lessen as the miles passed by. "What time do you need to be up tomorrow?" Noah delivered the question with no hint of emotion in his voice.

Gid said, "Base by nine. Still plenty of time to relax and party, you know."

Noah didn't say anything, as if he was ignoring him. Gideon slapped his shoulder, wanted his brother's attention.

He got it in spades, as Noah's angry eyes flashed in his direction at the same time he overcorrected on a turn. The swerve wasn't major, and Noah's reaction seemed out of place. His yell echoed in the van's big interior. "What the fuck is wrong with you?"

Another swerve settled them on the shoulder of the road, and Gid braced himself on the overhead grab handle. When his brother jerked the gearshift into park and shut off the ignition, the sudden silence made Gid wish he'd never taunted him in the first place.

"What is wrong with you?" Noah's question held less heat this time, as if he truly didn't understand Gideon's behavior.

Figuring it was a rhetorical question, Gid said nothing. Besides, what could he say? Apologize for being a dope of an older brother? He turned toward Noah, who had settled against the driver's door as if he planned to stay there for a while. His intense gaze made Gid feel uneasy.

"I asked you a serious question, Gideon. I don't get what's going on. Do you know how bad this is for you? Your liver is probably a mess. You've slept with almost every woman in town. And I've heard there are problems at work."

Gid closed his eyes and leaned his head back. Yes, he fucking well knew that. He could feel it. If he could run from his problems in any other way, he would. He banged his head against the side window, liking the thud it provided. He deserved it. He did it again, then once more for good measure.

With that clunk of clarity, pain. Memories of a bulky shape lurching out of flames and smoke. He'd never forget that vision. The man he couldn't save. The child's screams. It was hard to get any volume to his voice over the pain of it. In a whisper, he said, "Noah, I killed someone."

He felt time slow as Noah's face morphed from passive disapproval to active shock. Eyes widened, breath caught, movement froze. It was like watching something in slow motion. Gid couldn't say a word.

Noah said nothing. The only reason Gideon was sure he'd heard the words was the staggered expression. His brother probably didn't know what to say.

Noah faced forward, his movements hesitant. He toyed with his keys, and even in the darkness, Gid noted the shaking hand. He hated himself for how much he disappointed Noah. The engine caught and Gid faced forward as well, resigned to whatever was going to happen next.

The silence stretched out as his brother pulled into the parking lot of Gid's apartment building. He shut off the engine and sat still with his eyes forward. Gid waited, then posed the obvious question. "Are you going to ask?"

Noah shrugged. "I figure it was the booze talking. You didn't exactly go easy on the beer."

If he only knew. Gideon felt bitter laughter rise and he didn't bother to try to hold it in. His younger brother was so naive. A pitcher of beer as fast as he could drink it wouldn't take the edge off Gid's trepidation. He said, "You missed the shots of Maker's Mark that came before the beer."

Noah sighed. Was that a grunt of disbelief? Noah didn't get it, and the only way he would is if Gid told him the whole story. Something held him back, though.

When was the last time Noah looked at him with respect and admiration? He used to look up to him, back when they were kids and Gid was big and strong and knocked sense into anyone who messed with his younger bro. He shied away from the censure in his brother's eyes.

But what if he didn't come back this time? He wanted Noah to understand. In the darkness and fear, it suddenly seemed like everywhere he looked, someone might be watching. The shadows in the quiet residential neighborhood appeared to waver and move, as if ready to pounce. Gid sucked in air and blew it out, unable to hide the tremble in his voice when he spoke.

"Look, I know you don't understand, but every time I go out now, I'm scared. Scared something will happen to one of my crew. Scared something will happen to me. Just plain terrified."

Noah shook his head as if he didn't want to hear it. Hell, he was going to hear it. He was going to damn well hear it, and by the time Gideon was done, he'd damn well understand it, too. His life could be in danger. Gid tried again, hoping Noah would turn to see the fear in his eyes.

"I know what you're thinking. You're saying to yourself, he's drunk. He doesn't know what he's saying. I talk a good game and I put on a great show. But deep down, these days? It's all a front."

Noah shoved open the door and stamped his feet on the driveway as he rounded the van's hood. Gid didn't want to get out, but he didn't want to have this conversation out here, where anyone could be watching them. Anyone could have followed them from the bar. Damn it, Noah was going to listen to him if it took all night. His eyes lost focus as his thoughts slipped to a wall of flames and young screams.

Would the vision ever leave him? The man's bulky torso lumbering toward him as if unaware his clothing smoked and small flames licked at his scalp. A roar, either from the fire or its victim, had Gid rushing forward. He wasn't sure what he would have done, because he never got the chance. The man made a grab for him, and Gid flinched away in self-preservation. If they both went down, they would burn to death. But if he could get the man outside, they stood a chance of surviving. Until the child raced through the door and into the old man's arms.

"Come on, Gid. Let's go hydrate you with something healthy. You can get to bed and sleep it off."

He hadn't even noticed Noah with his hand on the door's outer handle. He stared at him, mute and shaking. He wasn't sure his feet would hold him if he put them to the ground. Noah didn't seem to notice as he continued.

"By the time you reach camp tomorrow, you'll be ready to take on any spark from here to the Canadian border."

Gid pushed back against the memory, shoving hard. He gulped in air, thinking he must be dreaming because he thought he could smell the stench of burning flesh, unlike any other odor on the planet. A cackling laugh. Screams, some of them his, as his crew dragged him away from the cabin engulfed in flames. No one deserved to die like that.

Noah still stared at him, resignation on his face. Gid attempted to pull himself together. Hydration. Hydration would be good. Anything to sooth a throat that felt as raw now as it had that day.

His brother watched him if as if weighing options. Finally, he nodded as if deciding something. He said, "Tell me what you need, Gid. You know I'd do anything to help you."

Gid heard the note of grim worry, the surrender to the inevitable. He felt it too. Noah would stand by him no matter what. He didn't want to add to his brother's burdens, but damn, he didn't want to be alone tonight.

Chapter 7

Dani leaned against the doorjamb, feeling the weight of worry telegraphing across the room. Nicolle had a predictable routine as she checked her gear, not so different from the one Dani followed each morning with her guns, her equipment belt, and her communications. She knew her twin was as capable and agile in her chosen surroundings. That didn't make knowing what came next any easier.

Running into danger. Nicolle wasn't supposed to run into danger. That was Dani's job. It's too bad her sister hadn't picked something else for a career, like librarian. She never wanted to send Nicolle off with anything but a smile, because she didn't want her worrying for a precious second on the line about what Danielle was feeling. She pasted a smile on her face, hoping it wasn't a false giveaway.

She asked, even though she knew the answer wouldn't be something they could count on. "How long, do you think?" The coffee in her cup tasted bitter on her tongue, and she nearly stopped her twin when she reached for the mug.

Nicolle took a sip and mirrored the grimace. "Ugh, you put sugar in it. What's that about?"

Dani smiled despite her worry, feeling the ache of too little sleep and too many stresses. A day off was a rare treat for her, and yet she felt restless and unsettled. Chalk it up to Nicolle leaving for the line. Ever since the incident, she worried. At least Nici worked in an office now, though Dani wanted to check out this assigned partner of hers, Kinkead. Something about him and those stories about trophies left behind at his fires wired her instincts. She retrieved her mug from Nicolle's outstretched hand and took a sip without losing her fake grin.

Nicolle didn't respond, her face serious as she continued to open zippers, riffle contents, and shut sections with rapid movements. Tension held her posture stiff, and Dani examined the line of her straight spine as her own anxiety grew. There would be one definite reason why Nicolle would be more agitated than usual as she set off for a longer fire deployment.

Dani swallowed the lump in her throat and asked the inevitable question. "You, ah, going out with any of the all-male crews?"

Nicolle turned her back, hiding whatever expression crossed her face. She didn't reply, but the jerkiness of her movements communicated her displeasure with the line of interrogation. Dani tried another tactic.

"Any new info on the firebug?"

Still nothing. Why wasn't Nicolle talking to her?

"You haven't answered any of my questions. Are you pissed off with me? Because I can't help it. Ever since – well, you know – I can't help but worry about you. You're the other half of my yolk."

One of their secret phrases, guaranteed to make them both smile. Some of Dani's anxiety melted at Nicolle's strained grin.

"I'm not mad at you. I have no idea how long, which you know. Yes, I might be out with all-males crews, but not like before. And you know as much as I do about the situation. Briefing concluded. I need to haul butt."

Dani reached for the heavier duffel and headed for the door, leaving the backpack for Nicolle. She hated this uncertainty, this goodbye, when they had no idea how long it would last. She wasn't joking about the yoke thing. If anything happened to Nicolle, she'd never be whole again. She settled the duffel in the back of Nicolle's pick-up with more care than it required, as if that would protect her sister. When she turned back, she couldn't help the solemn expression or sudden surge of intense affection.

"You'll be careful." She didn't want it to sound like a command, but it did.

"You be careful. I don't need a gun on my hip to do my job."

When Dani looked into the mirror of her face, she frowned. "Maybe that wouldn't be such a bad idea."

Nicolle blew out a sigh as she grabbed her for a tight hug, one Dani returned and held on to a little longer than she probably should.

"Be safe," Nicolle said.

"Be safe," Danielle echoed.

Nicolle turned her truck around and paused at the end of their driveway with a wave in the rear view mirror. Dani did what was expected, lifting her middle finger in a wave of her own. She bet it put a smile on her twin's face. That was all she wanted.

She stood long after the engine's noise fade away, unable to avoid the sinking feeling in her heart. The day off stretched in front of her with too many empty spaces. If Nici was off too, they'd go for a run, raid the grocery store for snack food, and indulge in a movie marathon. Dani always voted for blow-'em-up movies, but secretly, she enjoyed the chick flicks her twin usually chose. They'd share a big bowl of popcorn, douse it with lemonade, and follow all that up with some monster burgers on the grill. That grill was the only piece of cooking equipment Dani could use with any reliability.

But Nici wasn't here. Nici would be up in the mountains, chasing fires that colored the morning sky a hazy orange. It didn't matter how long Dani stood in their driveway and glared upwards. Her ill ease would not put out the flames any faster. Going to office on her day off was sounding better and better.

She tossed the remainder of the bitter brew in her mug at the bushes next to the drive. The sugar might help the scraggly plants. Dani had no idea what they were, though they would probably benefit more from the sugary coffee than she would. Nicolle refused to water things, saying they needed to have defensible space and a drought-tolerant landscape. Plants that needed water didn't survive. Since neither one of them knew a thing about gardening, empty spaces were the norm in their design.

Empty spaces, too many empty spaces. Too many gaps in her life too. What she had revolved around her work and her family, with a sprinkling of friends she wasn't that close to. Digging her fingers into her temples, Dani gave up the fight. Work it would be. At least there, she was in control.

An hour later, she realized the fallacy of that idea too. "Trajan, you're setting a bad precedent. You can't yell at the deputies for coming in on their days off when you do the same damned thing yourself."

"Yes sir, I realize that. But my situation is different."

The sheriff's pursed lips and huff of disapproval told Dani what he thought of her situation. Her work was important to her, and they never had enough manpower or time to break through on any number of cases. The arsonist targeting their county and the surrounding communities was a perfect example.

"I'm going to only say it once more, Lieutenant. Go. Home. I don't care what you do there on your off hours, but I don't want to see you here again until oh-seven-hundred tomorrow when you're on duty. Am I clear?"

Dani snapped a salute and said, "Crystal, sir."

The man looming over her desk didn't hang around for a second longer. She appreciated his position. As an elected official, he had to balance between taking care of his personnel and pleasing the constituency. The fact that additional funding was not forthcoming didn't make a difference to the people they served. They expected a deputy to be there when they needed them and to leave them alone when they didn't.

Once upon a time, Dani thought she might want to run for sheriff someday. That's was when she was idealistic, impressionable, and innocent. She lost all that not long after joining the force when she realized some people didn't want to be helped. That was the beginning of the change, and to this day, she had to live with the consequences.

She swept the files from her desk into her briefcase. If she couldn't work on things here, she would at home. Who knew that being a lieutenant came with so much paperwork? The impressive mound bulged her bag, but she added another stack to strain the handle anyway.

Half an hour later, she'd settled into her favorite spot in the living room, turned on the continuous loop of weather gabbers on the big screen, and sipped a glass of lemonade. Her kind of relaxing day off, with a stack of cases to review and documentation to sign. She pushed that aside, though, and pulled the smaller pile toward her.

Arsons. It wasn't her strongest investigative expertise. She relied on Nicolle to explain fire nuances to her. How things got started. Why they burned fast or slow. What direction they would race based on the weather. But there was one thing she knew better than her twin. How to catch a bad guy.

She flipped through the files of unsolved suspicious fires. Most even she could tell would probably be ruled accidental with time. Others awaited test results from crime labs backed up for months. The system limped along despite its shortcomings. She turned pages until her eyes crossed, but she saw nothing new.

The final file in the stack was thicker than the others. Its tab was well worn, as if it had been visited a time or twelve for a review. A fire at a cabin that resulted in two fatalities. The number of the elite fire squad assigned to the case sounded vaguely familiar.

The final page in the file before the photo sleeve held an interesting tidbit. A white rose had been found on a picnic table at the squad's campsite after the fire. The item had been deemed a memorial to the firefighters' hard work to save the pair in the cabin. The evidence was never analyzed and now missing, so the only information they had about it was hearsay.

Dani didn't believe in hearsay. She wanted facts, proof, and substantiation. But a white rose, and now red roses? What were the odds? She read on to the bottom of the page, lifting her drink for a sip. Her hand stopped before the glass reached her lips.

The name of Gideon Kinkead jumped off the page as if the words screamed. Kinkead, her twin's new investigative partner. He had been involved in that cabin fire, and now trophies appeared at his fires here.

Dani knew there was no such thing as coincidence.

Chapter 8

Gideon lengthened his angry stride, kicking up dirt in clots as each step pressed deep into churned soil. Another fire. Another suspected damned arson. And here he was on the front lines. Cap looked at him funny. He was beginning to feel paranoid, like everyone suspected him of something. Even his brother.

Or rather, Noah probably suspected him of overreacting. He'd told Noah about the man and child in the cabin, the ones who would haunt his dreams for eternity. His brother had relented and said it was an awful way to watch someone perish. What he didn't seem to understand, though, was how this was Gideon's fault. He'd insisted as much, until Gid blew his cool.

After that, Gid kept the rest to himself, slipping into silence when Noah wanted to talk about post-traumatic stress disorder and the tricks it can play on someone's memory. Noah talked until Gid couldn't stand it anymore, and he raced out the door without a backwards glance. The finger he raised in response to Noah's final words expressed his sentiments exactly.

Gid could concede the stupid plastic flowers were undoubtedly a bad joke. Whoever had been dropping them around had hopefully gotten the message that everyone on the squad thought the joke had gone sour. Of course, that fire investigator, Trajan, thought they meant something. It was in her serious face, her heated questions, and her distance. She'd listened to his story about the cabin and feeling like he was being watched, but she hadn't given that credence when it came to the fires.

But the letters were real. He told her about those, and she wanted to see them. Evidence, she called it. When he hesitated to reveal their location, Trajan had fallen silent, but the narrowing of her eyes and careful step back from him let him know what she thought. She didn't believe him.

He was convinced he was the target and not the cause. The only way to prove it was to catch whoever was igniting things and put a fire under the perpetrator himself. But first, he had to find him. Early reports indicated this fire had its origins at the top of the hill in front of them, and he wanted first shot at the investigation.

He brought his radio closer to his mouth to be heard over the general commotion of the camp's equipment yard. "Cap? Kinkead."

The radio crackled with Cap's booming voice. "Kinkead, I need you on the southeast line, and –" Additional static made the rest unintelligible. Gideon curbed his impatience. He didn't want to be on the southeast line. He wanted to be at the top of that ridge, finding the source of this fire. If there was another plastic flower in the vicinity, he planned to bag it and deliver it to a crime lab himself. He hoped that would support his innocence.

"Cap, I want to take a look at the ridge where the fire blew up. Before too much time passes." He stopped speaking, hoping Cap would understand the unsaid in his message.

Snaps and pings of unknown sounds with occasional garbled words filled the air, leaving Gid with the uneasy sensation of being cut off from what he knew and loved in the midst of everyone else's action. His feet carried him forward toward a line of small trucks dwarfed by larger vehicles with tanks on the back. One by one, they rolled out of formation, each one kicking up dust and debris in their hasty departures. He was supposed to be on one of those, headed for a jump off point near the fire's advancing line. He glanced up in the opposite direction of the ridge tops instead.

"Kinkead? Are you sure?"

His name and the question were clear and simple. So was the intent behind the message. If he found anything out of the ordinary up there, his ass might be kicked out and prosecuted faster than a snag torching. But if no one else was going to clear his name, it was up to him alone.

Gid keyed the mic. "Yeah Cap."

The pause might only be momentary, but it was long enough to send Gid's nerves into a state of renewed jitters. Then Cap's voice boomed through the comm as if he was standing next to him. "Okay Kinkead, take a truck and check on those two ridges. There are four cabins along the ridge, and two are occupied by full timers."

"Copy." He raced to the last truck in the line.

He turned the key at the same moment the opposite door of the cab pulled open. The burly form of a firefighter, his face obscured by the shield of his helmet, jumped inside with a heave and topple. The man behind the shield grinned in greeting. Gid stopped in the act of putting the truck into gear, staring at his passenger.

"What the hell, Curtis?"

The man shrugged, his grin widening. "Cap said you needed eyes out for you, so here I am. You know, to watch your back and all."

Gid wasn't sure if he felt relief or worry. Either Cap sent Curtis to keep an eye on him, to make sure he didn't mess with evidence, or Cap thought there was more danger ahead than Gid could handle on his own. He didn't like either choice. He shoved the truck into gear harder than necessary and put his foot down hard enough to jerk the vehicle forward.

Keeping a steadying hand on the wheel, he glanced back at Curtis with a curt nod. "My lead. We clear the cabins, and we check the fire source to make sure we don't lose any important evidence. You got a problem with that?"

He glanced at the road, then back at the firefighter. Curtis had his hands spread in the universal sign for no problem, then his eyes darted to the windshield and he swore as he braced against the dashboard.

Gid turned back to see what captured his attention in time to see a figure dive out of the truck's path. He swerved the wheel in the opposite direction, relieved not to feel the telltale bump of tires over flesh and bone. But that didn't mean the person was okay. He jammed on the brakes and tumbled out of the door before swirls of dust cleared.

Jogging around the truck, he gave himself a mental kick in the ass for being so distracted that he nearly hit one of their own. He knew better. Hell, he berated anyone in his crew who would act like this. He was so off his game, he almost hurt someone. Then his eyes fell on the tightly curled body and the red braid.

"Trajan, what the fuck are you doing standing in the middle of the road?"

She shifted on the ground, coughing and stretching with no apparent injuries, but that didn't make him feel any better. In fact, he wanted to kick himself harder. Trajan might not like him, but over the time they'd worked together, he'd developed a healthy respect for her knowledge and a brotherly sense of protectiveness for her wellbeing. The fact that she was easy on the eyes only made the days brighter even if she never would give him a social inch.

She rolled to her feet, and he worried she moved too quickly. A fall like that would jar anyone, and he wrapped a protective hand around her upper arm to steady her. Why the hell was she standing in the middle of the road anyway? He reached for the laptop she clutched to her chest, intent on keeping it from dropping out of her arms.

"What the hell are you doing racing through camp?" She spat out the words as she shook off the helping hand.

He should feel remorse. He should feel say he was sorry. But the anger in her face stopped his gentler feelings and let his own frustration speak first. He didn't bother holding back the snarl in his voice. After all, Trajan believed he was a torch.

"Curtis and I need to clear the ridge. The houses up there." He pointed through smoke that suddenly swirled and thickened, obscuring their view. He couldn't waste time. People might be hiding in those cabins. He didn't want to think about the rest.

"We don't need to be mowing down crew in the process, now do we?" She stepped away from him with a disgusted look on her face, as if being close to him sickened her. Not only did she not believe he was innocent. She didn't like him either. So be it.

"Kinkead, come on," Curtis yelled from behind them. The truck's exhaust mixed with the smoke and bit into his eyes, blurring his vision. His head pounded, and he wasn't sure if it was from the remnants of last night's liquor or the tension vibrating through his nerves. He had a job to do, and damned if this one wasn't more important than all the rest.

"Watch where you're going, Trajan," he said. She was in his way. Someone was always in his way. He'd never be clear of the incriminations, the assumptions, and the doubts if he didn't clear his name. He turned away before he said something he'd need to apologize for later.

"She okay?" Curtis saved the words until they left the boundaries of the camp. Gid didn't bother to respond. Curtis didn't pursue it, which was also a damned good thing. Gid didn't feel like talking.

How had his life ended up in this mess? He worked hard. Yeah, he played hard too, but he didn't hurt anyone in the process, except maybe himself. A little voice whispered an addition. Noah. His brother worried about him too much.

Gideon felt a new wave of remorse. He made his brother's life harder, not easier. He hadn't been completely honest with him because he, the older brother, thought he was protecting Noah by giving him fewer concerns.

In truth, it was because he, the older brother, was a chicken shit coward. Saying the words aloud, sharing the letters, would make it all too real. Despite the heavy turnouts and the heat of the day, he shivered. His sweaty fingers gripped the wheel harder as they bounced over the rutted road, their headlights catching twisting spirals of smoke in devil's dances.

Curtis pointed through the veils. "There's the turnoff. The first one's about two miles ahead."

>>>>>

The first cabin proved a waste of time, empty as if abandoned for seasons. Remnants of animal nests and chewed holes told the story as clear as a fresh breeze.

Gid trotted back to the truck, eager to get to the next site. He'd wanted to start nearer the origin, but Curtis's calmer sense prevailed. Clear the closer ridge, giving anyone left in the structures more time to get out. Driving faster than was probably a good idea, they reached the second cabin and pulled up as an older couple shoved items into the back of a sports utility vehicle. They waved distractedly as they slammed the back gate.

Gid got out and approached them, happy to see that they didn't appear to be people who would argue with an evacuation order. The woman ran toward him, panic evident on her features.

"I know, we left it too long. Can we get down the road?"

"Yes ma'am, you should be able to get out, but you need to leave now. Do you know of anyone else who's still in the area?" Gid glanced around their house, feeling frustration at what he observed. A well-kept property, a good firebreak, and neat surroundings cleaned of understory and debris. They'd done what they should to protect their home, but it wasn't enough. Someone was bent on destruction and didn't care who or what was in its path.

The woman flapped her arms in a distracted movement and waved in the general direction of the other ridge. "The

Pattersons are gone, on a river cruise in Europe, and their place is empty. They wanted us to go with them, but we couldn't afford it. Granddaughter's college graduation, that was our travel budget for the year. We were so sorry, because the trip looked so nice and all. But now I'm glad, because we wouldn't be here to gather what we can. Is the fire going to take the rest?"

The tears in her eyes and pain in her expression tightened a grip on Gid's heart. He hated this. This was probably all these folks had, and they would lose it. He keyed his mic.

"Four-eight? Got a structure on the ridge we're clearing. Good defensible space. Can you give us a hand?"

A voice came back almost immediately, confirming the transmission and the coordinates, with an ETA of seven minutes. Gid gave the woman a reassuring smile. When she reached up and kissed his cheek, he felt a blush color his face. He gave her a gentle push toward the SUV now idling a few feet away.

"We're going to save your home if at all possible, and these guys are pretty determined. Keep going down the hill and don't stop. Someone in the fire camp will direct you to the aid station where you can get settled until we get this under control."

A thick lump grew in his throat as the woman gave a final look at her home, tears streaming down her face. As the SUV pulled away, he saw her put her face in her hands as the man reached across the front seat to pat her back.

Yeah, they were going to catch this guy, and then Gideon would take great pleasure in giving him a punch in the gut for every line of worry in any resulting victim's face. He raced back for the fire truck with renewed energy.

"Two down, two to go," Curtis said, already directing Gid with a wave of his hand.

"Can you tell which cabin is owned by someone named Patterson? They're on vacation. That leaves one, and that one should be empty."

Curtis grunted and typed, his big fingers jamming on keys with an occasional lighter tap. "Head left at the T."

Radio noise filled the truck in spurts of sound. Over it, the rattle of gear in the back and the whine of the engine measured their progress. Where the road split right and left, Gid veered left fast enough to make both men rock in their seats. The right tires probably left the road, but he didn't care. This direction took them closer to the fire's origin, one more ridge over on the other side of a steep canyon. Once they'd cleared the cabins, they could investigate the source of this monster.

He wanted the bastard more with each passing minute. An unknown face, a mystery in motive, a person who had no morals.

"There it is. There's a truck out back and tools lying around. Someone might still be here." Curtis already had his hand on the door handle before Gid pulled to a stop.

"Wait." Gid gripped the man's sleeve. Something didn't feel right. The place looked too perfect. There was no sense of hurry. The truck was almost new but dusty, as if it hadn't been washed in quite a while. Who would leave a location like this with an active fire so close and leave behind a vehicle worth tens of thousands of dollars? The tools looked almost new too.

"Kinkead, come on. There's a truck. Someone might still be in there. We need to get them out. The fire could flash up the canyon any time now. We gotta check."

Curtis was right. Maybe only one person was here and they had another vehicle, and they could only drive one out. Or maybe they'd gone to town and couldn't return. Roadblocks kept everyone away from this area. He shook off the feeling of dread and pulled on his gloves. Mirroring

Curtis's movements, his boots hit the ground and he trotted toward the cabin's front door.

"I'll check the back," Curtis shouted, pointing toward the place where the truck was parked. He didn't wait for Gid's acknowledgment.

That sense that something was off swept over Gid again. Maybe he should call Curtis back, and they should examine this site together. His feet slowed as he stared around the walkway, taking in the ax leaned against a wood chopping block, the stack of completed firewood off to the side, and path swept free of pine needles.

That was it. The place was too neat, but not neat. Someone who cared enough to sweep the every-falling pine needles from a dirt path wouldn't leave an ax that looked brand new outside. They'd put it inside, away from any damage from the elements. His next glance located a garden hose wound in tight coils, but free of any needles as cover. The front steps were clean too, as if the person had just been here. He shook off the trepidation as Curtis rounded the opposite side of the cabin.

"No sign of anyone, but the truck motor's warm. Maybe they're inside."

Together, they approached the front door and Gid lifted a fist to pound on it. He pounded again, and the door swung open to darkness on the other side.

"Hello? Fire department. Is anyone here?" Gid listened, but heard no response.

"I'll check over there." Curtis already headed toward the smaller buildings.

Gid shouted into the interior again, taking a step inside and pulling a penlight from inside his jacket. It barely dented the deep darkness, as if someone had covered the windows with a deliberate intent to block all sunlight.

He heard noise coming from outside, and it didn't fit. An engine. The fire truck? What the hell was Curtis doing? He turned to the door and was only a step away when he saw the taillights of the vehicle they thought was abandoned barrel down the road.

"What the hell?" Curtis joined him in the doorway as they stared at the departing truck disappearing into smoke. He grabbed Curtis's arm.

"Let's get the hell out of here."

Curtis nodded, already moving to the fire truck. Gid took a last glance inside, wondering why someone would race away without acknowledging them. Could be there was something illegal going on here. He was tempted to check the interior again, just in –

The thunderous crack came without warning. The whoosh knocked him sideways with its velocity, and another gust pushed him toward their fire truck so fast that he couldn't catch his breath. Searing pain ripped at his shoulder and his leg. Heat licked at the side of his face, and he reached up an automatic hand to drop his shield as his body crumpled to the ground.

Gid lay there, stunned and disengaged. He felt like he'd been blown through a cannon and impacted into a brick wall. His shoulder burned, and his arm didn't want to obey his commands. The initial pain in his leg subsided with a rapid drain, and he couldn't bring himself to try to move it. It all hurt too much. Worst of all, he couldn't pull in a deep breath.

Curtis. Where was Curtis? He tried to turn his head, and he felt something impede his movement. Something lay over him, pinning him in place.

"Curtis? Curtis?" He shouted, but he didn't feel like he had enough volume to carry far. He pushed at whatever lay over him, feeling it shift as a new wave of pain darted through his leg. He kicked with the one he could feel, knocking free of a large plank of wood.

A few feet away, Curtis lay on his face in the dirt. He wasn't moving. He'd landed in one of those odd needle free areas of the yard. Gid pushed with his good leg again, trying to depress the button on his mic to call for help.

His arm wouldn't lift. He could either crawl, or he could try to contact someone, but he couldn't do both. Knowing that Curtis was alive suddenly felt most important.

A dispossessed feeling came over him, like he was out of his body watching his actions from a separate point of view. Why hadn't he paid attention to his instincts that something wasn't right? He should call this in, so someone could investigate it. And the truck racing away. Who was that?

He crawled another four feet, which felt like a mile. Six more and he'd be by Curtis's side. A fresh heat rushed at his cheek and he stopped, turning toward it. Then he saw the flames.

They licked up the pine needles like they were ice cream on a hot day. He couldn't see the cabin for the wall of fire. It danced across the clearing, feeding on debris and detritus with quick flashes. The stench of freshly burning wood made his lungs burn.

He had to get to Curtis. He had to get them to safety. The fire truck stood twenty feet away, its broad side of red a flash through dense smoke. He pushed again, ignoring the pain and gasping as heavy smoke reached inside his helmet to choke him. Another shove and he was next to the other man. He reached out and shook him, getting no response. He tried to lift Curtis's face shield, but crammed in the dirt, it was impossible. He couldn't tell if he was breathing under the heavy turnout, the back of which looked sooty but otherwise unharmed. He didn't want to believe Curtis could be dead.

Cracking noises pulled his attention away, and the tall pine across the small clearing went up with a roar. Flames shot into the air in an impressive display of power, and Gid could only stare at it for a moment. Madame Fire was an amazing thing to see in her glory, and he always knew a sense of respect for her brute force.

Then his mind flashed to his brother. He'd never forgive himself if the last time he and Noah talked, they'd parted with bad blood between them. With his good hand, he dug into the pack on Curtis's back and pulled out the fire shelter. Specks of little flashes of bright light and dark arrows clouded his vision as he tried to shake it open. He swore he wouldn't pass out.

He could not pass out.

What would his brother think?

That pushed him forward, and he yanked and tucked the deployed shield around his comrade. As he struggled with his own, flashes of darkness accompanied a narrowing corridor of light. He tried to dig a small depression in the dirt to hide his face, but it was too much. With a final tug, the corridor narrowed to a pinpoint, and he sent a silent apology to Noah for not fighting harder.

Chapter 9

Dani dismissed the deputies with a wave of her hand. They were no closer to finding the drug manufacturing site than they had been two months ago. It was her job to find those people. Protect and serve. She didn't feel like she had done a good job of that in recent months.

Her mind strayed back to the incident in the bakery. She'd suggested to Stuart and Sarge that they keep a camera handy to snap a close-up photo of the mystery man. She couldn't base an investigation on Stuart's spidey sense, no matter how accurate it might be. The feeling that the man looked familiar stayed with her. She needed evidence.

Working against her, he never made a fresh appearance, so a photo was out of the question. Identifications of prints on the mug were slow to return, and even when they did, she doubted they'd be definitive. Sarge, Stuart and the man all contributed smears to the ceramic surface.

The phone on her desk buzzed a jarring tone. She lifted the handset as she focused on the list of tips coming in from the line they'd set up to gather anonymous information on possible illegal drug-related activities. So far, nothing concrete.

Distracted by the frustration, she barked a greeting into the phone. "Trajan."

Nothing came through the line, as if she'd surprised someone. Then, "Dani, it's me."

She rocked her chair forward, her distraction forgotten at the subdued tone in her twin's voice.

"Nici? What happened? Are you okay?"

A deep sigh filled the phone, and Dani pressed it closer to her ear. If anyone ever messed with her sister again, they'd have to answer to her. Fear made her heart throb hard.

"I'm okay, but others aren't."

Relief flooded in first, followed by a moment of confusion. Why was Nicolle calling on the work line? They always had their conversations on their personal phones. Department policy on both sides.

Then her sister's words hit her. "Who was injured? How bad? What happened?" Dani couldn't hold back the rapid-fire questions as she tried to focus on the good part, that it wasn't Nicolle.

"That's why I'm calling. The feds are here crawling all over the source of an explosion that injured two of our firefighters. I am your official liaison, as in, officially official."

Which mean Nicolle was on the investigation. Dani realized she'd stood and taken steps to the door without being conscious of her actions.

"Sit down. You can't do anything here. Frankly, there are so many people trampling things, I'm worried we'll destroy evidence in the process."

Dani smiled despite the situation. "Listen to you, talking about evidence and everything." She dropped back into her chair with a slump, unwilling to let Nicolle know how close she'd had her pegged.

Another deep sigh. "Yeah, go ahead and laugh, but you didn't see the men. The only lucky thing we can say is that they didn't get burned."

Dani sobered in an instance, as the vision of Nicolle being one of those firefighters became too vivid in her mind. "Tell me."

She jotted notes as her sister talked. A remote cabin. Firefighters checking it for possible evacuation. An explosion of unknown causes. Serious injuries.

"How bad are they?" Dani kept her voice soft and even, though she wanted to yell the words into the phone. She never got over how dangerous Nicolle's job was. Today of all days, she didn't need the fresh reminder.

"One has a possible concussion and he was unconscious when the EMTs moved him. He could have been worse if the other guy didn't wrap him up in a deployment shield."

She hated to ask, but she made herself anyway. "And how is the other guy?"

Silence. It lasted so long that Dani wondered if the man would make it. A shaky breath, then Nicolle said, "Broken leg, something with his shoulder, smoke inhalation. He regained consciousness long enough to ask about Curtis, then lost the fight and hasn't woken up since."

"Curtis is the first man." Dani didn't bother to phrase it as a question. "Who's the second?"

Then she heard what she'd suspected before. A gulp as if Nicolle was holding back tears. "Kinkead."

Dani went rigid in shock. "Kinkead, as in the guy you believe might be the arsonist Kinkead?" She sat waiting for a response that didn't come. That answer was obvious, even if she wasn't a trained detective. Never wanting to shy away from the hard stuff, she asked the difficult question. "Do you think he did it?"

Nicolle didn't answer immediately. When she did, Dani heard the qualifying message in the words. "I don't believe he would, because I think he's a decent guy, all things taken together. I don't think he would do anything to deliberately injure one of us." She fell silent.

Dani waited for more, but nothing came. She could feel Nicolle's pain, and it wasn't just over the phone. That twin thing covered the physical distance between them. She sent a warm hug back into the stratosphere, hoping Nicolle caught it. A lighter sigh sounded through the phone.

"Anyway, I'm calling you officially because we're collecting preliminary evidence at the scene. We need someone to gather up the clothes and gear at the hospital for testing. You know, looking for residue and –" Her voice trailed off. If Kinkead was their firebug, he would have contaminated materials linking him to the blast on his clothes.

"I'll take care of it." She was already on her feet, sticking her head out and pointing to a nearby deputy. It happened to be Jake Kermarrec, because he was the only one not cleared for street duty since his accident. He was a friend of Gideon Kinkead, if she remembered right. But he was also as law-and-justice as they came. She handed him a slip of paper with her instructions, and he nodded with a deep frown as he read it. He exited the squad room without a backwards glance.

"What else can I do?"

Nicolle assured her there was nothing else, that the investigators had things otherwise well in hand, and the weather had turned their way and given them a break fighting this latest fire. When she ran out of words, she became quiet again. The uncharacteristic silence made Dani itchy and nervous.

"What can I do for you, sis?" She paced the room, willing her twin to give her a clue about what to say or do to make things better.

A brittle laugh, bitten off almost before it began, came through the line. "Nothing else. I guess I really needed to hear your voice, to know you're okay. This is one fucked-up mess, you know?" Another pause had Dani contemplating getting in a patrol vehicle herself and racing with sirens screaming to the site.

Nicolle's next words chilled even that idea. "You don't think it could be, uh, him, do you?"

There was no need to clarify who they were discussing. The man still haunted Nicolle's sleep and Dani's guilt.

"No, I don't think he's that bright, or that stupid. He's miles away from here, Nici, miles." Then she stopped in her tracks as recollection made her gasp.

"Yeah, okay. I just needed to hear you say the words too. I have to go. I'll call you later and give you an update, okay?"

Dani answered automatically and the connection clicked off before she had a chance to rope her thoughts back into an actionable direction. Then she whirled and yanked open the bottom drawer of a file cabinet, kicking her outer door shut as soon as she found the file. She snapped it open and pushed aside the papers on her desk, settling it front and center, open to the front jacket.

A photo. A physical description. A cloudy memory suddenly cleared.

The man in the corner of the bakery. The one who smirked at her and disappeared. The face her twin may never forget. He'd changed, but not enough for Dani to question her current identification of the resemblance. Her pulse sped up even as a cold shudder ran through her body.

The man who attacked Nicolle was in Flynn's Crossing.

Chapter 10

He hurt. He ached in places he didn't even know he had. What wasn't sore was either numb or in rigid pain with no in-between. He must be in hell, because heaven was supposed to be pleasant.

"Mr. Kinkead? Gideon? Are you ready to wake up for us?"

The kind voice was one he recognized from before. He imagined her to be an angel. She sounded like one.

"Gideon? Time to wake up, bro. You've slept for long enough."

He recognized that voice too. Noah. His little brother sounded pissed, so this couldn't be heaven. Gid tried to peel his eyes open. A flutter brought in brilliant lights overhead, too painful to contemplate.

"Douse the lights," Noah commanded, and his will was done. His little bro, a god in his own world. The idea brought a smile to his lips.

"He's waking up," Noah said. And hell yeah, Gid was. He never realized the power Noah wielded.

The idea made Gid frown in an attempt at concentration. He thought he was dead and preparing to burn in a never-ending bonfire of remorse. But Noah was here too, and he would never leave his daughters, nor would he burn in the fires of eternal damnation. That meant, shit, he was still alive.

The idea wasn't necessarily pleasing. Pain returned with a vengeance, confirming his suspicions. Gid groaned in response.

"Gideon, you can't hide from me forever." Noah's reference to their popular childhood phrase from games of hide and seek made Gid want to laugh. Even the tone was right, coaxing with a hint of frustration thrown in. He tried his eyes again, pleased to find he could hold them open in a room now lit closer to dusk than midday.

He focused on Noah's face. Shadows made a clear read of his expression hard to come by, but they also marked deeper grooves around his mouth and a pinch of worry between his eyebrows. Noah looked like he'd aged a few years. Had he been asleep that long?

He tried to speak, but only a weak grunt came out. Noah was by his side in an instant with a chip of ice, ladling it on his tongue. Sucking on that felt like heaven, and the trickle down his throat extinguished the burning sensation. When it was gone, his eyes settled on Noah again, begging for another one.

"Easy does it, okay? Squeeze my hand if you understand me."

Noah wrapped firm fingers around Gideon's, a feeling Gid found comforting. Gid squeezed, surprised to find it was more difficult than he expected. Noah gave him a smile and a nod in recognition.

"Do you remember what happened to you?" This time the question was delivered in a quieter voice.

Gid remembered. Hell yeah, he remembered. An explosion, getting blown across the clearing, and Curtis. What had happened to Curtis?

He was sure fear communicated itself in his expression, since Noah's shifted to worry. Gid tried to lick his lips and speak. "Curtis?" The single word came out in a croak, but at least he thought Noah would understand him.

Noah's face cleared and he squeezed Gid's hand. "Curtis is okay. You saved his life. You got his shield around him when he was unconscious." Noah paused, examining

Gid's face with some of his childhood hero worship showing. "How the hell were you able to do that?" The admiration in his tone rang out louder than the beeping equipment surrounding the bed.

Gid winced. He wasn't a hero. He had been so intent on his purpose for being on the mountain that he overlooked things. There must have been a propane line. He hadn't checked the cabin thoroughly, shutting off things a renter wouldn't think to do.

Then he remembered the truck racing down the mountain. The mystery driver who didn't acknowledge their arrival. The strange perfection of the setting.

He needed to have someone look for the driver and examine the site for illegal activity. Why else would someone to flee a scene when firefighters arrived? He shut his eyes, trying to pin down any other oddities from those moments, but a fog threatened to descend once more.

"Gid? Stay with me, okay? We won't talk about what happened. What can I get you?" Noah nudged Gid's hand once, then twice, growing more insistent. Opening his eyes again, Gid found his brother leaning closer.

He tried to smile, but his lips were too dry to force very far. Noah was again the man with an answer, dabbing a cotton swab with some kind of gel on it around cracks that felt like canyons. Gid let his eyes slide shut again.

"You stay quiet. Other doctors will be coming in to check on your progress. Then you'll be going to therapy. I want to get you up and moving. Lying in a bed for a long time isn't a good idea."

Gid wanted to laugh. He could remember when lying in bed for a long time with the right companion was the perfect way to spend a weekend. Or a good part of a week. This time, the smile didn't hurt.

"I can guess what you're thinking. Please leave the nurses alone, okay? And the therapists. And for that matter, the doctors. You had a female surgeon. She's damned great at her job, and we'd like to keep her around."

Wait, surgeon? He expected bruises and maybe a few cuts. But what was bad enough to require surgery? He tried to lift his head and look at his hands and feet, but the effort required was more than he could handle.

Noah placed a hand on his chest, holding him down with amazing ease. He felt as weak as a baby. His alarm must have been evident, because his brother delivered the news with regret in his voice.

"You broke your right leg in two places. You're pinned back together, but your rehab will take a while. You dislocated your left shoulder, but it's back in place and braced. More rehab. The burns on that ugly face of yours were minor and will heal in no time. All in all, you were very lucky."

Noah's face swam closer, a reassuring set to his mouth and his eyes expressing his confidence in Gid's potential to heal. But the smile faded as he searched for something in his brother's face. At about the point where Gid wanted to yell at him to come out with it, Noah said, "What happened up there, Gid? Investigators have been asking questions, and they want to talk to you. I can't hold them off much longer."

True to Noah's promise, a constant parade of medical personnel made their way through Gid's room that afternoon, and he was exhausted by the questions, prods, and tests. Everyone appeared satisfied with his progress, but he caught more than one curious glance sent his way. It was if everyone wanted to ask what happened. No one had the balls to do it, though, not even the surgeon whose looks were better matched to a fashion runway. When the door opened after another knock, Gid played possum. There wasn't a part of him that didn't feel bruised.

"Mr. Kinkead? It's time for your exercise."

The female voice delivered the message in a singsong, as if charming her patient into compliance. He shifted and opened eyes to see if she looked at delicately charming as her voice. His movements came to a full stop when he took in his visitor.

Grey hair in a bun, glasses perched on the end of her nose, and an ample figure filled the doorway from side to side and near to the top. The face wasn't kindly. She looked like a drill sergeant in some perverse army. The voice didn't match her demeanor, either, since she looked like she'd pick him up and toss him down the corridor if he hesitated for even a moment. Her fingers flexed as if preparing to do just that.

"Now, Mr. Kinkead, I bet you're eager to start your rehab. So let's take a little walk, you and I. You can tell me all about yourself. My name is Marge."

Marge gave him a smile he decided was evil and stepped toward the bed. He gulped and wondered if it was too late to pass out, this time for real. She chuckled as if she was on to him. "Now, now, don't you worry. You're a very important person around here, seeing as you're Dr. Kinkead's brother and all. Dr. Noah wants the best for you, and the best is me."

Damn Noah. Gid said that many times in his head over the next hour, as Marge pushed and prodded him into movement. His body failed him more than once, and those were the uninjured parts. He was sweating like an active fire hose by the time she wheeled him back toward his room. Damn Noah, and Gid would tell him as much when he next saw him.

As they rounded the corner of his corridor, he realized he'd get his opportunity soon, since Noah and Jake stood outside his hospital room door. They stared into the hospital room, frowning, as Jake relayed something on his phone with quiet, urgent words.

"Ah, there you are, Dr. Noah. I took good care of your brother, just as you asked. Now I'll get him settled in bed again if you don't mind. They did change his linens, didn't they?" Marge bustled between the two men and turned the wheelchair, preparing to back in through the door. Gid opened his mouth to voice his displeasure with Noah's prescribed treatment, and stilled in his chair when he met his brother's eyes.

Worry. Confusion. Fear. Gid glanced to Jake, reading big questions in his intense scrutiny. Jake stepped forward and put a restraining hand on Marge's arm.

"Ma'am, you can't go in there."

Marge stepped around the wheelchair and went toe to toe with Jake. Did the deputy just gulp? Gid would have enjoyed this, if Noah's face didn't carry that desperate expression.

"Marge, we're going to put Gideon in a different room. If you could move him over by the nurses' station for a few minutes, we'll get this sorted out."

Marge stared at Jake for a full minute, then nodded toward Noah and said, "Of course, Doctor."

She stepped back behind the chair and spun it again, and Gid glanced inside his old room. Curiosity won out over exhaustion as he wondered what could have caused the sudden change in venue. Then he gasped loud enough for Marge to ask if he was all right.

"Stop, please Marge. Stop."

He stared inside the room to the freshly made bed. Sheets were pulled tight in military precision, unlike the tossed mess he'd left behind. And on the pillow, something red gleamed like blood against the spotless white. His breath came in pants of disbelief, making him dizzy enough to spin the corridor on its axis.

By the time he found his air again, he lay in a different room. How Marge got him into the bed, he wasn't sure. At the foot of his bed, Noah remained oddly silent, as solemn as if he stood watch over a dying man. Jake asked probing questions, none of which Gid felt prepared to answer, before falling quiet too.

A red rose here at the hospital. How was that possible? According to Noah, he'd only been here for a day, and most of that time, he'd been out cold. Had someone hovered over him when he couldn't protect himself? The idea made him want to hurl the small cup of cherry gelatin he'd eaten during rehab.

He tried to block out Jake's looming presence by closing his eyes, but the deputy wasn't buying it. He waited, patient as a priest in a confessional, tapping that ever-present pen of his on that damned notepad. The fact that he didn't say anything more to prod Gid along made it even more annoying.

Why here? More importantly, how had someone gotten to him here? Someone knew what room he was in, and watched long enough to know when that room would be empty. That person had close contacts inside the fire department or the hospital, because that would be the only way they'd have his story. An apprehensive shiver slid along his spine. Jake must have seen the gesture, because he stepped closer and resumed his line of questioning.

"Who knew you were here, besides your captain and squad? Think, Gid. Who else could know?"

Giving another involuntary shake, Gid tried to focus, but every time he did, all he saw was that damned red flower. When Marge caught the drift of what was happening, she'd appointed herself his personal bodyguard. Noah didn't appear to be discouraging her either.

Noah. His brother wasn't saying much, leaving the talking to Jake. When he was paged to the ER, a look communicated his worry about leaving. Marge stepped to where he'd been standing as if she belonged there. Gid fought the comfort he took from her newfound dedication.

Gid pressed his eyes closed. He wasn't going to talk, not until he'd had a chance to think this through. Someone knew more about his personal life than he ever advertised. He couldn't even protect himself, much less Noah and the girls.

The idea someone would go after them brought a fresh wave of pain that had nothing to do with his injuries.

"Deputy Kermarrec, that's it for now. Mr. Kinkead has had a very full day already. As you can see, he's in pain. You'll have to return tomorrow with your questions." Marge's voice sent the message that she expected no arguments on the matter.

"Gid? The longer this goes on, the worse it could get. You know that, don't you?"

He opened his eyes and met Jake's frank stare. A pounding pulse made his grimace real as he shook his head. He moaned before he could catch himself.

She fought the urge to drive up the mountain a number of times over the past day. Patrolling local streets and widening her perimeter to surrounding county roads, she stared hard at any possible suspects or vehicles. She probably scared the daylights out of a few folks too, since everyone suddenly dropped their speed to regulation when a view of her SUV with its array of obvious cop paraphernalia protruding from the roof came into their rearview mirrors.

Radio noise droned at a constant hum, something every beat officer learned to tune out unless necessary. She had loved being a detective, a great stepping-stone in terms of experience and opportunity to the role she had now. But in all honesty, she'd loved patrol more. On investigations, they tended to see only the meaner side of life. At least on patrol, she often got to help people, and sometimes, they even laughed and joked with her.

When she picked up her number over the air, at first it didn't seem real. It had been years since she was on the roads with any regularity. Her number came again, and this time, she responded. The dispatcher notified her of a pass-through, and Kermarrec's voice came over the air.

"Lieut, I delivered the evidence bags to the lab. They're putting a rush on them, but they're backed up. The feds offered to expedite things, but I declined." Jake stopped as if waiting to hear if she agreed. When she did, he continued.

"I saw Curtis, the firefighter who had fewer injuries. I took a statement, because I didn't want things to go too long before we knew anything."

She admired a deputy who was decisive and thought on his feet. Maybe he'd be a lieutenant someday soon too. She didn't need to ask if he'd learned anything of value. If he had, it would have been the first thing he shared.

"I tried to learn what Kinkead knows, but he's not talking. Going to be a while recuperating." Jake paused again as if considering this. Then he said, "That's going to be a bitch for him."

Jake would know, since he spoke from recent experience. Dani respected his willingness to work while he recovered, even though it was limited duty.

"His brother, Noah Kinkead, is an ER doc at the hospital. He isn't leaving his side and he's very protective. He said Gideon can't remember the time around the blast. Says that's normal for trauma victims. And, well, there's the new rose."

She sensed there was something he wasn't saying. "And?"

A staccato sound came through the phone, and she could picture Jake tapping his pen on the little notepad he habitually kept in his uniform shirt pocket. "I might be over-thinking this, but I believe Gid told Noah something for the little brother to be hovering so much over the older one."

She turned into Main Street, intending a slow cruise by the bakery, just in case. She'd been out of the office long enough. This was a witch-hunt and she wasn't having any success from it.

"Like you wouldn't be protective if something happened to your brothers?" She didn't add, *or me with my sister*.

Jake harrumphed, and she took it for agreement. Of course, the other alternative could also be true. Gideon could have told Noah something, and now they both carried a secret. She wanted to meet them both in person and find out.

A dark tan pick-up pulled out of a parking space with abrupt moves, cutting her off. Who cut off a sheriff's cruiser? She considered following to the vehicle's destination and giving the driver a talking to when he turned to look at her. Then she thought about hitting the sirens.

His face first sneered, and then grinned. At this angle, the expression held menace. Sunglasses, the ball cap, the same leer. The man from the bakery. His truck shot forward and she shouted instructions at Kermarrec to join her pursuit.

Tires squealed, and they weren't hers. She'd already accelerated, keeping one eye on the truck, attempting to read the license plate covered in thick dust. The back window was covered in a thick layer too, as if it hadn't been washed for months. If she could get a car length closer, she'd be able to read the number.

Out of the corner of her eye, she caught a bright splash of color darting between parked cars. The colors jumped into the street and stalled there. She jammed on her brakes as two young girls stared back at her in horror. Their faces dissolved into tears when the SUV stopped a good ten feet away.

Dani looked from the crying girls to the disappearing backend of the truck turning in the direction of the freeway, and she slammed her open palms on the steering wheel until the pain overcame her need to scream out her frustration.

Chapter 11

"Not taking it." Gideon tried to hide the stab of pain making his leg jump inside its cast and knew he failed when Noah's frown darkened. But Gid couldn't explain it. The painkillers were great, almost too great. With them, he felt like he was floating. And when he was woozy, he wasn't watching.

Noah sighed and ran a hand over his hair in a rapid motion, his assessing gaze hard to avoid. "This will help the cramps and make it easier for you to rest. You're only two days post-surgery, Gid. I heard you refused the sleep aid last night too."

Gid shook his head. The physical misery was an ever-present reminder that someone had deliberately set out to create injury. Whether he was the target or not didn't matter. The effect was the same. Months of depending on someone else for help. Months of physical therapy. Months away from work he loved. Months of looking over his shoulder and suspecting a threat.

Where would he go? His apartment was no longer his, and even if it had been, the stairs were enough to prevent him from living there now. Any of a dozen of Flynn's Crossing women would be more than happy to put him up, but those helping hands arrived with obligations. Just considering the long line of female visitors who'd insisted they were close friends and needed to visit him made his aches worse.

Then there were his fellow firefighters. Fires continued to rage on the mountains, and damn it, he should be up there beside them. He saw the exhaustion on their faces as they took a few precious moments they should have spent sleeping to check in on him. They should be taking care of themselves, not worrying about him.

He wasn't sure who had been more pleased when he called a halt to everyone but immediate family, him or the nursing staff.

One side of Noah's mouth lifted in what looked suspiciously like a smirk as he said, "You'll be able to come home more quickly if we have your pain under control."

He felt the skin on his face tighten with the statement. Anger made his heart monitor beep faster at his bedside. He refused Noah's help before, and so help him, if his brother didn't get the message, he'd wrestle him to the ground and pummel him, casts and braces and IVs or not.

Gid shook his head with enough effort to make something screech in the machine by his side. Noah glanced at it but didn't appear concerned. His patience didn't appear to be flagging either. Gid tightened his lips, trying not to explode with fresh frustration. "I am not, repeat, not, moving in with you."

But what choice did he have? As if to underscore his predicament, his leg muscles twitched inside the cast again, and his pain sensors made him bite his lip to keep a gasp from coming out of his mouth. He forced himself to turn his face away as he said, "I need to sleep."

He felt Noah stare at him for a minute longer. Then noise levels and light rose briefly as the door to the corridor opened. The room felt as silent and dark as a forest cave when it swung closed. Gid imagined he could smell the tangy rise of new sap in spring trees, but without the rustle of a welcoming breeze or the feel of it on his face. He was empty and alone in his misery, and he welcomed it.

Two days after the explosion, Dani wondered if they were even further away from a clue than they had been before. Across the desk, Jake tapped an impatient beat with his pen as they pondered what he'd just reported.

Footage of the hospital's security cameras didn't specifically cover Kinkead's corridor. The nurses swore someone was at their station all the time, and no unknowns had entered Kinkead's room. They had eyes on it at all times, because that's what the doctor brother asked. Jake would have questioned the doctor brother about it, but a multi-vehicle wreck on the freeway kept him occupied into the wee hours. Noah had slept at his brother's bedside after that.

Her department couldn't spare someone to sit outside Kinkead's door around the clock. He wasn't an active suspect because they had no proof. He wasn't a potential victim, again, because barring the plastic flower, there had been no concrete threat. They lacked real evidence at every turn.

"Anything on the rose?"

Jake shook his head in response to her question. "We're building on what the fire investigators had done before us, but it's all been confirmed. The plastic flower is a generic type. No one sells them in Flynn's Crossing, but drive down the hill and there are literally dozens of potential outlets. Big box stores, craft places, table decoration designers. The flowers are manufactured in China and shipped all over the country. They could be purchased states away. We have no way of tracing them."

She picked up his frustrated rhythm with her own pen. "Prints?"

He shook his head again.

"Dozens of partials, but nothing we can run. Imagine how many times those things are touched. Someone packages them after manufacturing. A clerk unwraps them at the store, puts them in a display, maybe moves them or straightens them. Customers lift them and put them back. Cashiers shove them in a bag. I think it's a safe bet whoever is leaving these is smart enough to wear gloves. In a hospital, boxes of gloves are hanging on every room's wall. We did check the trash from Gideon's room and the surrounding public areas. Nothing we could trace." He slapped his notebook shut in apparent disgust.

Dani glanced at the stack of paperwork awaiting review in her inbox. Another virtual stack lined up in her computer. This should be her investigation, if for no other reason than Nicolle was on it too.

Ignoring the admin crap, she rose and said, "I'm going to pay Mr. Gideon Kinkead a visit."

It didn't take long to drive to the hospital and take the elevator to Kinkead's floor. She was happy to see security stood or sat at strategic points on the way to the nurses' station. The nurse looked as tough as any deputy on her force, and Dani felt a flicker of admiration at her dedication to orders. It seemed that no one, not even a sheriff's lieutenant, could get past the formidable woman. If looks were lethal, hers would have mowed down Dani in a second.

But this was an active investigation. A crime had been committed and the man who might be able to shed light on the details lay in a bed on the other side of this woman's crossed arms and tapping foot. The foot didn't make a sound since she wore thick-soled shoes, but the message came through loud and clear.

Dani tried her best conciliatory smile, which probably failed given the fact that her voice rose in frustration. "I need to interview him. We can't delay this any longer." Her shoulders ached from the parade-sharp stretch to straighten her spine.

"I'm sorry, but only family are allowed. Doctor's orders." The nurse shot a glance over Dani's left shoulder as she said it. Dani turned that way to pin her gaze on the man behind them. His eyes widened in apparent surprise as he stared at her, and she ran his face through her internal database for identification before it clicked.

A doctor, the one who usually met the ambulances or patrol vehicles. The case file scrolled through her brain next.

Dr. Noah Kinkead, a younger brother to Gideon. She should be grateful to him for taking care of her deputies on their all-too-often trips to the emergency room, but today, he was a barrier. The eager expression accompanying his too-rapid steps forward had her sliding a hand down nearer her weapon just in case he tried anything.

From behind her, the nurse said, "I'm sorry, Dr. Kinkead. I've told the deputy Mr. Kinkead can't have visitors, but she's insisting."

He waved a hand as he continued to stare at Dani. She stepped forward and into his personal space when he would have put a hand on her drawing arm. No one touched her like that, no one. She poised on the balls of her feet in case there was a need to take action.

Dani said, "You're Gideon Kinkead's brother?"

The doctor fell back a step as he nodded in confirmation. Did she imagine the flash of disappointment on his face? But of course he'd be upset. She was here to question his brother. She wondered what the good doctor already knew.

"Lieutenant Trajan, Doctor. I'm sorry your brother was injured. I understand he's doing better. I'd like to speak with him."

She offered her hand, noting his slight hesitation. His firm handshake lasted no longer than a couple of pumps, and her hands slipped back to rest on the equipment belt around her waist before she caught herself. Her boss cautioned her more than once to soften her approach, but it was difficult for her to remember the world wasn't filled with bad guys.

The doctor put his hands in the pockets of pristine dress slacks, rocking up on the balls of his feet as if balancing himself for a spring. He said, "Gideon continues to be in significant pain, and he's not completely cognizant of what he's saying due to his medications." A deeper frown crossed his features as he continued. "I don't think he's able to recall the incident, and I'd hate to have him mislead you because he isn't clear."

His eyes met hers, and she read the challenge there. Her official authority meant nothing to him, probably because in his world, this hospital, he was authority. She could press the issue, but what would that achieve? She nodded for no reason other than to convey her recognition of his power within these walls. Softening her tone, she added, "The sooner we have anything to go on, anything at all, the sooner the community will be safer from this person. This was a deliberate act, Dr. Kinkead. Even if your brother feels he can't contribute anything, I don't want to miss an opportunity to gather any intelligence he might have, however incomplete or minor."

Appealing to his community spirit. She figured that would be something he related to, given that he was an ER doc. His gaze flicked over her face as if he examined her features for artifice, and she kept her expression bland but sincere, or as sincere as she could be, given that she was trying to execute an end run around him.

Over the brother's shoulder, a woman in a long white coat approached and knocked knuckles on the wall to get their attention. When Noah turned at the sound, she said, "Dr. Kinkead, a word please?"

Noah nodded and gave Danielle a shrug with a small smile she took to be relief. The other doctor glanced at her, and her gaze sharpened as she took in Dani's uniform in a slow sweep. When their eyes met, she said, "I assume you're here to see Gideon."

She nodded, and the doctor shook her head emphatically in the negative. "I'm sorry you've wasted a trip. I can't let you interview him now. He's in considerable pain and we've had to sedate him."

The doctor put a hand on Noah's arm and pulled him away. It was as if they conspired to keep Gideon from being interviewed, and Dani had to wonder why that would be. In most cases, victims were only too happy to talk, seeing it as a way to help catch whoever did the bad deed. But neither doctor seemed inclined to cooperate. She didn't miss the worry on Noah's face as he and the woman whispered their way down the hall.

She glanced back at the nurse behind the desk, who looked a little too pleased Dani had been officially blockaded. It wasn't her fault, but that didn't make being polite any easier. She reached into her shirt pocket and produced a business card, making a slow arch with it as she met the woman's eyes without blinking.

"I'd truly appreciate your cooperation and help with this. As soon as Mr. Kinkead is able, I need to speak with him." She held on to the card for a second longer than necessary, making the woman pull on the cardboard when it didn't immediately release into her fingers. The nurse frowned, and Dani let go.

If it sounded like a threat, so be it. Someone was setting fires and bomb blasts in her county, and she sure as hell wasn't going to rest until she caught them.

Gid folded the bedcover into an accordion, then smoothed a hand over the same spot to flatten it once more. The repetitive gesture calmed him. He was glad Noah had left the ceiling lights up to full power when he left the room. Anything to keep the shadows away.

It was the surgeon's fault, coming in here and shouting out questions before Gid had a chance to wake himself from terrifying dreams of flames and blood everywhere. The shocked expression on the woman's face when Gid screamed at her let him know he's said too much.

In his nightmare, he was in a cabin with fire all around him. Only, he couldn't escape. Someone tied him to the chair as they shrieked bitter words.

"You're going to burn. You deserve this, because you let us burn. You need to die, and all of your family and friends too."

That's when he saw Curtis, his face a picture of terror, tied to an identical chair across the room. Flames licked between them, eating up the wooden floor like sawdust. Gid yelled at them to let Curtis go.

"It's all my fault. He's innocent, just a kid. Let him go. It's my fault. I killed them."

When someone shook him hard and said his name in a firm tone close to his ear, he tried to tell that voice to help Curtis. The kid didn't deserve this. It was Gid who hadn't insisted, hadn't dragged out the old man and the little girl, no matter what they wanted. His name came louder, along with a pinch on his arm.

"Gideon, do you know where you are? Do you remember who I am?"

He struggled to open his eyes. The coat the woman wore was so white, it looked like snow, and her face registered. The surgeon who performed his surgery. Gid couldn't focus on her name, not when the horror of the burning room and the picture of a wild-eyed Curtis hung in the air like so much smoke.

He shook his head as he fought off the restraining hand on his arm. The doctor stepped back, her eyes shifting to stare at the rapidly beeping monitor at the bedside. A hospital. He was in the hospital. A blast and fire. The fact that he knew he was safe here didn't make his heart rate drop much.

"How's Curtis? Is he okay?"

The surgeon glanced back and frowned, but didn't reply. Instead, she moved to a screen on a cart in the corner and typed in something on the keyboard. The doctor gave a huff of sound, muted against the noise of the monitor and sounds coming from the corridor that now registered with Gid.

"Gideon, I see that you have refused pain killers." The doctor examined him from across the room as if Gid was a particularly worrisome case. "Do you remember what you just said to me as you woke up?"

Gid was shaking his head before the words had faded from sound. He remembered, but he wasn't sharing it. "No, I was having a dream. And no to pain killers. I don't like how they make me feel. I like to be in control."

The memory of the nightmare flashed back. Being at the mercy of crazy people, even if they were ghosts, was not control. A whole body shiver ran through him, and with it, his shoulder screamed in pain and spasms ripped through his leg. He doubted he did a good job of hiding a contorted scowl.

When he looked at the doctor again, the woman was shaking her head in apparent disbelief. "Control? Like the control you exhibited when I walked in? Is that what you mean?" She sighed deeply and clicked the keyboard again. "Let me give you a piece of advice, Mr. Kinkead. Control is an illusion, and I should know. I'm a surgeon, and we always like to think we're in control. Until we're not, of course."

Gid opened his mouth to argue as she slipped out of the room. The letters had been clear. His life was in danger. The other threats flashed through his mind. Noah. His nieces. The only people he loved and the ones he knew he had to protect. If it came to it, he'd stand in harm's way and die before he let anything happen to them.

He rang the call button with urgent fingers. The faster he accelerated his rehab, the sooner he would heal. And the sooner he could guard his family.

Chapter 12

An hour later, Gid wished he'd never been so enthusiastic about getting on crutches. They were implements of torture, and harder to manipulate than any piece of firefighting equipment he'd ever used.

Worse yet, he suspected he smelled like the inside of an old boot. He hadn't realized how bad he looked because he hadn't been near a mirror since the accident. But the therapy room was lined with them, and when he first caught sight of his face, he nearly shouted out in surprise. Mottled green, yellow and dark purple warred with small cuts and scrapes. The rest of his body felt the same. After an hour with a female physical therapist who could have run a reality show boot camp with ease, he was soaked in sweat and could barely breathe. He wasn't fit company for anyone.

That made it much more difficult to see the woman walking toward him with purpose on her face. The older woman pushing his wheelchair at a leisurely speed, and Gid couldn't come up with a single way of avoiding the obvious.

"Trajan, what the hell?" A shift made him miserable again, and he grimaced with a new shot of discomfort.

Nicolle said, "What the hell, Kinkead? Though I have to say, you look like hell."

He thought about pounding his head against the metal supports of the crutches propped on his good foot, but gave up on the idea when it pounded all on its own with exhaustion. He said, "Yeah, I'm getting that a lot these days. Any word on whose pretty face I can mess for this?"

She gave him a sympathetic grin, as if she knew he wasn't going to be throwing any punches for a while.

"I think that by the time you're ready to rumble, we might have a name for you, but up until now, no."

He swore, then apologized to the aide. She patted his shoulder, and assured him it didn't bother her a bit. Then she added, "Would you and your young lady like to sit and chat for a while? It's very pleasant in the courtyard today."

"Why don't I push him? I think we could both use the fresh air." Nicolle was already rounding the wheelchair as the woman protested, and they were moving before he had a chance to convince them otherwise.

Nicolle spun the chair and backed them out of the automatic door, and Gid felt the cool breeze hit his damaged cheeks with a puff of air. Funny, but he hadn't noticed the astringent smells of medication and cleaning fluid until he was out in the open once more. He closed his eyes and inhaled deeply, happy there was no tinge of smoke hitting his nostrils. Things must be going well up on the mountain.

Up on the mountain, where he should be, fighting fires and taking care of his crew. Not sitting in a hospital or a wheelchair. It would take months for him to return to a readiness level that would allow him to work. That morose thought seesawed his emotions back to a dark place.

"I expected to see you before now," he said, trying and failing to keep the grumble out of his voice. Then he grunted as the wheels bumped over a crack in the concrete. He held up his good hand as she started to apologize.

"Not necessary. Trust me, I've been prodded, poked and generally made uncomfortable from the get-go. My brother says it will get better, but not before it feels worse first."

The outdoors seemed unnaturally bright after the artificial shine in his hospital room. He blinked and closed his eyes against the sting. He forced them back open with his next thought.

Danger could be hiding here. There was no way of knowing where it might come from. Someone might be looking out one of those dark windows overhead even now, and he could be powerless to stop any actions they chose to take. He almost ordered Nicolle to roll him back inside as his nerves jangled.

When Nicolle said nothing to fill his silence, he forced his eyes from rapid sweeps of their surroundings to her. She scrutinized him as if taking a mental picture of his injuries. "Why don't you tell me what you remember," she said.

He began to argue, because he wanted to know where the investigation stood. They could discuss what he thought he remembered, which was damned little, later. She needed to bring him up to date so he could fill in the blanks in his memory.

She held up a placating hand. "I don't want your recollection to be tainted. You haven't explained it to anyone yet, have you?"

He shook his head with sudden wariness at the concentrated expression on her face. She was a damned great investigator, from what he saw. Reluctance warred with the need to share his suspicions and assumptions with someone who might understand.

He said, "Some deputies were here to interview me, but Noah chased them off. He's very protective."

"Noah?"

"My brother. He's an emergency doctor here. He was on duty when they brought me in. He said it aged him ten years to see me on that stretcher. I'm kind of following his instructions for the moment, since I gave him such a bad scare."

Nicolle smiled. "The no-visitors rule?"

Gideon nodded. "Yup, that's Noah, though I didn't argue. I think he's worried the arsonist will come by and finish the job."

That idea made his stomach roll, and it had nothing to do with the pain he could still feel as a steady throb in every nerve ending. He was a sitting duck, a bump on a log, an easy target.

Nicolle tilted her head and examined his face once more, and he wondered what she saw. He knew what the mirror told him, but did she see his worry, his shame, and yes, his fear? She waited a few beats before saying, "You think the explosion was aimed at you?"

Gideon glanced around at their surroundings, a fresh billow of fear blowing over him. The courtyard was protected on all four sides by wings of the hospital. Two doors from the interior sat at opposite corners of the rectangle. Next to one, a narrow passage to the parking lot lay open to anyone's access from the hospital's exterior. It wasn't the most secure place in the world.

Nicolle's face fell into deep lines he rarely noticed as she reached into her tote. In moments, she recorded the date and time into her cell phone, noting their names before putting it on the bench where she sat next to his wheelchair. "Talk," she said.

He didn't want to do this, didn't want to share the hell he'd been going through with anyone else. He could never explain the fear, not even to Noah. Fear like this was not what firefighters were made of. The level of it felt like a paralysis.

But he had to tell someone. In his condition, he couldn't solve this puzzle on his own. He shifted in the chair and stared at the trees around them rather than watch her reaction to his admission.

"I've been getting death threats," he said.

Minutes after his admission, he ran out of words. He told her about the phone calls, with their clear death threats against him and his family. No, he hadn't recorded them, too much in shock at the hateful words delivered by a raspy voice to do much more than freeze. The letters were concrete, though, and something they might be able to go on.

She listened to his story in silence. Her face remained neutral. When she clicked off the recorder, her expression was as blank as the bare wall behind her, and Gid wasn't sure if she believed him or not.

Gid didn't like it, not one iota, but when Noah dragged him home, he could no longer avoid it. His brother had to be warned. The inevitable led to this.

Noah, pacing the living room of his comfortable little house, the one plastered with pictures of his daughters at various ages. Gid propped up on the couch with his leg elevated. The explanation, the long story about the cabin and feeling eyes on him, hanging in the air between them.

Gid said, "You can tell me I'm crazy. Imagining things. You know, the concussion blew a screw or two loose in my head and I'm nuts."

Noah asked, "Why didn't you tell me before?"

"I didn't want to worry you," Gid said. The words sounded empty, given their relative positions.

When Noah stopped and fixed him with a stare that only added to Gid's guilt, he tried not to squirm. "You told your work partner before you told your brother."

Trying to keep the defensive tone out of his voice, he answered as directly as he could. "Nicolle is solid, a good investigator and a good firefighter. She knows what to do with the information."

And it's my job to protect you, he added silently. Between your divorce and daughters, you have enough to worry about already.

Noah finally cut the pacing and stopped in front of Gid. He took a visible deep breath as if trying to get himself under control, and Gid was impressed. The resulting cool, impartial face must be the one he used at the hospital when things got hairy.

"First of all, I'm not sure how she got an opportunity to talk to you, since you weren't supposed to have any visitors. Then you tell her what's been going on, but not me. And to top that, you haven't talked to the sheriff's deputies I've been fending off, and they might want to know a little about this too, you know?"

Gid nodded, taking a pull on the straw Noah had stuck in his juice can. Extending his good hand with the palm up, he tried reason. "I'm sorry, Noah, really. I didn't think it was anything at first. Then I didn't know what to do with it. I didn't believe it. I mean, how would it sound if I said someone was stalking me but I had no proof?"

"What's different now?"

Gid took another sip of juice. What did make him believe? He sure as hell didn't at the beginning, thinking he was being pranked by someone in the squad. By the time he realized no one would be that cruel, things had spiraled out of control. He set the can down on the table with a clatter and earned himself a headshake from Noah. When his brother crossed the room and shifted the can to a coaster, Gid glared back. But seeing the worry creasing his brother's forehead up close softened his anger.

Gid dropped his eyes and traced a pattern in the skin of his leg, thinking back to that day when he opened the first envelope. Surprise followed the realization that this problem would not disappear by itself.

They both stilled when a cell phone rang from across the room. Gideon's phone, the one he'd stored in his pocket when the blast occurred. It worked despite the flight across the clearing and the cracked screen from where he landed on it. Noah offered to get it replaced, but to Gid, it was a talisman of his survival.

"Kinkead," he said, holding the phone at an awkward angle with his good hand. He was used to propping it against his left ear, currently impossible to manage with the brace on his left arm holding his shoulder in place. Who did he think he was fooling, assuming he could hide somewhere alone? He could barely get to the bathroom himself.

At the other end, Nicolle spoke in an irritated tone. "I'm coming over tomorrow, and I'm bringing investigators from the sheriff's department. I would make it today, but they moved the gear truck and I have to catch up with it to retrieve your threat letters. We want to make copies and send originals to the lab ASAP."

Gideon nodded. He knew there was no way he could avoid the deputies much longer, no matter what Noah hoped. "I'm not going anywhere, so yeah, tomorrow morning is fine." He raised an eyebrow at Noah, who shrugged.

Nicolle said, "I'll bring your gear by too, and we'll want to search it thoroughly. I'm sure you understand. Until then, we, that is the sheriff's department and I, would strongly suggest that you say nothing more about what happened, not even to your brother. The more times you repeat the story, the more opportunities there might be for things to reflect something other than a pure memory. Got that?"

It was easy to agree. Even now, fresh flashes of phantom pain came with each thought back to the cabin. He hadn't finished his explanation to Noah. "Okay, I won't discuss it anymore until then. I'm sure Noah's going to be pissed, because he wants all the details today. But he can wait until you get here." He signed off and tossed the phone next to the juice can, where it's damaged face reminded him he probably looked little better than the broken plastic.

"That was Nicolle. She asked that I wait to discuss things any further, even with you. She's coming by in the morning with my gear, and more questions. And she's bringing a sheriff's deputy with her. You can listen in on the whole thing, and then maybe we'll both find answers."

Noah opened his mouth as if he planned to argue, and shut it again with an audible snap as his frown deepened. He yanked a cord and blinds fell across the front window. Gid shivered against the memories, wishing he could yank something to blot out them out as easily.

Chapter 13

After a mostly sleepless night with spot fires of nightmares featuring a variety of bad guys trying to kill him, Gid thought that perhaps his brain would simply explode from worry. Noah didn't look much better, and the deputy seemed to pick up on their tension.

"I'm sorry. I'm sure this seems like overkill, but it's necessary."

Jake stood in the middle of Noah's living room, surveying the space as if assessing how many more people could fit there. Two more were scheduled to show up according to him, his lieutenant and Nicolle. They were driving together and had sent ahead a court reporter to transcribe the interview, and a sketch artist to lay out the site.

His brother hovered, as he had last night. The constant pacing got on Gid's nerves, but he understood the strain. He saw its evidence on Noah's drawn face. To distract them both, he said, "Noah? You okay, man?" That was a damned stupid thing to say, considering their circumstances.

Noah looked up but shook his head to dissuade any further discussion. "This is a sick, fucked up, shitty situation." His glance went to a large jar on a side table. Last night he'd explained its purpose. A quarter for each curse. The girls would probably both be able to go to college when they were done. Noah was up to a twenty and Gid wasn't far behind, and that was only over a few hours.

Did either of them truly rest last night? When Gid awoke from yet another fiery nightmare, Noah's eyes were watchful slits from his place in the easy chair across the room. Later, Noah grumbled and twitched as if from a bad dream as Gid sat in prickly wakefulness. This morning, they drank their coffee well before sunrise by unspoken agreement that the night was long past over.

Gid took another sip from his tomato juice, the last remnant of a breakfast he'd done little justice to. He had no appetite for the toast and eggs, his stomach churning with thoughts of recounting what he could recall about the blast, which was sparse at best. At least they could no longer label him a suspect, or that's what he kept telling himself. The juice rumbled in the heightened acid in his stomach.

"They're here," Jake announced from his post at the front window. The sketch artist smoothed pages on the easel. She'd arrived with a rough drawing of the cabin and surrounding area covering the first sheet. The pages underneath also carried lines on them, but she hadn't shared the contents. Not knowing made him more nervous than he already was.

Jake moved to the front door and opened it, nodding to the people outside. "All set up."

Gideon dropped his eyes to his lap, propping his hands on the couch to rise. He attempted to swing his leg to the floor before realizing it would be useless. He couldn't stand on his own, and his crutches stood against the wall and out of reach, Noah's purposeful doing. Avoiding a sigh signaling his frustration, his attention shifted on Jake's next words.

"This is Lieutenant Trajan."

When had Nicolle been given the rank of lieutenant? That didn't make sense. They didn't stand on ceremony, but he would have heard about her promotion.

He opened his mouth to congratulate her as his eyes rose to the woman standing just inside the door. She and Noah were shaking hands, but the woman's face was unsmiling. Tight with tension and deeper lines than he was used to seeing, Nicolle didn't look remotely happy. Even under the worst circumstances, she'd never appeared this grim.

He blinked in confusion as facts struck him. The uniform was a sheriff's tan and black, from the crisp slacks to the hat under her arm. Her brisk no-nonsense movements and firm steps carried her partway into the house without any apparent effort. Toned muscles were obvious, even through the uniform, which she filled out nicely in all the right places. She would probably hate to hear that. It was written in her expression, the firm straight line to her lips and the intense light in her eyes. She commanded respect, willing or unwilling, and no one messed with her.

She was a replica of all of the best physical qualities of Nicolle, but with none of the apparent humor. Something made him sit up straighter and wish he could stand toe to toe with her to see into the depths of her eyes. The stirring of intrigue made him focus his attention, but his eyes still didn't believe what his brain told him.

Nicolle Trajan must have a twin. That thought dropped his mouth open, and the lovely lieutenant picked that moment to turn his way. She scowled at him.

Jake said, "And this is Fire Investigations Specialist Trajan."

Out of the corner of his eye, he saw Noah spin to the doorway and freeze in his tracks, a hand partially raised. But Gid couldn't take his eyes off the curvy lieutenant, whose frown deepened the longer she stared at him. She didn't appear to be inclined to look away, but she didn't seem happy about it. If a glance could throw a person against a wall, he'd be flat and pinned. Funny, but the idea didn't bother him, as long as it was her body pressed up against his.

Warm curves. Hot legs shoved against his. A female form soft where he would be hard. Then he'd shift their positions and she'd wrap her legs around him and –

The lieutenant's eyes seemed to narrow, as if she could read his thoughts.

Gid heard the perplexed note in his own voice when he asked the obvious. "There are two of you?"

A woman's voice he recognized because of the smile evident in its tone said, "Yes, Gideon, two of us. Mirror images, so to speak." But the lieutenant's lips hadn't moved.

Gid flicked his eyes past the deputy to the woman standing in the door in a uniform he identified. The grin on Nicolle Trajan's face was a sharp contrast to her twin's cold stare.

Noah glanced between the two women, his eyes a little glazed and wide, as if he couldn't believe his good luck. His mouth snapped shut, and he grinned. Gid remembered with sudden clarity the description Noah provided of a red-haired woman he saw at a store. How he described her. The longing and the disappointment that he hadn't acted on it. Looked like his brother was going to get a second chance.

Lieutenant Trajan's sharp gaze returned to Noah with an assessing examination. She said, "We have met on more than one occasion, Doctor."

Ah, her voice. Rumbling and rough where Nicolle's was lighter and freer. It sounded like the lieutenant didn't speak unless necessary and didn't share her words easily. That was okay. She didn't need to talk a lot for what Gid had in mind. But she could scream if she wanted.

Gid wanted to pull back the lieutenant's attention and keep it focused on him. He could take the scrutiny, he'd be sure of it. He put as much heat as he could in his tone and the smoking hot smile. "Gideon Kinkead, ma'am, and I'm so very happy to meet you."

Her eyes swung back to him, eyes as deep and gray as fresh smoke from hot wood. An icy biting wind blew in next with her tone. "Lieutenant Danielle Trajan, Mr. Kinkead. And frankly, I'm not sure what to make of you."

Dani fought the urge to glare at her sister. Why hadn't Nicolle told them she was a twin? More to the point, why hadn't she warned Danielle that Gideon Kinkead was smoking hot? The pictures Dani saw hadn't done him justice.

Even seated on the couch, he projected strength and competence. The sling holding his arm and the blue cast wrapping his leg, the scrub of unshaven beard on his battered face, and the wolfish interest obvious in his expression should have turned her off. Instead, it made her pulse pick up with a shot of adrenalin like the zing when she entered the ring for a bout.

Gideon stared at her, occasionally flipping his eyes to her twin over her shoulder as if comparing them. He grinned in that self-deprecating way she supposed men thought would get them off with less than a warning. That didn't earn him any points in her book, or at least that's what she tried to tell herself. She pushed down the disappointment that he might be guilty. Frowning at him, she threw menace into her gaze, and his face sobered. Gideon shifted as if he didn't like this line of questioning but didn't drop his eyes from hers.

Dani stepped forward, using the man's position below her on the couch to press her authority. "Mr. Kinkead, I sincerely doubt you are without any information that can help us. By your own admission when working with my –" She bit off her words to keep it professional. She resumed, "With Investigator Trajan, strange things have happened on a few of your fires since last fall. And then there are the trophies."

"Trophies?" The other Kinkead, the doctor, interrupted with obvious surprise. The brothers hadn't discussed it. That, at least, was good. She had been worried Gideon Kinkead would not follow their instructions to stay silent.

Dani glanced at the doctor, then back at Gideon. She shook her head. "You haven't told Mr. Kinkead, the other Mr. Kinkead, about –"

"Doctor Kinkead, Lieutenant."

Dani pursed her lips at the interruption.

"What about the letters?" She delivered the questions on rapid fire in an attempt to catch the man in front of her off-guard. The sooner she figured out what his game was, the better. He threw an accusatory glance at Nicolle, and his expression looked like he felt sold out.

"You told her about those?"

"Letters? What letters?" The doctor interrupted again, moving closer to his brother. His stance, hands flexing at his sides but his knees soft as he stood there, drew Dani's attention. Noah Kinkead looked like a man ready to jump into the fight, and she realized there was more to him than she'd originally assumed.

Nicolle said, "Gideon's been receiving threats. Death threats, to be specific. They arrive before each fire. They appear to escalate in level of threat and in promised violence." The brisk tone wasn't fooling Dani. Something about this whole situation had her sister uneasy.

Noah swung back around toward his brother and took a step forward. She wasn't sure who he was mad at, his brother or the intruders, and she and Jake stepped forward as if recognizing a threat at the same time. Jake went so far as to put a restraining hand on Noah's arm.

"Why didn't you tell me?" Noah didn't bother to shake off the hand as his worried voice dropped with the question. Dani wasn't sure what to make of him, but he wasn't her focus, and she turned her attention to the man on the couch.

Gideon appeared uneasy, though the pained expression on his face held its own weight of worry. A protective glare came to his eyes as his face turned up to his brother's and she suspected that if he could stand, the two would be inches apart and snarling.

"You have enough on your plate with the girls, and well, everything else." Gid waved his uninjured hand as if this explained it all. But she didn't miss the flash of apprehension.

Gideon Kinkead was guilty of something, and she was going to find out what it was. When his eyes met hers, she tried to ignore the visceral response deep in her gut, the one telling her she didn't care what he was guilty of, as long as she got a chance to know him better.

>>>>>

Gid listened to the questions swirling around him, answering as best he could. But his focus remained on the accusations in his brother's voice. Noah had made the move north for them to be a family, and Gideon had done precious little to allow them to cultivate that connection. Noah felt hurt, and Gid couldn't blame him.

Guilt flashed over him. The girls, Elena and Charlotte, who he always asked about but didn't know much better than he had when they moved to town months ago. Noah, who worked too hard and played too little, and now seemed fixated on Nicolle as she too shot out questions. Most of all, though, he felt a weight of responsibility about not explaining all of this sooner. Maybe if he had, Curtis wouldn't have been injured. He looked down at his leg, and wondered if it cost him his career too. What would he do if he couldn't fight fires? He had no clue.

Jake's reasonable voice cut through the noise, followed by Danielle Trajan's, and Gid realized they were questioning Noah now. His brother didn't sound right. He focused on Noah's face and recognized the fleeting shadow before it hid behind professional objectivity. What did Noah have to be guilty about?

Gid shot out the words, not caring that they had an audience. Whatever was wrong, it was his job to fix it. "Noah? What's on your mind?"

The lieutenant too shifted her attention at his words. "Dr. Kinkead, do you have any insights you can share with us about the threats, the letters or the trophies?"

"He doesn't have anything to share, because I hadn't told him about all of it before. He's probably pissed with me. That's what you're seeing." Gid flashed Noah a warning look as he lifted his chin toward the cops.

"Everyone has secrets, Kinkead," said the lieutenant, though Gid wasn't sure to whom she directed the statement. A passing darkness crossed her face, a fascinating shift of expression that disappeared as quickly as it came. Gid knew he didn't imagine it when she frowned for a brief moment in her sister's direction.

"I get the impression there's something we need to know but no one's sharing." Jake scratched his head, keeping his eyes fixed on Noah as he resettled his uniform hat in place and tapped the pen in his fingers against his thigh.

"Kermarrec, why don't you get pictures of the letters? I assume you're fine with that, Mr. Kinkead?" Danielle pinned Gid with an intense look that dared him to say he wasn't. Given that he was itching to see what she was made of, he almost wished he could say no, to piss her off and see what would happen.

But he did the right thing because when it came to being professional, he didn't know how to be any other way. He nodded in reply. "Yes, I am. I kept them in plastic bags, in case they were needed for evidence someday."

The lieutenant cocked her head and nodded as if in approval. She kept her eyes on Gideon as she asked again, "Dr. Kinkead, are you sure there isn't anything else you can tell us?"

It was like she wove a spell with her eyes, eyes that reminded Gid of warm nights and hot thoughts. Thoughts that didn't belong in this room, though they sure belonged any place Danielle Trajan stood. Or laid down, like across a bed with dark sheets to highlight the creamy skin hidden beneath the starched uniform. The red hair, now in a tight braid at her neck, fanned across the pillows. Her lips, red from passionate kisses. Her voice, tense with anticipation –

He had to stop this. He was no more going to get into Danielle Trajan's perfectly creased uniform slacks than he was going to climb a mountain, and it had nothing to do with his current injuries. But if any woman was going to stir him to life again, he suspected she would be just what the doctor ordered.

Chapter 14

Dani watched Nicolle fumble with her computer in uncharacteristic clumsiness. Something in her disjointed movements issued a warning. Was Nicolle attracted to Gideon Kinkead? Nerves communicated as easily as any emotion between the two of them, and when Nicolle glanced up to find her watching, she read a blend of anger and excitement in her twin's eyes.

Who was she kidding? Dani had to be honest, because she understood. The draw Gideon Kinkead already had for her was completely out of line. She'd have to quash it, and she'd need to tell Nicolle to do the same. They couldn't be objective if they were involved.

She said, "Jake, I was curious about the Kinkeads' reactions. What do you think they're hiding?"

Dani focused in on her deputy, who stared back at the house with a puzzled expression on his face. "I get together with Gid every once in a while. Something happened last summer, though he doesn't talk about it."

"What about the doctor?" Dani moved so she too could keep an eye on the house.

Jake shrugged. "He moved up here to work at Armstrong in the ER. A good doc, from what I can tell. He took care of me when I was hit in the winter. He has two little girls and rarely hangs out with us because he's a single parent. I think there was a messy divorce involved."

Beside them, Nicolle sighed, and Dani forced herself to stay on track. Any discussion the two of them had would be private. They had a job to do, and that brought her back to the threats against him claimed by Gideon Kinkead.

"Jake, we didn't get the letters Gideon claimed he received. Take care of that, okay? I want them analyzed as soon as possible, even if it means bumping another case down the ladder."

Jake nodded and resettled his hat, hooking his fingers into his belt as he continued to eye the house. When his eyes shifted to dart between the two women, Dani felt herself tense. The speculation in his expression made her cringe. As if he read her pending censure, he raised a placating hand and walked back to the front door in stiff steps.

Suspects. Too many of them, and none of them solid with any evidence. Maybe the letters Kinkead claimed he had would provide something. Then again, pigs might fly someday too. Dani needed more access to determine if he was a target or a suspect.

Who was she trying to kid? She wanted to get closer to Gideon Kinkead and see what else might be hiding behind his striking smile. Even bruised and battle-worn, he looked blistering hot. And that was no way for a sheriff's lieutenant to be thinking about a potential suspect.

Gid shook his head. "Okay. I know what you're doing. You're trying to turn this around on me, and I deserve some of that. But don't give me shit. You're keeping something from me, and you're going to tell me if I have to beat it out of you."

When his brother threw pointed stares at the leg cast and shoulder brace, Gid couldn't hide a frustrated sigh. In this instance, his brother had him beat.

"I'll pay someone to beat it out of you then. Trust me, Noah, I am going to find out what's going on." But he smiled as he spoke the words, and was relieved to find Noah lightening up as well. Whatever he was going to say next, though, was lost when a knock sounded on the door.

Noah rose and opened it to Jake's frowning face. "Sorry, guys, but we need those letters. Gid, where did you say you had them?"

He gestured to the duffels sitting inside the door. "The one on the right, in the large inside pocket. You can't miss the plastic bag."

Jake bent over with a marked grimace, and Noah hurried over before he moved much further. "Let me. I don't want to see you back in the ER or hear you had a relapse because you dug through Gid's mess." He crouched low and shot a hard glance at Gid as if asking for any potential surprises.

But there weren't any. Just the letters, which they now knew about. Gid gave a small headshake and changed his gaze to Jake, noting the intense scrutiny with which he watched Noah.

"You know," Gid said, "I could have Jake interrogate you. I bet that would be fun to watch. Then I'd know what's going on with you."

Jake flashed Gid an unreadable look, then turned to Noah once more as if considering the statement. "What's going on?"

Noah shrugged, waving a large clear bag as if to dispel any interest. When he stood, he glanced again at Gid.

"Is this everything?" His warning was written clearly on his face.

"That's all of it."

Jake took the bag and examined the envelopes, as he seemed to try to read the pages through the plastic. Impossible to do, Gid knew, because he'd tucked the letters back in their envelopes before bagging them. Noah also looked more closely, and Gid caught a brief flash of relief on his brother's face. When their eyes met, he wondered why there seemed to be guilt on Noah's face once more.

Shaking open a larger bag mark 'evidence' in bold letters, Jake said, "So, you two didn't know about the twins? I thought everyone in Flynn's Crossing knew Danielle and Nicolle."

A spark of hope lit his brother's face. As long as it fell in the right direction, he'd be the first one to cheer his brother on. Noah said, "I'll need to ask Gid more about Nicolle." Gid nearly cheered, because he wanted to know everything there was to know about the lovely lieutenant.

When his gaze fell to the cast on his leg, he snorted at his delusions. He had no hope of romancing the woman in his present condition. He could entice her to spend time with him in their common interest in public safety, however. There was still an arsonist out there, and who better to help her catch a firebug than a firefighter?

Chapter 15

It took Gid a week to figure out how to approach her. He thanked Madame Fire that his brother chose this morning to explain his fears. Gid now had something to offer.

"Trajan."

Despite the knowledge that he was alone in the fire camp office, Gid glanced around to make sure. The no-nonsense voice answering the phone sounded every bit as stiff as she'd appeared in Noah's living room. He hoped behind her body armor and evil eye, Danielle Trajan had a softer side. She wasn't a woman to give things away easily, which only made her a more tempting challenge. Her air of someone who could handle herself in any tough situation enticed him.

"If you want something, talk," she said, and the demand in her tone made him smile. It was going to be a definite pleasure getting to know her.

"It's Gideon Kinkead. I have information for you, Lieutenant."

The pause on the other end lasted long enough for Gid to wonder if she'd already hung up. Then he heard a fast breath, as if he'd surprised her.

"Kinkead, good of you to call, since I was about to contact you. I have questions for you."

More questions made him nervous. His memory of the blast was still fuzzy, and he doubted it would become any clearer. But to spend time with her, he'd be accommodating.

"Kinkead? You still there?"

"Yeah, yeah, sorry. We can swap stories. Where and when? Though I have to warn you, I'm not inclined to make this a public discussion."

Silence met his words, and he could almost hear the gears in her brain moving in rapid-fire sequences.

He thought he heard a reluctant heavy sigh. "I'm not sure we should have this talk at the station, either." Another hesitation, as if she was undecided, then she said, "I'll pick you up."

He relaxed into his chair. "I have crutches."

"I have a truck," she replied, and he thought he heard a trace of humor in her voice. "Be ready in thirty," she said, the smile gone.

"Don't you need to know where I am?"

"Oh, I know where you are, Mr. Kinkead. I have my eyes on you."

The line went dead before he could respond, but that didn't keep him from grinning. When twenty-three minutes had passed, he was waiting on the landing at the top of the trailer's steps, as eager as he'd ever been for a fire call to sound.

Five minutes more had ticked off the clock when an over-amped pick-up pulled to a stop. She rounded the engine in a slow saunter that had his pulse picking up more speed as she seemed to slow her advance. The lazy grin he gave didn't have to be forced, and her foot faltered for a beat before she dropped her sunglasses and regarded him over the top with wariness in those smoke gray eyes.

This should not be happening on so many levels. She could decide he was a suspect. The lovely lieutenant could slap him in handcuffs, and it wouldn't be the fun kind. But she was here, and dressed as a civilian. The jeans and button-down shirt with rolled up sleeves gave him the first sight of her body without her usual armor, and he mumbled a silent prayer to the regulation gods that she hadn't picked him up in uniform. This view was much more pleasant, and he couldn't help it when his eyes slipped up and down her body in a glance he hoped she felt like caress.

"I can manage this, if you lend a shoulder," he said.

Danielle nodded with a jerk and moved with tentative steps, as if ready to engage in combat. It was the opportunity he wanted. Gid slipped forward just as she arrived in his personal space. That brought them chest to chest, and air flashed into his lungs with hard force. The woodsy aroma of tempting female overwhelmed him, drawing him forward in a sudden desire to sniff her hair. Warm forest and wildflowers made him want to nuzzle closer.

When he leaned in, he tipped his balance, and her hands shot out to support him. Hot palms landed on bare skin, and that warmth raced through him, starting at the roots of his hair and heading down to settle in the pit of his gut. A distracting blush lit up the lovely lieutenant's cheeks, and Gid would bet his next paycheck she hated the sudden flutter of her eyelids. Her previous kick-ass mode slipped long enough for him to note the intake of breath and frown that followed. She didn't like reacting to him, which made him want to make her do it again.

Yup, definitely should not be feeling any of these things.

"Thanks for coming for me," Gideon said.

The lieutenant dropped her hands and took a step backwards, eyeing him with a cautious expression as if analyzing his double entendre. Her gaze didn't give anything away when she said, "No problem. We need to discuss this case and any help you can provide to the investigation, Mr. Kinkead."

"Call me Gid. Or Gideon, though I'm not as fond of it."

She didn't reciprocate, which he found intriguing.

"I'll help you up into the truck," she said, her voice softer than it had been, but her frown deepening.

"No need, I can manage." He swung away before she could argue, because if she insisted on letting him lean on her, he'd give in to it.

He worked his crutches across the space, though the effort cost him. He swung himself up into her truck with only a brief stutter favoring his injured shoulder. Feeling her shrewd eyes on him, he rubbed a hand across his forehead to hide the sheen of sweat. By the time she slid into the driver's seat, he was grinning once more.

"So, where do you want to go? My treat. I haven't been able to get out much since the accident."

He delivered his words in a casual, friendly tone. Charm was never something he had to search for, and he upped the wattage for Dani's benefit. It looked like he'd need an extra helping to win her over.

Her frown was again in evidence as her hand rested on the keys. "We'll split the check. I suggest the diner outside of town. It's quieter there and we can talk, Mr. Kinkead."

"Gid, please."

As if in response, she shifted closer to the driver door and further from him. There was only so far she could go in the truck cab, and he planned to use that to his advantage. If his shoulder wouldn't scream with the movement, he'd be running his hand across the seatback and into the hair she'd pulled back with a single band.

"Should we get down to business? I have questions for you, and you said you have information for me." Her no-nonsense business tone made him eager to yank that braid. She fired up the truck without looking at him.

"You and Nicolle were a surprise, I have to tell you. She never mentioned she had a twin, or even a sister. And a cop. I'm impressed. Twin first responders. Tell me, are there more of you at home?"

Her lips pulled into a tight line.

"I could say the same thing about you and your brother. I mean, first responders and all. Are there more of you at home?" She pulled to a smooth halt at a stop sign and turned to watch him.

He couldn't help grinning now. "Is this how we're going to play it? I ask you questions, you dodge and ask me questions? Because I'm game if you are, but I tend to get what I want in the end. In the interest of full disclosure."

Glancing in the rearview mirror, she kept her foot on the brake and a dispassionate expression on her face as she continued to study him. He realized baiting her was the most fun he'd enjoyed with a woman in a very long time.

She said, "In the interest of full disclosure, I too tend to get what I want, and sooner rather than later, Mr. Kinkead. And for the record, I'm going to ask as many questions as I like and as often as I like, until you give me the truth."

That stopped him. He knew he should be careful. Her stare wasn't hostile, but it certainly wasn't welcoming. He kept his smile firmly in place, even if his stomach jumped at the thought he was playing with fire. The truck stayed silent as they continued their pissing contest. Only the approach of another vehicle shifted her back into driving mode.

Gid remained silent, and the lieutenant kept her counsel too. There would be plenty of time for questions and answers soon. He wanted to examine her face when he talked, and he didn't want them swerving into a tree when he told her about Noah's problems.

When they pulled into the nearly empty diner parking lot, Gid didn't wait for her help as she shut down the engine. His door was already open and he hopped down, holding on to the cab's back panel as he slammed the door. His pride ached, and he swore he'd make it inside without her help. He swung the crutches in long arcs to cover the distance without looking to see if she followed.

It worked well until he tripped and dropped his injured foot to the ground in response. Pain lanced through him as he put weight on the leg, but it was worth it when she slid an arm around him and gave him her shoulder to lean on. He had smoothed his face into a blank expression, but he couldn't do anything about the tension in his body as it pressed against hers.

"If you want to lean on the truck for a moment, Mr. Kinkead, that's fine," she said. He shook his head against her offer even before she finished speaking. He felt the damp sheen of perspiration on his forehead and tightened his mouth against the discomfort.

"Gid, please."

She examined his face before her eyes landed on his lips. He swore he felt them tingle. She said, "Danielle."

"Danielle. It suits you." He smiled wider and turned toward the restaurant, shaking off her helping shoulder under his. If they prolonged that contact, he could not be responsible for his actions.

"Are you always this stubborn?" She delivered the question so quietly, he wondered if she intended it to be under her breath.

"Pretty much," he grumbled in response.

The man behind the counter barely glanced up at their entrance and bustled to a table in the window to toss down two menus.

"Sorry, but this table won't work. We'd be better off with a booth in the back so I can put my leg up and out of the way." He winked at the man's sudden concentration, staring at Gid's cast as if this was the first time he noticed it. The man walked away at a fast clip. Menus landed on the plastic top of a booth that could easily hold six people. But it filled Gid's requirements, since a high back protected it from any prying eyes in the rest of the restaurant.

He settled in the booth and grinned up at her. Danielle hadn't stopped frowning since she glanced around the darkened area as if expecting trouble to pop out of the worn plastic seats. She stood there long enough that Gid felt compelled to ask, "Would you like to sit down?"

She waited, as if not wanting to give him the upper hand by agreeing too quickly. Baiting the lovely lieutenant was making his day.

She slid into the other side, and he immediately pushed toward the center until he was almost thigh to thigh with her. Her body heat washed through the denim she wore, and he had a fleeting wish she'd donned a dress or shorts so he could absorb it faster. As if she felt it too, she slid away. Keeping his grin to himself, Gid nudged close each time she moved, until she was at the edge of the banquette. When she frowned at the floor before shifting a glare to him, he shrugged. "I would like to put my leg up."

He lifted the cast with both hands and dropped it with a thump on the banquette. Her sudden change in expression, what he thought might be a fluster of embarrassment, made him want to know exactly what she was thinking. The frown returned, and when her eyes met his, her perusal would probably be the same if she examined dog shit on her boot. She might not be one to play games, but she intrigued him.

As did her looks, her attitude, and her feminine charms. She must have some, hidden deep behind that authoritative scowl and under her conservative casual clothes. She was as well stacked and toned as her sister. Nicolle was no slouch in the looks department, but her easy-going disposition made her appear open.

Sheriff's Lieutenant Danielle Trajan felt as accessible as a steep rocky ridge in an ice storm. But then, even those could be climbed successfully with skill and patience. And luckily, Gid knew himself to be a man with both when it came to women.

"What looks good?" He didn't glance down at the menu, letting the innuendo hang in the air between them. She was close enough for him to pick up her timber-laced scent, and he inhaled deeply because in the forest, he was at home.

Danielle's expression didn't change one iota. She didn't answer, continuing to study him. Her eyes flicked over his face as if memorizing it for a police artist's sketch. The turn of her head to accommodate their side-by-side position left her ponytail out of sight and the creaminess of her neck exposed. Gid wondered if her captivating scent would be stronger where milky skin disappeared under the fabric of her button-down shirt.

Her eyes shifted forward and she leaned away from him, reaching for a menu with apparent disinterest. That irked him. Women didn't usually lean away from Gideon Kinkead. Worse yet, this attraction he felt for one sexy cop was out of proportion. He wanted to slide his arm along the back of the bench seat and wrap it around her to draw her closer. Damn the brace and sling for getting in the way of that idea.

She licked her lips, and his eyes stuck on the movement. Shine and plumpness called to him. He watched the slow movement of her throat as she swallowed iced tea, still studying the menu as if she was preparing for an exam. She'd have the whole thing memorized if she stared at it this hard for much longer.

"What do you think about the meatloaf?" She didn't raise her eyes with her question.

Baby, I would lay you down on that meatloaf and coat you in the mashed potatoes, then lick them off you. Slowly. He was drooling in sudden hunger, and it had nothing to do with the food.

He must have been silent for too long, since Danielle suddenly turned her gaze on him with a questioning frown. Those dove-gray eyes narrowed when she registered his expression.

He knew how he looked. Hungry. Wolfish. His mouth was open and his breathing fast, because getting the lovely Danielle alone, truly alone, suddenly felt like an emergency of the first priority.

>>>>>

She observed his heated glance and tried to convince herself it didn't matter. It was all about the case, because that's all it could be about. The fact that Gideon Kinkead proved to be as nice and sweet as every woman in town said, and as affable a guy to hang out with as the men said, made it hard to come up with a reason to hate him. Add in the heat factor, and she thought she should ask her twin if spontaneous combustion could happen to humans.

She needed to hate Gideon. She needed that for her own preservation. She needed it for the case. What the fuck was she supposed to do with her need for him as a man?

The only answer that made sense to her wasn't something she relished, or so she kept repeating it in her brain. Get close to Gideon Kinkead to determine what he knew and how he knew it. She had good reasons. Gid had received death threats against him and against his brother and his family. He didn't appear to think his own personal safety was in question.

"Yeah, I know I'm in danger on a fire line, but I have a squad of nineteen others around me." He shrugged as if this explained everything.

"But you aren't on the line at the moment." Her counter made his lips tighten into a single thin line and she read the anger in his eyes. He didn't rebut her comment, and he didn't look pleased about his situation.

At least he answered her questions about the arsons and recent explosion without pauses. Dani had confidence in her ability to read people, and she bet his recitations were without pretense. Her objective assessment led her to suspect Gideon Kinkead was telling the truth.

Objective, her ass, or Gideon's very fine one. She nearly cracked her glass of iced tea when self-disgust made her drop it on the tabletop. The disgust part was because she'd broken one of her own important rules. Don't get emotionally close to a case, not to the victims and not to suspects with sympathetic circumstances.

She should reassign this one. She should step back behind the safety of her desk and the cover it provided. She should let the arson task force do its job and run as far from the enticements Gideon provided, as far away as she could.

Those were a lot of shoulds, and she was never good with that word. If her reasonable intelligence argued against becoming involved, it would make sense to listen to it. Something about the man made her lose her mind. He might be a victim, but it was more likely he was a suspect. It would make sense to stay close to him. Close at this point would be up close and personal.

When the check arrived, Gid grabbed it before she could, and he ignored her arguments to split it with a grin. A glance at her watch shocked her. Two hours had passed, and she thought they'd only been there minutes. Not only was she losing her senses, she lost track of time and professional etiquette. Was it wrong to hope he'd try to kiss her when she dropped him off at his brother's?

But Dani never got a chance to chastise herself about that because when they reached the house, he pushed open the passenger door, slid out, and reached in to extend a hand as if he planned to shake it. She reached out automatically. He might have held on a few seconds longer than necessary, or maybe that was her. With a ghost of a smile, he lifted his chin and swung toward his brother's front door.

By the time she reached home, she figured out her course of action. She ignored the personal sacrifice she was about to make as she typed the email and hit send.

Sacrifice, her ass. Somewhere in the back of her brain, she recognized the ludicrous logic. She always reminded her deputies to treat everyone equally, with respect and consideration within the letter of the law. Be compassionate and caring, but firm and objective. Yeah, on that last idea, she had the first part straight and the last part completely fucked up.

A ping sounded, and she slid a finger across the mouse pad to wake up the machine. Her email inbox lit with new messages, and the top one was a reply from the sheriff.

'Close personal observation of subject approved. Use all appropriate protocols and procedures.'

If her heart skipped a beat at the prospect of spending more time with one hot firefighter, she would ignore it. She had a job to do it. It was her duty, and Dani was all about duty.

Chapter 16

Gid waved his thanks to the helpful townie who delivered him to the firebase. He settled the backpack into a better position and hopped up the trailer steps with his crutches banging each edge. He hadn't planned on coming in today, but if he wanted to occupy Danielle's personal space, he needed Nicolle's insights to help him get situated.

As the door swung shut behind him, he eyed the trailer's hodgepodge of desks and partitions. Offset from side to side to give occupants the illusion of privacy, the array created an obstacle course for a person on crutches. Gid found he could only move sideways, making his progress clumsy and tedious, and he cursed when his backpack crashed into a box that tumbled to the floor, spilling its contents with a noisy clatter.

He hadn't realized how hard this would be. The crutches, the maneuvering, the weight of the pack making his shoulder ache. He cursed with more color when he nearly stuck his good foot in a trashcan set at a distance from one of the desks. When hands landed on his arm, he huffed out his frustration and prepared to shake the person off. Only as he began to do so did he realize how unsteady he was.

Nicolle said, "Are you supposed to be up so much already?" Her hands tightened on his arm as he struggled to remain upright.

Gid huffed and blew out another curse. "I can't stay cooped up. I don't care what the doctors say. I can't stand feeling helpless." He shrugged out of her grasp and took tentative steps into their shared cubbyhole, falling into a chair with little grace and nearly ending up on the floor when its wheels propelled it backwards.

"Fuck. I hate this. I need a walking cast but the doctor won't give me one for another two weeks. Two weeks. Can you believe that? I even asked Noah to put in a good word for me, but my brother is in cahoots with the ortho." He wiped his sleeve across his forehead and finally looked at her fully. "Well, someone sure looks happy this morning. Are you enjoying my show? Tickets cost three kisses, Trajan."

She barked out a laugh but blushed a deeper red as she settled into her own chair. He examined her features, noting the similarities to her twin in the bone structure and facial expressions. Not that Danielle laughed all that much, which was something he planned to change. The women even shared that sprinkling of freckles strapped across their noses and powdering their cheeks.

But there were differences too, and he could pick them out easily after staring at Danielle last night. He would have spent more time with her, but she extended no invitation for him to come back to her place and he certainly had nowhere to bring her. Something told him he'd be better off biding his time and letting her think their eventual closer encounters were her idea. If it was disappointment on her face when he turned to shake her hand last night, he could only echo the sentiment. Her scowl could stop a bullet faster than her body armor, he bet.

Tough, he'd give her that. Danielle Trajan didn't stand for any shit. Nicolle didn't mind being considered one of the guys, but she was female through and through. Danielle, on the other hand, might deck the first man who suggested she use her feminine wiles for anything. He needed to learn everything he could about what made the lovely lieutenant tick. His primary resource had her eyes closed across their shared cubbyhole.

He said, "Ah, Trajan? Nici?"

Her eyes popped open as if he'd startled her. Would Danielle look the same, dreamy with the whiff of a smile? He asked the first thing that came to his mind. "Tell me the truth, Nici. Does your twin ever relax and let her guard down?"

He got a reaction, but not the one he expected. After an initial start, she laughed as if this was the funniest idea she'd ever heard. Would Danielle sound the same if – no, when – he encouraged her to laugh as hard? Would the years fall from her face and make her appear younger and even more beautiful? What was she like when she was truly happy? He really wanted to know, and seeing the possibilities by watching Nicolle, he knew the wait would be worth it. But it would take time. Shaking his head to clear the image of Danielle, accepting and laughing in his arms, he opened his mouth to fire more questions at her twin.

Nicolle grabbed a folder and her laptop. She pushed both toward Gid and said, "No time for twenty questions, I'm afraid. Tell me, what do you know about incendiary ignition devices?"

He frowned at her obvious rerouting of the discussion. She chuckled every once in a while and shook her head as if something was unbelievable. When she answered none of his questions, he gave up trying.

Two hours later, he was glad he'd allowed her distraction, because they found it. A common chemical signature in the devices used to start a fire two months ago, and found at the site of his explosion. He wanted to contact Danielle immediately, but Nicolle beat him to it. The phone was to her ear before he had a chance to ask who she was calling, and by the conversation, he knew it was Danielle on the other end. His excuse to call her went up in smoke. Of course, as her twin pointed out, he was still a common thread linking the arsons together. The lovely lieutenant might still hold that against him.

He had to calm himself with the thought that at least they had a signature. It was something they could trace, with time and a little luck. What was that saying about luck? If you wanted to be hit by lightning, you needed to put up a lot of kites.

Gideon spun his chair to stare out their small window at the orange tinge of the sky. They didn't have time to fly a lot of kites. The arsonist could be lurking, waiting until the crews might have a handle on controlling this monster. Then he'd ignite a new burn and they'd be back to square one. If it was personal, who knew where that burn might happen? It was bad enough in the forest. If the guy decided to set something closer, say, at Noah's house, things would go from ugly to hell and quickly.

What would he do if he was an arsonist? Gid examined shifting colors in the sky, thinking through the implications. Wait around and see how much damage he did on the last explosion? How would he know otherwise? Strangers in Flynn's Crossing stood out, and strangers asking questions, even more so. People would talk.

But what if the arsonist was a guy who looked like a firefighter? People might not question him. What if the arsonist was on the inside? He realized with a sinking feeling that this is what people, probably including Danielle, thought about him.

A ripple of greetings rolled to them from the outer room, followed by a perfunctory knock on the partition. The space filled with a tall, boney man wearing a creased uniform and a hardhat that read 'Safety' across the front in bold lettering.

"Trajan, Cap said I'd find you here." The man moved forward and eyed Gideon. "Kinkead. Sorry to hear about your injuries. It's a bitch."

Gideon nodded as he shook the man's hand. Nicolle said, "What can I do for you, Clyde? I know you have jurisdiction here, so my findings are all yours." She updated him with their discovery from the morning. "If you'd like to step in with your big resources, feel free."

Gid noted the welcome in her tone, but the other man didn't seem to need it. His exchange was collegial and respectful. The old firedogs rarely like the younger women on the line because they said it slowed them down. That wasn't the case here. Gid bet Danielle garnered the same respect in the sheriff's office.

"Well, thanks, but I'm not here to shovel your embers. I came because I received a report on the test results for the materials located at the points of ignition for the cases we're calling arson. We got lucky."

Gid sat forward, trying to temper his eagerness. The sooner he could get out from under suspicion, the better his chances with Danielle might be.

Clyde frowned and pulled a sheaf of papers from his back pocket, referring to them over his glasses. "In one of the last arson fires, we found a common trigger mechanism, a cell phone. It's the disposable kind, so untraceable."

Everyone nodded, because that wasn't news.

"But a corner of the case remained intact, protected enough during the blast to let us lift a print. We got a hit on it. A con with priors."

Finally, they had a lead. Gideon said, "Did someone pull him in?"

Clyde's grin died. "No can do. He was released right before the fire in April. Mean bastard, by the sound of him. One Clovis Mitchell left the Idaho pen on a mistaken early release. And no one knows where he is now."

Well of course the fuck not. A lead with another dead end. Gid opened his mouth to ask more about the guy, but he didn't get a chance when Nicolle gave a loud gasp. Her paled face made him wonder if she'd be visiting Noah at work today.

Dani heard the edge of tension in Nicolle's voice, and it had nothing to do with the case. Or rather, it had to do with the person involved more than the case. The man who attacked her sister was a potential arsonist. Didn't that suck six ways to Sunday? A fresh wave of guilt washed over her, one she pushed through and tried to ignore as she considered her options.

She had an opening, one she still wasn't completely sure she wanted to pursue. Gideon Kinkead might be off the potential suspects list, at least for this fire. But then there were the roses. How did they relate, if at all? Was it someone's idea of a sick joke on Gideon? Or did they tie him to the crimes in some way?

There was only one way to find out, and that was, as her boss put it, close personal observation. She had to stay on Gideon until she knew the truth. And the truth was all that mattered, not what her body wished for.

Yeah, that thing. Reminding herself for the umpteenth time that the man was in a cast, Dani straightened her uniform and strode up the steps to the fire squad trailer. She didn't bother to knock. Being there on law enforcement business was enough.

Cap stood propped against a steel partition that looked like it may collapse under the weight of his beefy arm. He glanced up and stopped speaking, before his eyes darted to someone behind the barricade. As if on cue, Nicolle's head popped into view, and she wore a forced smile.

"Hey, thanks for coming over, but you didn't have to. We would have brought everything to you."

She didn't do much more than nod to acknowledge her sister's words. Instead, she felt the tight wad of worry her twin carried as if it was her own. And fear, though Nicolle wasn't showing it, at least not for the public to view. Dani dodged the obstacle course to join the discussion, and schooled her features into objective nonchalance before looking at the man seated sideways at a metal desk.

Gideon sat with his leg up on its surface, his chair tilted back at what appeared to be the probably tipping point. When his eyes fell on her, he gave that same lazy grin he had yesterday. And damn if that didn't wake up her girl parts and make her wish no one else was in the room.

He nodded his head and said, "Lieutenant Trajan."

"Mr. Kinkead, I'm happy to see you up and around."

"But you just saw me last night," he said, grinning now.

"Last night?" Nicolle's eyes darted with curiosity between them.

Gid said, "Yes, she picked me up for dinner last night. We had a great time. Too bad we both had to work today." His grin widened into a leer, and she knew he must be doing this on purpose. Everyone in the room shot knowing glances between the two of them as if they suspected there was more to this than met the naked eye.

Naked, in bed with Gideon. What a marvelous place that would be. But it wasn't what she could allow herself to think about. Dani had a job to do, so she scowled her best frightening stare at the man. In response, he winked at her.

Her twin said, "Why Danielle Trajan, you two-faced little sneak. And after the lecture you read to me."

Okay, fine, so she was protective. She had every reason to be. That monster was out there, and her sister was distracted by the doctor instead of watching her own back.

Nicolle chuckled again, but her face quickly lost its happy glow. She frowned at the file folder in her hand as she extended it. "The reports. It's all there."

Dani flipped through the pages, though some of it was going to require a more detailed read. Some of it was chemistry, which she'd need Nicolle to translate for her when they were alone. That was never her strong subject in school.

"So where are we?" She looked between the people in the room.

Cap said, "You got half an hour, then we move the trailer. Time to find somewhere else to park yourselves, guys. Tell me when you figure it out, Trajan."

Danielle and Nicolle said in unison, "Thanks," then stared at each other for a moment. This was usually the point where they both burst into laughter, but based on the combustible words on the pages in her hand, Dani didn't feel like it. Apparently neither did Nicolle, since her frown tightened and she started packing the papers on her desk into her briefcase with rapid fingers.

Dani glanced after Cap as the door slammed. "What was that about?"

Nici shook her head without looking up. "They're moving this to the new command location further east along the southern flank of the fire. I was hoping we could work at HQ with you."

It was Dani's turn to shake her head. "Our only available conference room is now filled with earnest twenty-somethings with laptops, auditing stacks of expense reports and other accounting shit."

The room fell silent as she joined her sister in packing files. She didn't look at the man behind the desk. Gid wasn't saying anything, but she felt his heat as if he stood next to her. She was definitely feeling the need to get close. She could always use helping him to his feet as an excuse, and if her body accidently pressed up against his in the process, well, that would be an accident.

Noises sounded from beneath them, and voices called out to one another outside. The trailer jostled, and Nicolle hefted up her briefcase, a backpack, and one of the boxes, heading for the door. She said nothing as it banged closed behind her.

"She's a strong woman, you know. Not just physically, but mentally and emotionally as well. Whatever's bothering her, I'm sure she'll muscle through it."

Dani froze in the midst of folding a box closed to find Gid regarding her with a thoughtful expression. Caring made his features softer, and his respect for her twin was clear.

"Let me get that for you," he said, and stood. Reaching for crutches she hadn't noticed in the corner, he had his backpack in place and both crutches under his bad arm, his good one outstretched toward her.

She narrowed her eyes on him. "A heavy box isn't the best idea." She lifted it with ease and held it with her arms extended. Her muscles didn't quake in the least, and he chuckled.

"Hey, a guy's gotta try, right? I mean, what kind of gentleman would I be if I didn't at least offer?" He made a passable imitation of a bow.

She found herself chuckling in return, and she caught the glimmer of happy surprise in his eyes. She surprised herself. He tickled her funny bone, and she thought she'd broken that long ago. Trying to hide her emotions, she said, "Come on, we have a case to solve. Now all we need is a place to assemble the team."

"Use my house. Or rather, Noah's house. There's plenty of space. And there's a kitchen."

She frowned again, her brief confused happiness evaporating. "I don't cook."

He looked at her, puzzled. "You don't? Wow. But I bet you do a mean take-out. No problem, though. I do."

She turned to weave between the desk, hearing the clunk and slap of him following in an uneven gait. What did he look like when he was hale and in one piece? She bet he prowled like a lion, with that sun-kissed hair flying past his ears and those big blue eyes flashing. "You do what?" She was enjoying the parlay between them.

He chuckled again, though there was a strain in the notes this time. She turned to find him maneuvering with difficulty between the tight spaces, and her first instinct was to drop the box to help him.

Then he lifted his face and their gazes met. His eyes said it all, cautioning her to hold her position. He wanted to preserve his dignity, and that meant doing this himself even if it wasn't easy. She had to respect that, and her grudging admiration for him scaled up a few notches.

Then he winked at her and said, "I cook."

Her insides performed a subtle flip as sexy thoughts raced through her brain. Oh I bet you do, Gideon Kinkead, I bet you do. But she only nodded in response and turned away, wondering what the hell she'd gotten herself into.

Chapter 17

Gid watched from his usual spot in Noah's living room as a cavalcade of vehicles took up the driveway and street. Some were marked and others looked civilian, but no one would need to guess there was law enforcement activity here. He probably should call Noah and warn him, but he was going to go with his gut, which said his brother would be pleased to have Nicolle under his roof as much as possible.

Not that Noah might see her with the crowd that had congregated. Clyde and Cap argued about fire suppression strategies with their faces close to a laptop screen. Occasionally, Cap would raise the stub of his pointer as a substitute for the middle finger, Clyde being the recipient of the gesture. The other man returned the salute before both laughed and returned to arguing.

A clerk from the sheriff's office manned a printer and pages fell off the machine as fast as it could run. She stapled them energetically and distributed each new stack. When she handed Gid the most recent installment, she smiled with more animation than the act required, and Gid smiled back. He looked up to find Danielle watching him with narrowed eyes and that blank cold stare. He winked at her, but she did not return the recognition.

The front door opened, and Noah entered the room with Jake on his heels. He stopped inside the door and looked around with a confused expression. Who could blame him? The man came home from a long day of emergencies to find his house overrun. He probably just wanted to put his feet up and have a beer with the TV playing. Gid dropped his eyes to the pages in his lap, not wanting to meet that gaze when it landed on him.

Danielle picked that moment to lean over him, and he caught that subtle forest scent of her skin. Or maybe it was her hair. The complicated bun she wore when she came to the fire trailer was gone, replaced by a simple ponytail. Its swing made Gid want to grab for it and put his lips to her exposed neck, then trail it up to her lips to see if she tasted as good as she smelled.

A nerve in his leg chose that moment to jump with a sudden stab of pain and he dropped his hand to rub the spot. Yeah, like he was in any condition to do any kind of loving. The lieutenant might have to wait a bit, but he didn't want to keep either one of them lingering too long.

>>>>>

Dani registered the moment when his face paled, a tight line of tension appearing between his eyebrows and drawing his face into a gaunt mask. He examined the pages dropped into his lap with apparent concentration, but his hand kneaded the thigh above his cast, where muscles looked as solid as rocks. Battered, but buff.

She needed to stop thinking about that kind of stuff.

She leaned over to see what he was reading with such intensity. A report about the chemicals used in the incendiary devices. Combustible properties, rates of burn, and possible residue patterns, the kind of thing that made her eyes glaze over, even though she knew they were critical factors in tracking their arsonists. It could be multiple cases, or copycats, or completely unrelated. The only thing they had determined for sure was they were all from manmade causes. These kinds of chemicals were not common to a household or garage.

Someone cleared their throat behind her, and she looked over her shoulder to find Noah and Jake standing inside the front door. Jake's impassive expression was a sharp contrast to the doctor's excitement. Noah stared at her with sudden hope in his eyes. When he realized who she was, he lost that bright anticipation.

"Okay, you're all set. You have hot food and cold, dinner and breakfast, just in case. When you need a resupply, let me know. Now that they've been here, the interns will be fine making the next delivery."

A flurry of white-coated activity erupted from the kitchen doorway. Roxy LaFollette, chef extraordinaire, directed the young interns outside with a lift of her chin. Her gourmet grocery store had been a regular lunch stop for Dani when she was still on patrol. That part of the county, with open rural roads and abundant wildlife, had always been a pleasure to serve. They'd become friends over a protein-rich salad one day, and while Dani didn't allow many people into her life, Roxy was one of those few.

"Roxy, you don't need to do that. I'll clean up later. I hope Noah understands –"

Nicolle burst out of the kitchen and stopped dead, her eyes locating Noah in a second. Dani wished she could twist her head fast enough to see his reaction, because Nici's mouth gaped like a fish. She snapped it shut on a sigh and said, "Hi."

Gid said, "Sorry, man. The squad HQ needed to move with the fire line. No room at the sheriff's office. We need to be here. There wasn't anywhere else to meet."

A few minutes later, they had Noah caught up on the particulars. The chemicals found at the sources of the last manmade fires were consistent with street drug processing facilities, which pointed their investigation in the good doctor's direction.

Dani said, "Based on what you told Nicolle, I made a couple of calls to resources in Southern California, and they tell me the gang you faced in that incident last year, Dr. Kinkead, is a major player in the manufacture and distribution of these same types of drugs. We've sent our chemical analyses to them for review, to see if they match anything they've confiscated. We won't hear back until tomorrow."

She kept her eyes on Noah's face to see his reaction to her assertion. While she wanted Nicolle to find a nice guy, she didn't want her sister in harm's way, and it appeared Noah Kinkead wore a target as well. He looked worried, and she couldn't blame him.

"I know that look. This didn't happen because of you. Noah, are you listening to me?" Gideon's voice rose and she detected the lace of anger in his words. She understood his frustration. When Nicolle had been hurt years ago, Dani had a hard time controlling her rage when Nicolle blamed herself and not the perp.

"Yeah, well, the drug angle only gives us part of an answer. There's the guy from Idaho. And what about the anomalies from the cases last year? I'm glad this is your turf and not mine, Cap." The tall man, the Federal fire investigator, slapped the commander on the shoulder once and disappeared out the front door as if a bullet was after him.

"Noah, can I talk to you for a minute?" Nicolle's voice, pitched low, was probably intended for Noah's ears only, but Dani didn't miss it. Nor did she miss the intense conversation shared by the two men as the doctor checked his brother's leg. Gideon remained on the sofa, his head back and eyes closed. He had ridiculously long eyelashes, shades darker than his blond hair.

She walked into the kitchen, because being too close to him made her think about stupid things. She was not a woman who liked to be stupid. Objectivity was critical, but it was difficult when she was finding all sorts of reasons to like Gideon. She had to stop this immediately. As a law enforcement professional, she could not become in any way attached to the man, even if he was her assignment.

"I don't need a lecture. I know, I know." Gideon's voice rose from the living room with a trace of exasperation. "I'm trying to watch it. I couldn't manage the papers with only one hand."

The words popped out before she could stop herself. "I bet you can manage a damn lot with one hand, Kinkead. Now is not the time to boast about your prowess."

She nearly bit her tongue off. Why the hell had she made that remark? It sounded like she was flirting with Gid, and again, inappropriate. There was nothing she could do to take back the words. She could only hope no one had heard her in the deafening silence. In that quiet, her stomach rumbled. Food, a common ground. She could make plates for herself and for Gid. She busied herself filling servings, avoiding a glance through the open door where she could see Gid.

Their dinner last night had proven that she and Gid shared the same tastes in meals, if their enjoyment of the burgers with mounds of cheese and hot peppers was any indication. They both ate their fries the same way too, loaded with ketchup. That was the only purpose for those potatoes in her opinion, as a conveyance for the condiment. Based on the amount of the red stuff they consumed last night, she bet Gid felt the same.

She made two identical plates and marched into the living room. So help him, if Gid said anything about her untimely remark, she'd break his other leg. What were the chances he was going to be a gentleman about this? She doubted that would be the case.

Gid had his eyes closed as if he was napping. Dani lightened her steps, not wanting to wake him. He looked exhausted. Guilt made her realize how wearing this must be on him. He'd only been injured ten days ago. That was hardly enough time to begin to heal. And getting around with one bad leg and a tender shoulder had to be a challenge.

He hadn't complained, though, other than to express occasional frustration when obstacles stood in his path. She had to admire his stamina. Not only was he physically in better shape than many of her deputies, he didn't let emotional issues like being under the microscope get him down.

She intended to place his plate on the table next to his seat and sneak away, but as she leaned over, Gideon's eyes fluttered. They didn't snap wide, and no confusion haunted them. Their slow sensual drag as they opened made the intensity even sharper when they focused on her, as if he'd known she was approaching all along.

She froze, bent over with her hand on his plate as it perched on the table. His lips lifted into a slow grin at much the same pace as his eyes had, and a vibration of heat dropped into her gut and churned. The man was intense in every sense of the word, and yet he looked so easy-going. This wasn't a ploy, she suspected, but the way he was wired, and damn if that didn't make him even hotter.

"You smell like an exotic candy bar, and I can't wait to take a bite out of you."

His words, low and gruff, made her glad she only had one plate in her hands. She willed it not to shake as she withdrew her other hand, intending to grip hers with both. He intercepted her fingers and before she knew it, he had them cradled in his tight grip.

His thumb moved in small circles on the back of her hand while his fingers laced with hers. He didn't blink and she found she didn't want to either. Black flakes speckled the light blue of his irises, which she found incredibly intriguing. She'd never seen eyes quite like his.

"What do you say we blow this joint and go someplace much more – private?" His emphasis on the final word had her heart jumping into overdrive.

Then her eyes fell, and they landed on the lab reports in his lap. She was here on a case, and he might be a suspect, or he was a target. She was a cop.

She disentangled her hand and rose to her full height. Taking a step back, she felt her regret first and his disappointment next. His face shifted into neutral, and she realized he wasn't going to make a big deal out of this. She wished he would so she could get mad at him for overstepping boundaries. It would make working with him easier, since she could keep a good mad going for days.

She took another step away as Gid watched her, concentrated but unspeaking. What would it be like to be the center of that private attention? She suspected she knew why all of those women in town sighed over him. She'd bet every dollar in her bank account that when Gid focused on a woman, it was like being in the sights of the hottest bullet at the range.

Her appetite for the sandwich had disappeared. She'd find Nicolle and make her eat it. She herself should go for a run or beat the hell out of a bag. She needed to burn off the sexual frustration, but she suspected the disappointment would take much longer.

Gid's energy zinged when Danielle's scent re-entered the room and closed in on him. She was one amazing looking woman, and she smelled almost as good. The analogy to a candy bar had been out of his mouth before he thought about it, and he liked the sudden surprise on her face with those words. He liked ambushing her. She clearly had a different set of expectations about him, and he was going to prove her wrong.

He popped a pickle into his mouth and crunched down, loving the spicy tartness that erupted on his tongue. Like the lovely lieutenant's sharp wit. That comment about his prowess had him smiling. Their attraction was not one-sided, and by the look on her face when she stomped out the back door yelling orders at Jake, she wasn't too happy about it.

That was fine with him. He'd change her mind. Still waters had nothing on the depths of one Danielle Trajan, and he loved swimming in deep water.

When Danielle returned from the backyard, she had her phone to her ear, speaking in a harsh tone Gid knew he never wanted to hear directed at him. When she punched a finger on the face of the instrument with a tight expression, he wondered if something new had gone wrong. He was about to ask when she grabbed her discarded plate and left the room, calling for Nicolle.

A moment later Nicolle and Noah reappeared, with Danielle trailing behind them. Gid's gaze flipped between the couple, trying to read them. Nicolle twisted her fingers and looked nothing like the accomplished investigator she was. Noah had a mad on that would rival Danielle from a few minutes ago. This whole place was going up in flames, and there wasn't a damn thing Gid could do about it.

He turned to Nicolle. "Did you tell Noah?" His brother deserved to know.

"Tell me what?"

Noah's cool words didn't hide the emotion behind them. Gid saw him rise on the balls of his feet as if poised to run. He felt sorry for his brother, not because Nicolle wasn't great, but because Noah was about to feel more rage than his life might have prepared him for.

Nicolle seemed to shrink, then shook it off and stood ramrod straight. She countered with, "We should eat."

"I'm. Not. Hungry. Tell me what?" Noah hadn't moved, but he leaned forward so far, Gid wondered if he'd fall over.

Danielle shoved past Noah and took Nicolle's arm, then pulled her forward and grabbed Noah. Neither put up a fight as she said, "Why don't you two go in the kitchen, eat something, and then we'll all talk." She all but propelled them through the room with impressive momentum. Now was not the time to get distracted by her muscles flexing the fabric of her jeans.

"Are you sure?"

Danielle stood hands on hips as the kitchen door fell closed, but didn't turn at his question. "Yes, I'm damned sure," she said, a worried tone in her voice.

They both fell silent, and Gid bet Dani was listening as hard as he was for an explosion of verbal magnitude. Her voice was a tense whisper when she said, "Did she tell you?"

Gid shrugged, though he wasn't sure she saw it. Her eyes stayed on the door and the near silence from its other side. If Nicolle spilled secrets, Noah was taking it well.

He hoped his brother would work past this. Nicolle was too good a person to be judged based on what someone did to her. Just like his situation, he realized, sitting up straighter. Those people in the cabin made a choice. That didn't make their deaths any less painful to contemplate, but damn it, he had to come to grips with the fact that he'd done all he could. Maybe when he convinced himself of that, he could convince the one sending the letters too.

"I should go in," Danielle said, moving a pace toward the door.

"Leave them to work it out, will you? We have other things to talk about."

She hesitated for a moment before turning back to him with a nod. "You're right. Okay, tell me what you want to dig into next. From a firefighter's perspective, what should we investigate?"

He crooked a finger to bring her closer, and she moved toward him. She'd get a shock when she realized what he had in mind. He patted the reports in his lap and she leaned over to look at the open page. When she did, he pulled her down to sprawl across him.

"Kinkead, what the fuck do you think you're doing?" Her hiss made snakes sound peaceable. Her eyes flashed with furious energy, making gold pinpoints in the smoky gray stand out like sparks at dawn.

"I think it's time for us to investigate why we seem to ignite each other every time we're close. And even when were not. Admit it, Lieutenant, you think about me much more than you should, given this case. And I have to say, the feeling is mutual. You are smokin' hot, lady. Now the question is, do we want to set a backfire to stop this thing?"

Her shock didn't fade as quickly as he thought it might, which was fine with him. Her rear nestled into his crotch, and the heat between them only made her enticing woodsy aroma more pronounced. Her pupils dilated until the gold glowed, and he felt the race of her heart against his chest.

Then she seemed to shake as if freeing herself from whatever linked them. A rough shove propelled her up, and Gid chose to believe that her hand landed on his equipment on purpose in the movement. Her face reddened. With a string of curses that would have made a fire camp applaud, Dani paced to the wall and slammed a fist against it hard enough to make pictures shake.

Gid grinned. Yeah, she was into him, and that pleased him to no end.

Her response was unexpected. "You and I are strictly business, Kinkead. We have an arsonist to catch. Too many bad guys and no luck finding them. We need to stay on track, which means staying focused. Don't you want to protect your brother? I sure as hell need to protect my twin."

That extinguished Gid's mood quicker than a hose set on high. He had to protect Noah. Someone was out to kill his brother, and he'd be damned if it happened on his watch, injured or not. The kitchen remained strangely quiet.

He shifted to ease his discomfort, making a point of ignoring the woman across the room. All he would need to do was look at her and he'd ignite all over again. He yelled, "Noah, haul ass out here. We need to get things organized and decide what we do next."

Chapter 18

Gid flexed his arm, rotating the shoulder until discomfort made him stop the motion. His discarded sling lay on the coffee table. He'd thrown the bandages used to brace things in place in the kitchen trash. Noah would be pissed, but he didn't care. He had healed enough, and he couldn't stand being this incapacitated any longer.

Because there were real monsters out there, after Noah, after Nicolle, after him. He could only wonder what Danielle was hiding, because it seemed everyone involved in this had secrets.

He used a single crutch to hobble to the bathroom, a trash bag in his free hand. He needed a shower, because he couldn't stand himself anymore. Wrapping the plastic around his leg took time, but the relief he felt from steaming hot water pouring over his body made up for the inconvenience. He only wobbled a little bit as he dried himself off. By the time he pulled on fresh clothes, he almost felt like a new man.

Almost, but not quite. The cloud still hung over his head, and he examined himself in the bedroom mirror, wondering how long memories of the past summer would continue to hold him back. His body wasn't his own. He felt like the ghosts in that cabin held it in their clammy grasps.

Funny, but it hadn't matter as much to him until now. Sure, it pissed him off, and the nightmares were enough to make him think about visiting a shrink. He didn't trust others to fix what was inside his head. That was up to him.

A vision of Danielle as she had been last night flashed into his mind like a sudden spark of ignition. The simple ponytail had slipped during the long arduous discussions, and he loved the way her hair fell in a sleek curtain around her face. What would it feel like in his hands? Better yet, would it be cool and soft as it brushed his body? The thought brought a shiver of anticipation before reality caught up with him.

She would never give him that opportunity, and more to the point, if she did, they'd never end up in any position other than him taking his usual excellent care of her. The women came first, no pun intended, and he let his fulfillment of their needs be enough. He could be very convincing, saying he was fine and didn't need anything more than their happiness. And since he made them very, very happy, most never questioned it. Everyone smiled in the end.

Except him. He never felt the emptiness of that until now. He'd done a damned good job convincing himself this situation was fine.

That would need to end now. The stakes were higher. He wanted Danielle, and he wanted her in every sense of the word. He was tired of the incident stealing this aspect of his life from him. He had done everything he could to help those people. They refused to leave. What was he supposed to do?

He growled that mantra to himself as he stumped back through the house, eyeing the couch with disgust. Just a few days and he was already tired of being an invalid. How the hell was he supposed to tolerate the rest of his recovery? He had to work, but his usefulness was limited by his lack of physical ability. The only thing he could do to help was track down whoever was starting those fires.

That concept brought him only marginal comfort, convinced as he was that the arsons were related to his letters and the roses. How was he supposed to track down a ghost? More to the point, hidden away as he was in Noah's house, how was the ghost going to find him? The mess of it made him want to throw things, but he settled for a growl of frustration and heaving yesterday's stack of analyses at the wall.

Before he had a chance to decide if that made him feel better, there was a knock on the door. He wasn't expecting anyone, which made the possibilities a mix of good and bad. His heart accelerated. He propped the crutch up again the wall within reach, leaving his hands available in case he wanted to throttle whoever was on the other side.

"Yes?" His fists clenched in agitation.

No response. He stepped to the door and placed his ear against it, but didn't hear anyone. Wanting to catch the person in the act, he yanked it open without checking the peephole.

A startled Danielle Trajan stare back at him, framed in the doorway's space. Her face looked uncharacteristically uncertain. Her hand reached for her waist and he considered himself lucky she was in civilian clothes. No gun to draw. The happiness he felt at seeing her was absurd and out of proportion. It made his whole day better, and he felt a buzz of energy chase his flagging libido to boot.

He put his hands on the top of the doorframe and leaned toward her in a casual pose. His shoulder complained and he wasn't completely steady on his leg, but he wanted to make a good impression on her. Yeah, he was definitely glad she was there.

"Hey, I was just thinking about you." He winked with the message.

Her face lost the uncertainty so quickly, he wondered if he imagined it. Her eyes narrowed as they swept over his body, and if she liked anything she saw, she gave no sign of it. That made him only want to try harder. Her lips moved into a sneer, as if she read his intentions. He waggled his eyebrows in his best evil villain imitation and grinned.

What the bloody fuck had she been thinking? Oh yes, she hadn't been thinking. She'd been feeling like she wanted a night of flat out exercise to burn off the fact that she couldn't get him out of her mind. She'd dressed for a run but got in the car instead, and her path brought her here as if on autopilot.

Dani hesitated at the front door only because she realized this behavior wasn't professional of her, not in the least. Working the investigation by quizzing Gid further had been an excuse, one she'd done a fine job convincing herself was necessary. Now that she stood on the doorstep of making a move, doubts rose up faster than a left kick she never saw coming. She couldn't say a word when he called out.

The fact that he threw it open looking as unsettled as she felt only made matters worse. Who was he expecting? If she was a bad guy, he gave her easy access. Then his face morphed into a genuine smile, and she didn't miss his relief.

He looked all too tempting, stretching to show off perfect abs peeking out below a cut-off t-shirt riding high. The muscles in his arms flexed. A trickle of moisture slid from wet hair down his neck and disappeared under the shirt down his chest. In her mind's eye, she followed its progress and wished she traced its path with her tongue.

Shit, what was she thinking? She was here about the case. The sooner they solved it, the sooner she could get him out of her mind and return to her normal life.

Normal suddenly didn't look anywhere nearly as good as Gideon. He even smelled tasty. She only avoided leaning closer for a better sniff by sheer willpower. Then he had to go and make things even worse by saying he'd been thinking about her too. They were both so fucked up.

She didn't say anything as she curled her fingers into hard pecs and pushed him inside the door. He fell back and stumbled, his good leg unable to compensate for the limited one in the rapid movement, and she grabbed his arm and whirled him around so she could take his weight as she kicked the door closed behind them.

He didn't fight her, but he waited a beat as if trying to get his bearings. She was about to haul him to the sofa and dump him on it when his words stopped her.

"Wow, that was impressive. You have some serious moves, Lieutenant."

She let her purse fall to the floor with a clunk, and grimaced when she realized the sound was her gun in its side compartment.

He looked down at the black bag on the floor with a considering expression. "And carrying, too. I feel safer already."

It made her want to trip him. Instead, she shifted their weight and shuffled a step, then tossed him toward the furniture. If he landed safely or not, it was not her concern.

She had to admire his agility when he spun himself as easily as a cat and landed with only a small bounce on the center of the sofa. He was still grinning, the bastard. His cast landed on the coffee table with a clunk and he spread his arms on the back of furniture as he gave her an up and down study that lasted too long.

"So what brings you out tonight, Lieutenant? Business or pleasure? Because I can assure you, I've had enough of the first to last a month and not enough of the second, particularly not with you."

Her pulse tripped. The man was a player. But then again, so was she. And she hadn't played in a very long time.

Staying silent, she slid up to the balls of her feet, crossed the room, and threw a leg over his raised one. When her foot hit the floor again, she bent and put her hands on the back of the couch, trapping him in place. Then she leaned down, and her lips landed on his in a message she didn't think he'd have any trouble understanding.

>>>>>

Thoughts raced away faster than a flash and burn. His brain shut down. Nothing to feel except a buzzing in his veins and a ringing in his ears that reminded him of the aftermath of the explosion. He couldn't hear, couldn't see, could only feel, and it had him salivating for more.

The lovely lieutenant could kiss. No introduction, no hesitation, no foreplay. Her tongue wasn't waiting for an invitation as it invaded his mouth. Her hands slid into his hair and she held him exactly where she wanted him. From Gid's perspective, that was perfect, a-okay, fine and dandy, because they were ending up exactly where he wanted them to be too.

He wasn't sure how long the lip lock lasted because he'd lost track of anything resembling consciousness when she leaned further forward and her breasts rubbed his chest. When she finally allowed them to come up for air, he ignored the twinge of discomfort in his shoulder and wrapped his fingers in her ponytail.

"You kiss with style, Lieutenant."

"Shut up, Kinkead."

If she was mad at him, she had a damned strange way of showing it, but he wasn't going to complain. What would she be like if she was happy to see him?

The thought scrambled his brain as she leaned in again, and this time, he met her halfway. He had a few moves too, and he wasn't about to allow her all the fun. His arms wrapped around her waist and he twisted, managing to sweep her off her feet and swing his casted leg to the couch at the same time. She landed on top of him with a grunt of surprise. He kept his arms where they were, in case she planned to jump off and run.

But she didn't do much more than brace herself and tilt her head, an assessing look on her face. Another snort of air accompanied what seemed to be a condescending lift of one corner of her mouth. "Looks like you have some moves on you too, Kinkead."

He let his fingers roam, not far and not fast, tracing the edge of her t-shirt where it had risen from their antics. He wondered if her skin was the same milky cream there. Smooth flesh met his fingers, along with more heat than the midsummer evening would call for.

He examined the dusting of freckles across the bridge of her nose extending to the tops of her cheeks. He bet she hated those in high school. He thought they looked sexy, tempting a man to trace every single one with a kiss. How far did they extend? Would he find them covering the toned belly or strong back, or down a shapely leg?

Inhaling the intoxicating scent of her deep in his lungs, he wanted to hold on to that fragrance as long as he could. At some point, she'd realize their compromising position and remember they could be discovered without warning. For some reason, that added a layer of intrigue only making him hotter.

"I appreciate your outfit, Lieutenant. Tell me, are those regulation, or did you dress up to see me?" He ran a finger around the elastic inside the waist of her gym shorts and felt even more satisfaction at her sharp gasp before trying to pull away.

"I came about the investigation. I don't know how we ended up like this. What the hell did you do?" She pushed with more force against his chest, but he didn't allow her to rise. As a reward, he felt her fingers curl into his muscles as if resigned to the inevitable.

"As I recall, Lieutenant, you threw yourself at me. Or rather, you tossed me. Nice move. You'll have to show me that one in slow motion some time." He reached up and placed a soft kiss on her lips, happy to see he'd confused her yet again. He continued, "And now, let's slow things down and get to know each other a little better. Because I have to say, you're rocking those shorts, but if I don't get them off you in the next few minutes, I'm not responsible for their future."

Her eyes grew huge, making him conscious of the grades of color in what he'd thought of as gray. It was more like a rainbow of grays, like smoke from different sources and with varying levels of heat. How much fuel it would take to ramp that up to inferno? He was going to concentrate on learning that about the lovely Danielle and make sure she had no reason to want to wander far any time soon.

Chapter 19

Light prodded and probed, making the inside of her eyelids glow with a red haze she associated with high heat. No way was she going to open her eyes, though, because she was nestled against a heady pillow of hard flesh and steaming skin, and she felt like her muscles might not work for at least a week.

Lax, sated, and without a brain cell to call her own. She had to give him credit. Gid lived up to his billing.

Her eyes opened to slits and swept the living room. Sunlight played at the edges of blinds that were thankfully turned shut, so they hadn't put on a public display. At least, she didn't think they did. She was a little hazy about when Gid limped over to the front window and covered it.

Beneath her fingers, the dusting of coarse hair on his chest rose and fell in time with deep breathing. His eyes were closed and those absurdly long lashes curled down his cheeks. The expression on his face was peaceful, almost boyish, and definitely tempting. If she woke him, would she get a chance to see what else he offered?

He sure offered a lot last night, but all of it for her. He'd coaxed her from orgasm to orgasm until she wasn't sure how many peaks she'd reached. She only knew she hadn't been so thoroughly taken care of in her life.

In one brief period when he allowed her respite, she'd attempted to return the multiple favors, but he'd trapped her hands in his and rubbed calloused thumbs over the insides of her wrists. The sensuous movement mesmerized her, until he had his wicked way with her again. She wasn't sure what she enjoyed more, the clever fingers that strummed over her like she was an instrument he wanted to tune perfectly or his clever mouth finding each and every sensitive place on her body, making her scream in ecstasy.

And yet he'd taken nothing for himself. She offered, she demanded, and finally, she begged. He only smiled and assured her he found his pleasure in hers. If she wasn't so pissed off because she hadn't been allowed to play too, she might think that was the sweetest sentiment she'd ever heard, damn him.

Her eyes swept the living room, looking for signs of his brother's return. Honestly, a squad of deputies could have rammed the door at certain points last night, and her crack investigative skills would never have noticed. So now, damn her.

Her eyes fell on the discarded clothing, hers, and the ripped t-shirt, his. She'd have to apologize for that and buy him a new one. She'd been a little – eager.

The aftermath of that move made her smile, and her eyes darted to his face to see if he slept on. It appeared he did, and she thought about the ramifications of reaching inside that unzipped denim to wrap her hand around him and –

"No you don't. I hear what you're thinking, Lieutenant. No need to rush things. Anticipation gives you something to look forward to."

He grinned, and she narrowed her gaze on him. Not that he noticed her censure, because his eyes stayed shut. His hands, though, ranged over her like he was memorizing her shape, as if he hadn't done that enough all night.

"Did Noah come home?" She kept her tone neutral, inspecting again for any sign of entry to distract herself. Nothing had been moved as far as she could tell, but given the condition of the room, a full assessment was impossible.

Her clothes, knotted but at least in one pile. The coffee table pushed against a chair. Another chair lying on its side. How had they managed that? Pillows from the sofa were strewn across the space, including one against the front door.

At least no one had come in that way, but would Noah have come in earlier and tiptoed around them?

She should feel embarrassed. She should be angry with herself. She should be raving mad at Gid.

Instead, all she felt was confused. And guilty. Like enough guilt to fill the department's evidence locker and have more left over for the squad vehicle parking lot. She could not figure out Mr. Kinkead. That made him dangerous.

She pushed against his chest, only avoiding digging into those tempting muscles by closing her fingers into fists. She'd left marks on him last night. Moon-shaped red bruises marred his skin, and those must have hurt like hell too since she kept her nails cut short.

His eyes popped open and settled on her without any trace of the confusion she felt. He swept his hands down her back and settled them on her ass, kneading the flesh with an easy spreading smile.

"Do you know you have a very sexy scream?" He found a knotted muscle and dug in deeper, and she tried not to mew in pleasure.

"I do not scream." But she had a hard time putting conviction in her tone when he moved his fingers. Another couple of inches, and she'd be screaming again.

"Yes you do. And I have to say, whatever you do for a workout looks great on you. Any time you want to toss me around again, Lieutenant, I'd be more than willing."

She stared at the sincere expression on his face. This wasn't what she'd signed up for. She was a one-night-stand kind of woman. This was not going to work out. Did it count as a stand if she hadn't held him in her hand, or her mouth, or inside her yet?

Dani blew out a breath and inhaled the aroma of over-sexed male. He smelled like the fires he fought, a rich mixture of spice and molten lava. She was sure when he erupted, volcanoes around the planet fell silent out of respect. She couldn't wait to see what that was like.

Her hands crept between them, heading south. With a chuckle, he caught her fingers and raised them to his lips, taking his slow time kissing each knuckle, then the back of her hands. His eyes never left hers as he kissed her palms. Then with regret on his face, he braced his hands on her shoulders and pushed her upright.

"Time to start our day, lovely Danielle. We have a firebug to catch." He turned away before she could read whatever emotion their separation brought.

This was fucking insane. He wasn't sure what had happened overnight. Gid wasn't the same man he had been only hours ago, all because of one red-haired witch of a woman.

He'd fallen under her spell. Skin so soft, it reminded him of clouds. His fingertips still tingled from their constant restless path over every inch of it during the night. When she fell asleep lying on his chest, her gentle breathing lent another aspect to that softness as air stirred against his chin. He combed shaking fingers through the silky curtain of her hair, grateful that she slept and didn't ask any more of him. He wouldn't know how to respond to her interrogation, and he had a sad, sick feeling he'd tell her the truth.

She stood now and made a process out of collecting clothes and righting furniture. He had to grin when he remembered her kicking the chair with the force of an orgasm that might have been the most beautiful thing he'd ever witnessed. More amazing than a high mountain sunrise or the flash of that same sun below the horizon at dusk. Hotter than a firestorm. More provocative than any risqué review.

He wanted to see it again, but he wasn't so sure about Danielle. To say she was distant this morning would be an understatement. She frowned at his torn t-shirt in her hand as if she wasn't sure what to do with it. He hoped she didn't regret their time together, because he didn't, not for a moment, and he wanted to do it all again and soon.

Emotions chased across her face, brief and fleeting, before her neutral bland expression, the one he'd come to think of as her cop face, returned. She held out the shirt, looking chagrined.

"Sorry. I'll buy you a new one."

He shook his head. "No need. Keep it as a trophy. You can wear it next time. You give me ideas with it in your hand, you know?"

She blushed, and wasn't that the most perfect image in the world? Tender pink drew another fiery shade to her natural ensemble. He reached back to stretch as a way to avoid diving for her and drew to a screeching halt when his shoulder protested the movement.

"Does it hurt?" She pulled on her shorts, minus underwear, with a fresh blush.

He shrugged. "No big deal."

She frowned at him, stopping with her hands on her hips and her feet planted in a stance that might work well on a firing range. "You might have done too much last night."

He couldn't help teasing her, all serious and dark with glowering beauty. "Oh, we didn't do nearly enough, Lieutenant, but again, that just gives us something to look forward to."

She lifted one corner of her mouth, and he wanted to kiss that little smirk. She pulled on her bra, and he wished she'd leave it off too. The sight of her in the altogether under her outside clothes was something he could come to enjoy without any encouragement.

She said, "You were pretty inventive, given the cast situation, Mr. Kinkead. Makes me wonder what it would be like if you weren't infirmed."

He laughed at that, unable to find a reason on the planet not to say what was already on his mind. So out of character, but so right, given the lovely Danielle and her special brand of investigative skills. "We firefighters are trained to work with what we have on hand, and I can be very inventive, Lieutenant."

At some point, however, he was going to have to tell her the truth.

If she drove the familiar streets slower than normal, she was allowed. She was being careful, given her sleep-deprived state. She could do a couple of investigative all-nighters and still function. When one of those nights included multiple screaming orgasms, her reserves suffered from severe depletion. Her shaky nerves and rocky emotions danced on a dangerous precipice, and she wondered if she could keep from spinning off the edge.

Okay, so she did scream. She knew she had, because her throat felt raw and roasted. Damn the man for that too.

He had been the perfect gentleman this morning, offering her a shower, breakfast, and a deep kiss at the front door. She turned down the first two and took the third with more trepidation than was her style. She hadn't experienced a morning kiss like that in years. She was a little dreamy-eyed when they opened the door. Bliss disappeared as soon as they saw it.

Bright red, lying on the doormat like fresh blood. Neither of them said anything at first as they stared down at the plastic rose. Gid then swore with so much color and feeling, she had to admire the range of his vocabulary. She felt the pleasure of the past hours drain away, leaving her cold and in cop mode.

The rose now lay protected in a set of large baggies on the front seat of her truck. She had taken the doormat too, though she doubted it would provide much in terms of evidence. It bore stains and debris from a hundred comings and goings. Gid was distracted as he gave her a final peck on the cheek, already on the phone to Noah.

He looked warrior angry, and she couldn't blame him. Whoever stalked him found him at his brother's home. If Nicolle's attacker learned where they lived, Dani would have been pissed off too.

She had to wonder if whoever was following Gid really was after Noah. It could be the gangbanger from LA. Then she discarded that idea as a long shot. While some of the incidents of presents left behind occurred in Noah's vicinity, most were solely focused on Gid. It made him a target, and that put Danielle on hyper-alert.

Plus, she'd used Gid. She'd used him like the player she thought he was, and he'd turned out to be nothing like what she expected. He'd been sweet this morning, implying there would be a next time. There would be no next time. Why did that make her feel even guiltier for leading him on?

Dani pushed back the other stark thought lurking like a shadow in the back of her mind. The rose this morning could have known origins. Gid could have put it there himself to throw her off track. The drop in the pit of her stomach, harder and scarier than any from a rollercoaster ride, let her know more than logic how far she'd already fallen.

Chapter 20

Gideon tapped the cordless phone on his knee in frustrated uncertainty. Any moment now, Noah would call and tell him where he was. Any moment now, he would come through that door. Any moment, he was sure of it.

But he'd been telling himself that since Danielle left, after carefully lifting the rose with plastic wrap on her hands and placing the mat in a garbage bag. She'd turned from sated woman into uptight cop so quickly, he could almost see a uniform dropping into place. She was out the driveway and out of sight without a backward glance at the house.

Not that this meant anything. Not that any of last night meant anything but the two of them letting off steam. The amount of steam, hers, had been phenomenal. He'd been too busy enjoying her reactions to feel bothered about the lack of his.

Through the open front blinds, he watched the street, willing his brother to appear. He'd checked at the hospital, but they would not confirm Noah was there. Gid appreciated the security, even as it pissed him off. Where was his brother?

A picture of the starry eyes shared between Noah and Nicolle flashed through his mind. Two genuinely nice people, but he wasn't sure either one of them was looking for a relationship. After what he shared with Danielle last night, the option was too weird to contemplate.

He paced as well as he could, given the crutch and his leg. Damn it, he needed to be out of this cast, and he needed it yesterday. Anger at his limitations gave him a place to target his worry. He was thinking about calling Danielle and asking her to check police reports when the minivan turned into the driveway. His brother sat behind the wheel for a moment before exiting and walking toward the house with a decided spring in his step. How could he have missed all of the messages?

Gid unlocked the entry and collapsed on a chair in relief. When his brother pushed open the door, he seemed surprised to find Gid staring at him. Relief that Noah was in one piece put a bite in Gid's words. "You didn't call me last night."

Noah's defensiveness was easy to read. "I'm sorry, I didn't know that at my age, I still had a curfew. Or that I needed to report my whereabouts to my brother, who often doesn't let me know for days where he is and what he's doing."

Gideon held up the phone and shook it for emphasis. "This is a phone. Until we get this thing with the arsonist cleared up, you call me. Where were you anyway?"

Noah walked through the living room, glancing around with a perplexed expression. His anger seemed to evaporate and he grinned, and damn if it wasn't a shit-eating grin too. What the hell?

"Oh man. I can guess why you're smiling this morning." Then Gid's eyes dropped to the couch, and he thought of the multiple rendezvous that had occurred on its surface and elsewhere last night. He could never tell Noah about that. His brother would never forgive him. Sex in the home of young girls, even when they weren't around, seemed like a sin.

And at some point, while he and the lovely lieutenant were otherwise occupied, someone placed a red rose on the step. They had been this close to catching him. More to the point, whoever was responsible for the trophies knew where Gideon was, and by default, where Noah and the girls lived. When he turned back to his brother, he couldn't hide the mix of feelings roiling him up inside.

"Bro, we have some things to talk about. Something happened this morning. And by the look of things, you weren't alone last night." He nodded at Noah in silent approval.

"Seems I'm not the only one," Noah said.

Gideon shook his head and stared at the couch once more. Good times, and probably never repeated. That idea left him even more depressed.

He kept his gaze on the couch, because he didn't want to see the pain and worry on his brother's face when he delivered the news. Guilt swamped him for bringing his troubles to his brother's doorstep. "Noah, we found another red rose this morning, on the doormat here at the house."

Silence met his words, making the sudden ringing of the phone more piercing in their stillness. Gid held it out to Noah, and by the time it rang again, Noah flopped back on to the opposite chair and connected the call.

Guilt gave way to anger as he watched Noah. His brother's face blanched as he listened to whoever spoke on the other end and an expression of terror filled his face. Gid wanted to tear the phone away and demand who it was, but his brother hit the speaker button, and a voice filled the room with hate and evil. By the time the call ended, they were both shaking. Gid pounded a pillow next to him, wishing it was the caller's face.

It was only after the call ended that he had the presence of mind to dial Danielle and give her a fast update. A single perfunctory knock sounded minutes later before the door pushed open, and the lieutenant marched in with her twin on her heels. Danielle angled over Gid's chair with a fierce look on her face.

"No discussion about the rose, not yet. I want to hear about the phone call first. And under no circumstances mention I was here last night." He wasn't sure if her hiss held embarrassment or frustration.

"Ah, cat's out of the bag on that one, I think." He grinned at her, because he couldn't help remembering how her stern face melted in passion.

Danielle gave him a confused look. "There is no evidence of me being here. Remember that. Say nothing."

Jake arrived moments later, and she began issuing orders. Gid stayed where he was, watching her in her element. Magnificent, to say the least. He grinned before he caught Noah's ghostly face and remembered why they were all here.

Nicolle stood close to Noah, close, but not touching. After they shared a penetrating stare, neither one of them looked at the other, but Gid knew. The energy jumping between them passed faster than escaping sparks on a high wind.

Danielle's occasional curses harmonized with Nicolle's quiet gasps as Noah related the call. Gid closed his eyes, unable to get the voice out of his mind. The venom in it was unmistakable. The man whose brother had died of gunshot wounds under Noah's care. Rage, he called himself. Rage was what Gid felt too. Powerless, that's what he was, powerless to stop this madness. His fists clenched in his lap as Danielle coaxed more information from his brother.

Gid now understood Noah's fear for the ones he cared about. For his daughters. For Gid. Noah suddenly grabbed Nicolle's hand in his and lifted it to his lips. And now, perhaps for Nicolle too. He wondered how Danielle felt about that, and he couldn't resist giving her a searching look, one she returned with equal tension. She was not smiling. Gid suspected she didn't approve of her twin's sudden profound interest in a man with a target on his back.

That was exactly what Gideon had too. He didn't have much to offer anyone. In fact, he was probably even more at risk. A city guy like Noah's gangbanger Rage would stick out in this rural town. Would he have the kind of reach to hire out his dirty work? On the other hand, the firebug Gid searched for probably knew how to blend in and never make his appearance obvious.

As if reading Gid's mind, Jake said, "Do we think this guy has anything to do with the fires?"

Gideon took up the conversation. "He mentioned being able to burn the town down if he wanted. He knew about the wildfires. Much as I didn't think it would be anything related to Noah when this started, he might be able to pay someone to start them."

Jake frowned and shook his head as if he disagreed. Danielle said, "What, Jake? He would be capable of hiring a torch, and it would be a nice way for Rage to keep his hands clean."

"That's not what I mean." Jake hurried through the words as if expecting to be interrupted again. "That's not why I'm here." He turned and looked directly at Nicolle. "Remember what we said about the town picking out people who don't belong? We had three calls yesterday, and all of them indentified a stranger matching the picture and description we circulated last week. I'm sorry, Nicolle. The witnesses are people we know and trust, so they're credible. And they all put your missing inmate on Main Street, asking specific questions about you."

Nicolle's gasp and flight into Noah's arms took no more than a couple of seconds, but it was long enough for Gid to realize none of them was safe. Not Noah from Rage. Not Nicolle from the man who had attacked her. Not Danielle because she would die for her twin.

And not him, because he still had a stalked in the shadows.

Chapter 21

Gid felt bad. He felt bad for throwing his crutch across the room and shattering something in a pique about his helplessness. He felt worse when Noah had to clean up the mess. Gid re-read the single page bearing the lab's insignia, and that didn't make him feel any better.

'…no fingerprints or other biometric data.

Unable to confirm match to previous evidence. Item available from numerous outlets in the greater Sacramento area.

Unable to identify recent or unique evidence from doormat.'

Nothing. The recent rose got them nothing. Another wildfire only fueled by speculation.

It could be Rage sending another message. It could be the mystery firebug. The only person Gid thought couldn't be responsible was the inmate after Nicolle, but now that she was involved with Noah, he wasn't sure about that either. It could be any of them, or it could be someone they didn't yet have a handle on.

He turned his worry back on his brother, demanding to know how he planned to stay safe. Gid couldn't understand why his logical assertion that Noah needed protection brought about conflict. Noah all but roared the words. "You have no clue what I can do, or what kind of protection I need."

Noah grabbed his keys and headed for the door, commanding Gid to follow. Gid did, but more out of a need to defend Noah in a temper than any other reason. When his brother calmed down, and he would, Gid would be able to reason with him.

Or so he hoped. Driving seemed to take all of Noah's attention, and by the whitened grip of his hands on the steering wheel, he wasn't calming down. Gid kept his mouth shut, not wanting to distract his brother while he was obviously upset. When they pulled in front of an industrial building and Noah all but jogged for an unmarked door with a black bag in his hand, Gid swung along as fast as he could to keep up.

Gid had never seen him hold on to anger for this long. Noah was the good brother, the calm one, the objective one who reflected before he acted. The fact that he didn't hold the door and it almost swung shut on Gid's fingers made him realize this was a side of Noah he didn't know.

A rank, sweaty odor permeated the inside of the building, smelling not unlike the pile of discarded clothes left by firefighters after they'd been in the field for too long. Darkness loomed in far corners, and a few scant overhead lights did little to chase it away. Gid had only a moment to register Noah's disappearance through a swinging door to the left, and he wondered if he was expected to follow. Then his eyes fell on the center of the space, and he had trouble processing what he was seeing.

Chain link fencing surrounded a raised platform. On one side, a gate served as the only opening. A man approached it and unfastened the gate with the harsh clang of metal on metal. This wasn't the type of place Noah frequented. Unless he was here to see a patient. That had to be it.

Noah reappeared wearing gym shorts and a sleeveless t-shirt, and Gid's eyes popped wider. His brother was ripped. He'd pass for a firefighter. Glancing between Noah and the cage, Gid still felt like he was in a twilight zone of confusion.

He made his way over to his brother, conscious of his crutch and sloppy gait being the only sounds in the room. Absorbed in stretching, Noah didn't seem to hear him approach, but he didn't jump when Gid said, "What is this place?"

"It's a gym."

"I see that. You want me to wrap your hands?" Gid reached for the roll of tape hanging on a hook, expecting a positive response.

"No."

Gid stopped, watching Noah spin away and back as if warming up. He said, "You should wrap your hands. You don't want to get hurt." He waited, expecting his brother to reconsider.

Noah swung around and stepped close enough for Gid to read the rage in his eyes. He had a visceral reaction, wanting to go at it with Noah because then he'd know for sure if he could take care of himself. But Noah was in complete control, and his measured reply was delivered in such a reasonable tone, Gid couldn't argue.

"When they come to find me, I won't have time to wrap my hands. I won't have time to do much of anything other than fight. When they come for me, I want to be prepared no matter what I'm doing at that time."

Turning without waiting for a response, Noah pounded up the stairs and slammed the cage door with a thunderous reverberation. When the thrashing began, Gid had to admire his brother's apparent skill. He seemed to be as good in destroying a man as he would be in saving him. If that wasn't the biggest surprise he'd had in a long time, he'd eat his cast in one sitting.

Dani fielded unproductive calls as Nicolle drove. Her twin needed the workout. They both did. Privately, she wanted to push Nicolle to her edge, to be able to fight off any attacker who thought to mess with her in the future. It didn't hurt to be prepared herself either.

By the time they reached the gym, she determined there were no credible leads on any of their suspects. Sightings of the man they assumed was Nicolle's inmate Mitchell had evaporated. Rage was nowhere to be found. Tracking the source of the call to Noah's house led to a burner phone and therefore untraceable. Nothing new on the roses front. No new fires to report, but then, Gid wasn't on the lines now.

She entered the gym with her thumbs flying over the phone. Reporting herself off duty, she registered the grunts of a fight in progress. The clutch and dance of bodies drew her attention to the ring, where she recognized their trainer.

"Looks like Devin's having some fun," Dani said, stopping in the cover of darkness with Nicolle at her side.

"Or getting his ass handed to him. Look at that guy's moves. He's small, but he's quick and accurate. Have we seen him before?" Nicolle took a step closer.

"Yes, yes you have."

Dani lunged in front of her twin on instinct as they turned toward the voice. Her eyes widened in surprise when she realized who sat in the folding chair at the edge of the circle of light, his expression a combination of pissed off and wonder.

"Kinkead? What the fuck are you doing here?" Running on the pumping surge of adrenalin, Dani paced up to him and all but straddled him in the chair.

Gideon turned his attention from the cage to her face. "I'm still a little unclear about this, but I think Noah's showing me he doesn't need me to protect him."

Dani whipped her head around to the cage and stared at the shorter fighter. It didn't fit her picture of Dr. Kinkead, not in the least. A glance at Nicolle confirmed her equal surprise.

Maybe they shouldn't be surprised. Maybe, like her twin, Noah wanted the ability to defend himself if danger came at him again. It would be a logical reaction. The way Noah kicked out and landed his opponent on his back still felt out of character.

"Who is this Devin guy?" Gid's question, full of suspicion and brotherly protection, made her pull herself together.

"You haven't heard of him? Mixed martial arts champion. He doesn't compete anymore, but he offers training. He's very particular about who he takes on, preferring people who want to learn for legitimate self-defense purposes rather than those aiming to follow in his footsteps in the competitive ring." That was the principle reason she and Nicolle came here. They wanted to learn from the best, and Devin was the best.

She forced herself to look away from Gideon, his mussed hair a glow of gold in the sparse overhead lighting. His attention seemed to be glued on his brother, and she realized she stood too close in his personal space. Moving four feet away did nothing for the rapid beating of her heart, though. It was the surprise of finding the Kinkead men here, she assured herself, or the remnants of adrenalin from hearing a voice call out.

And man-oh-man, was she ever lying to herself. How had she looked, towering over Gideon? Nicolle would call her on it, of that she had no doubt. Her twin would pick up the vibes. Dani's crush would come out.

She glanced at Nicolle to see how bad the smirk was on her sister's face, but her twin wasn't paying attention. She stood at the base of the steps, staring up at the heaving breaths of the good doctor as if she was in a museum examine a priceless piece of art. Dani had to admit that he did look stunning with all that rippling muscle and beaded sweat. And by the dance of her feet, Nicolle couldn't wait to take her turn with him.

Sparring be damned. Nicolle could take care of herself. Dani wanted to take care of someone else. She felt hyper-aware of every breath Gideon took beside her.

"Go on, if you want," Dani called out. She wasn't sure Nicolle heard her, though she said something to Devin standing at her side. Dani felt her bristle with sudden anger, then something else, a surge of energy so explosive, it was a good thing there wasn't any tinder around. The frown on Nicolle's face deepened.

"How good is she?" Gideon's question held humor and awe. He clearly didn't seem put out by the fact that the Trajan women could kick some ass too.

Dani pushed in close to him, drawing his attention away from the ring to focus on her. She felt the zing of awareness in his regard, and she liked that too, maybe too much. Reaching out to place a hand on his injured shoulder, she pressed ever so slightly and was rewarded by his wince. She wasn't sorry for it. She wanted him to know she could take him, any time.

"She's damn good, strong and quick. We're evenly matched, which surprised me in the beginning. It shouldn't have, since she has to be fit for her work too, but still. Do you know any self-defense moves, Mr. Kinkead?"

He stared into her eyes, unblinking and constant. Her heart kicked up even faster with the intensity of his gaze, and she wondered what he'd be like, hale and hearty.

That was stupid. By the time he was fully healed, their fleeting interest in one another would have faded. He didn't do long term, and neither did she. Still, a woman could wonder.

Then he smiled at her, a full-on lazy grin that deepened the fine lines at the corners of his eyes and the sexy grooves surrounding his lips like accent marks. She swore he was laughing at her. He didn't need to throw her across a ring. That wasn't the power he required. He only had to turn on his considerable charm.

"Do you want to stay and watch them beat the shit out of each other? Or would you rather adjourn to a place where we can get a workout?" His hesitation before the final word made it sound almost dirty. And hot damn if that didn't take the safety off whatever resolve she had left.

"What the hell?" The seething anger in Nicolle's voice made her glance in her twin's direction. Nicolle stalked toward them, and Dani wondered if she looked as guilty as she felt. No matter how hard she tried, she couldn't summon her cool cop control. It didn't help that she snapped the hand caressing Gideon's shoulder after her message behind her back like she was hiding it.

Before Nicolle could question her, she went on offense. She said, "Gideon says Noah's itching for a fight. I say go give him one." She hoped her face looked as impassive as her words. What did Gid's face give away?

"What's going on here?" Suspicion made her twin's voice unusually loud. But Gideon answered before she could respond.

"She's been telling me about Devin, and about how you two have been training with him. I think it's a great thing, learning to defend yourself. It gives you an element of surprise if you ever get overtaken again."

Dani felt the surge of anger encrusted with guilt. Her twin didn't deserve these constant reminders, even if Dani lived with them. That was the last thing Nicolle wanted. But before she could calm the waters, Nicolle had spun, kicked off her shoes, and jogged to the cage. The clang of the gate didn't raise Noah from his dark thoughts, and Nicolle advanced on him with predatory steps.

"I guess we watch for a while, just to make sure they don't kill each other." She hadn't been aware of Gideon's rise from the chair or hobble over to stand next to her until he spoke in her ear. In the ring, Nicolle grabbed Noah's arm and twisted, just as his head came up with an expression of shock easy to read even from this distance. Her twin wasn't going to go easy on him. By the expression on the doctor's face, it didn't appear he wanted it easy either.

She said, "Yeah, I guess we watch them for a while. Someone needs to be around to soak up the blood."

Next to her, Gid's quick chuckle made her smile.

He wasn't sure how or when it happened. Maybe it was when he shifted with the discomfort of balancing on his crutches, and Danielle brought him the folding chair without saying a word. Maybe it was when Noah landed a particularly jarring slam against Nicolle, and Gid felt the lovely lieutenant's anxiety as if it was his own. His hand had come up to stroke her lower back to ease that tension. Instead, he felt it grow in her and in him.

Man, he wanted this woman. Why it was turning out like this, he wasn't sure. She didn't move away, and he swore she even leaned into his hand. As the match continued, she left for a few minutes, returning through the gym's outer door with a large backpack in her hands. When the combatants left the ring and Noah stalked to his duffel, Danielle moved to her sister. From this distance, he couldn't hear their exchange. He hauled himself to his feet and crutched his way over to where Noah hid under a towel.

"I have to say, that was impressive fighting, bro, very impressive. How long have you been doing this?"

Noah mumbled something but kept the towel in place. He didn't seem inclined to hold a conversation.

Gid glanced over at the women, who seemed to be having an intense discussion of their own. He hoped to hell he'd read this right. Otherwise, he was going to have egg on his face and major explanations to make.

"Can you give Nicolle a ride? The lieutenant and I need to have a discussion."

That popped Noah's head out fast. "What the hell, Gid? You're hardly in any condition to be chasing after any woman, and let me remind you, she is Nicolle's twin sister."

Not, 'she's a cop' or even that she was a lead investigator on the arsons. No, it was the fact Danielle was Nicolle's sister that made Noah's hair kink. Gid only wiped the grin off his face when he noticed the heated look his brother shot to the twin he had been fighting in the ring. Enough heat to qualify for a fire.

"No can do, Gid." Noah's sudden assertion had him swiveling his attention back. His brother's hungry expression didn't hide the sadness behind it. He continued, "We'll drive like we came in. If Nicolle wants to see me later, I can swing by her place. But you aren't in any condition to do anything other than return home and rest." With that, he lifted the duffel as if it weighed nothing and paced toward the door.

The desire to argue gave Gid a new sense of urgency, and his ability to wield the crutches improved with inspiration. He was only a pace behind when Noah paused with his hand on the outer door's handle.

"Don't be an idiot, Noah. As you can see, Nicolle can take care of herself. More to the point, you can take care of both of you. I'm proud of you, bro."

Noah turned with shock on his face. Didn't his brother know what he thought about him? They weren't the most communicative of families, but Gid thought he let it be known how great he thought Noah was. Evidently he didn't say it often enough.

Nicolle paced over to stand next to Noah, flashing a curious look between the two men. Gid felt Dani at his side like a heat source. Their attraction could not be one-sided. He didn't turn but reached out to put a hand on her lower back. The sudden restraint of movement convinced him he was right.

"We're all set," Gideon said, as Nicolle shifted closer to Noah. She looked as hungry as his brother. Gid fought the urge to raise a hand in a fist pump.

"Are you sure?" Noah hadn't turned from his position at the door.

"Noah." Gid put a double shot of warning into the single word. Noah and Nicolle wanted each other. Gid knew what he wanted, and that was Danielle. By the way she returned his stare with marked intensity, she shared that desire.

When the sun suddenly fell across the gym's concrete floor, he didn't register the words the others were saying. He was busy watching the spark of anticipation on Danielle's face. Whatever happened tonight, it was going to be hot, and he wasn't about to try to extinguish that flame.

Chapter 22

Limited conversation marked the miles on their return trip. Glances in the rearview mirror didn't reveal the minivan. Dani wanted to keep Nicolle in a protective cocoon. At the same time, she felt hyperaware of the man sitting next to her. His brooding presence dwarfed the interior of the truck cab. Based on his unsettled expression, his thoughts were as dark as hers.

Why had she agreed to this? Nicolle's eagerness to spend private time with Gideon's brother was only an excuse. It was a good one, but Dani had to be honest. She wanted Gid with as much edgy anticipation. It was only sex, and she was an open book. She hid no secrets about it.

Her internal argument withered as she remembered the folder locked in her desk drawer at home. There was no real reason to lock the desk. Nicolle would respect its privacy, but Dani's possession made her jittery. The words were volatile enough by themselves. The one thing Dani swore she'd never share with her twin, the secret she didn't want to see the light of day.

Not her finest hour. No matter how many times she analyzed the situation, she wasn't sure she could have changed the outcome. It overwhelmed her at times. She had sworn she would never let anyone past her carefully constructed boundaries to know the role she had in Nicolle's tragedy.

They stopped at one of the few lights in town, and Dani drummed her thumbs on the steering wheel. As soon as she realized that mark of impatience, she wrapped her fingers tighter in a deliberate move. Her cop face was firmly in place. She said nothing, not even glancing at Gideon. If he made one smart-assed remark, she would stop the truck and dump him wherever they were. He stayed quiet, as if he knew she was processing emotions faster than a high velocity bullet until they were sitting in her driveway with the engine ticking over as it cooled.

"You seem tense. If you aren't happy with this, you can drop me at Mallory's. I'll find a place to crash for the night, no problem."

Gid's tone gave away no clue about his feelings. He sounded like he could enjoy a night together with her or without her on equal levels of interest. It reminded her he was a player, and so was she. No strings. No commitment. None of that word she always thought of as ugly when it came to her, relationship.

Except it didn't seem ugly now. Could she allow him past her defenses for anything other than casual physical contact? The sex felt anything but casual to her.

She pushed open her door and exited with an abrupt slam. Rapid steps carried her from her parking slot toward the front steps. The creak of the passenger side made her pause once more. Did she want to do this?

Hell yes.

He closed the truck door with exaggerated care as she turned in a slow rotation to watch his deliberate progress. His eyes stayed on her as he crossed the distance separating them with four crutch swings. She turned away so he wouldn't see the nerves overtaking her. Her hand fumbled in the lock for the first time ever, and she had to step back to pick up her keys from the porch mat.

A whoosh of air marked the slam of his body into hers. She spun, her hands still in the air, and slammed again, this time into the tense awareness on his face. When he dropped the crutches and grabbed her instead, his words were rough, echoing the frenzy inside her.

"How long does it take for pizza to be delivered?"

The out of place question threw her for a moment. The hard lines of his body pressed into her. Her nerves misfired in needy response. She tried to form a coherent thought. "About half an hour. They stop delivering at nine, so we have time."

Which would be just enough time for round one, and she dove in to put her mouth on him. She forgot what she was thinking, because his lips were as firm and demanding as she remembered, and her hands were no longer in the air but woven in his hair. If he grabbed her out of urgency and appetite, she returned his attack with equal attention. That clever mouth made her knees weak and her pulse sounded a jungle beat.

Demand warred with the desire to savor him. He was one hundred percent maximum force male, and his recent injuries did nothing to reduce his potency. His strength called to hers, and she tightened her arm on his waist to draw him closer. His hands ran down her back to knead her butt, and his fingers toyed with the waistband of her leggings.

Danielle broke off the kiss, burying her face in his neck as he eased two fingers inside the stretchy material and stroked her skin with fingers that were torch-hot. He placed a kiss where her neck met her shoulder, slow and gentle with a dip of his tongue, and a shiver ran down her spine. She leaned back then, examining his face with as much concentrated intensity as she used to gauge a criminal's honesty.

Dusk made the blue of his eyes more pronounced, like the deep water in some tropical ocean. She wanted to jump in and learn the secrets in those depths. Why did he stare at her? Could he see past her bravado to the wounds underneath?

Inhaling on a deep gasp, she said, "Are you staying?"

He mirrored her strained breath. "Only if you want me to."

She gave a single nod, stepping back with her arms extended because she didn't want to let go of him. Gid seemed willing to allow her to drag him. Then she frowned and looked at his crutches on the ground. When she let go to retrieve them, she felt a shiver of cold despite the heat of the night. She handed them to him with a lift to her chin, daring him, though for what, she wasn't sure.

Looking away, she said, "I should order that pizza. What do you like on yours?"

Flipping the switch to turn off her emotions was harder than usual. She found her keys on the ground and dealt with the door, striding inside with more command than she felt. Her steps took her to the gun safe and her homecoming routine. There was calm in the normalcy, a calm she was far from feeling.

The sound of Gid's crutches squeaking on the floor told her he'd followed. She wasn't sure he would. She knew she was running hot and cold and sending mixed messages. Any moment now, he'd ask for a lift into town, to find a more enjoyable partner for his evening. Any moment now –

Or strong hands would wrap around her upper arms and spin her away from the cabinet to face him. His expression would be fiery as he lowered his face to hers. Her pulsing need made her skin feel too tight and sent her good sense fleeing like a criminal up for his third strike. She didn't even want to look at him, afraid of what she might do. Any moment now –

The tremor in her fingers was nerves. She didn't want to knock him on his back and jump on top. She couldn't wait to peel him out of those shorts and rip the t-shirt over his head. All that rock hard flesh to play with. Her fingers curled at the prospect until her short nails bit into her palms. She considered how fast she could swing him around and topple him to the sofa.

"This is nice," he said from behind her.

"Nici and I share it. We bought it together when she realized her investigator position meant her home base would be in Flynn's Crossing. It only has three bedrooms, but two of them have attached full baths."

God, what an idiot. She babbled on like a realtor giving a home tour. Biting her lip to keep from spewing more nonsense only reminded her of the way he nipped at her mouth when they kissed in the driveway.

"I wasn't talking about the house," he said, sly humor in his voice. "But it's nice too."

She whipped around to face him, only realizing she'd adopted a shooting stance when his eyes widened and looked her up and down. When those eyes lighted on all of her important parts, she felt each pause like a caress. The intense gaze locked on her face, and any trace of humor fled his expression.

"Bacon and chicken," he said.

She blinked, unable to process his words.

"On my pizza. I like that chicken and bacon thing, I forget what they call it."

She blinked again, trying to bring his words into focus. Pizza. Shit, perps could take lessons in cool from Gideon Kinkead.

Unless he wasn't as hot for her. The man standing with more steady ease on crutches than most men managed on two good legs didn't appear to be about to perish from need for her. It was just sex. It would be great sex, and this time, she wasn't going to allow it to be one-sided. She'd have her pleasure, but so would he. She would make sure of it.

She emptied her face of expression and assumed a bored tone. "Chicken and bacon, got it. You want anything else? I can guarantee there's cereal and milk, but I can't vouch for much more than that in the fridge."

He tilted his head as if her words amused him. "I assume the cereal's for breakfast. Unless you've changed your mind about my staying. Lady's choice, of course."

Lady's choice? Oh yeah, she could make her choice right now. Prime male flesh in her bed, and fast and furious. They would need sustenance. When she smiled at him with heightened awareness, he returned it with a slow growing grin of his own. It was the sexiest smile she'd ever seen, and her body turned into one big throb of wanton heat as easily as if he'd set a match to her.

"Holy fuck," Danielle said, dropping back to the pillows. She had yet to let go of the slats in the headboard, and Gid kept the smile of pure male satisfaction to himself. It wouldn't do to gloat.

"Yes, I believe it would qualify. Did you hear angels singing?" He allowed his smile to show then, though the lovely lieutenant didn't notice. A slim arm now covered her eyes as her breathing slowed from pants to a gentler wheeze. The pale skin on its underside tempted him to get closer for a taste, but he decided to be a gentleman and let her find her balance again.

Plus, he was hungry, based on the growls of his stomach.

They never did get those pizzas earlier, because as soon as she had smiled at him, he forgot about playing it cool and taking things slow. He'd been having that conversation inside his head, since she seemed to be slowing them down too. Slow would be a good idea. He was still trying to figure out how to keep his little secret when her smile did him in.

He wasn't sure who made the first move. He enjoyed the hell out of peeling those gym clothes off her body, his hands free to run down soft skin that belied her underlying strength. That she was fit and toned, as muscled and able as Gid, was never a question in his mind. Having a partner who could wrestle him to the floor without even breaking a sweat was a turn-on.

If her moans had been any indication, she didn't mind that first round on the living room rug, not in the least. When her heat clenched around his fingers and she exploded with a cry of completion, he thought it might be the sexiest thing he'd ever heard. Giving a strong woman this kind of pleasure added a whole new layer to the game, and he was ready for many more hours of play.

Gid felt his heart rate accelerate as he thought back to round two. She nearly undid him with her crafty hands and patient lips. When she slid down his body, he didn't have to fake the sheen of sweat or the agitation that came with her near-discovery. Only a rapid swap of their positions, his mouth finding her core with precision at just the right moment, kept Danielle from knowing.

She'd been quite creative in her suggestions for round three, and he really wished he could accommodate her. He didn't need to glance down to know nothing was happening in the erection department. He could feel it – or rather, the lack of it. As he kept up a patient attack on her mouth while his hands roved everywhere he could reach, he cursed that day when everything changed for him. He might even have heard the victims' screams. Or Danielle's. He wasn't sure.

"You are quite the dedicated public servant, aren't you?" The slur of her voice from the arm covering part of her mouth sounded breathless and content.

"It's part of a firefighter's code, you know. Caring for our resources, preserving the public's trust, and serving in a manner that respects everyone's rights. Don't you have the same line in your cop manifesto?"

Her arm fell away, and luminous eyes met his. He swore the gray glowed with inner heat. Despite not being able to perform, he found his interest piqued. Maybe they could go around for one more.

"I see that look, Kinkead, and I'm going to handcuff you to the bed if I have to. I need a break. What are you, superstud? I'm either doing things wrong, or you're due for an explosion of your own."

She seemed to realize what she said about the same time he felt like a bucket of ice water landed on his head. He didn't need explosions. He'd rather not repeat that experience.

Her hands covered her face and scrubbed at it. "Damn it, sorry. I wasn't thinking. You see? You fuck up my thinking. I didn't mean that to come out sounding so crass."

He shifted to a sitting position, rubbing the thigh above his cast with an absent motion when his feet touched the floor. His shoulder only ached a little, and he no longer felt any pain in his leg. He was sure that would change when the cast came off and rehab to regain full use of it began. The sooner he returned to full duty, the better. These empty days gave him too much time to think, and everyone knew where that would lead.

"Gideon? I said I'm sorry." A hand massaged up and down his spine. It was a nice gesture, and Danielle sounded sincere in her apology. Everyone walked on hot coals around him, and he was getting damned tired of it.

"It's okay. I don't expect the world to treat me like an invalid or a crazy person. In fact, I was hoping I could get a little more investigative work to fill my days. I can only do so many hours of rehab before they kick me out of the gym because they're tired of my gorgeous studliness."

He felt the bed shift as she rose and walked around to stand in front of him. She was comfortable in her nakedness, as much at ease as he was in his. Another way they were matched. He had to stop finding ways they clicked, because eventually, one or both of them would move on.

"You're supposed to be recuperating," she said, though their activities probably didn't count in his rehab routine. That would be a kick, sex as a rehab workout. He needed to ask his physical therapist about that. Good thing the PT was a guy.

He lay back on the bed, stretching his arms and only grimacing once, when folding his hands behind his head made his injured shoulder twinge. She must enjoy looking at him, because her eyes never strayed. The hunger in her gaze was unmistakable.

"Did I seem to need additional recuperation time to you?"

She chuckled and shook her head as if she wasn't sure what to make of him. But he also caught a puzzled pinch to her face as she turned away, as if he disappointed her. He guessed why as he reasoned it was more than enough to give her a night of unlimited pleasure. At least that's what he'd been telling himself these last months.

"It's too late for pizza, and I'm starving. Are you up for cereal? Or I can try not to burn something." She disappeared into a closet and reemerged in a thicket green robe, short enough to make him want to run a hand up her thighs and pull her in for another taste.

"Kinkead, pay attention. Food. Cereal or cinders?"

He shrugged off the vision of her standing in front of him in that robe and his mouth on her making her squirm. "If you burn anything, you have a fully qualified firefighter here to take care of it. But I'd vote for trying not to burn something."

She chuckled again and disappeared into the adjoining bathroom. He heard the shower come on, and he flopped backward on the bed with a groan as he thought about water running down Danielle's curves. If he moved fast enough, he might find a garbage bag large enough to wrap his cast, and he could slide in there with her.

And do what? The voice in his head issued the question with enough derision for Gid to snort in agreement. He sure as hell wasn't able to slide into Danielle, and with a sudden moan, he realized he needed to get his problem fixed, and pronto. He really wanted to be physical with the lovely lieutenant in every way, and his body better cooperate.

>>>>>

Parts of her were tender, and rough abrasions from Gideon's end of day beard stung when soap hit them. Her nipples ached, though it might be for more attention. Dani didn't care, not one bit, not about any of the discomfort or the resurging need. She had bigger problems to handle.

What was it about Gideon that made her so wanton and crazy? This was no wham-bam and out the door kind of thing. In fact, she was almost ready – okay, she'd better eat something first – but almost ready for another go-round. That kind of sexual energy wasn't her thing.

Besides, unless she'd been so self-absorbed and unobservant that a truck could have crashed unnoticed through the living room, Gid had yet to experience any kind of fun. He seemed to enjoy giving her pleasure, and she hadn't missed the smile of self-satisfaction when he drove her nuts, but the pleasure had been all hers.

That was something she planned to change, as soon as she fed them enough to survive until morning. She could safely fry eggs and make toast, if the bread wasn't growing anything disgusting.

She wondered what other women did for him. Beyond their ability to feed him better than she would, she wished she knew the secret to breaking his tight control. For a moment there, she thought she had him, nearly in the palm of her hand and with her mouth on patrol south, but he turned the tables on her. He was quick, cast and all.

Gideon had never let her touch him with the reciprocating intimacy. Maybe that was part of his game. Dani didn't want to think about how often he practiced those famed moves on the women of Flynn's Crossing, even if no one uttered a bad word about him.

She didn't want to be one in a long line of females under his charms. With a jolt like a taser, she realized she wanted to be the only one he couldn't resist. What was she thinking? There would be no opportunity for that. He'd be gone soon, and she'd have moved on. That's what people like them did. The idea made her perversely sad.

"I'm going to see what you have in the kitchen and get a start on our dinner."

She jumped at the sound of his voice. Through the haze of the shower door's glass, she could make out his form, dressed and standing just outside the bathroom. His head was bent, as if he wanted to give her privacy. Such a gentleman. Such a stud. And she was going to be such a schmuck for him, which was a whole new reason to string together a silent line of curses and pound her fists on the tile walls once he stepped out of view.

But hiding here would do her no good. She had to face her feelings, which meant facing Gideon. She was never a coward to run from a fight.

With another sudden insight, Dani knew she didn't want to run. She wanted to fight, and for something she never thought she wanted. A relationship. The idea made her rinse off soap with more speed than she may have ever used and catapult out of the water for a handy towel.

Chapter 23

"No, seriously. That's where they hid?"

Dani liked his laugh, the way he used every note of it to convey his full humor while the lines near his eyes crinkled into canyons. Gid appreciated her stories of life as a sheriff's deputy. She'd even told him the one about the old man who thought she was a stripper sent by his grandson. He'd nearly choked on his eggs laughing at that one, and she would be ready with mouth-to-mouth. She would be even if the situation didn't arise. The longer she spent in Gideon's company, the more comfortable she became.

Why did he have to be a potential person of interest in these fires? The sooner they solved the arsons and the rest of these cases, the better. Nicolle deserved a chance to be happy. Dani didn't want to consider her own opportunity.

Pushing her fork around the empty plate, she let silence fall at the dining table. Stretching out his leg at an angle to her chair, Gid didn't break the quiet, as if he could read her mind and wanted to honor her concern.

"Your brother is a good guy, right?" She lifted her eyes to examine his face for the truth.

"He's a great guy, as great as they come. A bona-fide hero in the Emergency Room, a terrific dad, and an excellent friend. I just wish he'd told me about everything before this. Maybe I could have helped him out sooner."

Gid shifted a tall glass almost empty of soda from hand to hand on the table. His contemplative expression matched her mood to a tee. They both worried about their siblings, ever the protectors. She placed her hand over his and squeezed before she realized she did it.

"You did everything you could once you knew. And you'll continue to do that. Don't worry, Gideon. Someone like Rage won't be able to keep his mouth shut if he comes gunning for Noah, and trust me, Flynn's Crossing will spot him."

He used his other hand to stack on top of their joined ones and this time, he squeezed. "You're worried about Nicolle, and I understand, but she's safe with Noah. In fact, they're probably great together. I mean, they can both cook, so they stand a better chance of surviving."

His goofy smile made her insides do a back flip. Yeah, there was that. They only had something more substantial than cereal to eat because Gideon, to his credit, turned the random contents of her fridge into a very edible scramble. Dani didn't even burn the toast to accompany it.

Right now, though, the food was doing an unhappy dance in her stomach. Guilt overwhelmed her once more. Someday, Nicolle would find out that Danielle hadn't done everything in her power to make sure that bastard Mitchell was off the streets and safely away where he could do no harm.

"What is it? Don't be worried about Noah and his situation. You saw him in the ring. Between him and Nicolle, I doubt any bad guy would last longer than seconds."

The patient understanding in his face as he tried to convince her was as heroic as the work he did. She wondered if he knew that about himself. He was a hero too. She, on the other hand, had a skeleton buried, and the bones were starting to work their way out of the ground.

She broke their clutch of fingers and slid her chair back, waving Gideon back into his when he began to rise. She did her best to sidestep her concern. "I have to say, those two sure looked like they would climb all over each other the minute we were out of sight. Do you think we should call them and see if they made it to Noah's house? I mean, it's three in the morning, but still."

Sliding silverware into the sink, she didn't hear Gideon approach until his arms bracketed her in place. When he pressed his body against her back, she felt every hard muscle and wanted to melt into the captivating heat.

"Is it Nicolle you're worried about? Do you think starting something with Noah will be too much for her? Noah has sound instincts, Danielle. He won't take things any further than they both want."

She didn't squirm out of the way, but instead ran water over their plates and left the mess in the sink. Later, when she was alone, washing up would be a good way of trying to calm her nerves. As she dried her hands on a paper towel, Gid spun her in place, but this time, he didn't press in closer.

He examined her face in slow sweeps, his light blue eyes shining with resolve and questions. "If this isn't about Noah and Nicolle, what is it about?" If anything, his lack of closeness only charged the moment with greater energy.

She waved her hands to dismiss him. "Maybe it's Nicolle. I mean, I know that look in her eye. Maybe she'll want to take things too far all on her own. Will Noah be ready for her?"

He didn't answer her teasing smile with one of his own. The solemn expression didn't change, but he did step nearer. Just one more step and they'd be pressed together from hip to chest. She could work with that.

"Why do you look guilty?"

She dropped the faked smile and wondered if she would have to drop Gideon too. He saw too much. She'd let him in too close and now he saw her secrets.

But secrets are safe as long as you don't share them, her inner critic whispered. Dani was sick of having a secret she couldn't share, not with her twin, the one person with whom she shared everything. And certainly not with the man standing in front of her with questions in his gaze.

>>>>>

He didn't want to push, not if she didn't want to talk about what bothered her. But Gid would bet a month of paychecks plus overtime that whatever bugged Danielle tore her apart inside. He could see it in her eyes. Others might not notice, but she had this incredible soft and caring interior she tried to hide under the gruff, tough outer hide of her cop persona. He knew the job made her that way, but something had hurt her and made the extremes worse.

He wrapped an arm around her shoulders and drew her alongside him. His crutches were in the living room, so he used the excuse of her support to lead her there. He pulled her down on to the couch. He didn't let her scoot away when she tried to, leaning her over instead so she was forced to fit under his arm. When she placed a hand over his heart, he wondered if she could feel how fast it beat for her.

He had a problem. He had the hots for the lieutenant, and she had her own agenda that might not include him, at least not for the long term. Hopefully Noah was having better luck. His brother deserved it, and so, he suspected did Nicolle.

"Tell Uncle Gid all about it, little one. You will feel better, and I swear," he placed a hand over hers, pressing it tight to his chest. "I swear I can keep secrets better than just about anyone. I promise no one will ever hear anything from me."

She leaned back into his arm and stared into his face. He didn't have to fake the sincerity. He could keep secrets, as evidenced by how long he hid behind the cabin fire last year. If he could only exorcise the voices screaming inside his head, he might stand a chance of making a decent life with this woman.

He jammed on the mental brakes. Who was he to think about anything longer than short term? Danielle's interest snapped to attention by something on his face, and he swore she looked like she wanted to interrogate him. The look faded when she shook her head and turned to stare without focus across the room.

"I bet you can keep secrets, Kinkead. I never hear anything but compliments about you. I've interviewed your squad mates and they all agree they'd want to be on any line with you, and the riskier, the better, because they know you'll have their back. The women you date sing your praises. I see the respect and admiration in your brother's eyes. You are a stand-up guy all around, aren't you?"

She didn't seem to expect a response as she linked her fingers in her lap and continued to stare away from him. How could he answer her? He wasn't sure what surprised him more, that she interviewed everyone without telling him or that they all stood up for him without question. He didn't deserve that kind of praise.

Her fingers turned white with pressure, and he put a hand over them and tried to unlace them. She glanced down as if just realizing what she was doing and shook her head. When she lifted her face to his, he found it very easy to drown in her eyes.

"I have a secret, Gideon, and I need to get it off my chest. Promise me you won't tell anyone, and particularly, never breathe a word about it to Nicolle. It would kill her." She drew in a huge sigh, and then blew it out. "And that would kill me."

He nodded, wondering what could possibly be so awful. He doubted it was as bad as she thought, so he would listen, and he would comfort her. Anything to keep her next to him and bring back that rare genuine smile.

Looking back at her hands, Danielle said, "I'm the reason Nicolle was injured."

That made no sense to him whatsoever. His face must have telegraphed the thought because Danielle frowned at him. "Not in the way you're thinking. Don't be literal about this. It's my fault. Got it?"

No, not in the least. Again, he let his frown say it all. She leaped off the couch to pace the living room rug, the same one that had seen such pleasant action only hours ago.

"I'm not sure you know a lot about the culture of our sheriff's department. Things have changed for the better in the last few years, but when I came on the force, it was a sexist, demeaning environment for women."

"Which makes your rise to lieutenant all the more impressive," he said, with real sincerity. He found more and more reasons to like her, which scared the shit out of him.

She shot him a bewildered glance before shaking her head. "Well thanks, but hold the praise until you hear the rest of this." Danielle hesitated as if struggling with her explanation. On a deep sigh, she continued. "We got a domestic disturbance call out in the very rural east end of the county, where houses and therefore neighbors are few and far between. Ergo, screams aren't heard and injuries can go unnoticed. It was a classic case of domestic abuse. I mean, the woman was so badly bruised, I wondered how she escaped internal injuries, but she refused medical treatment." Her words tumbled out in accelerating speed to match her quicker pacing.

"Listen, Danielle, if you don't want to talk about it, I –"

She held up a hand like a stop sign and he fell quiet. She didn't meet his gaze, though.

"I was brand new, fresh out of the academy and still on probation, and the other deputies on the call were seasoned. They'd been out to that address before, though it wasn't clear who called us in this time. No one lived close enough to hear the beatings. The man laid out a story about how clumsy the woman was and how she also wanted to take a strap to him during her time of the month, and that got a chuckle out of the guys. All I could see was the terror in the woman's eyes, but one glance from that pig and she cowered. She even agreed when he taunted her with his story."

Danielle swung by the table and chugged the remaining soda. The force she used to slam the glass back on the surface made the remaining items jump.

"Since the guys weren't doing anything and seemed too chummy with the man, I maneuvered the woman to the side and talked to her. I tried to get the real story, but she insisted it was like the man said. Then she got scared, and she whispered he'd kill her if she pressed charges. I tried to find a way to convince her there were shelters she could go to for protection, but she kept coming back to his death threats as if they were real. She was terrified, and nothing I could say would sway her."

She stopped and took up a stance in front of him, and while it might look like she was in control, he read the quaking tension in her body. He almost dreaded hearing more.

"What happened? And don't spare me anything because you think it will bother me. I've seen some pretty awful things myself, in case you forget."

She nodded one quick dip and continued. "I couldn't get anyone to listen to my concerns for the woman. In fact, the old sheriff, the one voted out in the scandal with underage girls, laughed at it, and other deputies did too. I was the only woman on the case." She shook her head, her expression contemplative. "I guess maybe I was naïve. I went back out there another time by myself to check on the woman."

He did not like where this was going.

"They were both there, unfortunately. The woman screamed at me to leave. She didn't want any help. The man threatened me and told me in no uncertain terms what he would do to me if I came out there again. I realized I was being stupid, going out without back up. The pleading expression on the woman's face about did me in. I left, and when I had a partner on patrol a few months later, we did a health and safety drive-by. The place was deserted."

Gid shook his head. It didn't make any sense. Unless he misunderstood, pieces were missing.

Danielle dropped on to a dining room chair and stared at the floor. "Fast forward to years later. Nicolle supervises an inmate crew. I don't know the guys or their names, but there are strict rules about who is allowed in. You probably know that better than me."

Gid nodded, unwilling to break up her explanation with the myriad questions swimming in his head.

"She gets attacked, and it's bad, very bad. A guy named Mitchell is the attacker. It happens on Federal land, so he ends up in the Fed system and in an Idaho pen. Something bothered me about the case the whole time, but it took me a while to put my finger on it."

"I don't see the connection. Yes, he should never have been on the crew, but Danielle, that's not your fault." He thought he was being reasonable.

Danielle threw her hands in the air and slapped her thighs on the way down. She stalked over to him and towered in front of him, hands on hips. "Don't you get it? Something always bugged me about Nicolle's attacker, so I ran him through some databases, and bingo, I got a hit. Mitchell and that guy in the woods years ago were one and the same. He should never have qualified for that inmate crew. We already knew what he was capable of, but I could not get that woman to press charges. I should have tried harder to get her help. But he threatened me, and look what happened. Years later, he gets to be on this crew and who's the supervisor? Nicolle, my identical twin. Do you really think he couldn't tell we're related?"

He examined her features closer. He already knew the differences between them, and now that he knew, he would always be able to tell them apart. It was evident in their contrasting approaches to the world. Someone who didn't care about their personalities would miss it.

He began nodding slowly at first and then with more conviction. "So you believe he took his spite against you out on Nicolle?"

She nodded, misery making her face sink. "I never told her I figured out who he was. I didn't want her to know, not when she was in so much physical and emotional pain. I'm a coward, Gideon, because she's always been the only one I could count on, the only person who I knew always had my back. I can't lose that. She's all I have."

The silence after her declaration stretched for minutes, time when Danielle stared with abject grief at a blank section of wall. Gid thought the only reason she wasn't openly sobbing was that she was made of stronger stuff, stronger than anyone he thought he'd ever known. She was as protective of her twin as he was of his brother, and as scared of losing her as he was terrified that someday, Noah would not need him.

He rose and hobbled in close to her. She didn't reach out to touch him, and he left space between them too. Somehow, this declaration needed to be said when they weren't leaning on each other.

"She isn't all you have, Danielle."

She looked confused. He almost smiled at the total and complete puzzlement on her face. He took one of her hands, and she let him, frowning down at their grasp.

"You aren't alone no matter what, Danielle, because now you have me."

Chapter 24

Why was it that all hell broke loose every time there was silence? She thought it was because when hell came, it made things seem still and quiet beforehand. She swore the world dragged into slow motion, then stopped with his words.

She could feel heat coming from Gideon's hand to warm hers. The tick-tock of something mechanical in the house came next. He regarded her with steady conviction, and Dani wasn't sure she'd heard him right.

She had – him? Her brain couldn't handle the words as he continued to regard her with steady sureness.

Her cell rang, followed by a heavy hand in rapid knocks on the front door. She couldn't command her muscles or her voice to respond. Gid hadn't passed judgment on her story, and she felt grateful for that. She needed space to process what he said.

Banging sounded again as she broke free of him and dove for her phone. Relief that it wasn't Nicolle's caller id morphed into something else when she heard the voice of one of her deputies calling out to her.

"Lieutenant? We've got a problem, and you're not going to like it. I'm waiting outside." That was enough to get her moving.

Gid snagged her hand as she passed for the front door. "Clothes?"

She stopped long enough to look down at herself, and grabbed the robe she had discarded on the sofa moments before. Gid pulled on his t-shirt and traced her footsteps. They both probably smelled like sex and her hair was undoubtedly a knotted mess, but there was nothing she could do about it. Her deputies would think what they wanted to think.

The pounding resumed, harder this time. Pictures on the wall on either side of the door rattled and jumped in response. "Coming," she yelled, and the deputy must have heard her, because the commotion fell silent.

Her hand was on the lock when she glanced at Gideon. If she read the stubborn expression on his face, he didn't plan on hiding. The hell of it was she didn't want him to either. His words still hung in the air like drifting smoke, and if that wasn't an appropriate metaphor, she'd eat her baton.

"It's probably nothing related to this," he said, though he didn't look convinced. He had as much at stake as she did, and he couldn't be as unconcerned as he tried to appear.

She straightened her shoulders and assumed her usual cold-eyed stare as she glanced out the peephole. The deputy had taken two paces back for better identification in the light on the porch. He looked as aggravated as she felt, with relief evident as the handle turned.

"Landowski, what is it?"

He tipped his hat and closed the distance between them. "Sorry to bother you in the middle of the night, ma'am, but we have a couple of problems. Dispatch couldn't raise you on your phone, so I came over to tell you myself."

She glanced down and noted the five missed calls. Gideon had kept her too busy to hear a ringing phone, and not only once. She winced at this, conscious of how this must appear to the deputy as he strode by her into the living room.

Landowski's eyes swept the room, stopping abruptly when he noticed Gideon. "Oh, hey Gid. Um, sorry, man."

This would be all over headquarters by the end of shift, because Landowski had a gossip mouth on him like a chatty high school girl.

"No problem, Paul. Just keep it between us, okay?"

Paul nodded, but his eyes looked a little too interested to make Dani feel comfortable. Gideon evidently felt the same way, because he hobbled over to the deputy with more speed than Dani thought he could manage, the cast clumping on the floor. He put a hand on Paul's shoulder, and from her distance, she noted the bite of his fingers into the deputy's shirt. Gid said, "We don't want inappropriate stories of any kind to get around town, now do we?"

While he hid it well, Dani noted the sudden stillness in the deputy's stance. Nothing moved, not until he nodded slowly. Whatever code passed between the men, the message was understood. She wondered if it would be enough to keep this quiet.

Paul turned and pulled a notepad out of his shirt pocket, flipping it through a few pages with a large finger before settling a hand back near his weapon. She'd seen the stance many times before. A report was coming, and it wasn't anything she was going to like.

By the time he was finished speaking, Dani was already racing to the bathroom for a quick shower. Behind her, she heard Gideon assuring Landowski they would be down to the station in minutes if not faster. She didn't even wait for the water to heat before she soaped her body and hair as one. This could not be happening. Bad to worse didn't even cover it. Rinsing just as the water grew warm, she reached for the knob to turn it off with a hard yank, and stepped out to reach for a towel.

The sight meeting her eyes caused her to freeze, momentarily forgetting the mess she faced ahead. Gideon stood at her sink, attempting to clean up with a wet washcloth. Despite the situation, she paused long enough to watch a droplet of water run down his chest. When he turned and caught her in the act, he didn't smile. Instead, he shifted over to her, wrapped an arm around her shoulders, and pulled her in for a quick, hard kiss.

She didn't have time for this. But damn if she didn't want it anyway. When he pulled back, he looked into her eyes as if waiting for her to comment. When she didn't, he lifted one corner of his mouth. It wasn't a smile, but she felt better seeing it.

"I have your back, Danielle. Whatever comes next, we'll protect Nicolle and Noah, you and I together. I meant what I said. You have me."

He dropped his arm and left the bathroom without waiting for a reply. That was a good thing, because she wasn't sure how to make sense of the cascading feelings and confusion swirling inside of her.

Danielle paced the parking area in front of the sheriff's headquarters. Gid would have paced too, but the crutches prohibited the rapid movement he wished. No question about it, today he would demand the doctor change this cast for something he could walk in, and if he refused, Gid would cut the damn thing off himself. He could wrap the leg back together with duct tape if he had to. He needed mobility, particularly now.

The minivan pulled into an empty parking space, and he and Danielle raced to its doors. He yanked open the driver's side as Dani did the same to the passenger front.

"About damned time," said Gid.

"Off the streets, now," said Danielle.

Nicolle didn't seem to resist as Danielle pulled her toward the doors, and Gid did the same with Noah, only to have their progress halted when his brother stopped. He couldn't pull him along, not with the cast, so he added urgency to his words.

"Come on, Noah. Now." He tried to add that same resolution to his expression, but his brother's appearance suddenly made an impact.

"What happened to you?" Gideon dropped his hand and stepped to the side, turning Noah to the wash of interior lights.

"Nothing. Listen, we need to keep Nicolle away from this. It isn't her fault, and she's not involved."

Yeah, about that. Danielle had called it, and Gid wasn't going to disagree. He'd told Noah the truth on the phone. Rage had shown up at the hospital, asking for him. That was enough to spur his brother into action, and he brought Nicolle along at Danielle's request. Gid wondered how long it would take her to tell her twin the rest.

"Gid, what is it?" Noah stepped in closer when Gid would have backed away.

"Danielle didn't want to tell her, not on the phone. That guy, the one who attacked her. He's been spotted outside their house."

>>>>>

Noah paced the room like an angry bear, and Dani couldn't blame him. She had more pent-up anger than she knew what to do with, and it was only because she had to remain cool and in charge that she didn't give in to her desire to break something, preferable the neck of one of their bad guys.

She eyed Nicolle, who was putting on a damned good show of being in control. The slight tremor in her hands as she took a drink from a bottle of water gave her away. Dani wanted to take her by the arm and lead her someplace to hide until this was settled. But she knew Nici wouldn't allow that.

"What do you mean he's been seen in town? Isn't he in violation of his parole? Can't you pick him up?" The pissiness in Noah's tone was enough to pull Dani's attention back to him.

She said, "To pick him up, one of my deputies or the local police need to see him. He's done a good job hiding himself, though how he's doing that, I don't know. An unfamiliar dog gets reported in this town faster than I can find this asshole."

When Nicolle spoke, her voice was as steady as Dani's, but her concern shown in the way she stared at Noah. "And Rage? You said there are multiple warrants out on him. Including murder, wasn't it? Doesn't that provide cause enough?"

Dani nodded, wondering how she was going to explain this shit storm on top of a shit storm to the sheriff. Things spun out of control faster than a speeding cruiser. Gid put a restraining hand on her shoulder from his position propped on the credenza behind her. Dani stilled and fought the urge to lean into his hand for comfort. It bugged her, even as it made her feel more secure.

She wasn't the one who needed people. They needed her. She could stand on her own two feet. She only needed to make sure her twin was okay. Had Gideon meant what he said? She still had no time or ability to process his words. Thoughts raced, crashed, and reassembled, but she couldn't make any better sense of them.

Gideon seemed to have more presence of mind. He said, "I called Dawson and told him you had been called out of town."

That was going to go over like a ton of bricks. Noah's expression became chilly as he stared at his brother.

"You called Marcus? Why?"

Gideon returned the stare. She respected his action, not that she was in any position to deny him. She'd called Nicolle's boss herself. She didn't meet her sister's eyes as she delivered her verdict.

"Cap knows you're not going to be at work until we catch this bastard," Dani said. She pulled a page from some random duty report and made a notation on it, as if this was a done deal.

"Hell no," Nicolle bit out, her fury more evident than Noah's. "I am not going to be scared off work because this jerk is on the loose. I can protect myself."

Dani grabbed a notepad, unwilling to look up and let her twin see the worry she felt.

"I can protect her," Noah said, sliding his hand into Nicolle's.

Dani allowed her eyes to flick to that grip before she resumed writing. Despite their situation, she admired the doctor for his determination.

"And I can protect Noah. So you see, there's nothing to worry about," Nicolle said.

Dani didn't miss the challenge in the tone. She kept writing until she was done, and waved the page she tore off the pad at her twin.

Nicolle didn't move. Dani's eyes drifted down to the linked hands, noting how both tightened their grip as if they thought someone would try to rip them apart. Nici was the touchy-feely type. Dani had never been one for holding hands with a guy. Despite everything else, she felt a stirring of envy.

She said, "Shit, Nici. Take the paper. It's directions to an address in Tahoe. You and Noah go there, hang out for a few days, and stay out of sight. Gideon and I will clean this up. Then you can come back and resume whatever it is you're doing." She waved the page at their hands but still didn't look up to their faces.

"Damn it, she's right. Do it, Noah. You two can have a little vacation. We've got this." Gideon's voice took on a pleading note. She appreciated his back up. His words echoed back in her head.

'I have your back, Danielle.' And *'You have me.'* But how far did he mean that to go?

Nicolle's stubborn denial snapped her eyes to her twin. Dani didn't have time to argue before Noah said, "Let's do it, Nicolle."

Something flashed between the two of them, something Dani couldn't catch. If it was up to her, she'd send an armed escort to the cabin and put them both under lock and key, but she didn't have the manpower to justify it.

"Okay," Nicolle agreed, with a meekness that was too sudden to make it real. Dani wanted to question her further, demand that she comply and stay put, but Noah had already taken the paper from her hands.

"This is a good idea. Nicolle and I will hang out and leave the two of you to handle this. We'll check in daily and see how things are going. Do we have time to pack some clothes?"

Dani nodded, trying to read their intentions in their faces. She glanced at Gideon, who grimaced as if he too was suspicious. Noah and Nicolle were out of Dani's office before seconds had passed.

"What the fuck?" Gideon's question made it clear he didn't believe them.

Dani tapped her pen on her teeth, wondering if she should lock them both up until things cooled down. But there was no probable cause, and she had to follow the rules. The isolation of the cabin was the best she could do on short notice. Even so, she thought there was too much spring in the pair's steps as they hit the outside door. She turned to meet Gid's worried look with the only words that made sense.

"That was too easy."

Chapter 25

How he managed to get away, she wasn't sure. In fact, she had a half-thought he was not returning, as Gid flew out the door on his brother's heels. She'd scared him off by not saying anything. Men like him needed to know their interest was reciprocated or they'd take off like dust on the wind.

She didn't have much time to think about him anyway, not with a man in violation of parole roaming her roads and another wanted for murder cruising her streets. She had a community to protect, and she notified her peer officers in the surrounding jurisdictions with personal phone calls. Everyone with a badge was on the lookout for these guys, even Animal Control.

Damn that twinge of envy every time she thought about her twin. But Dani assured herself she was happy for Nicolle, as happy as her sister would be if the conditions were ever reversed. They never would be. She had a tendency to run over the men she met, and they ran away faster than a speeding patrol unit when they experienced her steely will. She wondered what secrets Nici and Noah were sharing, alone in their eerie overlooking the lake. Dani hoped it was everything. Once they cleared the air, Nicolle would have a chance at a relationship with a nice guy.

A knock sounded on her door, but she kept her eyes on the computer screen, sifting through Rage's known aliases and priors to see if there was any connection close by they could exploit. "Yes?"

A mixed gait advanced into the room without words, and she felt the annoyance she always did when someone wasted time. Her deputies and the admin staff all knew they should report fast and get to the point. None of them had time for delays or nonsense.

Her ready string of curses already hung from her lips when her eyes lighted on Gideon. He wore different clothes, including a pair of jeans that hugged everything like they'd been sewn on him. His hair was still wet and more surprisingly, he didn't have a crutch.

She leaned forward and looked down, noticing the boot with Velcro straps that replaced his cast. While it didn't look comfortable, he could walk on it. She turned her face up to comment, meeting his gaze only moments before his mouth met hers.

The kiss was hot and she never saw it coming. Its hint of desperation might be coming from him or her. She wanted to act like it was nothing, but he didn't stop, cupping the back of her head to keep them locked together. She should move away, because anyone could walk by and see. She should stop them because she wasn't sure what the hell she was doing.

Gideon broke off the kiss, but he didn't let go of her. The blue in his eyes throbbed despite the glare of overhead lights. She didn't want to look away. One side of his mouth tipped up in a smile, and the corners of his eyes crinkled to match the deep grooves darting from his lips.

"Hey, I missed you. Any news?"

He leaned away, and Dani closed her eyes to hold on to the feel of him a moment longer. Fuck it, whoever said a word about seeing that display was going to go a few rounds with her, and the result wouldn't be pretty. But no interested faces peeked in the door.

Gideon leaned his fine rear end on the desk's edge, close enough for her elbow to nudge him without any effort. His eyes stayed on her face, and he seemed to be enjoying what he saw.

"I really did miss you. I had plenty of time to think while I waited for the doc. The only thing I kept coming back to was you." He frowned as if that thought troubled him.

"I, ah, I thought about you too. When I could. Which wasn't often. I've been, ah, busy." Where was her habitual cool? She felt like she could use a bucket of ice on her head, though it might turn to steam in seconds.

"Yeah, busy. I get it. So, any news? Any sightings? Did the kids make it to the cabin?"

Kids. Dani shook her head, knowing Nicolle would knock Gideon's block off if she heard that appellation. In fact, she doubted Noah would stand for it either.

She met Gideon's scrutiny with a stare of her own. "In summary, Nici and Noah are ensconced in the lovers' nest that is the cabin. We may have to pry them out of it once this is done. It's a wonderful place."

Gid's eyebrows rose close to his hairline, and he said, "And you recognize the potency of this place – how?"

Heat filled her face before she could call it off. She should be able to control her emotions. When she met Gid's direct and very interested stare, she lifted her chin in response. "First hand knowledge."

The man poised over her let out a huff of a chuckle. "And you told me it was a wilderness spot. I guess I should know better. And?"

His hand inched closer, covering hers and squeezing. She tried to concentrate on what she should be explaining.

"No further sightings. In fact, not even a suspicious car to tie to Rage. I'm trying to get a warrant to trace his financial records, but it's been an uphill battle. The sheriff said he's got that one now." He might have better luck than she did, given that he was a hunting buddy of the judge in question.

"And Mitchell?"

She shook her head, watching the close circles his thumb made on the back of her hand. The sight was sexy enough. The feel of it sent her insides tumbling from a tall mountain.

"We've got to do something. I can't just sit around. I have to take care of this, for Noah, and now, for you and Nicolle too. I have something to show you."

She looked into his serious eyes, wondering why he included her in the equation. She could take care of herself. She'd tell him that, just as soon as she could get her tongue unglued from the roof of her mouth.

"Trajan? Oh, Kinkead, good that you're here. Guess you're off the hook for this one."

Gideon straightened and turned forward, and Dani rose to face the sheriff standing just inside her office door. He didn't look pleased.

"Off the hook for what, sir?" Gideon seemed to bristle next to her, and she narrowly stopped herself from reaching out a hand to grasp his and restrain him.

"Trajan didn't tell you? We've got a new arson fire. She's your alibi. Unless the gossips got it wrong."

She heard Gideon inhale a deep breath and hiss as if he was ready to argue, but she beat him to it.

"Damn Landowski." She bit off what she was going to say next when the sheriff grinned.

"Yeah, he gossips like an old woman, but I've never known him to get a story wrong. So congrats, you two. Kinkead, watch out for this woman. She's tough, so you have to stand up for yourself, but I'm guessing you're up for the job."

He spun and left before Danielle could get words out of her mouth.

"What the hell just happened?" Gideon turned to her, his face a mix of confusion, anger, and goofy grin.

She sank into her chair, wondering if it was too late to escape to the cabin and beg Nicolle and Noah for a room.

>>>>>

With a new keenness, he wanted to know all of her secrets. Every single one of them would intrigue him, and once he thought he knew them all, she'd pull out a fresh set to surprise him. He liked the idea of surprises, as long as they included the enigma that was Danielle Trajan.

"She's not responding." Danielle tapped a pen on the desk. It was her only outward sign of agitation. Her composed face and the casual lean into one side of her chair appeared deceptively calm. To the public, she might seem to be in control. Gid knew better.

"Maybe they're busy," he said, grateful for the walking cast that allowed him to move toward her with more speed.

"She should still be monitoring her phone, no matter what."

Gid put a finger under her chin to raise her gaze to his. He noted the annoyance and spoke before she slapped his hand away. "Come on. Do you honestly think either one of them will hear a call when they're wrapped up in each other?"

He wished they were somewhere private, any place other than here. They had been at this for a night and a day, and the new evening crept in the sole window in the office. He didn't want to think about the time Noah was spending with the woman that Gid would bet anything his brother loved. He tried not to fan the spark of envy.

Danielle's mouth opened enough to allow him a peek of her pink tongue as it ran over her teeth, and he wanted to lean down and suck that tongue into his mouth. He wanted to see her come unglued in his arms. He needed more than anything to be able to show her how much he cared about her. His secret be damned. She'd learn of it soon enough. If he could explain it to her, perhaps she'd understand and take pity on him. With time, maybe they could overcome it.

More maybes. He needed to find a new word for the uncertainty that lurked everywhere he turned.

Danielle swallowed and picked up her phone again. "I need to talk to Nicolle." She glanced at him and then the door.

He got the message, but he didn't walk away. Somehow, he felt leaving would drive a wedge between them. He didn't want Danielle to have an opportunity to get her balance again. He wanted to persuade her to leave the station, come home, and allow him to distract her for hours on end, but he doubted she'd agree, at least not until she thought they'd exhausted every avenue of finding the men threatening their siblings. That could take a long time.

"Gideon, please." There was no pleading in her tone. She met his eyes, and he noted the exhaustion and tension tightening her face. She would feel better once she talked with her twin. Reluctantly, he recognized he'd feel more at ease once he spoke with Noah. When he nodded, he enjoyed her brief grateful smile.

"I should get in touch with Noah. I'll be outside when you're ready."

How much she'd be ready for, though, he wasn't sure.

Gideon's gait as he walked out her office door wasn't quite a swagger, but it was closer than he'd had with crutches. Dani had no doubt it would continue to interest her, and that alone was enough to bother her. If Noah was now an important part of Nicolle's life, Dani guessed she'd have to adjust to seeing Gideon occasionally. She had no illusions about how he would react to knowing he was still a suspect in her book. The sheriff might believe he'd been with her all night, but she knew differently. Gideon had slipped away for a time, and she bet he didn't think she had noticed. The fact that he said nothing to clear up that inconsistency meant he thought he had something to hide.

She was so fucked up. Involvement with a possible criminal went against every cell in her being. But she couldn't seem to help herself.

She tapped the phone again, adding another line to her last text.

'Talk?'

'Unless ur busy?'

She had no expectation of hearing from Nicolle this time either. There was nothing she could do about it, other than send a patrol unit by the cabin to see if they were okay. Dani didn't oversee the eastern end of the county, but the lieutenant there would be sympathetic. They all had families they worried about.

As she debated the need for a drive by, her cell phone buzzed on the desk, and she grabbed it with one hand and tapped the green button to accept the call as she recognized Nici's number. She didn't even realize she was standing and staring out her office window until the length of the dusky shadows registered. A full day had passed since Nicolle and Noah had left.

"Finally. You need to keep your phone handy and monitor texts and calls. This isn't a game."

Then she nearly bit her tongue off in an effort to stop the torrent. It wasn't Nicolle's fault this was happening. That was all on Dani, a fact she should remember.

The pause wasn't lost on her, and she nearly jumped in to apologize when Nicolle responded. "Well hello to you too. Yes, we're fine, thanks for asking. I'm guessing you haven't been home since this started, which means you're hot and itchy for that sexy firefighter. I have to admit, I can understand your frustration."

Dani blew out a breath she hadn't been aware she'd been holding and coughed a laugh at the same time. Nicolle never took her moods to heart, which was a blessing. At least one of them was balanced.

"Sorry, sis. Yes, I'm frustrated, but not for the reason you think." Still, she glanced in the direction Gideon had wandered, noting he wasn't in any part of the squad room she could see. She missed being able to watch him, something she'd beat herself up for later.

Dani focused outside on the brick wall of the building on the other side of the parking lot. "I wanted to give you an update. There was another fire, but they jumped on it and got it under control. No sightings of either Rage or Mitchell. I have everyone on the lookout." She inhaled deeply and delivered the final message. "And Mom knows about you."

Silence. Then, "Mom knows about me what?"

She didn't think Nicolle was being deliberately obtuse, but then again, the calm tone said differently. "About you and Noah."

"So she also knows about you and Gideon then too." The reasonable notes in her twin's voice made Dani calm a little.

"Yeah, that too, not that there's anything to know."

A chuckle sounded through the phone. "Yeah, and pigs fly. I've seen them, little pink pigs with blue wings flapping through the air."

It was Dani's turn to chuckle, and her eyes followed the progress of a man in the parking lot. Gideon paced back and forth, the uneven gait giving him a rapid prowl nonetheless. Yeah, pigs were flying all over the county now.

"It is fucking frustrating, and that's all I can tell you."

Gid paced the length of the parking lot, grateful to be able to move. Anything to expend some of his barely contained energy. He wanted to be out there, catching someone, though the allusive who and where were completely uncertain.

"I mean, how hard can it be to locate a black guy covered with gold bling and probably driving a car that stands out just as much?" He realized how that sounded, but this was Noah he was talking to.

"Gid, that's profiling."

Gid cursed in response, surprised when Noah said nothing to admonish him. "I'm not being prejudice. Would you like to hear what I think about the white guy who attacked your girlfriend?"

Noah didn't say anything.

"Did you hear me?"

"Yes, I heard you, and since I share your sentiment, I don't need to respond."

Gid waited for more, but Noah wasn't confirming or denying. He stopped pacing and checked the face of his phone to make sure they were still connected. They were, which meant Noah wasn't going to help him.

"So, she is your girlfriend now, am I right?"

A deep sigh came through the phone as Noah said, "She's the woman I care about deeply, and I plan to continue caring about her even more as time goes on. Satisfied?"

Despite their circumstances, Gid found himself smiling. He liked Nicolle, admired her skills and talents, and was in awe of her sense of humor and honesty. Noah had a thing for Nicolle, which meant she was now family, and Gid took care of everyone in his family.

He glanced back at the station, wondering what Nicolle was telling Danielle. He doubted she'd share it with him, not without significant persuasion. They had a job to do, and the thought forced him to glance around the parking. Even here at the sheriff's headquarters, someone could be watching.

Noah's aggravated words came through the phone. "Where do we go from here?"

Gid nearly groaned, saying, "You and Nicolle don't go anywhere. Danielle and I have this."

"And how is the lieutenant?"

Gid answered with silence. He wasn't sure what to say.

"Gid?"

"She's pissed, fine, but pissed. Listen, I have to go. Danielle's waving me over."

With curiosity echoing in each word, Noah said, "Where are you?"

"Doesn't matter. I'll check in with you later. Until then, lay low, okay?" Gideon paused, then added, "Take care of yourself, bro."

After the briefest of pauses, Noah said, "You too," and hung up before Gid could respond.

He didn't have a chance to empty his expression as Danielle strode to his side with rough purpose in her step. She examined his face without asking how the call went. Gid doubted she would miss his frustration. They had family to protect and they were getting exactly nowhere. It was time for action, and he was happy she sought him out. The worry on her face told him she felt the urgency too.

But her next words surprised him. "Let's go home, Gideon."

She turned and walked away from him as if she knew his response. He only hesitated a moment before following her. Because, yeah, he had it that bad.

Chapter 26

He wasn't sure what he expected. Would Danielle drop him off at Noah's? She remained silent on the drive, and when she pulled into her driveway and exited with only a glance in his direction, he thanked the fire gods for their divine intervention.

She gave the drive and surrounding yard a cautious visual scan, as if seeking anything out of place, and apparently satisfied, she went to the front door and opened it. She didn't look back to see if Gid followed, and he felt a moment of hesitation. Her boss's innuendos about them being an item hadn't pleased her. What were his intentions? He never thought he'd find himself interested enough in any woman to want to stay. He never expected to be in this position, and he had no skills to navigate the dark forest in front of him.

"Are you coming inside?"

He must have been thinking too long. Danielle stood in the doorway, wiping her hands on a bathroom towel. Her hair was down and she had already changed her clothes into shorts and a t-shirt. The combination showed off her toned body. Give her a tan and she'd look like a surfer's wet dream.

He crossed the drive, taking care to step gingerly on the gravel. The last thing he needed would be to take a tumble, the physical kind. Gid suspected he'd already taken the metaphorical one and hadn't even registered the fall.

Danielle backed up, keeping her eyes steady on his as he closed the door. Reaching behind him, he turned the lock, and its distinct click sounded overly loud in the silence. She grimaced, and he wondered if this wasn't going the way she wanted.

Instead of moving toward him, she turned and walked to the kitchen, leaning on the counter. "Have you ever noticed that the shit hits the fan when it's too quiet? It's like tragedy inhales and it takes all the noise with it. Then it blows out and we all suffer."

He drew closer, noting new lines of worry pulling her brows together. "We'll find them, Danielle. It's only been a little over a day. They can't stay hidden for much longer. I'm betting that by tomorrow at this time, it will all be over."

Her eyes rose and captured his, and he felt her worry like a furry thing burrowing between them. "It might be over, but at what cost? Can we keep them safe? I can't stand the idea of Nicolle being scarred any more than she already is."

Gid wrapped his arms around her and pulled her in close and she didn't fight him. She sank into his hold like she was now that frightened creature seeking refuge. Running a hand down her hair, he only wanted to soothe her and take away her fears. He could bear the brunt of worry for both of them. Whatever emotions she hid, she didn't need to hide them from him. Gid swore Danielle would have nothing else to fear.

"I don't think Nici understands why she needs to be out of harm's way. All I want to do is keep her safe, Gideon. If I can't find the bad guys, I can draw another ring of defense around the good ones."

She tried to push out of his arms but he wouldn't let her. That brought her attention back to him with questions in her eyes. Instead of saying anything, he leaned in and placed a soft kiss on her plump lips.

She tasted like fresh air on a cold morning, crisp and bright and surprisingly enticing. He was used to heat, given his profession. Coolness had a different flavor, and he found he had grown addicted to it in the last few days. When he ran his tongue across the seam of her lips, her mouth opened, and he dove in for a deeper taste.

Her tongue danced around his until he wasn't sure he had the strength to stay gentle. His skin felt like it was growing too tight the longer he kissed her. Nerve endings twitched and he wanted to crawl as close to her as he could, wanted to be inside her and never let her go. He pulled back to catch his breath, and missed their connection when she let her eyes drop to his shirt, where her fingers clutched fabric like it was a lifeline.

"Danielle, I –" He never got any further, because she put a firm hand over his mouth and shook her head. He wasn't completely sure what he'd planned to say.

"Gideon, we have things to discuss. I still haven't told you everything, and I want to clear the air before things go any further." She stepped back then, and he was surprised enough to allow it.

Fair enough. He had matters to explain too. She might not be all that interested in him afterwards. He didn't fool himself on this. Yes, they had a mind connection, but they needed the physical side too. Danielle deserved it, and he wanted it more than anything.

He had to put the past in the past, far enough away so that it was a speck in the rear view mirror. He might never forget the sounds of screams or the smell of burning human flesh, but he had to stop letting it define his life.

She pulled the coffee maker forward on the counter and glanced at him, her question obvious in the single raised eyebrow. He nodded. He doubted he'd doze much, not as long as Noah was at risk.

Danielle stopped before putting in any grounds, staring at the machine as if she wasn't sure what to do with it. Then she shook her head. "What am I thinking? We need our sleep. Neither one of us will be able to function, much less think clearly, unless we're rested. The kids deserve that." She pushed the machine back with enough force to knock it into the tile backsplash and turned for the fridge.

Unless elves visited to restock it, that would be empty. Throwing together something when they last ate here had been a feat of magic. There wasn't much else to pull from.

"Maybe it's a night for pizza," he said. Memory of the last time they had almost shared that dinner washed over him, making him take a forceful step forward before catching himself.

She regarded him with wariness. "Gideon, we have to talk. I mean, really talk. I need to keep my distance. You're still a suspect."

That stopped his progress as firmly as if she'd put a boot to his chest. "A suspect?" He heard the incredulous disbelief in his voice, but he couldn't help himself. "A suspect in what?"

Danielle waved her hands as if missing the words she needed. Guilt flushed her face, and she held her eyes open too wide. When he considered the implications of what she said, a shot of anger raced through him.

"Wait, I get it now. You think I could still be responsible for the arsons. Despite the state I was in, and despite what I've told you. You confirmed the cabin fire, and you read the reports. You know I was often not even available to start a fire because I was fighting one someplace else."

He ran a hand over his hair, feeling the longer ends and wrapping them in his fingers to tug. He hated the game playing. In the interest of honesty and full disclosure, she should have mentioned that little fact. Before they went horizontal would have been best.

"Why didn't you tell me? Why didn't you say something before all of this?" Gid swept a hand between them, and Danielle blinked at him. There was no doubt she knew exactly what 'all this' meant.

Instead of defending herself, Danielle turned away and straightened her shoulders. He wasn't sure what he expected, but not her chilliness. More than that, he wasn't sure what he wanted her response to be. Denial would have been nice.

But her silence spoke louder than words could. In her eyes, he remained a suspect. He wasn't sure how this could even be possible. Did the cops believe he started the fires, blew himself up, and left himself those damned roses?

That reminded him, and the envelope burned in his pocket. He'd found it in Noah's stack of mail in the box at the curb. It bore no postage, meaning someone left it there, and it was on top of the other mail, meaning someone left it after the daily delivery. The single line of type on its surface already sent the message about what was inside. *'Gideon Kinkead, Killer.'*

"Are you going to say anything?" He took a step away from Danielle, who seemed intent on the contents of a cabinet he knew was almost empty. She was avoiding him.

He'd had enough of it. He ripped the paper from his pocket and crossed the room with a forced stomp that made his leg ache. She didn't turn, and he waved the envelope in front of her face, making the paper crinkle and snap like new flames.

"How do you explain this, then?"

In profile, her expression remained passive and uninterested, but he noted the reaction when her eyes lighted words. The sharp focus widened them again, and she reached to take the envelope with slow movements.

"When did you receive this?" She stopped before taking the paper, turning and opening another cabinet and pulling out a box of resealable plastic bags. She slipped one on each hand, then added a third, opened on the counter. She tugged at the letter in his fingers, surprise on her face when he let go of it suddenly.

But he wasn't going to give up the hurt that easily. He wanted her apology. More to the point, he wanted her to believe him. He related the prior whereabouts of the envelope as she slipped a knife into plastic bag and struggled to slit the top.

"Just rip the damn thing open. You know it will have no identifying marks like the others. Whoever this is, they're good."

She shot him a single glance, and in it, he read the mix of her emotions. Concern, professional focus, worry, frustration. If any of that was a personal connection to him, she wasn't showing it.

The stiff plastic of the bags on her hands made retrieving the page inside the envelope difficult, and she fumbled it for a few precious seconds while he looked on with growing impatience. He reached for it, intending to hurry the process along.

"Give it to me. I'll pull it out, and then we'll know how my prints came to be on the paper."

But she turned away and the letter was now out of reach. "No, Kinkead. Don't you see? If you don't touch this and we keep it in pristine condition, it could be more evidence to prove this has been a series of crimes against you, not perpetrated by you."

Proof. She wanted proof. His word wasn't enough for her. He understood others would need evidence, but it hurt more than he could say that she didn't believe in him.

She regarded him steadily, and if there was a trace of pleading in her eyes, he chose to ignore it. He didn't care about the others, but he cared about what she thought more than he could imagine.

He waved a hand to indicate she should proceed and walked away. He didn't want to know what was inside. He actually didn't care anymore. A weariness that felt all encompassing made his leg feel as heavy as lead, his shoulder throb like a toothache, and his body scream for respite. He only wanted all of this to be over.

Over, and then what? He didn't want to stare at Danielle, to see her in a keen cop orgy of new evidence, but he couldn't seem to help himself. He wished she'd look at him, but her face remained close to the page she was only now coaxing out of the envelope. Whatever the letter said, it no longer mattered to him. Danielle didn't believe him, and that was the only thing he cared about.

She was proud of her hands for not shaking, proud of her body for staying upright and strong, proud of being part of a profession that had trained her how to be feeling one thing on the inside and showing something completely different to the world. Because on the inside, she knew things were cracking apart, fissures so wide and deep that no bridge would ever cross them. Chasms that would separate Gideon from her.

Already, he ignored the letter. Hands covered his eyes as if he needed to press them back into his head. She echoed that emotion but she also knew hiding wouldn't expose the truth. That truth was what she was after.

She couldn't tell him her heart already knew he was innocent, not when she was in charge of the investigation and his participation remained one gigantic question mark. It wasn't enough for her to believe him. Others needed to as well.

Her fingers barely trembled when she unfolded the single page of plain white paper. It looked like any piece of generic printer paper, and the words on the page looked like they were produced by any of a number of machines. Gone were the days when notes like this could be associated with a single unique typewriter. Electronics made evidence possible to refute.

"What does it say?" Gideon's voice sounded like he no longer cared. She'd done that to him. She should have said she believed him.

She read out the sentences in a low tone. *"How does it feel to burn, asshole? What will it be like when you watch someone you love explode in flames? I hope you hear their screams for the rest of your days."*

Gideon made a rough sound, part curse and part exclamation. The guttural notes reminded her that despite everything they thought they knew about this case, despite the threatening presences of Rage and Mitchell, there was still another big unknown. The arsonist was still a mystery.

He hadn't moved from his place at the table. "We need to find this guy, whoever he is. I'm beginning to think we've been distracted by the ones who are stalking Noah and Nicolle. They are still out there, but this bastard is too." He pressed his fingers harder, and she wondered what he saw against the darkness of his eyelids.

He'd described it, but she reasoned that until someone experienced this up close, it remained an exercise in supposition. He knew the reality, being blown across the clearing. He'd been there when the people went up in flames. She wondered what went through his mind when he thought back to those experiences. It must tear him apart inside.

"I believe you," she said. Where the words came from, she wasn't sure, but they carried conviction.

He didn't move. In fact, she wasn't sure he was even breathing.

She dropped the single page into the plastic bag to rest with the envelope. She would turn this over to the crime lab, though as Gideon had said, there was probably nothing on it. But at least his prints wouldn't be found on the page. Circumstantial or not, that had to mean something.

Evidence told the story, a credo she believed in. Direct evidence was missing in this case. No one had ever seen Gideon Kinkead do a single thing wrong. In fact, it could be argued that he'd rushing into danger to rescue any potential victims, and that caused him to be injured. Were those the actions of a guilty man?

"What do you believe?" She thought she heard pain in his muffled words. His hands still covered his face, so she couldn't read his expression.

"I believe you didn't start any fires. I believe you aren't the arsonist. I believe that the arsonist, whether it's a bad guy we know about or one we have not yet identified, is making you a victim too."

Shedding the bags on her hands, she crossed the room and knelt next to his chair. "Please, Gideon, you have to believe me. I think I always knew you were innocent. Maybe it was the damned rose in the hospital that tipped things over the top. I'm not sure. In my heart, I've known, and that's why I've been trying to protect you."

His hands lowered slowly, and he blinked as if the dim light of the room was too much for him. He watched her with a cautious expression, and she had no idea what he was thinking. She did the only thing that seemed natural, leaning in and settled her head in his lap.

Moments later, a hand settled in her hair and stroked it with a feather-light touch. She didn't want to move and break the moment. They could stay this way for hours as far as she was concerned. This was the closest she'd felt to anyone other than her twin.

"You know, that cabin fire broke something inside me. It broke something inside my head and my heart. I'm not the man I was before, and since then, I tried to hide that fact through actions that weren't exactly responsible. Danielle, look up. I need to see your eyes."

She leaned back on her heels and kept her hands on his thighs to anchor them together. This moment was important. Without conscious consideration, she knew it would decide everything between them.

Gideon gulped, but he didn't look away. "There are things I still need to share with you. Not about that fire or about the arsons, but about me. You've undoubtedly heard things and I want to clear the air. There are reasons why I act the way I do, and once you hear them, you might not want to have anything else to do with me."

Her heart sped up to pounding as a thousand possible implications for his words ran through her mind. But she held on, because she wanted nothing more than to be everything for him. She hoped that would be enough.

He met her gaze steadily, if with some unidentified embarrassment. Danielle realized he was waiting for her to respond, so she nodded, taking any questions out of the motion by making it quick and assured. She felt anything but on the inside.

Was this what Nicolle felt with Noah? No wonder she didn't want him to know about the rape from anyone else. When everything hung in the balance, you wanted to form the words yourself. That way, you had no one else to blame if things resulted in a major fuck-up.

Into the silence, her cell phone rang. Then it beeped with an incoming text. Another call followed, and the pings of her voicemail messages sounded in quick succession. She wanted to ignore them, but the moment was broken as soon as they both realized something could be wrong with their siblings.

She rose, letting her hands linger on him for as long as possible. Somehow, his fingers became entangled in her hair as if he too didn't want to let go. She pulled the phone toward her and looked at the display. When she toggled the text to life, she swore.

"What is it?" Gideon was by her side as if he flew there.

"I can't believe this. Why didn't they stay put?" She was already tucking her personal weapon into a large purse.

"Noah and Nicolle?" Gideon seemed to make even quicker work of checking the peephole and unlocking the front door, sweeping up a backpack she hadn't noticed leaning next to it.

"The patrol unit doing a drive by didn't find them at the cabin. Then Jake reported from the hospital. Noah just showed up for work. I have no idea in hell where Nicolle is, but I can guess she's headed to fire command. What kind of jackass stunts are they pulling?"

But she had no one to answer her words. Gideon was already stomping toward the truck. He hesitated as if thinking about driving, then stared down at his leg for a moment before continuing around the vehicle. By the time she locked the front door and raced across the drive herself, he had his seatbelt fastened and a grim expression on his face, facing forward and staring out the windshield.

"We have to deal with this, once and for all. I'm sick of wondering when something's going to blow up." He gripped the dash as she pulled a tight u-turn and hit the accelerator.

She couldn't have said it better herself.

>>>>>

"Rage showed up at the hospital, and Noah went there anyway. Un-fricking-believable. Why didn't Jake arrest Rage?"

Gideon kept his hands locked on the dashboard. It helped to hold on to something, grounding him in some kind of reality when things appeared to be spinning out of control. What was his brother thinking?

Same thing as he was, a reasonable voice said in his head. Ending this thing, so he could get on with whatever grew between him and a woman. The irony of their situation wasn't lost under the hysterics. He and his brother were hot for a pair of twins. Go figure.

"Hospital security monitors the cameras inside and out. They have multiple feeds, so they can't watch everything in real time. They had someone else viewing the recordings and Rage showed up again about five hours ago. Someone notified Noah, and I plan to have a little talk with them as soon as I have their identity. They are interfering with a sheriff's investigation."

She rounded a corner on two tires, and the truck settled back down with a spurt of gravel. They were minutes from the hospital. The phone beeped again, and she handed it to Gideon without slowing.

He glanced at the screen. He recognized the number. "It's Cap. He asks if you knew Nicolle was at fire headquarters. She's settled in as if she plans to work for a while."

Danielle swore, and Gid couldn't avoid a sudden smile of appreciation. She could out-curse seasoned firefighters without blushing at the words. His kind of woman.

"What are you smiling about? Damn it, I can't be two places."

He put a hand on her shoulder, and she paused long enough before her next turn to glance in his direction.

"There are two of us, Danielle. You go to Nicolle. I'll cover Noah. Is Jake still there?"

She nodded, looking distracted. The next glance she sent him was grateful. "Jake said Dr. Dawson is there too and he doesn't plan on leaving. I'm not crazy about the idea of more civilians in the line of fire." She stopped speaking with a stricken look. "Sorry. I could have picked better words."

Gideon shook his head, leaning forward so she could see his face without missing the road. "Don't worry. From what I've heard about Marcus, the man can handle himself."

Danielle frowned and sucked in air. "Does he own a gun?"

Gideon shrugged.

"Does Noah?"

He shook his head emphatically. "Doesn't believe in them. That's why he's turned to martial arts."

Danielle's frown deepened. "Unfortunately, a good kick isn't going to stop a bullet. Maybe I should go to the hospital with you first. Cap has Nicolle in his sights, and she hasn't been there long enough to attract attention. I could –"

He didn't let her finish. "I'll take care of Noah. You head to the fire camp. You need to be with Nicolle."

She pulled to a screeching stop in front of the emergency entrance and put a hand on Gideon's arm. "Stay smart, okay? We have things to talk about, you and I. Don't make me want to kick your ass because you aren't able to sit there and listen."

Gid stared at her, seeing the sincerity and worry in her eyes. Instead of saying anything, he leaned in and gave her a single hard kiss. It stoked every fire inside him, and he shoved open the door and stepped down before he gave in to the desire for more. As he closed the door, he looked back at Danielle. Fingers touched her lips and her eyes were wider than they'd been moments before. Dazed and confused, he'd bet, which was a solid approximation of how he felt.

"Be safe out there," he said, then turned and raced to the automatic doors as they slid open on silent tracks.

Dani didn't have enough time to get her emotions for Gideon in check by the time she reached the fire base, and she hoped Nici wouldn't notice. She forced herself to compartmentalize and focus on the task. Showing her identification to a guard on the perimeter, she drove into the camp yard.

Even in the darkness, it was a beehive of activity. The cover of night would only make it easier for whoever wanted to sneak up undetected. Not on her watch. She located the mobile headquarters trailer and barged in, noting faces turning toward her without really looking at them. Cap's broad back blocked her view of Nicolle's desk, and she felt a wave of gratitude that the man took the safety of his people so seriously. When the door crashed back into place, a gnat's wings could have been heard to flutter in the place. Silence, never a good sign.

"I've got this, Cap," Nicolle said.

As soon as she saw her twin standing at her desk, Dani shot back, "No, I've got this, and you're going back to the cabin."

Cap's gaze flicked between them and he wisely stepped out of the way, just as Dani marched up and came nose to nose with Nicolle. She wasn't sure if she wanted to kiss her twin or lay her out with a good side punch.

"We had a deal. You, out of sight, and me, doing my job." Dani hadn't bothered lowering her voice. Cap herded people out of the small trailer with a bark of command.

"You had a directive. It doesn't work for me. So I'm here, doing my job." Nicolle took a step back and returned to her seat, cool as could be.

Dani swore up one side of the alphabet and down the other, making up words when she couldn't think of anything new to say. Nicolle smiled, which only made her madder. Like a generator without fuel, Dani ran out of energy. The cascading emotions of the past few days overwhelmed her, and she pulled a chair over from a nearby desk and fell into it.

"Why didn't Noah have the good sense to stay in place?"

Nicolle's direct stare, wide-eyed with a cocked eyebrow, let Dani know how stupid her twin thought the question was. She knew the answer herself. For the same reason Gideon wanted his mess over with. For the same reason she wanted their half-truths to come out. So they could all move on with whatever they each had at stake in this.

Dani groaned out loud when she realized what was at stake for her was her heart. It belonged to Gideon. That dumb bastard better survive this without any new injuries, because she wanted to take him to the floor herself. After all, he'd already done the same to her.

Chapter 27

Dani rubbed at the tension in her neck, unable to calm herself despite long days that should have brought exhaustion. What little sleep she was able to get sitting upright in their cozy living room with her gun in her lap had been broken up by nightmares of fire, too much fire. In that strange half-aware state where she realized it was a dream, she expected it to be Nicolle walking into the fire. But it wasn't. The form heading toward the wall of flames was Gideon.

She startled awake with a scream forming on her lips. Gid needed to be safe. She couldn't afford to lose him any more than she could Nicolle. More than anything, she needed to tell him that. Somehow, love crept in on silent feet when she was distracted. The next time she dozed, she must have yelled aloud, because the next thing she knew, Nicolle was shaking her awake with the gun safely out of reach.

"What is it? Tell me, and the nightmare will have no power over you. Come on, that's what you've always told me."

Nicolle's concerned face was her own mirror image, and yet, time and experience had changed her. She still smiled more easily than Danielle, and her face bore fewer wrinkles of worry. But underneath all that, Dani could see the sadness that never seemed to pass.

Unless Nicolle was with Noah, or speaking about him. For that matter, the ease on her expression at times when she was quiet was probably due to thinking about the man too. Dani could relate, if only things were as easy between Gideon and her.

Since Nicolle didn't appear to be walking away and since she still had Dani's gun in a hand outstretched in the opposite direction, Dani told her. Nicolle's expression turned sympathetic as her voice grew soft.

"Gid knows better than to walk into a raging fire, but if he has to, it's something he's trained for and there's a good reason he needs to. The people on his hotshot squad consider him the best of the best. That's why they were willing to give him a pass on the weird behaviors these past few months. None of them begrudge him the time to recover from what he experienced."

Dani wrapped a pleading hand around her sister's wrist. "Tell me about it, Nici. I mean, Gideon told me about it himself, but that was an emotional account. I need to understand what a firefighter feels out there. Do you ever get scared? Do you ever wonder if this time, the fire wins and you pay the ultimate price? How do you still do it? I need to understand."

Nicolle examined her face, and Dani wondered if she could read every emotion churning inside her. She probably could, just as she could read the feelings in Nici's heart. They already understood what each felt without resorting to words.

Putting the gun on the dining table with ginger fingers exhibiting her distaste, Nici gave Dani's shoulder a shove and wiggled into the room between the wide chair's arm and her twin's body. They curled into each other, as naturally as they had in the womb. It had always been like this. When one hurt, they both did.

"When you get the call, it isn't like you want there to be a fire. Wildland fires are dangerous, deadly and always world changing. Land that scars today may never recover in our lifetimes. Trees older than generations of us are gone in what seems like a blink of an eye. It makes you feel very insignificant in the overall scheme of the universe."

Dani nodded against her sister's bent head. "Then how do you do it? How can you be so courageous?"

She felt the chuckle rather than heard it, and she raised her face to stare at Nicolle. Her twin gave her a half-grin. "I seem to recall having this same conversation with you a long time ago, but I was asking you the questions. I wanted to know how you could run into gunfire, knowing a bullet could injure you or get you killed. Do you remember what you told me?"

The recollection came to Dani with sudden clarity. It was after a particularly messy case involving a backcountry meth lab. Her department's original assessment of the size of the operation hadn't done it justice. The officers responding were outnumbered and outgunned. Dani had been one of the first to arrive after the initial deputies were pinned down under fire. She hadn't thought about the risk, not once her head dropped into action mode. She did her job, the one she'd been so highly trained to do.

She nodded, thinking back. It was what she was trained to do. That didn't mean she didn't feel fear from time to time or wish like hell she didn't have to go after yet another bad guy. That train of reasoning brought her back to Gideon.

Dani said, "When you head into a fire, it's what you're trained to do. You save people and the things they find important. You save the forests because they are essential in our natural existence. You save the planet, because that's your chosen profession and what you do."

Nicolle did laugh this time. "You make us sound like we're Robin Hood, but yeah, that's about it. No different from you. Yes, sometimes we have to do things that are more risky than usual, but we're well trained and we do know how to approach problems. That doesn't mean there is no danger, but it's more controlled than you think."

Her twin was so brave and so noble. Dani could feel it now as well as understand it. She couldn't keep it in any longer. "I'm the reason all of the bad stuff happened to you."

She read the surprise in her twin's feelings as easily as the uptick in her heart. "What are you talking about?"

If she was going to face her consequences, she needed to come clean. "I'm the reason Mitchell was allowed to be on that inmate crew. You were attacked because of me. It was all my fault."

Nicolle sat still, frowning at her like she'd lost her mind. "I think you're going to have to explain that to me with a few more details."

She didn't want to look at her sister as she unrolled the whole sorry saga, so Dani climbed off the chair to pace from the door to the kitchen counter, back and forth. Her steps were as slow as her words at first, and then both picked up speed. She wanted to get it over with. If Nici hated her after hearing this, she hoped she could mend their relationship with time.

Just as she needed to mend her relationship with Gideon.

Dani ran out of words when her pacing brought her to the front door, and she stopped facing it. She didn't want to see the pain and disbelief she was sure filled Nicolle's face. Her twin had lost so much.

Nicolle's voice was low when she finally responded. "You think you're to blame for Mitchell not being judged a low risk. And you think he mistook me for you. And you are mad at yourself for not recognizing him sooner when you saw him."

Dani nodded, feeling sick misery wrap her in icy fingers.

"Danielle Trajan, come here," her sister said.

She turned but didn't raise her eyes.

"I said, come here. What do you think I'm going to do, floor you like I can in the ring? Dani, listen to me. You are not to blame. The only one to blame is Mitchell. He did this. You need to let go of a past you can't control. You're the one who taught me that."

She lifted her face to find forgiveness and love in her twin's eyes. Nicolle extended her arms, and Dani ran into them and held on tight. Nicolle's soft words were a balm on her soul. "We're so alike, it's scary sometimes. I blamed myself too, but I never realized how much pain this caused you. Let it go, big sister. Eight minutes and thirty-eight seconds doesn't mean you're invincible. You're the other half of my yolk. I love you, you are not to blame, and you need to let this go."

Nicolle punctuated her words with hard shakes, hugs that Dani held on to as tightly as she could. She wasn't sure if she wanted to laugh or cry. Relief burst through her and she felt the weight of her secret lift off her shoulders. As Gideon had said, the truth would make her feel whole again.

Gideon. The truth. The truth was, she loved him, she believed him, and she needed to tell him.

Nicolle gave her another squeeze, pushing her far enough away to stare into her face. "You're so dedicated to your work. We both are. I think we both need to lighten up and enjoy life more. There will still be fires. There will still be bad guys. We can't stop them all, nor should we try to on our own."

Dani nodded. Crimes were committed, and criminals needed to be stopped before society grew unruly. Most of the time, those criminals were merely people who were too stupid or undereducated to realize what they were doing meant they would eventually be caught. The smart ones hid deeper. Thankfully, they were few and far between.

The idea brought her upright and spinning away from her twin. "They're too stupid to be doing this."

Nicolle frowned at her in confusion. "Who's too stupid for what?"

Dani paced to the table and retrieved her gun, checking the safety by force of habit before tucking it into the back of her jeans. "Stupid isn't the right word. Mitchell and Rage want revenge. They wouldn't plan the kind of taunting attack on Gideon we've been seeing. The roses. The letters. The escalating fires. They're a deliberate plan. The bad guys we know wouldn't plan. It's the one we don't know that we need to worry about."

The confusion on her twin's face cleared and she nodded, slowly at first and then with more force. "Yes. I agree, now that you put it in that context. The science behind the incendiaries alone would indicate that. This is why it was so easy to cast Gid in the role of firebug to begin with. It took training and mental agility that, I agree, is not something Mitchell has. Rage is probably the same from what Noah has told me. Come on, we need to go to the hospital."

Nicolle was already on her feet and heading for her duffel. Dani did the same with her backpack, holding out the gun. "Take this. I'll feel better."

Nicolle stopped and frowned at the weapon with obvious disgust. "I don't do guns, Danielle, you know that. Besides, you'll be there."

Dani shook her head, her mind racing to link the facts together faster. She needed to find anyone who had contact with Gideon Kinkead in the line of duty who might believe they'd been wronged. The facts had to be there. She just needed to dig deep enough to find them.

"Take the effing gun. I'm dropping you off and I'm going to the station. I have to get a computer search in progress, and I don't think I can do it remotely because I'm not yet sure what or who I'm looking for."

Nicolle dangled the keys to Dani's truck from her fingers. "Do you want help?"

Glancing at the clock, Dani shook her head. "Go to the hospital. Take the gun."

Nicolle got that stubborn line between her eyebrows and shook her head. "I have Noah. Jake's there, and who knows how many off-duty officers from how many jurisdictions. There are probably more guns than patients there. I'll be fine. When Noah's off-duty, we'll come and help you. Do you want us to find Gid and bring him too?"

Dani nodded, though she didn't say what she knew. Gid stood guard at that hospital too, and more than anything, she wished she could slip inside and into his arms, even if just for a little while. She needed to tell him how she felt and clear the air between them. But she had a job to do, and the sooner she got to it, the faster she could catch the guy trying to kill the man she loved.

Gid leaned into a corner of the waiting room, intentionally trying to act like he was watching nothing when he tried to see everything. He glared at each person entering the space as if that would alone send them on their way, and in more cases than not, it was enough. His brother wouldn't be very busy tonight, not while he had anything to say about it.

He hadn't been able to convince Noah to stay home, and that pissed him off. It had been a long week, with Danielle bound to Nicolle like they were conjoined twins instead of identical. All four of them were on edge, and Gid missed Danielle like hell. But his brother's desire to stay in public and draw out the bad guy won out over his lovesick need. Besides, Gid knew he was fighting a losing battle in the love department, because Danielle didn't believe in him.

He crossed the waiting room to a counter where Noah made notations in a tablet computer. The large form of Marcus Dawson appeared at his right shoulder, and Jake came up behind Gid.

"I can't believe Rage hasn't made a move," Gid said, letting his frustration show in his tone. Screw them if they wanted to argue about that.

He played with the cell phone in his pocket, thinking about calling Danielle to ask if she was having any better results. He had so much to say to her, but both of them were distracted with these screw-ups. The waiting, not knowing if she'd accept things as they stood or would kick him to the curb, wore on him more than standing in this room. If only Noah would have the good sense to go back into hiding, and Nicolle did the same, he and Danielle might find time to talk.

Who was he kidding? He didn't want to talk, not right away. He wanted to strip her naked and make love to her in the best way he could. He'd tell her he loved her and they could see where things went from there.

When Jake said, "Relax, he'll show eventually," Gid focused back in on the tight group of men. He tried to offer an accommodating nod when Jake and Marcus both threw in their opinions that this was the best way to catch Rage. As they walked away, Gid could only reflect on how it might be easy for them to say. Noah wasn't their only brother.

He turned to that man who stood with deceptive calm in his sparkling white doctor's coat. Noah wouldn't need his fists or his kicks. Gid was happy to take on that responsibility, though he doubted even a doctor with Noah's talents would be able to put the result back together again once Gid was through with him.

He sighed in resignation. Who was he fooling? He wasn't able to help, and he might as well be a picture on the wall for all of the good he could do.

"You're doing everything you can, Gid. I know that. And while Nicolle is chafing under Danielle's constant surveillance, we understand it's for the best. Eventually, both guys will show. And we'll be ready for them." Noah tipped up on to the balls of his feet in an aggressive posture.

"You should get back to work, Noah. You're a good doctor, and it's clear everyone here respects you. I understand why you need to be here, more than you realize." Gid saw the surprise on his brother's face before he turned and walked toward the outer door. He couldn't help wondering if he'd ever command that kind of respect, or if he'd ever return to the profession he loved as much as Noah did medicine.

"Gid, wait up." Noah put a restraining hand on his arm. The honesty in his open gaze was enough to stop Gid in his tracks. "Thank you for everything you're doing. I know this costs you, and I appreciate it. There's no one I'd rather have at my side than my big brother."

Gid felt his eyes warm, refusing to think tears formed there. He wasn't sure how to respond. Noah didn't seem to expect anything, and when the outer door slid open, his attention was distracted by the entrance of a woman who brought a big smile to his face.

Searching the emptiness behind Nicolle, Gid wished it brought his deliverance too. His brother wrapped his arms around the twin who was so different from her sister. Gid loved every one of Danielle's differences. He loved the whole package, and it was time to tell her that. When Noah was done for the night, Gid would make sure he had a ride to wherever Danielle was. Where she was, he needed to be too.

When the receptionist approached Noah and Nicolle, it broke up the tender moment. Gid eyed them with a newfound respect. They'd faced enormous tragedies in their respective pasts, but they'd done a better job of surviving them than he and Danielle had. Danielle never forgave herself for what she thought was her fault in her twin's suffering. Gid would never forget the screams of death. Even walking down the hallway in full sight of hospital staff, Noah and Nicolle's hands remained linked, and indulgent smiles followed them.

Jake's voice sounded over his shoulder. "They make a good-looking couple."

Gid nodded, keeping his eyes on his brother until he turned a corner out of sight.

A hand squeezed his shoulder, and he turned to look into Jake's amused face. "Now, about you and Danielle. Do I need to ask your intentions?"

Gid spluttered out an expletive that had Jake's grin widening.

"Dude, you know I'm asking because I've seen you in action. You know, a new woman every time you go out hunting and none of them lasting more than a night. I have to hand it to you, I've never heard a bad word said against you. But you know, this is Trajan we're talking about. I don't want to see her hurt."

Gid bristled at the unsaid, that he would be so careless. "What's it to you?" He took a step forward and shook off Jake's hand.

The deputy shrugged. "She's good people, that what. She's worked harder than anyone else to earn her stripes. She was the only woman with the balls to shatter the glass ceiling in the department, and that's saying a lot, since we've had some real ball-busters moving up the ranks. Besides that, though, she cares about every single person, not only those under her command but throughout the department, the community and the county. Hell, she even cares about the bad guys."

Yeah, Gid could easily see that. She even cared about him, or at least, she said she did. Her feelings might not come close to what he felt, but that was something he'd accept if he had to. He could change her mind about a lot of things, if she only gave him that chance.

The disruptive jingle of plastic badges shook him out of his thoughts as the young receptionist hustled up to them with big worry on her face. "Ah, deputy? We need your help. Dr. K's given the security assistance call."

Jake was already moving down the hall. Gid didn't know what kind of call they were talking about, but if it involved Noah, he was going too.

The deputy stopped long enough to put out a hand, halting Gid's progress. "No, you stay here. Better yet, go back to the staff lounge."

Gid shook his head, ready to argue, when two other deputies in civilian clothes passed him by and drew up next to Jake. The three of them conferred in low tones as they rushed down the hall on soft footsteps.

Damned if he was going to wait around like some wimp. He couldn't go as fast as they did without sounding like an elephant, but he could wander more slowly in their direction.

Sticking his head around a corner, he saw the officers surrounding the closed doorway of an exam room. He was too far away to hear Jake's words, but in quick succession, he heard his brother's faint voice from the inside. The deputies exchanged hand signals and raised weapons, and Gid wanted to scream at them to be careful because Noah was in there. One of them eased toward the door and paused with a hand on its shiny handle.

A scuffle and gunfire sounded from inside the exam room, and at the other end of the corridor, Dr. Dawson came barreling toward them like the former all-pro linebacker he'd been. Sudden pandemonium made Gid shoot forward. A deputy kicked open the door and Gid didn't wait, diving in after the big doctor and the officers.

What he saw in a quick glance made him stop breathing. He couldn't, not when Noah was bleeding on the floor. It took him a moment to process the fact that it wasn't a lot of blood, but that didn't mean anything. Then he saw the gun lying a few feet away, just out of reach from where Jake had a be-jeweled man pinned. He recognized Rage from his numerous mug shots.

Gid reached down and picked up the gun with two fingers, holding it away from his body and pointed toward the floor. It made him sick to see it. He fought the urge to drop it in the container with soiled bed linens, hoping someone with authority would take it from him and quickly, before he lost the battle with his disgust.

In the next heartbeat, Nicolle was by Noah's side. Gid wasn't sure where she had come from, but she didn't look like she would be pried away from his brother any time soon. The two of them consoled each other as Marcus checked over a laughing Noah. Gid sank back against the wall as Rage was escorted out of the exam room without gentleness. A young woman under a bed babbled and cried, and more medical staff and deputies poured in than the room could handle. One of the cops took the offending gun from him with a cursory nod of thanks.

Gid backed out, not because he didn't want to see Noah, but because there was nothing for him to do. His brother had taken care of business all by himself, and he deserved the circle of attention and praise being heaped on him, along with the good-natured lectures about taking things into his own hands. There would be time for Gid to add his admonitions later.

A new commotion near the waiting area drew his attention, and Danielle turned the corner at a run. Her feet scrambled to a quick halt that would probably leave skid marks on the smooth floor, but Gid wasn't checking that now. He stared at her, realizing she had a look of panic on her face. He smiled at her in what he hoped was a reassuring way, and she started moving again, more slowly this time, until she stood in front of him.

"They're okay," he said, stroking escaped hair back from her face. Then he tugged on the braid down her back to bring her closer.

"Oh thank god," she said, exhaling hard enough for him to feel a breeze over his skin. The next moment, she grabbed his face and locked her lips to his with that familiar feeling of a torch lighting. A second later, she was gone.

Chapter 28

Statements took time. A review of the hospital's security procedures would be necessary, but with Rage in custody, it could wait until morning. Reports, however, were best done while information was fresh. Dani had a difficult time feeling sympathy when she and Jake took an initial statement from Rage.

"I'm gonna sue his ass, that's what I'm going to do. Both their asses."

Dani regarded the man handcuffed to the chair long enough to let him know she wasn't buying his crap. "That will be something you will need to discuss with your attorney, Rage. Or should I say, Mr. Dakota. I understand you talked to your legal counsel. I'm sure he'll be interested in the report about you brandishing a gun in a hospital and threatening to kill everyone in the room. When is he scheduled to arrive?"

Rage snarled and jerked on the handcuffs. "Bastard. Said he can't represent me up here. I'm gonna sue his ass too. I been supporting his sorry-assed business for years now, and what does he do? He's not representing me in my hour of need."

Dani bit back a smile. She would bet a month's pay the attorney was happy Rage was in another jurisdiction, not that this would matter for long. Murders trumped attempted murders as long as the case was solid, so Rage would soon be remanded to the custody of the Los Angeles Sheriff's Department. Justice would be served, even if it wasn't happening on her turf.

"Tell me about the fires," she said.

Rage frowned at her, sitting still for the first time since she began her interrogation. "Fires?"

Hairs on her arms stood up. The man looked puzzled, and she didn't think he was hiding anything.

"Why did you start the fires?"

Rage scoffed and shook his head. "Can't pin those on me. I didn't start no fires. I don't even like matches. If you looking at me for those, you be missing the point."

That was what she was afraid of.

The conversations with the injured woman, Nicolle and Noah took longer. The young woman had been dragged north from LA, and she couldn't wait to disappear before Rage could find her again. Jake interviewed Nicolle and Danielle took Noah, and their preliminary statements were clear and concise. If either one of them were the worse for their experience, they did a damned fine job of hiding it.

"One down, one to go," commented Noah, when Dani was finished with her questions.

She gave him a strained smile. "You were pretty impressive in there, Dr. Kinkead. You were also lucky. That could have gone either way, and someone would have been digging bullets out of you or Nicolle or both. Do me a favor and leave the vigilante justice to the experts."

Noah merely nodded but didn't reply. She doubted Jake would have much better luck convincing Nicolle to back down. Dani wasn't sure what scared her more. If they succeeded, it meant her twin would come face to face with her attacker. If they failed, well, that didn't bear thinking about.

When Dani hustled Nicolle and Noah toward the outer doors hours later with instructions to go home and rest, the sun was shining high in the sky. It looked too bright outside, too pretty a day for so much drama. She sensed eyes on her and turned to find Gideon leaning against the hospital's shadowed wall, staring at her with hunger in his gaze.

She felt it like a gravitational pull. It wasn't unlike what she felt when she looked at him. Would that be enough to keep him around? She doubted it, but she was willing to give it a try.

As she walked toward him, she felt the weariness flow through her. Part relief that at least one of their problems was now answered. Worry about her sister came next, because they still didn't have Mitchell. An arsonist was still out there.

And then there was Gideon.

He had stepped away from the wall into a more private corner out of sight of the main entrance by the time she reached him. When he extended his arms, she walked into them without hesitation. Putting her head on his shoulder was the most natural motion in the world, and she let him embrace her without speaking.

Gid stroked her back, her hair, and her face, and still, she didn't want to move. She cursed the body armor that made it impossible for her to feel the nuance in each touch of his fingers. She wanted nothing more than to forget their situation and let the warmth of this perfect moment wash over her. But she had work to do. In the brief time she'd had before the hospital attack, she hadn't found any obvious links. She needed to make something break in the investigation, because until she did, Gideon remained in danger.

Pushing back against his arms, she looked into his face. "I have to go to headquarters." She heard the reluctance and longing in her voice, and by the frown on Gideon's face, he did too.

"How many hours has it been since you slept? You need to rest, or you can't operate at full speed. Come on, I'll take you home."

She wanted that, but she couldn't. Still, she also couldn't help asking, "Which home?"

Gid shrugged, already walking them toward a patrol unit parked in a loading zone. "Whichever one Noah and Nicolle aren't using. I'm not picky about that."

She nodded and stopped as they reached the unit's driver door. "I do have to go in, Gideon. Believe me when I say I would rather be anywhere and be there with you. But I have work to do, and the sooner I get it done, the sooner we can both move on."

A shot of worry crossed his face as he nodded. "Okay, I'll go with you."

She shook her head before he even finished. "No, go home. I'll drop you off at my place and give you the keys. Nicolle is at Noah's, so you'll have the place to yourself. You rest. You still need to heal, Firefighter Kinkead, and that's an order I'm sure your boss would back up."

He shook his head with a stubborn impatience. "No, I go where you go until this ends, and then we figure out the rest." He hesitated and glanced around as if checking to see if they were being overheard, then opened his mouth to add something.

The mic at her shoulder squelched with her call identification before he could speak, and Gid frowned at the interruption. "Don't get that," he said.

She smiled at the idea even as she keyed the mic and listened to Dispatch's response. Affirming her return, she stepped back from Gid. "I'm going in."

He stepped around the unit and was in the front seat before she had a chance to argue. "Then I'm going too."

She was going to upbraid him for the sentiment but she was only human. She kind of liked the idea that he wanted to be near her. She liked it a lot, and that should worry her even more.

>>>>>

In the end, he was glad he'd insisted. He told himself that, as boredom wore away what energy he had left. His perch on the credenza in the corner of Danielle's office wasn't exactly comfortable. He'd slept on rocks that were softer.

But he had to admit he loved seeing her in her element. Deputies and admin staff came and went, and Danielle efficiently dealt with each issue. Her dry humor showed now and then, something he hadn't had a lot of opportunity to see. She wasn't the badass she wanted him to believe she was. In fact, watching her like this made him like her more, and that in turn made his love grow.

He stood and stretched, and noted with some enjoyment the fast hungry glance Danielle took as he did so. Let her look. He'd give her a hell of a lot more to look at and soon, he hoped. She licked her lips with a quick fidget in her chair as she returned to her examination of a report, and he had the fleeting thought that maybe no one would notice if he closed her door for a while.

She snapped shut a folder and tossed it into a tray on her desk. "Ok, LA is working on transport for Rage. Everyone's statements for the incident are filed. I have deputies doing drive-bys on Noah's house, just to make sure nothing else goes to hell overnight. I'll check on them in the morning and make sure they're okay. Nicolle needs to stay away from work until we catch Mitchell."

"You think she'll do that?" Gideon slid off the credenza and rounded the desk to stand behind her. His hands went to her neck and he rubbed at tension that felt like steel bars under his hands.

"Hell, that feels good. And to answer your question, she'd better. I'm older and I know better."

Gid laughed at the comment, earning him a frown over Danielle's shoulder. In response to her dark look, he said, "I don't know about your sibling, but mine hasn't listened to that line for years. We have age between us, unlike you and Nicolle. I believe your sister will do what she wants, and I for one think she has a lot of sense between her ears. She'll be careful. I've seen her in action, and she can take care of herself. Plus, she'll have Noah."

Danielle sighed and leaned into his hands, and if the occasional passerby glanced into the office with curiosity, she must not have noticed it. When her head tilted back, he noted her closed eyes. Underneath them, dark shadows made her skin look ghostly in comparison.

He pulled her chair back abruptly. If this dedicated woman would not take care of herself, it was up to him to take care of her. That meant home, dinner and bed. A glance outside told him they were just shy of sunset on another long day.

He put his hands under her arms and hoisted her out of the chair, happy to hear her surprised squeak. "What are you doing?"

"Taking you home, feeding you, and making sure you sleep. Come on, Lieutenant, even the big bad boss needs to rest now and then." When she opened her mouth to argue, he added, "You won't be any good to Nicolle if your brain is fogged with fatigue."

She snapped her mouth shut and scowled as if she saw the wisdom of his words but didn't like them. "Give me a minute to make sure I'm covered, and then I'll buy what you're selling, Kinkead."

He made a big show of looking at his watch as she marched toward the door. "Sixty seconds, Trajan, and I'm counting."

He knew he didn't imagine the quick flash of a grin she hid crossing the threshold, and that made him even more eager to get them someplace alone so he could share everything that was on his mind.

Chapter 29

Dani didn't complain when Gideon insisted on ordering delivery Chinese for dinner. She dozed as they waited while he rubbed her feet. She wanted to be awake to appreciate the small circles and deep presses of his thumbs on the soles, but she was beyond exhausted. She barely noticed the doorbell when food arrived, and it was only because Gideon pushed a plate under her nose that she roused enough to take a bite. That single taste made her realize she hadn't eaten well over the past couple of days, and she was ravenous.

She polished off two full servings and was reaching for a refill when she realized Gideon grinned at her. His arm extended across the back of the couch, his leg was propped on the coffee table, and he had every appearance of a man at ease and loving life.

The thought flashed across her mind so fast, she didn't have time to push it away. She wanted everything with him. Even when he returned to the fire line once his leg was healed, she wanted a chance to build a future. She clearly could not do that if there was any chance he was their arsonist.

"What are you thinking?" His soft question matched the quizzical expression and the half-smile still lingering on his face.

Her hand fell back from the takeout carton and without meeting his eyes, she wiped each finger on a paper napkin until it shined clean. "Nothing. Just tired, I guess."

A finger tipped her chin up until her eyes were forced to meet his. Blue flashed with humor and curiosity and something else. She didn't want to analyze it. In fact, she didn't want to think at all.

"Take me to bed, Gideon."

If the request startled him, he didn't show it. He stood without hesitation and extended his hands to her. Glad that on this level at least they were on even ground, she allowed him to pull her up, and when his arm came around her waist, she did the same. The brush of his lips in her hair had her closing her eyes with longing.

He had to be innocent.

"You need to sleep, and honestly, so do I. I'll tuck you in and make sure you're snoring, and I'll get settled on the couch."

She tightened her grip on him. "No you don't. You're with me tonight, Kinkead, and that's an official command from a sheriff's lieutenant. We're going to bed together."

Gideon stopped at her bedroom door and turned her to face him. She looked into his eyes, and his serious gaze almost made things worse. "I have something to tell you first."

She put her fingers over his lips, willing him to be quiet. If he was going to confess anything, she'd rather he wait until morning. She wanted one more night with him. He pushed her hand away and wrapped his fingers around her wrists so she couldn't block his words again.

"I have something to confess to you and I want to say it now, so you can tell me if it changes things."

She closed her eyes, because she didn't want him to see the desperate feeling growing inside her. Her emotional defenses were exhausted, much more so than her body. She didn't want him to tell her his truths. She thought fleetingly of calling Nicolle and asking her to come over, because then Gideon could turn himself in to the fire investigator instead of the cop who loved him. She couldn't bring herself to admit out loud that she might love a bad guy.

"Don't say anything, Gideon. Once you say things, you can't take them back. Once I hear them, I have to act on them. I hope you understand."

When he didn't respond, she opened her eyes to see him watching her with disappointment. "I'm willing to risk it," he said, keeping his hold on her wrists.

"I could throw you across this house," she responded, making a move to break his hold. When he released her without hesitation, she wondered what move he planned to make next.

He could be an arsonist, her inner conscience whispered. He looked torn all of a sudden, and he glanced at the bed and then back at her. "I'd rather throw you on the bed and curl up around you, if you don't mind. I guess everything else can wait."

She nodded, willing the tears to fade. She must be more exhausted than she thought, because she almost gave in and told Gideon what was really on her mind. She loved him, and she was worried his secrets would tear them apart.

Every dream he had that night involved pillars of fire and the high-pitched screams of a child. He woke more than once, sweating through the briefs and t-shirt he'd left on at Danielle's request. She slept like the dead through his nightmares, thank god, and lay curled in a ball with her t-shirt hiked up enough to show the curve of a breast. He reminded himself she needed her sleep, much as he'd like to peel that shirt off the rest of the way and wake her with sensuous kisses.

She hadn't let him say it last night. By the time they lay in bed, she was already half-asleep, and he wanted her conscious and coherent when he told her he loved her.

He'd never said it out loud in his adult life, not to his family and certainly not to a woman. This would be a first and he wasn't sure how to handle it. Blurting it out without any preamble seemed crass and cowardly, but Danielle wasn't making it easy. Even if he stuttered the words, they could figure out what happened next.

She might laugh. She might cry, which would be worse. She might not care at all, regarding him with undisguised pity. Danielle Trajan was a woman who didn't appear to need anyone or anything to make her complete, and that included him.

Unable to watch any longer without touching her, he slipped off his soggy clothes and wrapped his body around her tight ball. She murmured something in her sleep but didn't change position, only nestling against him in deeper breathing. He let that tempo fill him, matching his breaths to hers. Her hair smelled like wildflowers under his cheek, and the soft curves he craved filled his arms. His mind emptied of any conscious thought, and with that, he dozed.

He wasn't sure how long they lay like that, cocooned in the darkness and warmth. He did not dream again, which was a relief. Contentment flowed through him like a babbling brook, and he let his mind idle on the idea that this was how it could be, and not just tonight.

"I love you." Despite his best intentions to make a big deal out of it, he whispered the words. Saying them often might make it easier when she finally heard him. "I love you."

Her sigh carried no coherent response. He pulled her tighter into his body, feeling the stirrings of emotional desire that never went away completely when he was around her. Practice would not be a bad thing. He tried the words again. "I love you." The hair at her ear tickled his nose.

This time, she murmured a response, though he couldn't tell what it was. Leaning over her, he tried to listen harder. Nothing more came from her lips.

She was heart attack beautiful. If he could stare at her like this for the next six dozen years, it wouldn't be long enough. Brushing hair back from her forehead, he noted the creases of a frown even in sleep. She worried too much and about everyone but herself. That was okay. He would be here to take care of her.

"I love you," he said again, with more conviction this time.

"It doesn't matter." Her quiet reply made the room seem darker.

Against his better judgment, he had to argue his case. "It does matter. I love you."

Her eyes stayed closed but her breathing changed. The depth of the crease between her eyebrows deepened to a chasm. "It doesn't matter what you did. If you started those fires, it doesn't matter, because I still love you."

Then her breathing deepened again, and she fell silent. If she was talking in her sleep, Gideon bet she had no idea what she revealed. In her eyes, he was still a suspect. She said she loved him, which should make him elated. Instead, he felt like he couldn't inhale, like after the explosion. Only this felt a hell of a lot worse.

Dani could play possum with the best of them, but this time it was a thousand times more difficult. His words had come to her dream-like in sleep. She thought they were a dream, until she felt his hard body press against her back and his heat penetrated every nerve ending like an electric current. When he said it again, she responded without considering her actions.

He hadn't said anything since. Did he cuddle in closer, or was that her hopeful imagination? She tried to imitate a dead sleep, and the feel of him made her long for anything but.

He had to be innocent.

She wanted to look at the clock. She wanted to turn to face him and kiss him until neither one of them were thinking anymore. She wanted him to say it again, so she could respond and explain.

She loved him.

"What the hell?"

His mumbled words came without warning. His body pressed against hers and she felt the stirring of something growing rigid against her bottom. Even if he hadn't responded, he wanted her, and for that, she was grateful. She could make up something about her words in the light of morning, or feign a dream she no longer remembered. But for now, in these dark hours, she could pretend they were two normal people who wanted each other.

She stretched, and his arms dropped away from her. The thin light coming through her blinds was enough for her to see his confused expression when she rolled over to look at him. He wasn't looking at her, though, but rather, down at himself. She followed his eyes and couldn't help but smile.

He was hard and ready, and even in the shadows, she could read the pulsing throb under skin she wanted inside her more than anything else. The morning would bring its challenges and risks, but for tonight, they had everything in each other.

She stroked his face, bringing his attention to her. Confused amazement filled his features before his gaze turned as ravenous as she felt. Tracing his lips, she wanted nothing so much as Gideon on her, kissing her, trailing his talented hands over her, and pumping into her as if they had no past.

"I don't understand," he said, though he shook his head as if it didn't matter. His gaze moved down her body, and she stretched further, allowing the t-shirt to ride up and show as much skin as possible. A devilish look came to his face as he reached out a hand to caress her belly. He reached higher, sweeping off the shirt, and his fingers trailed back to the waistband of her panties.

"Condom?"

She lifted her chin to the night table, and he reached back to it and opened the drawer, rummaging inside. The telltale crinkle of foil made her smile again, but she didn't have time to enjoy the moment, because he was on her like a desperate man.

The heat coming off him and into her made her think of the picture she had in her mind, Gideon walking into a wall of fire sane men would run from in a panic. When his lips closed on a nipple and tugged, she forgot about the dream, and let that fire engulf her.

The need to be inside her rose above all else, but one thing pounded through Gideon as hard as he wanted to pound into Danielle.

He loved her, and she said she loved him, though the conditions of the rest of it were cloudy in his brain. He wanted to please her, make her come like the explosion he knew he could bring her, but it had been too long, and he wanted her so much.

"Hurry," she said, the panting in her voice making his blood boil hotter.

"I will. Give me time. I want to take care of you." He tried to slide down further, to please that core of her in a way he knew would make her wild. She seemed to have other ideas as she grabbed his hair and yanked.

"Now, inside me. I can't wait, and by the feel of it, neither can you."

Who was he to do anything but obey? He drove into her in one stroke that had him seeing stars. Danielle gave a triumphant cry as she began to move in rhythm with him.

God, he had missed this, but then, he hadn't ever had anything like this before. No experience in his past prepared him for being lost inside Danielle, sharing a passion that was both physical and emotional. He'd never been one with another person. With each deeper stroke, he vowed he'd make it last.

But she had different expectations. She lifted her hips to meet each of his thrusts until coherent thoughts shattered in his brain. He knew he chanted words, repeating the mantra again and again.

"I love you. I love you. I love you."

He couldn't hear past the roar like flames crackling in his mind. When the fire consumed him, he yelled her name, and over the explosion, he wasn't sure if she screamed or if it was him.

Chapter 30

She could tell it was daylight out, but the probable time was a mystery in the darkness of her bedroom. Dani felt soothing warmth and wanted to crawl deeper inside it. She pushed harder against the wall of muscle and when her hand settled, she felt the beat of a heart under her fingers.

Gideon. Who knew he had that much passion in him? For that matter, who knew she had it in her? No one ever made her feel like this. She didn't want to move, except to have him again and again. That should bug her, but instead, she felt oddly content and more than a little shy.

He loved her.

She trailed her hand down his body, following the line of hair down his chest and belly to his very happy morning greeting. Gideon was erect, hard, and throbbing in her hand, and she couldn't help her gentle strokes becoming more firm as her blood sped up in anticipation.

His hand came down and closed on her wrist like a vise. "Stop. It's too much."

He pulled her hand away and rested it on his hip, holding it there. She was sure she could break his grip, but this wasn't about a power struggle. His voice sounded strained and angry.

"What's wrong?" She wished she could see his face, read his eyes and figure out why he suddenly seemed pissed with her.

"You don't understand." He spat out the words and rolled away from her, ending up on his stomach with his face buried in a twisted pillow.

She felt the sting of his rejection, and sat up to reach for a blanket to cover herself. This wasn't the kind of discussion one had naked. But Gideon's body lay on the bunched fabric, and despite her tugs, he didn't move to help her.

She tried to locate her shirt. She had a vague recollection of it disappearing into the shadows, but where to, she wasn't sure.

"Did you mean it, any of it?"

Gideon's muffled words made her freeze. He had heard her last night. She wondered if she'd spoken out loud, since he hadn't commented further. More to the point, she wasn't sure she had heard him correctly either. It might have been her desire speaking.

Feigning nonchalance seemed the cautious approach. "Any of what?"

He bolted up and sat facing her, anger making his expression harsh. "What you said. Did you mean it?"

"Well, did you?" Her breathing labored as if an elephant sat on her chest. Gideon seemed like he was not faring any better.

"You don't understand," he shouted.

"So make me understand," she shouted back.

They fell silent, staring at each other and breathing in gasps like they'd run a marathon flat out.

He looked away just as she was going to. She wasn't sure what they were fighting about, but she didn't want it to come between them. Summoning thoughts of that happy feeing she'd held only moments ago didn't make things easier.

"It began with the fire," he said, his voice quiet. He didn't seem to be staring at anything in particular, his eyes unfocused and his face to the empty wall.

When he didn't say anything else, she found herself drawing closer to him without touching. "With the explosion?"

He shook his head. "Last summer. The cabin where the people died."

Dani forced slow breaths in, exhaling just as slowly. If he was about to tell her what she thought he was going to, she wanted to cover her ears and say nonsense words so she couldn't hear any of it, as she had as a kid. But she was a cop now, and if he was about to admit to a crime, she had to listen.

He shook his head again, closing his eyes. Agony made his features contort, and she wanted to run her hands across his face and tell him it would be okay. But she couldn't. Sitting back on her heels, she tried to focus on his words and demeanor.

"I still dream about them. The old man, so proud and disdainful. The little girl, her eyes wide and without fear, as if she thought what the man said must be true. She would not leave him, and his hand wrapped around hers so tightly, I doubt I could have pried them apart."

Dani leaned closer despite her professional intentions, watching the play of emotions on Gideon's face. His eyes dropped closed, with strain drawing thick lines from the corners. The hollows of his cheeks dipped into more pronounced shadows under a fuzz of day-old beard. Deep lines radiated from the thin tight line of his lips. She wanted to see those lips full and laughing, those eyes shining with good humor and his face full of life once more.

"The old man was convinced the fire would not touch them, and nothing I could say or do would change his mind. I tried luring them outside, hoping the sight of the wall of flames would send the message I obviously couldn't get through. I backed to the door, stepping on the porch, and noticed the roof was on fire. I tried to go back in to grab them, but a rafter collapsed across the opening. Bars covered other windows, and I couldn't break them free. The last thing I heard before I had to back off with the fire bearing down on us was the girl's screams."

Dani waited for him to say more, but he stayed silent. She swiped at her face, feeling tears she hadn't realized were falling. Gideon's expression stayed pained and broken, as if he lived it all over again. More than anything, she wanted to make it right for him, but she was afraid there was more she needed to hear.

"I still hear those screams in my nightmares," Gideon said.

"Do you have those dreams often?" Her voice sounded as husky and troubled as his to her ears.

He nodded.

"When did you last dream about that fire?"

He opened his eyes then and planted a tortured look on her that was cutting in its despair. "Last night. I'm surprised you didn't hear me. Noah tells me I scream when I'm in it."

She had been dead to the world, driven to deep dreamless sleep because exhaustion had overcome her. "I didn't hear you. Maybe you don't always scream."

He gave a sharp nod but didn't seem convinced. Then he shook his head. "Anyway, since then, nothing happens. You know, in the equipment department. Until this morning."

She wasn't tracking. Her perplexed expression must have told him that.

He rose off the bed and paced the room. "In the sex department. I could not achieve or maintain an erection, as the television ad says. I keep the ladies happy, but it's a one-sided situation, if you get my drift."

Dani rubbed her forehead, trying to sort things out. She didn't expect this conversation. She focused in on the one fact she could verify.

Creeping across the bed on hands and knees, she smiled at him in sudden clarity. "But you performed this morning, and with great vigor, I might add." She felt almost giddy, thinking about their wanton behavior.

Gideon shot her a new look, and she recognized the heat in his eyes. An answering rise ignited her, and she wondered what the next round would be like. Fast and hard, or slow and tender? She'd vote for either one.

Difficult reality burst through the bliss, and she remembered he hadn't said anything about the arsons since that cabin fire.

"That's the thing, Danielle. I haven't been in action like that since the cabin. It was as if my body shut down, and while I was happy pleasing the ladies, I could never encourage them to return the favor. You do something to me, in here," he tapped the center of his chest, "and it changes everything."

So this is where they would say it, she assumed. The shared vows of being in love. The sudden flighty birds in her belly flapped their wings as if the devil himself chased them. Love.

But Gideon didn't look pleased about it. He eyed her closely, and she wasn't sure what to make of the glare that followed. "You still think I could have started the fires," he said, an accusing tone in his voice.

She collapsed back on her heels and wondered how she could salvage the situation. "I'm a cop, Gideon. I'm trained to explore the angles and avoid tunnel vision. Thinking you know before the evidence is in creates bad assumptions. Stop looking too early, and the real bad guy gets away. Wait to act until it's too late, and you have the same outcome. I have to follow the evidence."

He regarded her like she had grown horns in the last few minutes. "What ever happened to innocent until proven guilty?"

She turned away because she couldn't stand the censure in his eyes. If their positions were reversed, she suspected he'd have an easier time giving her leeway. "That applies to the legal system, not to law enforcement. We have to be suspicious of everyone," she said. She pleated and unpleated the messed top sheet, asking herself why she hadn't kept her concerns to herself.

A rustle of movement drew her attention to Gideon's backside. He bent to gather his clothes without bothering to cover himself, and she had to admit, the view was spectacular. When he turned, she saw he was still aroused, probably hard as a baton, and she longed for the ability to turn back the clock. If she'd just kept her mouth shut, they'd be engaging in something other than the brutal staring match currently underway.

He glanced down at himself, and a hiss escaped his lips. When he met her eyes once more, the expression on his face held disgust and yearning. "Yeah, despite all of this, I still want you and I want you bad. Isn't that just a fucker? But while my body might be into it, my head and my heart have someplace else to be."

He turned and stormed out of the bedroom, and she scrambled for the closet and grabbed a robe. It happened to be a fuzzy winter one, but she didn't care. She couldn't continue to discuss this naked, and she didn't want to waste precious time finding something more appropriate.

He was already dressed by the time she made it into the living room. He was pulling a boot on the uninjured foot, the walking cast already wrapped in place on the other. When he stood, she swore he looked taller. He watched her steadily without a shred of emotion in those smoldering blue eyes. Then he tipped an imaginary hat and unlocked the front door.

"Where are you going?" Great, now she sounded like a melodramatic rom-com heroine.

He paused with his hand on the handle, but didn't turn. "I'm leaving. I think it's best if we don't see each other again. I wouldn't want to be accused of swaying your objectivity while the investigation is in progress." He shrugged as if the outcome made no difference to him.

When she couldn't come up with anything to say, she thought about grabbing his arm and begging him to talk it through with her. But she had more pride than that. She had laid down the rules, so she had to be strong enough to live by them.

"Can I give you a ride somewhere?"

He shook his head, opening the door. Outside, birds sang like it was just another day. "I'll walk, and if that's too much, I'll hitchhike." He shrugged as if he didn't care one way or the other.

She took a step forward, willing him to turn and look at her. She wanted to see his face, to read his eyes and find out if she'd pushed him too far. But he didn't turn, so she said, "Where will you go?"

Another shrug as he said, "It doesn't matter, not unless you have another fire start in the next few hours. Then I'm sure you'll verify my whereabouts." He stepped on the porch with the words, and in the time it took her to cover the distance to the front door, he was halfway down the drive. He made quick time, his gait stilted but rapid, and before she could figure out how to keep him, he was around the curve of the road and out of sight.

His leg ached like a bitch, probably because he'd decided walking would be a good way to burn off the hurt in his heart. So far, his heart still hurt, and his leg now matched it.

He thought about calling Noah, but he didn't want to disturb him. His brother would be having much better luck in the love department than Gid knew he'd ever have. The one woman who kept him wanting to come back for more didn't believe in him. Wasn't that a fuck and a half?

His newfound ability to make love to her wasn't what made him want her even more. It was because she had scruples and principles and values and all of those other things that spoke about her character. He admired that in her, even as he hated that she didn't believe in him. If he was honest with himself, he could see her point of view. He hadn't exactly been forthcoming right off the bat. Secrets, too many of them, had created the barricade between them.

By the time he'd crossed town and climbed its hills to Noah's house, he wondered if he'd done the right thing in leaving without hashing it out. He could have given Danielle the benefit of a doubt. He knew she must be torn between duty and attraction. That didn't make it more palatable. He could ask Nicolle her opinion, but he didn't want her interceding on his behalf. He and Danielle needed to work this out on their own.

The minivan stood in Noah's driveway, and Gid hesitated. He didn't want to discuss this yet, not with his brother and certainly not with Nicolle. But he had nowhere else to go, and it only made sense to rest here. He knocked and waited, hearing nothing from inside. He knocked again as he used his key, calling out for his brother as he swung the door open slowly.

The interior had a hollow empty feel, and no one responded to his second shout. It only took a couple of minutes to determine the house was unoccupied. Wherever Noah was, he hadn't driven. It didn't take long to figure out he must be with Nicolle. Even in his depressed frame of mind, Gid had to give his brother a silent hurrah.

He dragged himself down the hall into the bathroom. The shower couldn't wash away his disappointment. By the time he collapsed face first on Elena's little bed, Gid decided Danielle was right. Compromising personal values never felt good. He fell into a chaotic sleep, dreaming of screams and fire and Danielle snapping steel cuffs on him while she laughed.

>>>>>

Dani texted Nicolle more than once, only to erase the messages before hitting the send button. She wanted to talk with her twin, but she didn't want to burden her. What the hell, she might as well go to work, even though she wasn't on shift today.

It took her longer than usual to get ready. Every time she looked at any part of the house, she saw Gideon in her mind's eye. The bed was a shambles, but she couldn't bear to make it. It still smelled like him, and it scented the air with them making love. If she had to wash her face and calm her reddened eyes a few times in the process of getting ready, who would be there to judge her?

The judgment on Gideon's face had been enough, and she might never forget his parting look. When this was over, she would make it up to him. She knew in her heart that he had to be innocent, but the cop in her had to be sure.

Who the hell was she fooling? When this was over, Gideon would have nothing to do with her, and it was her own damned fault. She wouldn't blame him, not one iota. Her chaotic thoughts ran in an endless loop over the same jagged ground.

The station seemed oddly silent as she walked in, and she could have been imagining the curious glances in the squad room. No one said much of anything to her, and she fell into her chair and pulled a huge stack of paperwork toward her. Might as well make use of the day. Here, at least, she knew what she was doing. She submerged herself in the tedious task of catching up on reviews and reports without anyone asking her why she was there.

Chapter 31

"What's going on, Gid?"

Gid shrugged in reply to his brother. It was the same question Noah asked each day for the last four, and yet he didn't seem frustrated by the lack of a concrete reply. Noah seemed more than happy to have him underfoot, but Gid found a way to make himself scarce each evening so that the lovebirds had a nest to call their own. If Nicolle eyed him with sympathy and seemed inclined to discuss something with him more than once, he waved her off with a scowl.

He didn't want to know how Danielle was doing, though he longed to ask if she discussed anything with her twin. Did she miss him as much as he longed for her? Was she sorry about the way things ended between them? There was no doubt it was the end, at least in his mind. She might think she loved him, but she didn't love him enough to give him the benefit of a doubt.

Most nights, he walked down the hill to a seedy bar on the outskirts of Flynn's Crossing. The people who hung out there didn't ask questions. He drank in peace, though he found he didn't like it as much as he had in the past. Nothing was the same without Danielle, and he had to learn how to move on.

Today, he thought about asking Cap if he could do anything at fire headquarters, and he meant anything. He'd clean the toilets if that was what it took to get back to work. He had too much time to think, and there were only so many hours of physical therapy a guy could do in a day.

Noah didn't think it would be wise, and he made that clear as he and Nicolle left for her day of work. He was adamant. Gid could not hitch a ride with them.

"You still need to heal. There's also the issue of the pending investigation. Cap says the sheriff's department wants to clear up evidence on the past arsons."

Yeah, Gid bet he knew who put that bee in Cap's bonnet. Danielle wouldn't want him near headquarters, not until she'd decided one way or the other if he was guilty.

Noah didn't ever ask Gid his opinion, and he could tell by what his brother said that he was convinced the arsonist was the guy after Nicolle. That was the reason Noah pulled double duty, working night shifts at the hospital and spending the day tagging along with Nicolle wherever she worked. Elena and Char were due home in a couple of days too, which would make everything more complicated.

Gid needed to find somewhere to live, though he dragged his feet each time he gave that any consideration. In the best of all worlds, Nicolle would be moving in with Noah and the girls, and they'd be one big happy family. That meant Danielle would have space, and before the shit storm of doubt blew up in his face, Gid had seen himself moving in with her. They'd make a cute couple, even if they'd probably be fighting half the time. He could live with that, as long as he got to make up with Danielle after each bout.

The day extended out in front of him like a big open field, and he had no way of filling it. He could go to the bar early, but that route had lost its charm. He didn't have much of a taste for it anymore. The ladies kept an eye on him, but he'd lost interest in them too.

Funny, now that he had found he was capable again, he didn't care. None of them was as smart or as beautiful as Danielle. None of them had her rare laugh or her sharp wit. He wasn't ready to settle, not by a long shot.

He lugged his boxes and duffels out to the living room, since he had to vacate Elena's little bed soon anyway. He needed to find a place to store his things, and the small back closet would have to do. The last couple of boxes were the heaviest, and his heart felt just as heavy as he thought about why.

His files. He kept an analysis of every major fire he'd worked on. It was more of a hobby than anything else. In those boxes, he also kept the files on the one fire he wished he'd missed. The cabin.

He deposited that box on the coffee table now, tearing open the tape with the multipurpose tool in his pocket. He hesitated with his hands on the flaps. It wasn't as if he needed to read the file again. He'd read them so many times, the pages were worn in spots. Gid had them memorized, and the words would not have changed.

Still, he pulled it out again. The pictures of the victims hadn't faded over the months, not in fact and not in his memory. The little girl still looked like a cherub. The old man, still as gruff and mean. His picture had been taken years before. Hers was from school that year. The final one of their interlocking charred remains was the one he stared at the longest.

The father had evidently skipped before the child was born, and the mother had left the girl with her own father so she could work. She'd been a small time singer someplace like Vegas. Gid often thought with regret about what she must still be feeling, losing her father and her daughter in one afternoon. He still wished he could have forced a different outcome.

This time as he waded through the pages, he found himself looking at things differently. He still felt guilt and sorrow, but the personal penitence each examination had caused him before had faded. He had always known on an intellectual level that their deaths were not his fault. He didn't start the fire. Officials had determined the old man had started it. Whether or not it had been deliberate was impossible to say. The ignition material had been in his possession. According to the investigators, he had run a still, and as a hunter, had smoked his meat. There were many different combustibles on the property to start a fire. The missing mother had been no help, though it was said she had grown up in that cabin too.

Gid tossed the photos back in the box and put his face in his hands. Maybe if he'd shown all of this to Danielle early on, she would understand there was no way in hell he'd be a firebug. He couldn't stand the idea of anyone being hurt in a fire. He didn't even like the idea of wildlife being injured. People who knew him well knew he could never be an arsonist. He lay back against the couch and allowed his mind to drift. As it usually did, his mind drifted to Danielle, and he wondered how he could have so completely fucked up something that could have been so perfect.

"Lieut, you need to hear this."

The admin who ran into the room with that statement ran back out again just as quickly. Dani was on her feet, moving fast in response to the woman's unusual urgency. Everyone in the squad room filed out rapidly, and they were all headed toward the same point, Dispatch.

The calm voice of the woman taking the call seemed out of sorts with the fierce nervous energy in the room. Despite that, no one spoke, and more than a couple of people glanced her way as she hurried to lean over the dispatcher. She read the situation on the screen from the bottom up and was ready to whirl for the door as soon as she hit on the names.

Nicolle. Nicolle and Noah and a fire. And someone injured, burned.

"Trajan, stop. It's already over."

The sheriff caught her arm as she would have rushed past. "She's okay, a little roughed up, but okay. Same for the doc. The weather guy got the worst of it, but that's not the important part."

She felt her legs want to give way when he said those words. Nicolle was okay, and Dani forced herself to bend over with a deep breath and hold it for a three-count. Slowing herself down would be important, particularly when Nicolle needed her.

"They got the guy, Trajan. He started a fire there. They got him, and you'll love this. It's Mitchell."

Okay, she would not cry. Nicolle was safe and they caught Mitchell, and she'd sort out the who and what later.

"Of course, he might not have started the other fires. He swears he didn't. Keep up with the other leads. Nothing's over until the evidence sings for us."

She walked out of the room without realizing she was moving. Mitchell had started a fire, which meant Gideon did not. She wanted to go to him, but she had no idea where he was. Her sister needed her too, and that decided her racing footsteps.

>>>>>

"We are fine, Dani. Really. Look, I have a little bit of a blister, nothing major. Noah's had the crap beaten out of him, but he's the one who's in better shape. I think the emotions are taking a toll on me."

Dani kept her arms around her twin. Nicolle really was going to be fine. She'd barely have a mark, according to Noah. He looked like he'd been through a cage fight to end all fights, but he as the one who checked on Nicolle's vitals himself as if he wasn't going to let her go for a moment without his personal attention.

"Check on Peter, would you please? I want to know how he's doing."

Noah nodded, sharing a stern glance with Danielle. "Make sure she stays put. I'm afraid she's going to be cruising the halls if I don't keep an eye on her." He planted a fast but firm kiss on Nicolle's lips and disappeared out the door.

Nicolle sighed, and Dani smiled as she heard it. That was a sigh of longing and desire if she ever heard one.

"Don't ask, and don't say anything. And don't tell me you weren't going to, because I can hear the wheels spinning in your head as clearly as if they were in my skull. We still have things to work out, Noah and me. Now, tell me what happened with you and Gideon."

Nicolle turned the tables on her so fast, Dani didn't have a chance to drop an unconcerned look on to her face. At the mere thought of the man, she felt herself flush. She saw hope on the horizon, a chance that all of this could be cleared up and soon. They'd stand a chance, if Gideon would still consider it.

"Danielle?" Nicolle's tone was almost strong enough to push her to responding. Instead, she looked her twin in the face and countered, "Nicolle?"

The door burst open, and on instinct, Dani spun to put herself between her sister and whoever was coming in. Her body wouldn't respond to her command to relax when the man stopped just inside and pinned her in his worried gaze.

"Gideon, we were just talking about you," said Nicolle.

Gideon stared at Dani for another beat, but she didn't have a chance to figure out what he might be thinking. In another second, his gaze switched to Nicolle, and he clomped his way into the room as if Dani wasn't there.

"Trajan, you are having way too much fun with my brother. Not to mention, you're both getting beaten up in the process. Do an old man a favor, will you? Take it easy for a while. I don't think my heart could stand another round of shocks like this."

He elbowed Dani out of the way, and she wondered why she didn't try to stop him. He gave Nicolle a hug and moved back, avoiding Dani's gaze with deliberate care.

Nicolle snapped her eyes between the two of them, and by the look on her face, Dani guessed she had a dozen questions, and that would only be the beginning of the interrogation. Any concern she had about that fled when Gideon finally looked back at her.

He didn't have any specific expression on his face. He stared at her long enough for her to wonder what he was seeing, even though she thought she kept her feelings well hidden. There was no doubt who he spoke to when he said, "You have anything you want to say to me?"

Struck dumb by the pain she could sense in his question and see in his troubled blue eyes, Dani only shook her head. Gideon nodded once, heading for the door without a backward glance. Over his shoulder, he said, "I'm going to check on the weather geek and Noah."

The door swung closed again, and Dani still felt like she had turned to stone. Why hadn't she said anything to him when she had the opportunity? Something like, "I believe in your innocence." Or better yet, "I'm sorry." Or what she really wanted to say, "I love you, Gideon Kinkead."

"Dani, what is going on?" Nicolle's strong grip on her shoulder didn't turn her. She only shook her head, fighting for composure. She'd fucked it up again, and she had no one to blame but herself.

Chapter 32

The little party was just what the doctor ordered, Gideon decided. The girls were home, complete with their noise, attitudes, and curiosity. Gid had spent the better part of the last few days in their company, giving his brother a chance to rest and recover. It was amazing how much energy it took to keep up with a sullen almost-teen and an active youngster who was nosey about everything.

Of course, Nicolle was around whenever possible too. Char had taken to her like a duckling to water, and Gid was happy to see them settling in together like they'd been long time friends. Elena was proving a harder nut for Nicolle to crack, though if anyone could do it, he'd put his money on her.

Noah seemed happy. More than happy, actually. Content. A couple of times, Gid caught him watching everyone around the dinner table with a fond tear in his eye, that eye landing on Nicolle last and staying there the longest. Those two seemed to be doing okay.

He and Danielle, on the other hand, never stood a chance. He'd tried without success to come to terms with it. When Noah or Nicolle asked about what happened, Gid shrugged and changed the subject, and when that didn't work, he went for a walk.

More and more, he found himself walking to that one seedy bar. He didn't make conversation there, and people rarely tried to talk to him. He nursed a single beer, and sometimes only a soda. He watched whatever rot was on the television, though the sound was never turned up loud enough to hear.

And he thought about Danielle.

He'd had a vague hope, unrealistic as it turned out, that catching Mitchell in the act of starting a fire would end the war between them. Danielle could admit Gid had never been the arsonist, and he would forgive her with grace. But when he asked her at the hospital, she hadn't said a word.

He wasn't going to give her that chance again. That didn't keep him from watching her when he thought he could get away with it. The party was the perfect opportunity, since Nicolle had insisted her twin attend. Danielle didn't look happy to be there, and if she took every chance she could to give him a wide berth, okay. He didn't want to be too close to her either.

Being close reminded him of things he couldn't allow himself to think about. The irony wasn't lost on him. After months of not being able to perform, his organ had decided to perk up every time Danielle swung into view. Or he heard her voice. Or he thought about her. Irony wasn't a grand enough term for it.

Gid eyed his boss as he talked in quiet tones with a serious-looking Char. Gid had asked more than once to return to work, but the old barriers were still standing. Ongoing investigations, Cap said. He didn't want to blame Danielle, but he did anyway. It was easier to try to be mad at her than to think about how much he missed her. It was hard to be in her orbit as he was now without telling her he loved her no matter what.

Char skipped out of the room hand in hand with Jake's wife, and Danielle made a move to follow, but Cap stopped her with a glare. She turned her attention to Nicolle, and her frown turned into a scowl when the discussion turned to saving Peter's life and bringing Mitchell down.

"What were you thinking, throwing yourself over a flaming man like that?" Danielle's eyes snapped as she asked the question, and Gid had to agree. He'd had the same discussion with Noah, but secretly, he was proud of his brother for taking care of business. If that made Gid feel like the extra wheel on the bus, so be it. None of them needed him anymore. It would make it easier to move on once he could go back to work.

Danielle's attention was on Noah as he related the series of kicks he'd used to subdue the assailant. She was so close, yet so far. Gid might as well be in another county or even another state. Absorbed in the conversation, she probably didn't realize she'd slipped closer to where he sat. All it would take to reach her back would be an outstretched arm. He watched her mouth form words, his focus drifting to how serious she was about the discussion.

"And the next one?" Danielle's eyes flicked in his direction as if she wished she could use the kick on him. Gid wanted to believe she didn't care, but when she did something like that, he realized she might still be thinking about him but in all of the wrong ways. That did nothing to brighten his outlook.

"The outside behind his knee. Same principle. Look, I can arrange for you all to visit the dojo and my sensei can tell you all about this."

Cap shook his head, wonder on his face. "I might have to have this guy come drill our female firefighters. The men, pah, they're on their own then."

Everyone laughed. Gideon plopped his foot in its walking cast on the table with a thud. "I want that last move, bro. They need that last one in movies." If he couldn't beat them, he might as well join them. Better yet, he'd join that dojo of Noah's and learn a few more moves of his own. If Danielle happened to be there at the same time, what could he do about that? It was a public place.

Danielle rolled her eyes at something and made a deliberate slide away. That didn't mean he couldn't sniff her scent, all of its strong pine and wicked female wildflowers.

Laughter followed, though Gid wasn't tracking with the conversation. Danielle didn't seem amused either. He stared at her, willing her to turn in his direction. She either didn't hear his mental plea, or she ignored it. Her eyes followed Noah's quick peck on Nicolle's cheek, and Gid swore he saw envy on her face.

She did not want to be here, and she prayed for a call from Dispatch to pull her away. Dani wanted to support Nicolle, but this was tough duty.

Being in the same room with Gideon was hard, harder than she had imagined it would be, and harder than almost anything she'd ever done. Who was she kidding? Being on the same planet was difficult.

She studiously ignored the man she wanted to stare at. He looked good when she stole a glance as he was otherwise occupied. She wasn't paying any attention to the activities in the room, stuck instead on the lazy good humor relaxing his face. When he jumped up from the couch with an excited, "Be right back," she thought it would be a good time to escape.

She couldn't go far in the small house, but at least she could avoid the temptation of watching him like he was the last meal on the planet and she was starving. She told herself to have more pride, but that had fled the moment Gideon Kinkead walked into her life.

She could say she was sorry. She could beg his forgiveness. She could tell him she loved him.

He might laugh in her face.

A commotion that sounded like someone toppling the contents of kitchen cabinets scattered her thoughts and drew her back to the living room. Noah stood at one end of the room, a guitar in hand. His fingers raced along the strings and a cacophony of noise sounded from a speaker on the floor. Gid pounded on pots and pans like the devil was in him, and in the middle of the room, Nicolle had a wooden spoon held to her face and she howled along to the music.

Oh god, her sister was trying to sing, and they might all suffer traumas because of it. Cap wailed on a harmonica, though rock and roll was not that instrument's best match. Gid banged a pot with a flourish, and Dani cringed at the noise. Nicolle laughed in her face when she pulled her to the floor, dancing like this was the best music since Kaane Scott and the Rebellion.

She wanted to play along. It would nice to lose herself in the beat, which Gideon did an acceptable job keeping despite the primitive drum set. Noah's voice wasn't half-bad, and his daughter's was terrific, a fact that seemed to surprise everyone.

But it was Gideon she couldn't look away from, and she gave up trying to hide it. So what the hell if he wasn't looking back? She could enjoy the view. It would appear they would be thrown into one another's company in the years to come, based on the way Noah and Nicolle ogled each other's laughter-filled faces.

Perhaps it was because she concentrated on Gideon that she picked up the moment everything changed. His body tightened, even as he kept playing another few beats. Then he stopped mid-beat, staring at the front door. On instinct, she turned, and then she heard it too.

Someone beat a fist on the door and called out to them in a demanding voice.

Everyone fell silent as Noah slipped off the guitar and opened the door. Dani didn't recognize the man, but Cap and Gid did. Cap grimaced at his radio, turning up the volume as he asked the man, Brody, what was going on.

"Sorry, Cap, but I knew you'd want to know about this." He nodded as if in apology to everyone in the room, but his eyes hesitated when they rested on Gideon. Dani watched Gideon's face as it became cautious and still. Dread seemed to fall over his expression like a wet towel, and his eyes lost their spark of energy.

"What, Brody?" Nicolle's question refocused Dani back on the man, and she noted a white trash bag in his hand.

The firefighter shifted in obvious discomfort, his gaze flashing to Gideon once more. "Another fire, arson based on the flashpoint and velocity of the burn." He hesitated again.

"Spit it out, Brody," Cap said, already pulling his communications belt across his body. Gideon rose from the couch and threw the wooden spoons on the table with dull bounces. He looked like he wanted to fight.

"We found this, Cap." He lifted the plastic bag, and this time, the glance at Gideon was deliberate.

Gideon's obvious tension made his words come out fractured. "Where did you find it?"

Brody held the bag out in front of him as if he hated it. "On your desk, Kinkead."

Dani swung to Gideon in time to see the surprise in his reaction. Close on its heels, his expression became wary as he suddenly met her eyes.

She wanted to tell him it would be okay. It was someone's idea of a sick joke. Anyone could have left it there. But she knew what she saw in the bag, and Gideon did too. A red rose. Her bet would be plastic, generic, and print-free.

Dani couldn't say anything. Gideon's nostrils flared, as if he read her indecision as a conviction. His eyes still on her, he said, "It's not over." He kicked the coffee table hard enough to turn it on its side and raced out of the room.

"Gid," Noah yelled and started to follow.

"No, I'll go," Dani said and didn't bother to ask herself why. She outpaced Noah and raced in Gideon's footsteps, easy to hear as they hit the back porch, then muted by the lawn.

She stopped at the top of the back stairs, watching Gideon pace the length of the yard as if heading for a fire. He reached the fence and turned, kicking at the grass. A tuft flew up and caught in the breeze, and when it fell to earth, he snapped his attention to her like he knew she'd be there all along.

"It's not over," he said again.

Dani nodded her head. She couldn't tell him differently.

"I didn't leave that, Danielle."

She wanted to say she knew that too, but she didn't. Cop-sense held her tongue. In Gideon's mind, she must have held it too long, because he paced back to her with fury in his eyes.

"I could not have left it, Lieutenant Trajan. I was with the girls today, all day. You can ask them. Better yet, ask your sister if it was on my desk. She was at headquarters today, working. Then she came home, where I was, with the girls. Noah was here too by then. I have witnesses as to my whereabouts." He snarled the words in a tone that dared her to argue.

She couldn't. She also couldn't explain why she could not take things at face value. There had to be an investigation. She prayed this time they'd find a print on the damned plastic, or anything to give them a lead.

Any lead that didn't point to Gideon, her inner voice whispered, and she pushed it down. It made her sick to be torn like this. She wanted to believe in him without any reservations.

He whirled away from her again. When he reached the fence marking the boundary of the yard, he didn't turn back. She waited, because she wasn't sure what else she could do. She had to say something, but exactly what was unclear.

The back door opened and in another few seconds, Dani felt a hand between her shoulder blades, rubbing in consolation. She didn't need to turn to know it was Nicolle.

"It wasn't there when I left today, Dani. I would have noticed, because I had to pick up a file off Gid's desk. I would have noticed."

Dani nodded.

"What's going on between you two? Noah and I are worried. Tell me what we can do to help you fix it."

Instead of responding, Dani walked out from under her sister's hand. She couldn't discuss this further. She had a job to do, and no one was going to like it, least of all her.

>>>>>

Gid found a stump in the far corner of the yard and settled on it to wait. It wouldn't take long for everyone to file out of the house, now that the party reached its abrupt conclusion. Nothing like a good stalker arsonist to kill the love.

Disappointment stronger than a raging river coursed through him. Danielle hadn't said anything to accept or deny his innocence. She had no words of comfort. He hadn't needed to turn to be aware of her departure. He felt it like someone had taken a chainsaw to a major limb. When Nicolle came over to console him, her assurances left him stony and cold. She might believe in him, but her twin did not, and that was the woman who mattered to him.

"Is this seat taken, or can anyone join the pity party?"

Noah held a bottle of beer in front of Gid's face, wiggling it back and forth. Gid grabbed it without saying thanks. Noah would understand.

"Someone's stalking you, Gid, and we need to figure out who it is and stop them."

His brother was a superhero twice in a week, and now he had turned into the enforcer. It was Gid's job to protect the youngster, not the other way around. He took a long drink of beer, but it tasted bitter in his mouth.

"Stick to medicine, Noah. I've got this."

A grunt of disagreement sounded from the man sitting on an overturned bucket next to him. "Yes, it looked like that to me. Danielle left, Nicolle's upset, and the girls are wondering what they can do to help. Elena even threatened to make dinner. I don't think any of us will survive that."

Despite his anger, Gid felt his lips curve into a half-smile. "I should order pizzas. It's the least I can do since I'm the one who ruined the party."

"Damn it, Gid, you didn't ruin anything. Whoever is after you is the one to blame. This can't go on. If no one else is going to solve this, we will do it ourselves."

Noah's hand landed on Gid's, a form of the pledge clasp they'd used as children. Gid didn't want to pull Noah into this any further than he already was. His mind made up, Gid stood and broke the connection.

"Not your battle, little bro. Go take care of your girls and your woman. I'll give you guys some space for the next few days and get a motel room somewhere. Just let me get a few things together and you can give me a lift."

Noah stood as well, and his mouth was open to argue before Gid even finished. "No, that is not the way this is going to play out. Don't you see? This is exactly what someone would want to do, drive a wedge between you and the people who love you. You cannot leave. I forbid it."

Gid barked out a laugh though he didn't feel true humor. "That line might be something you try with Elena or Char, Noah, and come to think of it, it's not very effective there either. I'm leaving. You can either give me a ride, or I'll walk. Relax, it's not forever. I'll leave my crap here, so you know I'll be back."

Without waiting for another round of argument, Gid walked back to the house. It was strangely quiet, and even the girls were in hiding. He poured the beer down the kitchen sink and left the empty on the counter. Through the window, he saw Noah hefting his bottle toward the tree stump. The spray of liquid from the inside rivaled a fire hose when it splattered. Then, as if he knew he was being watched, he met Gideon's eyes and shook his head. For a brief second, Gid wished they could continue the fight.

Chapter 33

Four hours later, Gid sat on the lumpy mattress and stared at the television. The motel didn't receive an array of cable channels, and the only thing remotely interesting was a wrestling event. Staged for sure, but at least he was learning some new moves.

Pizza sat cold in its cardboard box, and Gid thought it tasted like it was made out of the same material. If the delivery guy glanced around the room with some trepidation, Gid couldn't blame him. This spot didn't have a stellar reputation, but it worked for him for the time being.

It was what he thought he deserved. No one could tell him differently. Noah had argued this decision for the length of the drive, until Gid hefted the duffel and backpack from the back seat of the minivan and slammed the door. He didn't drive away until Gid closed the motel room door. He probably hoped for a change of heart once Gid noted the less than comfortable accommodations.

But his mind was made up. Danielle wasn't answering his calls or his texts, so he had no opportunity to explain anything, though he wasn't even sure what he thought he could say. His life had been looking up, only to crash down again. When a tree fell in the forest, it sure as hell made a big boom.

Snapping off the TV, Gid picked up the pizza box and opened the door. The smell of the food was beginning to nauseate him, and the trash dumpster wasn't far away. Still, he examined the area carefully. Someone could have followed them here, and they could be hiding and waiting for a moment like this. If he could only figure out who it was, he could present that person to Danielle on a platter.

He hustled to the dumpster to get rid of the box, and speed-walked back to the room. Slamming the door was probably overkill, but his elevated heart rate and vibrating tension demanded it. How the hell would he now kill the next few hours? Sleep was not going to be a possibility.

He thought fleetingly about the dive bar up the street. The few ladies who partied there were friendly enough. That idea left a worse taste in his mouth than the pizza. No one would compare to Danielle.

She was the only one he wanted to convince. Noah and Nicolle were already on board, but Danielle's stubbornness held her back. He had to find the arsonist and she would then have to take his calls.

He picked up his phone, checking to see if he'd missed anything in the short walk to the trash. Nothing, of course. He doubted she was even concerned about him. Whatever he thought she felt, it must not be enough. The text box was empty, except for the list of messages from Noah. Same on the voicemail. He nearly hurled the phone across the room, but it was his only lifeline, and he knew sending it to a crashing end would be suicide.

Dropping to the bed again, he pulled a pad of paper toward him and dug out a pen. While he didn't agree with Noah's involvement, it didn't mean Gid himself couldn't spend his sleepless hours analyzing this from every direction. With a grid approach, he stood a better chance of narrowing down the potential list of suspects.

The blank page mocked him twenty minutes later. All he could think about was Danielle. The curve of her cheek. The frown she wore when she thought hard. Her too-rare smile. The bar was looking better and better if for no reason other than as a distraction. Gid tossed the pad on the bed, shoved his phone into his jeans pocket, and thumped to the door. At least they had a satellite dish at the bar.

"You got a what?"

Dani winced as Nicolle screeched the words, and she couldn't blame her. When Dani showed up on Noah's doorstep with the offensive pages in hand, she felt the weight of her twin's anger along with his.

"Ma'am, our search is limited to the possessions of Gideon Kinkead. Doctor Kinkead's items are not part of our search. If you could just step aside, please, and let us do our job, we'll be out of everyone's way very quickly."

Dani didn't acknowledge Landowski's better handling of this. Concertina wire wrapped her insides and pulled tight, and she felt the slice of it to her core. Things had snowballed out of control, and she had to do her job.

Nicolle stepped aside, but Noah still regarded Dani with a steady unflinching gaze. "He's not here, you know. He's trying to work this out on his own. He won't even let me help. If I know my brother, he feels like he has to take care of it, fixing things by himself as usual. Would it have hurt to try to support him, even if you have to do your job?"

He didn't sound that impressed with her profession at the moment, and though she couldn't show it, she tended to agree with him.

"Doctor, if you could show us where your brother stays when he's here, we'll go through his things and be on our way." Landowski took off his hat and held it under his arm. The respectful gesture earned a frown from Noah, but he stepped back and waved them inside.

"Gid has been sleeping on the couch, so you're welcome to look around."

Dani stepped inside after the deputy and stared at the couch. She'd made out with Gideon on that couch, but whatever fondness she felt for it would have to be submerged. There was no room for sentimentality when they had an arsonist to catch.

"I cannot believe you're doing this." Nicolle's hiss in her ear told her they were far from done with their discussion on this subject.

"I'm trying to help. If I clear Gideon, we can concentrate on whoever is trying to frame him. This arsonist has to be stopped."

"What do you mean, 'if'?" Noah's question wasn't even delivered in a whisper.

"Excuse me, sir, but where does he store his belongings? I don't see anything that would indicate he had things here."

She'd have to buy Landowski a steak dinner for being so polite and considerate. She should be doing a better job of that herself, but her emotions got in the way.

"He has some boxes in the back closet. That's all he has. He doesn't exactly have a lot of stuff since he's in the field most of the time. I'll show you where it is."

Noah and Landowski shuffled off, and Nicolle grabbed Dani's arm when she would have followed. "I thought you cared about Gideon."

Dani shook off the grip. "I do care about him, more than I can explain." She tripped over the next words." I love him, Nici. This is how I have to deal with things. I have to clear his name. I just have to."

The desperation in her tone, the part she tried to hide, was obvious to someone she shared a lifetime with. Nicolle grabbed her and hugged her hard, and Dani's arms came up and returned the gesture. She wanted to cry, but that would have to wait until she was out of uniform.

"You should talk to him, sis, and make him understand why you have to do this. Though honestly? I don't understand it, so I'm not sure you can make him see the value either."

Dani hiccupped in an effort to avoid impending tears. "It's my job. He wouldn't run away from a fire any more than I would run away from a case. It doesn't matter who is involved. In fact, the stakes are higher when it's someone you – you –" She couldn't stutter out the word.

"Someone you love?"

She nodded at Nicolle's completion.

They stood back and stared at each other for a moment, and Nicolle raised a hand and brushed at the tears Dani hadn't realized she'd released. She was a wreck, no doubt about it. She needed to pull herself together and do it fast, because she wasn't helping anyone like this.

"Lieutenant? It's a stack of boxes. What do you want to do with them?"

Landowski's voice sounded muffled and distant, and Nicolle grimaced. "It is a small stack of boxes. Six of them, to be exact. Noah shakes his head and says that his brother has never been the kind of guy who acquires things, but come on. No childhood memories or paraphernalia? I think Noah keeps it all for both of them."

Dani nodded and wiped at her cheeks. She raised her voice, thankful it sounded more level than she felt. "Let's take them in. We can open them at the station and see what we find. That is, if it's okay with Noah."

Chain of evidence demanded certain procedures, and even though it was the middle of the night, Dani didn't want to wait another second. She and Landowski cataloged the boxes into the evidence list, returning to the station for a preliminary analysis. She roused a crime scene tech to dust for prints on the tape closing the boxes. The investigation could not wait, not when this case could combust again at any moment.

She slit the tape on the first box, and she and Landowski peered inside. Uniforms, fire gear, boots. Poking through it didn't produce anything unusual. Box number two was no more informative, though it held civilian clothes.

"This one has photos and stuff, Lieut. Looks like Gid does keep some personal items. Hey, look at this picture of Gid and Noah as kids."

Landowski held out the photo, and while she knew she shouldn't, she took it. The latex gloves on her hands stuck to the old print, though she couldn't have let go of it no matter what. Smiling up at her, two blond boys, one much smaller than the other, sat on a beach. Sand coated them and ice cream dripped from cones in their hands, but that wasn't what caught her attention.

Gid had that same fierce protective expression she'd seen countless times over the past weeks. While he grinned in the picture, the look also dared anyone to try anything with his baby brother. His arm wrapped around Noah's shoulders, and he sat tall and straight as if letting everyone know he was in charge.

She traced the edge of his face, thinking he was the cutest kid she'd ever seen. He might have been about eleven or twelve years old, and she remembered him saying that their dad had died when he was ten. He was already filling the shoes of the man of the house, the protector, looking out for his brother.

Just like she felt about Nicolle, though her twin didn't buy it. When you were the first-born, it was your role to protect the siblings who came after you. That's just what you did. She and Gideon had more in common than anyone would believe.

She glanced around the box as she placed the photo back inside. A stack of report cards caught her eye, and she lifted them out. It wasn't the kind of thing she would have expected Gideon to keep, but he had. Flipping through them, she noticed his grades were good. That didn't surprise her. She knew he was a bright guy.

A bright guy. The idea halted her actions as effectively as a gunshot would have. She and Nicolle had talked about this. The arsonist was not a bright guy. In fact, the early igniters had been primitive, and certainly not the kind of thing one would expect a seasoned firefighter to use. Circumstantial, almost to the point of being a hunch, but it made her feel better.

"Here's the opened one, Lieut."

She glanced at the box in front of Landowski. They had discussed this at the house. It was the only box without a seal. The tape across its top flats had been slit cleanly. Noah didn't know anything about it, but rather than dive into it there, they'd loaded it into evidence with the rest and brought it in.

"What's inside?" She stepped closer, curious.

Landowski used the pen to lift one flap, and they put their heads together to examine the contents. Brown envelopes, the kind large enough for a sheaf of papers, stood neatly on their sides. Some were skinny and some were fat enough to stress seams. She grabbed one midrange and pulled it out.

On the outside in bold printing she recognized as Gideon's, a location and a range of dates covered the envelope's opening end. She slid out the contents on the desk, and her mind stalled on what she saw.

Fire scene photos, lots of them. During and after. Reports about the fires containing analyses of ignition source, fuel loads, and various other factors that would gauge why and how a fire burned the way it did.

She left Landowski to pick through the rest of that stack and grabbed another one, the fattest this time. She looked at the location and date, and her mouth went dry. She recognized it because she had reviewed this case herself. She'd done that because the man she loved had been involved.

The cabin fire.

She was more anxious about the contents in this one and she sprayed them out of the envelope like a deck of cards. Photos. Reports. Yellow legal pad pages covered in more of Gideon's writing.

"Looks like he analyzed these fires."

She'd forgotten about Landowski, absorbed as she was in Gideon's notes. The subjects of his scrawling included suspected causes, known ignition points, burn patterns, and fire fighting techniques used.

Her heart jumped into her throat when she came upon a different type of scribbling. Here, Gideon's hand looked agitated and the script was not as precise. Some of the sentences rambled, but she got the gist of it. Gideon tried to reason out what he could have done differently to convince the old man and the girl to leave. When the final sentence ended with an abrupt series of hard dashes, she wished she had been more understanding about what he'd been through.

"You know, he could have been figuring out how to duplicate the fires," Landowski said in an even tone.

"Or he could have been analyzing how to fight them more effectively."

The deputy gave her an impassive stare.

"I have to go to him," she said, pulling off the gloves and tossing them toward the trashcan. She missed, and she didn't care.

"I'll come with you and help you take him into custody."

She whirled on the deputy. "I'm not arresting him. This could be anything."

Landowski gave her an uncertain nod. "So, person of interest."

She waved a dismissive hand, already on her way out the door.

"What should I tell the sheriff?"

She didn't pause to deliver her orders. "Tell him whatever the hell you want, Paul. I don't care. Gideon needs to know he's not in this alone. I've got his back."

She heard a muttered, "What the hell?" It should matter that her deputy and soon, most of her squad and her boss would think she lost her objectivity. That was as bad as losing her mind. But her thoughts were suddenly clearer than they had been in days.

She loved Gideon, and the rest of it did not matter.

Chapter 34

He didn't think one beer would make his head ache like this, but his recollection was foggy. It was one beer, right? He remembered walking into the bar, and he ordered his usual on tap. Then things got cloudy.

Gideon tried to roll over, but his arms and legs wouldn't work. He seemed to be kind of upright, but things were crooked. In the darkness, he wasn't sure which way was up.

Where the hell was he?

The room had a stale odor to it, but it didn't smell like that lousy motel room. He forced himself to concentrate, a feat made more difficult by the fast pounding in his blood. A drunk had never felt like this. He must be out of practice.

That had to be the answer. He had been trying to get back on track, and he'd done a damned good job of it. Danielle had been his inspiration. He wanted to be the best possible man he could be for her, because he loved her.

The slurring thought in his mind crashed into the wall of his skull and he moaned. Danielle didn't love him, because she didn't believe in him. If she really loved him, she would have stood by him no matter what, because that's what people in love did for each other.

"You killed them!"

The screech came out of the darkness and he screamed in response. Pain shot through his brain like someone had planted a Pulaski in deep. The combined sounds echoed hollowly around the room, and he only had a moment to wonder who else was there before something hit him in the face and he blacked out.

>>>>>

"I need you to open number seven for me."

The sleepy clerk eyed Dani with suspicion. "Don't you need a warrant or something?"

Dani slammed her fist on the counter. "Do you want me to get the SWAT team here to break down the door? I'm happy to do it. I'm sure the owners of this fine establishment would see that as a blessing."

Yelling seemed to be her modus operandi tonight. First, she yelled at Nicolle on the phone as she demanded to know where Gideon was. When Noah came on the call instead, asking why she wanted to know, she roared at him too. Then when he told her where Gideon was staying, she screamed out of frustration.

Her tires shrieked as she pulled to a stop in front of the seedy motel. Pounding on the door of room number seven, the door Noah reported Gideon had slammed shut, brought no response. It took precious minutes to wake the clerk. When he handed her the key with reluctance, she didn't bother to thank him. She was already running down the motel's covered path.

Why he would go to this hellhole when there was a perfectly good bed at her place? She caught herself when she realized she didn't exactly make him welcome with her attitude. That was about to change, as soon as she could find the idiot.

Her fingers shook as she tried the lock. The flimsy thing was barely legal. In fact, SWAT would not have been necessary. She could have kicked this open without much of an effort. She turned the handle and pushed it with another call.

"Gideon? It's me, Danielle. We need to talk."

Nothing but darkness. The place felt empty, but to make sure, she turned on the light and the measly low-watt bulb in the ceiling shed a pale light. The room was deserted.

"I could have told you he wouldn't be in here."

The reedy voice behind her belonged to the waddling clerk, who scratched his chest and then his balls as if to emphasize his knowledgeable status. She wanted to grab him and shake him to make him talk faster, but she took a deep breath instead.

"Why would that be, sir?"

The clerk made a huffing sound. "Well, I saw him walking down the road, a little after ten o'clock." He seemed pleased he could provide such in-depth information.

Dani stared at him, the hard, irritated cop stare, and he stopped smiling. "Do you happen to know where he might be going?" Gideon on foot couldn't have gone far.

The clerk pursed his lips, and so help her, if he scratched his balls one more time, she' d make sure he had them someplace where he could reach them more easily.

"Well, some people like to go get a meal at the McDonald's down the road, but they'd be closed by then. There's the bar, though. They don't close until two in the morning, but you'd know that, being as you're an officer of the law and all." He smirked at her.

She took a quick glance around the room, her eyes settling on the backpack and duffel. It didn't look like Gideon had unpacked, and she couldn't blame him. She would want to keep everything in plastic bags in this place. A yellow legal pad on the bed claimed her attention, and she walked over to it slowly as if it would bite her. Empty too. But the type of paper matched.

"Is he some kind of fugitive from justice, sheriff? Is there a reward for finding him?" The clerk rubbed his hands together, obviously anticipating his elevated financial status.

"No, he's the person in danger." She checked her watch and pushed past the man. He leered at her, and for that, she would call the building department in the morning and have the place inspected. There had to be a long list of violations.

She barely paused as she threw a card at the man and didn't bother to see if he caught it. "If Mr. Kinkead returns, please tell him to call me immediately."

The man bent to pick up the card and stared at it for a moment. "Ah hell, you're not even the sheriff. Am I going to get in trouble for this? And hey, you never said about the reward."

Dani turned the key in the ignition and had the SUV in reverse without saying another word. When she slowed at the stop sign, she considered adding the lights and siren, but she could see the bar from there. It wasn't far, maybe a mile down the road. The Five Spot, as upscale as that motel had been. If Gideon was drinking there, she worried about the swill he was getting.

She hit the door with her hand and it swung open like a saloon in an old western. The place was nearly deserted and very quiet except for grating old country music. No sound came from the television over the bar, and the torn pool table was bare of any game. The few patrons moved at the speed of turtles to blink at her, but there was little interest in their eyes. They returned to their drinks with blank stares.

None of those patrons was Gideon.

The only person who gave her the least bit of interest was the man behind the bar. One hand was out of sight, and she bet he had it on a baseball bat or a gun. She couldn't blame him, not in this part of the county. When he ran his gaze up and down her uniform, he relaxed and placed both palms down on the bar where she could see them.

"Can I help you, deputy?"

She covered the distance to the bar in rapid steps and stood in front of the man, hands on her equipment belt and close to her gun. If he read it as a threat, so be it. She suspected her career would face scrutiny it might not survive from her actions tonight, but she didn't care. Being nice was the last thing on her mind.

She described Gideon as plainly as possible and asked if he'd ever been in, but the man was already nodding.

"Yeah, he comes here. Been coming here every night the past couple of weeks. Quiet guy. Buys one beer, drinks it so slow it's warm by the time he's halfway, and then leaves it. Why? What's he done?"

In for a penny. "His life is in danger, and I'm here to escort him someplace safe. Do you know where he is?"

The man looked uncertain and turned to the bar. "He was here, but he left. Hooked up with a woman, I think her name is Irene. Hey, anyone know anything about that woman with the curly brown hair?"

A couple of the patrons shrugged, and Dani nearly yelled at them too. No one knew the woman, but the barman clearly thought she was important.

He stared down the dimpled wood surface again, frowning. "It was weird, but maybe it was because she kind of egged him on to drink the whole beer. Never saw him drink the whole thing before, but maybe there's a reason. We get a lot of those around here, if you know what I mean."

Dani got in his face then, because she was out of patience. "What are you talking about?"

The man put up his hands like she planned to arrest him. "He was slurring his words and falling down drunk, but it was only one beer, I swear it. I don't serve people if they seem to be drunk. Guess he can't hold his liquor."

She'd seen Gideon drink a whole beer on more than one occasion, and she'd never once seen him drunk.

"Where did they sit?"

The man lowered one hand to point at the end of the bar. Two glasses, one a taller beer glass and one a shorter liquor type, stood side by side. Her heart rate picked up as she took slow steps to their position.

"He drank out of this glass?"

"Yeah, that's the one."

She sniffed the glass, and the odor of beer was obvious. But there was something else there, something that seemed off. It could have been the dirty bar, but she feared that wasn't the case.

"Get me a bag, a new, clean bag. Or a clean towel. Move it, damn it."

The barman scurried to a room in the back and brought a whole box of reclosable plastic bags. As he yanked one out, the rest fell to the floor. Dani plucked it from his fingers, turned it inside out, and grabbed Gideon's empty glass. She picked a second bag off the filthy floor and did the same with the shorter glass.

She was already racing out the door when the bartender said, "Hey, you going to pay for those?"

In for a pound. She gave him the finger as she hit the outside door.

>>>>>

Slivers of light pierced his vision, and he screwed shut his eyes in response. It hurt to look at anything, and his body felt like he'd been the punching bag in the dojo cage. Water would have tasted good, and he thought about risking another movement to get a drink.

Opening one eye, he could see an outline, a rectangle with light showing around it. Must be the motel room's outer door. That would mean the bathroom was behind him, but his head wouldn't move to turn to it. Maybe he could crawl. In training and drills, they had to crawl under boards and barbed wire, and he was good at moving fast in tight spaces.

But he couldn't move. Trying to figure out why confused him. It was easier to close his eyes and sink back into oblivion.

Danielle sprang into his mind. He felt especially close to her in the darkness. Maybe that was because their relationship was like that, murky with edges of unidentified something that made assessing their positions or movements difficult. He wondered if she thought about him in any way other than as a suspect.

He missed her anyway. So what the hell if she didn't believe him? He'd convince her. They were wasting time. Noah and Nicolle had it right. Jump in with both feet and get on with it. Those two would survive. About him and Danielle, he wasn't so sure. But he loved her, Madame Fire help them both, and he had to try.

A new odor wafted into the room, and he sniffed. He sniffed again and with greater attention when the odor identified itself in his fuzzy brain.

Smoke.

He struggled against whatever held him, feeling that dense pounding in his blood as his wooziness increased. His last thought was of Danielle, and how much he wished he could reassure her once more how much he loved her.

>>>>>

"Tell me what the glass smells like."

Dani sniffed, and tried her best to describe it for Noah.

"Bring it to the hospital. We'll meet you there. I can get the lab to run a tox on it faster than your crime lab can."

She banged her forehead on the steering wheel as she started the engine. When she turned to back out of the space, her eyes fell on the other plastic bag.

"Can you do me a favor, Noah?"

"Anything, considering you're saving my brother's ass and I love your twin. Either would earn you more than one favor."

She chuckled, even as tears stung her eyes. "Bring two cars. I'm going to have Nici run something by our techs. I need fingerprints checked, and I need them done fast."

She didn't wait for Noah to reply. Activating her mic, she asked the dispatcher to put her through to the lab. She explained what she needed, and why she needed it so fast, and the tech quickly agreed to accommodate her out-of-line request. She merely shrugged when the woman said she'd have to put the unusual requisition in a written report. What came after the penny and pound?

She tried Gideon's phone, leaving a in voicemail when he didn't pick up. Breaking more rules than she cared to think about, she texted him one-handed as she sped toward the hospital. When he didn't respond, she stared at her cell phone and nearly slammed it into her dash for good measure.

Her next call was to the computer geek on duty. A bored voice greeted her as she identified herself.

"What can I do for you, Lieutenant? Kind of late, isn't it? Or early, depending."

"I need you to check the GPS on a phone. Here's the number." She rattled it off rapidly, knowing the tech would have no problem typing even faster.

The man hesitated. "Ah, I need a case number. Or a warrant. Or something. I can't just ping someone's cell phone without cause."

She took a deep breath to hold back her frustration. Now she was in for the whole damned mint.

"A man's life is in danger. Would you rather see him when he's in the morgue and we have to call him a victim? Get me the location, and yesterday. Send it through the scanner if it makes you feel better."

The tech mumbled something unintelligible, but Dani didn't care. She screeched to a halt in front of the Emergency Room, and Noah and Nicolle came running.

"What's going on? Where's Gideon?" Given his obvious thick panic, Noah did an admirable job of holding himself together. If the positions had been reversed and it was Dani panicked about Nicolle, she wasn't sure she would be able to imitate his cool.

"I don't know, but I'm trying to find out. Here, Gideon drank from this glass. See what you can get from it. Nici, race this down to the crime lab. They're expecting you. Give them this." Danielle scribbled a series of letters and numbers on a piece of paper. "It's a case file. If they get a hit on the print, have someone check the names in that file."

Noah opened and sniffed the glass. "Oh fuck, this is bad. Yeah, there's something in here. It could be any of a dozen date rape drugs, but they all have similar effects. They knock a person out, and their muscles don't respond when they wake up. Nasty shit. I'm coming with you."

Dani didn't give him a chance to round the SUV. "Noah, I can't wait for the results. Get them to put a rush on it, okay? Nici, the same. I've got a very bad feeling."

She caught Nicolle's strange look. "Bad feeling? You never say that. You go by the evidence. You say gut intuition leads to tunnel vision."

The mobile display unit beeped and a locator map appeared on the display. The notation below it only read, *'Found it.'*

Dani pushed the gearshift into drive in a movement rough enough to make the transmission whine. "Fuck the evidence," she said, and she tore away for the mountains.

Chapter 35

The light was much brighter this time, and when he opened his eyes with care, it didn't hurt like stabs of a shovel. He still felt woozy and he thought he might heave his guts, but he also might survive.

"Well, well, well, look who finally woke up. I was kind of hoping you'd wake up earlier, so we could have a nice heart to heart before I burned you like you burned them."

Gideon blinked to focus his eyes, and in the corner, he made out the form of a person. The form rose and came closer, and he could now identify the features. The curly hair was a tip-off, though it looked more muddy than brown in this light. The creepy woman who kept coming on to him at Mallory's months ago hovered over him.

Her face pulled into a snarl. "What? Nothing to say? You still off or something?"

Events returned to his memory in rapid succession. "You drugged me."

The woman snickered. "Yeah, and it worked like a charm. I wasn't sure about it, but the guy I got it from said it was primo stuff. Got to remember that if I ever want to kidnap a guy again." She cackled once more, and the madness in it made Gideon feel cold in the heat of the day.

Heat. It felt hotter than it should have, and on instinct, he sniffed and smelled it. Smoke, the kind from an intense, hot forest fire. He had no idea where they were, but the fact that a fire was close-by was unmistakable.

"Aren't you going to ask me?" The woman drew close, so close that he could smell the ripe odor of a body in need of a shower.

"Why?"

She smiled, and the odd light in her eyes reminded him of the old man.

"You don't remember? You killed them, and now you're going to pay."

The ice in his veins froze solid and every nerve along with it.

"I don't understand."

The sick smile disappeared, replaced by rage. Her hand flashed out and hit him square on the cheekbone, and from the brute pain of it, he realized she'd slapped him before.

"You let my little angel burn. You killed her, just like you killed my pop. You could have saved them, but you didn't. It's all your fault."

The cabin rose in front of his eyes like a nightmare and the sounds of the little girl's screams made him wish he had something to throw up. As it was, dry heaves contorted his body. He was tied to a chair, and that chair was fastened to something else and it didn't even rock. When the heaves subsided, he closed his eyes and put his head back.

"Oh no you don't. You're going to see this. I'm going to make you see it, because it will be how you die. You think only you firemen know anything about fires. Well let me tell you, my pop knew a thing or two, and I got his gift."

The woman raised her hands and wiggled her fingers, as if dexterity alone would be able enough to light a match.

Reason with her. That's what the good guys always did on the shows when the crazy bad guys had them pinned down. He remembered Noah's cool kick, but his legs were tied too tightly to be of any use.

Reasoning it would be.

"I'm sorry for your loss, Mrs. Glass." He never knew what she looked like.

The woman adopted an injured look. "Oh for god's sake. Don't give me any of that false grief crap. I heard it all before. They all tried that with me, and I told them I would get even someday. That shut them up."

She looked smug, and Gideon was at a loss on how to proceed. Maybe a different road completely.

"I have to be honest with you, Mrs. Glass. I have nightmares about that fire. I tried to convince your father to leave, but he refused. He was sure he and your daughter would be safe. I tried to force him, but he fought me. If it brings you any consolation, he died because he wanted to be there, and your little girl did not suffer." He would keep the agony in those screams to himself, because he could not bring himself to be that cruel.

Her lips curled into a snarl, and she raised a hand as if she'd slap him again. He stared at her dead on, because this was now out of his hands. But before her palm connected, she stopped. Her eyes grew crafty and sly.

"I know what you're doing. You don't want to be around in the end. Too bad. You're going to feel the burn. I made sure of it. Look what I have planned for you."

She waved her hands with a flourish, drawing his eyes to a table. The light was bright enough for him to see what was assembled there.

A wired device, probably an incendiary, large enough to ignite the canisters of accelerants lined up next to it. He could smell the gasoline from here. Wires ran between the canisters and the device. Other packages wrapped with red warning tape were clearly explosives. The bomb would make a big boom, and if he couldn't get out, he would be at the center of it. The fire that followed would take care of any pieces of him that remained.

"You can't be serious," he said, thinking that at least it would be over quickly. Waiting for the explosion would be the worst form of torture.

"Like a heart attack," she said with a crazy smirk.

Dani turned off her mic when the sheriff's voice boomed there was no proof Gideon had been kidnapped and she needed to get her ass off the mountain. Powering down the mobile display after she found the location seemed like a good way to avoid distractions. She thought about turning off her phone too, but she wanted one way for back-up to find her.

That would take a while, though. The fire was up the road a good distance and moving away, but that didn't mean unauthorized vehicles had access. She was so unauthorized, her badge might as well say Mars on it. When the road was blocked by her own department's people, she turned around and allowed them to see her taillights disappear past a curve. She found a rutted logging road and headed back in the direction she needed. Her back-up wouldn't be as motivated.

She had parked a distance away so her approach could be unseen. No vehicle stood by the cabin. To some eyes, it might look abandoned, but she noted the trampled ground by the door. Recent winds would have picked up leaves and twigs and moved them around carelessly. Someone came and went here.

Gideon's cell signal came from inside.

She crept low around the perimeter of the clearing, keeping out of sight of the windows. No glass filled their frames. In the low light, it was impossible to see the interior.

Changing positions again, Dani scanned the surroundings. At a distance, a dull darkness caught her eye, and she moved toward it on careful feet. A truck, old and paintless, stood about forty yards from the cabin. While it didn't look like much, she suspected it ran fine. Fresh pine needles outlined tire tracks, marking its arrival from the direction opposite the road. Another path through the woods.

She thought about disabling the truck, but it would waste precious time. She had no idea what condition Gideon was in, and he was her first priority. Make that her only priority. Someone else could worry about whoever held him here. She crawled back, searching out an angle where she could get a view inside without being seen.

Her mind went into calculating cop mode. Would there be booby-traps along possible access points? Was the kidnapper working alone? Which angle of approach would be best? She could immobilize one person, but a second might be ready to hurt their prey.

Her heart stuttered along with less efficiency. Was Gideon injured? Was he still alive? She shut down that line of questioning before it detonated her.

Her search took her to the north side, away from shadows fed by pale sun filtering through the smoke. When she crawled under the window, she breathed slowly to control the hard thud of her rapid heart. Think like a warrior in the cage. She had to find him to save him.

"Did you like my roses? I picked them for you." A maniacal laugh sounded from inside the cabin, and Dani held her breath, waiting for a response.

"You left me the flowers? Why?" Her heart sped up as she heard Gid's voice. He was inside and alive, and that was all she cared about.

"Why to remind you, of course. All those fires were mine. I wanted you to remember my little angel after each and every one of them."

Dani tracked the sharp sound of boots across the wood floor to an opposite corner of the cabin.

"See here? My pop taught me how to make this too. The clock ticks and then it all goes boom. I left your phone over there, by the way. You can't reach it, but I'm betting someone will be tracing you and they'll find something to use to identify you. But if they don't, hey, I don't care. Did you know I had to give a DNA sample so they could match tiny burned bits of my little angel and my pop to it? Nothing else left to identify."

Dani inhaled through her nose and held it for a count of three. When she blew it out through her lips, she made sure she was soundless.

"I am sorry, Mrs. Glass. I can understand how this has hurt you. As I said before, your father insisted they were staying. I cannot force someone to leave."

"Hell yeah you can. You pick them up and you carry them. You're a big strong fireman, and you could have done that. You could have rescued my little angel. You know she comes to me in my dreams sometimes? And she tells me, Mama, you have to make this right. So I'm making it right."

A scraping sound in the cabin came close to the window, and Dani fell back a few feet to the hidden area behind a solid wall.

"Now, you just sit there and think about what you could have done differently. You know, like rescue them. I'll leave you to your prayers. Of course, you're the devil himself, so who would listen to you?"

A demented laugh sounded an octave too high for normalcy, followed by a slam. Silence, then rapid thumps and scraping, along with a string of loud curses. Gideon.

Dani lined up her weapon with the window and leaped through the open space.

Gideon felt new sweat join the fear layer as he struggled against the bindings. Whatever they were, they were strong and tight. A sharp pain seared his shoulder, and he realized he couldn't do anything about getting himself free.

That left two options. Get to his phone somewhere behind him, or get to the bomb and try to disarm it. With his teeth.

He fought harder. When a shape flew through the window at him, he thought he'd lost it completely.

Danielle landed on light feet and her weapon swept the small room. Gideon stared at her, unsure she was real. She could be remnants of the drugs.

Her eyes met his and softened. Her weapon was back in her holster and her hands were on his cheeks, and she was kissing him.

Yeah, if this was the last dream he had before death, he would take it. But her mouth was warm, and she smelled like forest and meadow, and the butt that landed in his lap as she continued to maul his mouth felt curvy and soft.

She pulled back and looked at him, suddenly frowning. "You're hurt." She ran fingers over his cheekbone, and it stung like hell.

"You're here." He wanted to be sure. "Why?"

Her eyes dropped as if she was embarrassed. "Because you're here. Because I was an idiot for not listening to my heart over my head. Because I love you." She inhaled on a gasp and moved behind him. "There, are you happy?"

Gideon suddenly couldn't help the grin. Then came a laugh. She stopped sawing to cut the ties on his legs, and came around to face him with hands on hips.

"Why the hell are you laughing?" She might have been interrogating a serial killer. The idea sobered him.

"Is it always going to be like this? You know, crazy between us? Because just for the record, I'm up for it if you are. I light up like a torch each time you're near me, or I think about you, or I –"

He didn't have a chance to finish when her lips landed on his again. The thrust of her tongue made him consider playing hostage and cop with her at some point in the future. It was incredibly hot.

Heat registered like a tangible thing, and he jerked as far back as his restrains allowed.

"What now? Maybe I need to give you a lap dance or something." She sounded annoyed.

Despite the circumstances, Gideon grinned up at her. "Now, now, Lieutenant, you're in uniform."

Her face fell, and she looked away with a troubled expression. "Yes, but maybe not for long."

They had to stop playing games. They might not have long unless he got his hands on that bomb.

"Untie me."

She raced around him and sawed at the ties again. One by one, they broke free, and Gideon massaged his hands to return as much feeling as possible. As soon as she had him unbound, he jumped up, teetering unsteadily. Danielle shoved a shoulder under one arm and wrapped her other around his waist.

"Come on. My SUV isn't far. I can help you down there, or I can drive it as close as I can. Then we need to get out of here and see if we can catch her."

He turned and kissed her hard. "You go. I need to take care of this."

Danielle looked confused for a moment, then scanned the room. When her eyes fell on the table, she grew solemn.

"Is that what I think it is?"

Gideon broke their embrace and hobbled over to the table, already trying to figure out if he could disconnect the leads without detonating it. Danielle pulled in close next to him. "What do we do first?"

Gideon didn't bother looking at her, though he did drop a hand to her thigh and squeezed for a moment. "You go. I take this apart. Simple."

Danielle didn't change positions. Her voice sounded like a command. "We disable it. We leave together. Simple."

He opened his mouth, but never got a word out. She barked, "Don't argue with me, Gideon Kinkead. I love you, and I am not leaving you here."

"You have a bad guy to catch."

"Let someone else have the glory."

He grinned, even as his fingers refused to cooperate fast enough. "See if you can find a timer."

She walked around the table on soft feet. When she'd made the circuit twice, she shook her head. "I don't see anything." She stood up and glanced out the window. "We could run for it. There is no one else around for miles, unless you count the crazy lady. We can get out of the danger zone."

Gideon shook his head. "No can do, Lieutenant. If this blows, it will start a new fire, and with this much fuel, it will be weeks before it's out. I can't let that happen. Do you have a knife?"

She handed him her multi-purpose tool, and he grinned when he realized it was the same kind he carried. Yet another way they were so well matched. He'd have to tell her about all of those ways once they got out of this.

He hesitated at the final wire. He was almost positive he had the order correct, but the only way to know would be to cut it. He turned to Danielle and grabbed her close.

"I love you, Lieutenant. Remember that, whatever happens. Now run."

Instead, she tackled him to the floor and kissed him until his ears were ringing. When she came up for air, tears poured down her face.

"I love you, Kinkead, and I am not leaving. You will cut that wire, and we will waltz our way out of the woods." She kissed him again, and with a final hug, pulled him upright. "Let's do it."

He put the knife under the wire again, but before pulling it through, he turned to her and stared into her eyes. "I love you, Danielle."

She nodded. "I love you, Gideon."

He leaned close and kept his eyes open, and she kept hers open too. Their lips met and he snapped the wire with a quick movement.

One count. Two count. Three count.

Silence.

He felt her lips twitch.

No boom. Four count. Five count. He exhaled.

This time when she tackled him, he didn't resist. After all, she had handcuffs.

Epilogue

Dani paced the observation room. One-way glass wasn't the most flattering, but Gideon still looked like a hero no matter what.

The sheriff towered over the interrogation table, his pose a classic intimidation technique Dani had used herself a few times. Gideon didn't seem to care. He remained respectful but adamant.

"I did not have anything to do with any of those fires being started, other than being the object of Mrs. Glass's looniness. I fought them, but I didn't start them."

The sheriff tapped the folder on the table. "Tell me again why you have all of those files about previous fires in your possession."

Gideon sighed and glanced at the glass as if he could see her. He couldn't, but that didn't stop her from smiling encouragingly. As if he felt it, one corner of his mouth lifted in a slight grin.

"I study the fires so I understand how to fight them more effectively next time. I study the causes so I can add to the eyes on the ground for the investigators. Many cases are solved because firefighters notice something when they first go in."

As if it pissed him off that Gideon had an explanation for everything, the sheriff lifted on his toes and leaned in close. "And the bomb-making articles?"

Gideon began to look annoyed, and Dani thought about intervening. The sheriff and other investigators had been over this ground numerous times, and everyone else was satisfied with Gideon's answers. Only the sheriff still held a chip on his shoulder. Everyone else thought Gideon was a hero.

But then, intervening would not be wise. She'd told the sheriff what she heard, but she wasn't sure he believed her. She'd received a well-earned dressing down for all of the rules she broke. She was sort of surprised it didn't include a demotion, but it could be the sheriff was waiting. For what, she wasn't sure.

She didn't care either. She had Gideon, and Gideon had her. As he said, Madame Fire help them both, because they seemed to bring out the crazies in each other. And yeah, it would be decades. She'd handcuff him if she had to.

A knock sounded on the interrogation room door, and the sheriff glared at Gideon one last time before lifting the folder and exiting. Gideon's eyes immediately hit the mirrored window and he grinned at her. Even knowing he couldn't see her, she grinned back.

The door opened abruptly and the sheriff walked in. "Trajan, I don't know what to tell you."

There couldn't be anything to hold Gideon. She'd demand to see the evidence herself. They couldn't hold him on suspicions. Besides, there was Mrs. Glass.

The sheriff stood in front of the window and shook his head, hands on hips with splayed feet. "I don't know what to make of your behavior, Trajan. I don't know what to make of Kinkead either. You're both crazy."

He turned around, and she struggled to find words to explain it. "I understand, sir."

"Yeah, you two deserve each other, that's for sure. Just for the record, the prints on the glass you gave to your sister match one Irene Glass, mother of the child and daughter of the old man in that fire, just like Kinkead said. We searched Glass's apartment and found all sorts of fun stuff. She had enough there to start a few fires, make at least a dozen bombs, and blow up city blocks. No sign of her, but they're tracing her credit card. Seems she's smart enough to make bombs but too stupid to realize she's leaving a trail. She's on the run near Tonnapah, Nevada. Locals are going to grab her up for us. So I guess there's nothing left for me to do but release this guy into your custody."

The sheriff grinned. Danielle gave him a glance lasting a scant second before focusing on Gideon.

As if he knew what the outcome would be, he stood stiffly and walked to the door. She met him in the hallway, wrapped her arms around him and slammed him into the wall. When she kissed him, she felt his wide smile.

He tightened his arms and drew his head back, watching her with that same lazy grin he'd given her the first time. "Why Lieutenant, is that any way to treat a prisoner? I have rights, you know."

Dani grinned back, letting out a long laugh. "Not in my jailhouse, Kinkead. You ain't seen nothing yet."

She locked her arms around him as he did the same to her. This time when they kissed, neither one of them found the breath to laugh.

THE END

Excerpt from LOVE'S FIERY PRESCRIPTION

Check out Book 9 in the Flynn's Crossing series, **LOVE'S FIERY PRESCRIPTION**, to experience the love and suspense from Noah and Nicolle's perspective – and learn how they conquered their demons and slayed their dragons!

Prologue – January

He strummed his fingers along with the song. That riff, the one leading into the chorus, was always the blazing hot part. Of course, it sounded best when the guitar player rocked it loud enough to deafen people in the next county. He and Gideon had tried to imitate it, the lyrics delivered in a wild screech, the guitar yowling and the drums' percussion strong enough to make rakes and shovels bang against the rack hanging on the garage's back wall.sad – "

Gideon, one of the reasons they left LA. The accidents he claimed were nothing more than that. Lives lost, lives Noah wasn't there to save.

His ease evaporated and he glanced up and down the aisle as he thought about the other big reason, the one he hoped he'd left behind. He noticed nothing obvious, but a threat could lurk anywhere, stalking his family. Even now, the tension never left him.

"Come on already, Char. Father is getting fidgety."

Noah swallowed the worry, realizing he wasn't living up to his promise to himself. Be in the moment. This time was about the girls. He used to be Daddy, or at least Dad. Elena decided those names were gauche. She wanted to call him Noah, but he had to draw the line. He was grateful his younger child didn't yet look at him as if he was an alien from another century, yet being the operative word.

Elena tapped her foot out of time with the overhead music and watched her sister with marked exasperation. Charlotte was having a hard time selecting a binder for school. In the last few months, his outgoing bundle of energy had developed numerous decision-making issues, from what to wear each day to which books she wanted to read. She'd become quiet, too quiet. The psychologist assured him it was a method of coping with upheaval from the divorce. Noah understood the why, but he didn't know how to fix it, another source of ongoing frustration.

"Would you like me to help you, sunshine?" He knelt next to Charlotte and examined the binders in their selection of styles and colors. His little girl smelled like her favorite lavender shampoo and bubblegum body wash. She leaned into his shoulder and he felt her nod as he inhaled with a pang. Up the aisle, Elena expelled another frustrated sigh and popped her gum. The popping accelerated as her eyes focused on her cell phone, her thumbs typing faster than her jaw could chew.

His daughters brought him immense joy. He wouldn't give up time with them for the world, which made him eternally grateful this job came along. It provided an opportunity to move the girls away from the less savory aspects of life in Los Angeles. He wasn't sure his kids felt the same way, but they'd come around. Or so he hoped. He hoped Gideon would come around too.

"Father," Elena popped to emphasize two elongated syllables, "why can't we study online at home? Lots of kids do it. Amelia goes to school online and then she can travel all over the world with her mother. If I'm going to be stuck in this effing hick town in the middle of effing nowhere, I should be able to go to school online so I can interact with people who are more my type."

"Elena, language." He sighed, knowing this was a futile reproof. It didn't matter how many times he asked her to watch her tendency to curse. He'd even taken away her cell phone for a week.

"It isn't like it's even a swear word. I mean, you say worse. I've heard you."

Yes, unfortunately, she had, on the phone with his ex-wife. Trying to be a good example, he set up a curse jar, and whoever said a bad word had to put in a quarter. He hadn't yet figured out what would happen to the money. Coins were beginning to accumulate.

"Char, honey, how about this binder? Will this work for you?" He tapped a white one at the beginning of the rainbow of choices, and his daughter nodded solemnly.

He grabbed two for good measure and stood, placing them in the shopping cart.

"Father, I cannot believe you picked white. Only morons get white. I mean, really." Elena stalked over to the cart and picked out the binders with two-fingered distain. "Charlotte needs appropriate colors, or she won't fit in."

Her irritation sent the message loud and clear. His eldest thought he was a clueless dork and therefore unfit to do something as straightforward as picking out the correct binders for school. Elena took over the job of helping Char, debating the merits and reasons why each color might or might not work, and Noah realized they'd be there for a while.

His daughters' heads bent together in intense conversation. He'd do anything to protect them. Slay any dragons and neutralize any threats. He just had to see them coming. He couldn't always be at his girls' sides. Horror could ambush them on any street corner, at any alley entrance, even in a pristine green park.

The piped-in music changed to a heavy metal classic delivered in show tune fashion more appropriate to a dentist's office, but despite its presentation, he bopped his head along with the rhythm. Music always soothed him, and today, he needed to restore his sense of calm. This move north to Flynn's Crossing made him almost as jittery and unsure as the girls. Unsure wasn't in his genes, or at least up until last summer, he didn't think it was.

He hadn't always been clueless either. In almost everything else in life, he was the bomb. Wait, did anyone say that anymore? He couldn't help nodding and bumping along to the beat. If that made him un-cool, so be it. He was a clueless embarrassment to his girls, who were sure they knew more than he did.

Swaying with an occasional snap of his fingers, he let his eyes roam the stacks of paper and dividers extending down the aisle. This early on a rainy Thursday morning, they had the place to themselves. His shoulders shook in a little shimmy when it came to the chorus. He grabbed a package of highlighters and pulled off a passable dip and dive with the fake microphone, mouthing the words to the music. As absorbed as they were, neither of the kids noticed. No one else would witness his rock and roll tribute.

Except for her.

He stopped bopping, his eyes snagged on the person at the end of the aisle. She wore a grin that said she'd seen the whole exchange. The song moved on to the next verse, and as if she was part of the band, she bobbed her head back and forth in a parody of a back-up singer. The movement made her braid of light red hair toss on her back. Her lips parted when it came to the chorus, and he found himself grinning and playing along. Together, they lip-synced the words until they were cut-off by an announcement paging any available associate to assist a customer by the printers.

The woman shrugged at their interruption but grinned, and his smile grew in return. She looked vaguely familiar. Was she someone he knew? From here, the expression on her face spelled fun and mischief. What color were her eyes? Even hidden by a tan jacket with a logo on the front, he could tell her body was fit. She was tall, but then, he wasn't, and she might have to lean down to kiss him.

Where the hell did that come from?

Did he need to put a quarter in the jar if he only thought the words?

It didn't matter. He hadn't kissed a woman in so long, he couldn't remember how long it had been. He kissed his daughters, and he kissed his mother on those rare occasions when she breezed in and out of their lives. He occasionally did a cheek buss with colleagues who were good friends. But kiss a woman, as in full lip-on-lip action?

"You aren't listening, Father. We're done. God, will you stop being such an embarrassment?"

"Quarter in the jar when we get home," he said to show he was listening.

"Charlotte is getting blue binders, because blue is cool. I, on the other hand, will have red, since red is my power color." Elena sashayed down the aisle as she delivered the information, already giggling and typing into her cell phone as she passed around the corner out of sight. Char followed on dragging feet, leaving dark heel scuffs on the off-white tile floor.

Noah knew how she felt. The last few months hadn't been a party for any of them, and through it all, he hadn't taken a break to breathe. Now he wanted to stay here and play rock and roll star with the intriguing singer at the other end of the aisle. Elena would never notice, and he'd be spared her derisive comments in front of the first woman to catch his eye in ages.

She stood where she'd been lip-syncing, that sunny smile still on her face as she examined his family with friendly curiosity. When his eyes met hers, she raised her hand and gave him an enthusiastic thumbs-up to go with the grin. A moment later, she disappeared toward the back of the store, as he stood motionless.

He felt a small hand on his and he turned his palm over automatically and closed his fingers, giving Charlotte a squeeze of recognition. When he looked down, her serious eyes filled her watchful expression. It hurt his heart to see her so silent and somber.

She shot a glance down the aisle, and her instant smile lit up his world. She leaned in and he leaned down, because whatever she said would always be important.

"Daddy," she whispered, "that lady looks like fun."

About the Author

I love to hear from readers, so feel free to contact me through my website, www.yvonnekohano.com, or directly on Facebook as Yvonne Kohano, on Twitter @yvonnekohano, and at yvonne@yvonnekohano.com. Please leave an honest review of this novel at your favorite book discovery site of choice.

A HOLT Medallion Award of Merit recipient in Romantic Suspense, Yvonne enjoys channeling her characters' voices and passions as they overcome real world problems and discover love. Her Flynn's Crossing contemporary romantic suspense series is set in a fictional northern California foothills town not unlike the one where she used to live. Of course, the beauty and wonders of the Sierra Nevada Mountains and the surrounding counties play costarring roles in her work.

The first six books in the Flynn's Crossing series follow the developing love interests of the girl tribe, a group of successful women who work through real world conflicts and challenges to find acceptance and love - with some suspenseful happenings thrown in! In the next six books, single guys in the wolf pack find their true loves, but not without their own issues to conquer. Periodically, Yvonne will be adding seasonal novellas to the series, featuring the first person voice of a character from one of her previous books experiencing an event that we can all relate to.

www.ingramcontent.com/pod-product-compliance
Lightning Source LLC
Chambersburg PA
CBHW021201250626
47155CB00008B/2621